The Good Death

Also by Nick Brooks

My Name is Denise Forrester

The Good Death

NICK BROOKS

Weidenfeld & Nicolson
London

First published in Great Britain in 2006
by Weidenfeld & Nicolson

A CIP catalogue record for this book is available
from the British Library

ISBN-13 9 780 297 84905 6
ISBN-10 0 297 84905 0

Typeset at The Spartan Press Ltd,
Lymington, Hants

Printed in Great Britain by
Clays Ltd, St Ives plc

Weidenfeld & Nicolson
An imprint of the Orion Publishing Group
Orion House, 5 Upper St Martin's Lane, London WC2H 9EA

The Orion Publishing Group's policy is to use papers that
are natural, renewable and recyclable products and made
from wood grown in sustainable forests. The logging and
manufacturing processes are expected to conform to the
environmental regulations of the country of origin.

www.orionbooks.co.uk

For Leona

Of touch they are that without touch doth touch,
Which Cupid's self from Beauty's mine did draw:
Of touch they are, and poor I am their straw.

'Astrophil and Stella', Sir Philip Sydney

One

Rose always said Madden had a reasonable eye for a body. From his Silver Anniversary crash couple – neither of whom would have recognised the other could they have seen – to his own father, supine on the gurney, resplendent with his own particular brand of trauma. There was something special, something different, about every single one. A quirk of disease or some kink of condition inevitably produced a result that was wholly unique in every single cadaver he had yet set eyes on.

And of course he had his favourites. Which professional did not? Which anatomist or surgeon could claim that they had never fallen in love with one spectacular example, a thesis in itself, a revelation? At least, no one serious, no one committed to their craft, their science. Madden was no different. He couldn't have done this job if he wasn't fascinated by them all, each in their own way. That was the truth of it. It was something he'd shared with Kincaid, even if Kincaid had never believed it. And it was Kincaid himself who'd introduced him to his very first.

It had been a perverse meeting. Madden lost his virginity to a ten-year-old girl, her insides fresh, firm and slippery, displaying none of the discoloration or swelling, none of the distension and downright ugliness, that were associated with the organs of the more mature client. Without doubt, Madden's own internal tissues reflected his age as readily as the small pouch-like breasts that had gradually appeared on his chest over the years, or the barbs that sprouted from his nostrils and earlobes in inverse proportion to the gradual depilation of the rest of his body. He was at least fifteen years younger than Kincaid – too late to claim that he had his whole life ahead of him – but not ready to slip off this mortal coil just yet. No, Rose would yet go before him. He often thought of dying alone, without wife or family to say goodbye to, but had never found the idea disturbing.

'You don't need anyone,' Rose had remarked to him once. 'You might as well be a lighthouse keeper or an astronaut.'

She'd said it intending to hurt, but his indifference was complete. He couldn't have been either of those things, he'd told her, because he'd become a funeral director. It was a vocation.

Rose told him she thought being a surgeon was a vocation. She thought funeral services was just work.

She was right of course. But the job had its perks. Kincaid turning up today was one of them. Few people stopped by Caldwell & Caldwell's offices so early in the morning, so Madden was a bit taken aback to see him for what must have been the first time in a long while. He was remarkably un-affected by the intervening years. Maybe a bit thinner on top, a slight thickening around the midriff. Other than that, he was noticeably well preserved, his nicotine-yellowed moustache trimmed as exactly as Madden remembered it. After he got over his initial surprise, Madden resumed the reassuring tone he took with everyone who stepped through the front door as a matter of course, though it was an odd sort of pleasure to have the great Kincaid here with him now, in Madden's own place of work.

'Dr Kincaid,' Madden said. 'Or should that be Professor Kincaid? I must say it's been a long time. As you can see I'm out of touch with academia. Perhaps you're Dean of the Faculty now.'

Madden would have liked to stare straight into Kincaid's

eyes, but something prevented him. Something he thought he'd buried along with everything else in his past. Obviously not. Here was the good doctor, still as capable as ever of disturbing him, of making him uncomfortable by virtue of his presence alone. Maybe Kincaid would always be capable of making him feel like that. Maybe feeling like that was no more than he deserved. Well. They'd see. After all, just to have Kincaid here at Caldwell's spoke of a certain shift in the dynamic of their long relationship. Kincaid was here for a reason, and no matter what Madden felt about the man personally, as a professional he wouldn't allow such feelings to interfere with his work. That was beyond question. Business was business, and that was that.

He forced his gaze to meet Kincaid's. His pupils were blacker than ever, completely dilated, almost no white visible at all. Ridiculously, Madden caught himself winking at him. The act brought with it a rebellious flush of euphoria and a mild nausea.

'Can I get you anything? Tea, coffee. *Espresso?*' he asked. 'We have a machine.'

Kincaid was silent. Madden smiled, taking the doctor's hand, as if to shake it, then drew away, letting it fall. It wasn't appropriate: the esteemed physician hadn't offered his own. Kincaid, unmoving, continued to stare with dilated eyes at nothing in particular.

'Don't mind if I have one, do you?' Madden placed a cup under the machine and switched it on, and it began to fill with dark liquid, the sound from the percolator comforting in the early morning silence. When the coffee was ready, Madden placed it on the side of the gurney and began to wheel the body through the curtains to the elevator that would take them down to where the mortuary was. This particular gurney had a castor with a tendency to stick, and he'd routinely complained to Caldwell Snr that they'd be better off with a supermarket trolley. Fat lot of use complaint was, though,

Caldwell Snr being even more dead than Kincaid, were such a thing possible.

Madden fancied he could read the final years of Kincaid's life as if they were contours on an Ordnance Survey map. Or more accurately, as symptoms in a diagnosis. That would be what he'd have preferred to call them. It was strange to look at him now, lying there on the trolley, so completely dead it almost took your breath away. It had certainly taken Kincaid's. Madden snapped on the strip-light, the porcelain and stainless-steel surfaces of the morgue blinking reflectively back. He stood, one hand on his hip, the other holding the espresso, regarding the corpse on the mortuary table. Now, in the laboratory brightness of the morgue, he could read a familiar story stretching out before him on the slab. It was one some other mortician might yet come to read into Madden's own death: certainly the denouement was at least as probable as anything else. Kincaid, over six foot tall in his stocking soles, had been undoubtedly robust. Today, though, he seemed somewhat diminished, less than the sum of his parts. This, too, was true of every other body Madden had seen. Kincaid was unusual in that his manner of death wasn't preordained for him. If the progress of his illness hadn't been checked before now, Kincaid would have suffered – how long, eight more weeks, ten? – but he'd taken the quick way out. And all this only a few scant months since his bowel irregularities had taken him to visit a gastroenterologist.

Kincaid must have known what the outcome was likely to be even then, what with his family history. A large obstruction on the intestinal wall. Metastasised tumour. Blockage of the tract. Surgery. A third of the colon removed. Spontaneous diarrhoea. Pointless chemotherapy. The liver a raddled mass of carcinoma. Denial. Shock. Denial. Anger. Denial. Grief. Denial. Denial. Denial. Septicaemia. A lingering, oblivious walk into that good night. Never any acceptance from the good Kincaid. No doubt he'd felt the irony of the situation keenly. A neuropathologist and also a star turn in under-graduate lecture halls and after-dinner speeches at the Lodge. Spend half your life digging holes in people's brains, only to shit yourself to death in public.

No, not such a fate for the good Kincaid. Instead of waiting for a painful and undignified end, the good doctor opted for the *good death*.

Madden had seen plenty of suicides in his time, too. It was, he admitted, something he'd never understood. He'd always imagined sticking it out to the bitter end, whatever that happened to be. The thing that appalled him most was the act itself, the guts it took. The idea that his own hand might sway at the last crucial second was what put him off. That he might just blow half his face off with the gun, then continue to live; or that he'd chuck himself into the path of a Tube train and simply bounce off and have to live the rest of his life in a wheelchair unable to masticate his own food.

No thank you. There was more to life than that. And it was maybe not bravery at all. Only that final swallow of the pills, that necking down of the arsenic. The sugared-almond crack of the cyanide capsule.

He gazed at Kincaid, the widened eyes, only his lower lip describing the faint blueness of asphyxia. Oddly, the tip of his nose was red. But then he'd always liked a drink. Madden sipped his coffee, momentarily entertaining the idea of taking a snifter in it himself. He kept a bottle in the black medical bag that he never used for anything else.

He could picture Kincaid, strutting back and forth in front of the lecture-hall podium, gesticulating to a blackboard scrawled with some enlisted student's annotations in villainous Latin or Greek. Even in those days of black and brown suits and carcinogenic fogs blooming from the city's chimneys, Kincaid had seemed of an earlier time, an officer of the Raj, all mutton-chop whiskers and quinine, his mannerisms and *bons mots* the results of weary practice and sycophantic under-graduates always ready to get the gags. Madden could recall his jokes to the cadavers in his anatomy class, repeated every year for the benefit of the new students, the *enough malingerings*, the *sit up straight when I'm talking to yous*. He had laughed along with everyone else at first. Nerves. He'd sat at the nearest seat he could find to the door, ready to bolt should he feel his breakfast demanding exit. Funny to think of now, this many stiffs in the body bag. Kincaid, scalpel in hand, extravagant as any magician on stage at the King's, standing in for another surgeon. As at home in cardiovascular detritus as in more cerebral matter. Madden could recall his bullet-pointed style of speech – if not the formulae, then the specifics – aorta; superior vena cava; right coronary artery; pulmonary artery; left main coronary artery; circumflex coronary artery; left anterior descending artery . . . He had learned the terms by rote, like French verbs at school.

Strange the language of biology should be so functional once filtered through the Anglo-Saxon. Perhaps that was something else he shared with Kincaid; a preference for the Latin and Greek. Perhaps that was one of the reasons Kincaid had seemed part of a passed order even then, and why Madden felt himself part of a passed order now. How could one describe the heart in all its valentine beauty without ever using a lover's language?

'Futility itself,' he could hear Kincaid say, as he often used to. 'As well to dine on mutton as barley. A congenital defect may suffer on such fare, but improvement is unlikely. The moral? Make hay while the sun shines.'

He stripped the sheet from Kincaid's body and walked slowly around the mortuary table, leaning over to inspect the cadaver occasionally, or pausing to sip from his coffee cup. Kincaid was lean and angular, his arms folded across his stomach, almost cupping the small roundness there, as if to protect his vulnerable intestines. He gazed with concentration at Kincaid's face. It was hardly marked, only a few lines at the side of either eye, and above those the brow, perpetually furrowed, a look he'd worn in all the time Madden had known him. The overall impression wasn't one of an old man, of withering: it was one of agelessness, as if in death his body was regressing somehow, becoming childlike again. Rose had that same look. It wasn't restricted to the faces of the dead.

He had certainly gone to some effort for the occasion. He wore a dark blue suit, immaculately pressed. Madden wasn't much of a dresser himself, and couldn't place the material. Lambswool? Mohair? Expensive anyway. Beneath the jacket he wore a waistcoat and a pale pink shirt under that, initialled gold cufflink at either wrist.

L.K.

Lawrence Kincaid.

On the right wrist he wore a watch with a white-gold face but a plain, cracked brown leather strap. Madden smiled to himself at the sentimentality of the man. No doubt he'd kept the wristband to remind himself of his humble roots, of where he'd come from. The touch was Kincaid, through and through. He wore no shoes, only plain cotton socks of charcoal grey; his body had been discovered sitting upright outside the covers of the bed he'd shared with his wife for over fifty years. It had been her who had found him. Very calmly, she'd loosened the plastic bag from around his head and neck, and before calling the emergency services had spent a while simply sitting with him. Apart from removing the bag, she had touched Kincaid only to lightly brush his hair. She'd wanted him to look dignified when the paramedics and police came for him. So she told Joe Jnr when the body had been delivered to Caldwell's.

He had been holding a photograph taken at their wedding between his hands, but there was no trace of it today.

Madden began undressing the doctor, unbuttoning first the

7

suit jacket, and then the trousers, careful not to mark or damage them in any way. It wasn't difficult for him to undress a corpse unaided: Kincaid was certainly big, but he wasn't especially heavy or corpulent. And he had no choice anyway. Joseph – the bastard – might not swan in for an hour or more, and Catherine was off again. He couldn't understand that girl. She'd been absent so frequently of late he wondered whether she'd ever been able to cope. It wasn't every seventeen-year-old that could. And after his last run-in with the girl, Madden was sure she wouldn't be coming back any more.

He decided not to worry about it: there was every chance that Joe wouldn't turn up till the afternoon, and he wasn't likely to be any help when he did. Catherine, of course, had never been much interested in the work. Even if it meant greater inconvenience for himself, Madden didn't think she would be sorely missed.

It was only with the considerably obese that Madden ever had any real problems, and – depending on their state of advancement – they could usually wait until he could track Joe down. Kincaid was no trouble, and Madden folded his clothes and placed them, carefully labelled, with the others in the cloakroom reserved for the defunct. He removed the watch, heavy gold signet ring and wedding band, which both slid easily from his fingers unaided by lubrification. Was that the word? *Lubrificante* was the one he had in mind. Once he had tagged them and placed them with the others, he was left with only the body itself, literally two-thirds the man. The other third had left some time previously. Surely that was what people meant when they spoke of the departed?

Apart from his chest, he was almost hairless, and the growth that remained around his genitals was sparse and greyish white. From below the lower rib on his left side a colourless weal stretched down into his groin. Of course. His pubic area had been shaved for the bowel operation and was only just growing back when he'd died. As likely as not, he'd have remained manfully bushy even in senility if the Fates had allowed it. Madden smiled. The dead man's genitals had tucked themselves up, their cherubic blush shying them away from the mortuary chill. Only the good doctor's hands reflected their years. Both were deeply lined and creased, the long fingers aptly skeletal, the nails almost luminous in their unnatural white, knuckles misshapen by arthritis. Though to say the nails looked unnatural was wrong. Of course, their look was entirely in keeping with Nature. On the right hand the index finger and cushion of the thumb were hardened and calloused. The fingers of an academic, though it was possible that the wielding of surgical instruments had made an impression too. Madden finished his coffee and prepared to begin drainage of the body.

There was no doubt that even now Kincaid was an attractive man. He'd seen to it that Madden's work would be straightforward, unproblematic. All it would take would be the sealing of the openings, a stitch between nasal septum and lower lip to keep the mouth shut, and the application of a little make-up. Some foundation here, some blusher there to give a healthy glow, and he'd look as good as new. As close to new as he would ever be capable of getting now. He set about mixing a scrub for the body.

The slow awareness of something disturbed him. After all this time Kincaid didn't trust him to perform even this simple duty to standard. Madden had almost forgotten the feeling. Not quite, though. Kincaid had managed to save his body the worst ravages of his disease. He had kept himself good for the grave. A handful of sleeping pills and a plastic bag taped over the head had done the trick, and left him looking pretty good in the process. At the very least, he had saved Madden the effort of doing the job himself.

He peered once again into the dilated pupils, now beginning to cloud. Kincaid had been dead for seventeen hours. The presence of rigor mortis was slight, though it hadn't completely left the limbs yet. He lowered his face to Kincaid's and inhaled. Tobacco and whisky. Probably a single malt, if he knew the good doctor, but it was sadly not possible to identify which. A Lowland, perhaps. Before straightening up, Madden placed his lips on the mouth and kissed it. There was the sweetness of a Lowland there, possibly. He glanced at his watch and decided to crack on. He was expecting another two arrivals later on in the morning. A diabetic coma and an industrial decapitation. He'd no idea where he was going to find the time. There weren't enough hours in the day.

Two

Joseph Caldwell turned up at midday. He was chewing on an apple and flicking disinterestedly through invoices, the radio on and the temperature in the office already climbing. Between pithy bites, he was complaining about the necessity of a fully functional air-conditioning system. Theirs was on the blink again, couldn't make up its mind whether it was going to work or not. Every funeral home needs the temperature reliably regulated, he was saying. It was one thing for the front of house to be a bit warm, but they couldn't have the cold room being affected. The last thing they needed was a speeding up of putrefaction. Their client base wouldn't stand for it.

'We'll have to get it sorted,' Joe said. 'Creates a bad impression if it's too warm front of shop.' He took another bite of his apple. Like his father, he had the habit of sniffing loudly and closing his eyes after making any kind of statement, something that Madden found very hard to bear. In sufferance, he would concentrate on any other distracting sound, ensuring he made no eye contact with him whenever they were forced into dialogue.

'Folk'll think the refrigeration's scuppered through in the deli.'

Madden looked up. 'The deli?'

'You know. Cold meats and that.' Joe spat a pip into his palm, then flicked it at the wastepaper basket. 'Mind you, some of the salamis we had in here last week were pretty far gone as it was. Pretty ripe, some of them. Phwoar.'

Madden paid no attention, listening as he was to the report on the radio, something about a young couple who'd become involved with a Presbyterian mission charity. The cult had persuaded them to hand over all their savings, abandon their homes, jobs, friends and parents and move to a compound in the middle of the South American rainforest. There, they had spent their time singing, evangelising the locals – all of whom were Catholics already – and trying to avoid a miserable death by starvation, for them and their three small children. The charity was soon turned on its head as the camp were forced to accept food and aid from the local population, a people who had hardly enough to feed themselves, never mind anything left over for these strangers. The Indians never stayed in one place for too long, and relied on hunting a great deal to supplement their diet. The young couple and all at the camp resented having to rely on the help of the Indians, and found their mix of paganism and popery too much. It was the ultimate humiliation for them. The insects more than anything else had got to them. The husband had described bizarre and 'relentlessly huge' caterpillars of all different colours. Assured that the creatures were 'harmless and delicious', and food being a commodity they didn't have, both he and his wife had eventually given in and tried a handful of the larvae. No, no, the Indians told them. The larvae are extremely poisonous. Only the mature grubs can be eaten. And then, really, only when there was absolutely nothing else. Why were the *extranjeros* eating the grubs when they were surrounded on all sides by food? The grubs were awful. The Indians told them this when they found the camp, after being away for a few weeks. The children were fine, if a little on the thin side. None of them would go anywhere near the grubs. But the young couple, and virtually all the other adults in the camp, were very, very ill. Two or three died, and were buried quickly by those well enough to handle a shovel. The fear of disease was very real.

'See what I'm saying? This is a funeral home. We've got to be beyond reproach.'

Madden strained to hear the end of the item over Joe's voice. He'd thought he'd heard that some of these Indians could be cannibals. Even so, he doubted that they would eat their own dead. Especially if the body were poisoned. Perhaps they dipped their arrows in the blood instead. They must, after all, have to be a very practical people to survive in the jungle.

'That rainforest lot have got it right,' Joe went on. 'Get them under the ground and do it quick. No faffing about. It's risky as far as the funeral services and the consumer are concerned.'

Madden was unsure what Joe meant. His habit of tuning out whenever Joe was around sometimes left him at a bit of a loss as to what they'd been discussing. It wasn't important, though: Madden felt he had the measure of Caldwell's well enough after forty years. He felt he could deal with any crises that might arise.

'The air-conditioning is nothing to do with me,' he said. 'I cannot be held responsible for the inadequacies of inanimate machines. As you know.'

Joe Caldwell frowned. 'You don't have to tell me that,' he said. 'I know all right. I was brought up in this business. Know every inch of it, so I do.' He took another bite of his apple and chewed furiously at it, mouth tight shut. He rocked slightly back and forth at the same time, like a polar bear in too tight a cage.

'I was just saying. It wasn't an accusation,' Madden said, running a handkerchief over the back of his neck. The heat was getting uncomfortable, even the tinted windows seemingly unable to slow the inexorable temperature rise. The display flowers in their vases were already looking defeated, a few petals already fallen and the rest a thirsty, stricken lot. Madden sprayed water over the blooms, trying to freshen them up, though their lack of lustre was as much a by-product of being in this office as anything else.

'Glad to hear it. Partners can't be making accusations at each other, can they. Bad for business.' Joe Caldwell appraised Madden, his blond hair flicked into a Tintinesque comb at the front. To Madden, Joseph Caldwell Jnr epitomised a certain kind of boyishness; an ill-founded confidence in what little he possessed of a kind of retarded attractiveness. It was strange that there were others who found him appealing: he didn't seem to be short of admirers. It irritated Madden that it always seemed to be himself who had to answer their calls when they rang him at the home. More than once, he had suggested that Joe invest in a mobile phone, so that he might monitor his own calls in the future, leaving Madden and Catherine the Absent free to carry on with the work they were being paid to do. Joe's reaction was typically over the top. Was Madden suggesting that his calls weren't important? The calls he got were vital business calls! How was he meant to run the place if he couldn't answer vital business calls! That was exactly what he was suggesting, Madden told him. A mobile phone would mean he could be contactable wherever he was, at any time. It would mean he'd have to spend less actual time at this office, he would be able to do the rounds more . . .

Joe had strained to come up with a reason not to, but Madden knew that the idea of spending even less time here was an appealing one. But then Joe said, *What could be worse than being* contractable, *twenty-four hours of the day? It'd mean less free time, not more* . . . He was right, Madden had agreed. The business must come first. Joe Jnr must remain, as he'd said, *contractable*. Madden had savoured this triumph, minor though it was. Even so the calls had continued, and Madden had continued to answer them.

Catherine the Irritant had butted in with some snide remark when Joe was out of earshot, which Madden had ignored determinedly. An old woman, that was what she had called him. Yes. She'd said he was nothing but an old woman. It was with Herculean effort that he'd stilled his tongue.

Why did he no stick up for himself? she'd said. *She'd have cracked Joe Jnr's sacks if he spoke to her that way . . . Madden wanted to get a life*, she said.

If I had your life, I might, he'd thought at the time. *If your life was mine, that is.*

He squirted the petals with his bottle.

'How many're downstairs at the moment?' Joe asked. 'Did the other two turn up yet?'

'No sign. If they're not in during the next hour, we'll have to send one back.' Madden was joking, of course, but Joe ignored it.

'Christ,' Joe said. 'Can you not manage the three of them? You're about done with the suicide, aren't you?

'Done? He's only been here since this morning. But we're getting a bit of a log jam. And I'd like to get home before midnight tonight. If I had some help, I could get all three drained and injected. That'd only leave make-up. Assuming they're not too far gone. One's a decapitation. *You* try making that look natural.'

Joe sighed and rubbed his forehead, staring down at the table top. Madden waited, but knew Joe would not offer any assistance unless asked directly.

'Any likelihood of Catherine putting in an appearance today?' he asked, knowing already there was none whatever, and resigned to another late evening. He could call Rose after lunch and sort it out with the home help. Mrs Spivey could stay on for an hour or two. Yes. He was sure she could.

Joe stood up straight and spat a lump of apple across the room, his plumpish cheeks swinging about like loose testicles. He tossed the core into the wastepaper basket behind reception.

'That midden,' he said. 'I doubt she'll be in the rest of the week. That's a fortnight already. Probably her allergies or something. I've no heard a peep fae her. I reckon she might be allergic to something in the morgue. A chemical or something. Formaldehyde.'

Madden nodded. 'It's possible. There's a lot down there that can irritate. Not just the embalming chemicals either.'

Joe looked at him blankly. 'Then what else?'

Madden shrugged. 'Tissue gas. A splash of noxious fluid. The work itself.'

'Christ,' Joe said. 'That's all we need. That really is all we need.'

'What?'

Joe closed his eyes and sniffed. 'A mortuary assistant who's allergic to dead people.'

Madden rubbed a hand across his brow; it felt itchy and sweaty. It had occurred to him that perhaps he was allergic to dead people too. He was definitely allergic to Joe, in a way he had never been to his father. Joseph Jnr was undoubtedly an unprepossessing lump of a boy with an opinion of himself as bloated as a three-day corpse, but at least he had some *vitality* about him. In his last days Joseph Caldwell Snr always seemed to Madden like a man who was in the premature grip of rigor mortis, and he had the feeling that perhaps he was too. He was unsure of when it had begun its gradual creep through his musculature. Perhaps it had been when Rose had lost the baby. Perhaps even before that, before they had got married. He was sure there must be some particular moment, but he found it impossible to place. It always seemed to him as though he had only imagined so much of the past, that he lived moment to moment, with no continuity beyond routine. Lately, he'd begun to have difficulty concentrating on his work, something he'd never known before. But now, he wasn't sure when that had begun either. Yesterday? Last week? Maybe it had started this morning when Kincaid had arrived. Maybe he'd always been like this. He was sure that wasn't the case, that this miasma would disperse. At the same time, he had the feeling that something terrible was going to overcome him, that something awful was going to befall Rose. He felt it most in his chest, a kind of stiffening, the rigor tightening there. He would feel himself drawn upstairs from the morgue to the warmth of the parlour, the light, the flowers that needed watering. At those times, if he was alone, he would lock the front door and pace up and down by the reception desk, the telephone off the hook, clenching and un-clenching his fists, repeating the same words over and over to himself in a kind of ritual daze, sure that the tightening in his chest was just a figment of his own imagination.

There are three stages, a voice he didn't recognise as his own would say to him. Three. They occur after death, not before. So you cannot be suffering from rigor. It is impossible. What you are feeling is not what you think you are feeling. It's an illusion. There's no reason for this, it would repeat over and over, there's no reason whatever. He would continue to pace and talk aloud to himself, placating the other voice, appeasing his panic. Although he wasn't a religious man – if anything he'd say he was the opposite – the repetition of the words seemed to have become prayer-like over time, so much so that he would seem to recover, calmed somewhat when the ridiculousness of his thoughts finally became apparent to him. The three stages. Primary flaccidity, rigor mortis, secondary flaccidity. He surely could be no farther gone than primary, he would say, and then recite to himself Gaskell's version of the Lord's Prayer. He'd called it the Prayer of the First Flaccidity:

> *Our father*
> *Immaterial is the cause*
> *Once death has taken place*
> *Now a relaxing of the eyelids, of the lower jaw*
> *The extremities shall move freely*
> *As though no longer hinged*

Their musc-yules sound, their joints unwound
The leg bone connected to the ankle bone
Dem bones don't walk around
Forever and ever
Amen.

Gaskell would undoubtedly have made a better surgeon than poet, but the words still seemed to release Madden from his panic, and he would begin to relax again, the tightness in his chest gradually loosening. Good old Gaskell. He knew what Madden was thinking, wherever he was now. That the time element would vary if his body was in a cold environment for a longer period, between two and eight hours for rigor mortis, or if his body was in a warm environment for a shorter period. The process beginning in the eyelids, descending to the lower jaw, thorax, upper extremities. And then down; the abdomen, the lower extremities. Voluntary muscles, involuntary muscles, the age of the individual unimportant. And like the condition he imagined himself to be suffering from, once Madden had prayed to himself, the process would gradually ease off, beginning this time at the feet, moving up the legs, ascending to free up his chest, finally allowing both eyelids to become flexible – no, *sensible* – once more.

'Anyway, I'm going to have to leave you to it for a while,' Joe said.

Madden nodded, but said nothing, the news on the radio distracting him: a body discovered in a nearby marsh or something. Joe seemed put out that he didn't ask where he was going, but Madden had long been used to his unexplained comings and goings. Anyway, what was there to say? It was Joe's business now, even if he didn't mind running it into the ground.

'I have to see about Catherine, get the flowers sorted and that,' he said. 'See if we can't get her to come in some time tomorrow, or later in the week. Either that or sack the silly bint.' He winked at Madden, no doubt the idea that they were cheeky co-conspirators an appealing one for him.

As he was opening the door, he leaned back in for a moment to add something.

'I know you're busy and that, but would you mind talking to Whatsisname's wife?'

'Whose wife?'

'The suicide's. His wife said she was going to come by, today or tomorrow. She said she wanted to talk about the service with someone.'

'Can't you do it?' Madden said, unnerved. 'I thought the talking was where you excelled.'

Joe shook his head emphatically. 'Flowers, man,' he said. 'Got to see about the flowers, deal with Catherine. Off again on ma mad travels! You'll be fine.' He winked again and disappeared out the door, a brief slash of bright sunlight being shut out with its closing. The radio droned on into the stillness.

Kincaid's wife didn't appear until late that afternoon, but Madden was unable to work with his customary speed for the rest of the day, nerves on edge and his pins-and-needles playing up so that he was constantly wringing out his hands. For five or ten minutes after this he would feel some life in them, but the tingling never took long to return. It was the physical effort of some of the heavier labour which seemed to cause it, and he had never managed to find any very successful curative. His rhythm had been broken by the constant inter-ruptions of the phone, the necessity of dealing with the arrival of the other two bodies, and his dread at the prospect of having to speak to Mrs Kincaid, whenever she decided to come by.

What was particularly concerning was the problem of identification. He often forgot names and faces these days, and it had been forty years at least since he'd set eyes on her.

He knew how foolish he was being, that Mrs Kincaid couldn't be angry with him. He'd done nothing wrong this time; her husband's death hadn't been down to him. His conscience was clear on that score. Likely, Maisie wouldn't even remember him. She must be in her eighties at least, for Christ's sake, and she'd no doubt be too upset to concern herself much with him. All the same, the idea that she might recall him bothered him more than he cared to admit. Normally, he had little to do with the families of the deceased, finding the practice of embalming or otherwise treating the dead a more natural use for such talents as he possessed. He'd never been, as Rose never tired of reminding him, a people person. But in truth, he found it too much a strain to be of much help anyway. Speaking to a member of a dead body's family, whether a blood relation or partner, interfered too much with his perception of the deceased as simply that: dead, inanimate, *work*. He'd never been one for emotional displays – not for a long time anyway – either in himself or others. Rose was as much as he felt he could reasonably deal with, and even that was exhausting, so much so that he found it difficult to sympathise with her to any great degree, too draining; as though she were a parasite feeding from him. And usually it wasn't necessary for him to be present should a family member wish to query some small detail of the process: that was what Catherine had been for, and she had performed adequately enough until recently, when she'd abused him for the last time. It was ridiculous: he'd only brushed against her for a second, he'd said.

Just you keep they deid body fingers of yours away fae me! I know what you're up to. Don't think I don't know what you're up to!

Even Joe was of more use than himself in the conversation department. Though Madden had initially been unsure of him, Joe's father had been one of the best, able to put anyone – no matter the degree of their distress – at their ease with only the simplest of words and manner. It was as though his whole demeanour spoke of peace, of rest, of the natural and the supernatural walking hand in hand as they inevitably must. It was a different story below stairs, though. He swore at the bodies, handled them with no apparent respect for title or rank, be they banker or bum. They all got the same treatment. Madden had seen him spit on corpses, occasionally even stab them with a scalpel in some out-of-the-way spot no one was likely to see. But very *slowly*. Joseph Caldwell had done everything very slowly and very quietly. His own dying had been carried out so slowly and quietly that no one in his family – least of all young Joe – had noticed he was unwell. In the end, his wife had asked him why he wasn't getting up for work that morning, and, his face pointed upwards at the ceiling, he'd said, 'I'm going to be deid in ten minutes, that's why.' Sure enough, ten minutes later he was – to use his own expression – brown breid. His wife had remarked to Madden later that his body had turned icily cold literally seconds after he'd stopped breathing, it was amazing. In his own way, Madden had found a great deal to admire in Joseph Caldwell Snr. None of which was going to help him deal with Mrs Kincaid.

Again, he found himself struggling to picture her. He remembered she'd been an attractive woman – forty years ago – but he couldn't seem to pin her features down and make them stay constant; they swam and merged with all the other past faces in kaleidoscopic flux. All he could clearly remember was that Gaskell had said she'd been a 'great little dancer' – he'd often seen her take the floor at the medical faculty balls, dragging a put-upon Kincaid about the hall like so much dead weight – but now Madden couldn't recall whether she'd been that *little* at all. He imagined people had said she'd been *flighty*, or *feisty*, or *headstrong*, but that might simply have been a trick of memory or imagination. He could see her birl about to the Cumberland Reel or the Dashing White Sergeant, but the face was an amalgamation of Kincaid's own, Gaskell's and even Carmen Alexander's. He could even see himself, watching her from the side of the dance floor of the old Men's Union, half of heavy in his hand, suffering behind a too tight tie and his father's navy blue suit, so underfed he was painful to behold.

Even then, dancing had been for others, something he'd never got the hang of. Once he'd actually pretended to faint when a girl, plumpish and acutely embarrassed, had asked him to be her partner for an Eightsome Reel during Ladies' Choice. He'd stumbled down the stairs and hid in the lavatory, nursing his half until he'd felt that the threat from the opposite sex had passed. It was on the way back up that he'd bumped into Gaskell for the first time, standing at the double doors that opened out on to University Avenue. He was wearing an olive-green suit, his thin blond hair already down to the ears, though the hippy era was still a good few years away. The green suit had marked Gaskell as someone different even then, someone who liked to be the centre of attention. It had been made of corduroy. A decade earlier and he'd have been called a beatnik, if he hadn't been beaten up in the street first. As Madden had passed, following the *hee-euchs!* back to the ballroom, Gaskell had blown a smoke ring from a white cigarette, one of those old dead brands, maybe a Woodbine or Capstan Shanty. Senior Service. He was evidently aware of an audience, and Madden was momentarily disgusted by him, the nocturnal white of his skin and the angular cheekbones. That the man had blown the smoke ring purely for Madden's benefit caused him to blush.

'Quite right, get back up there and dance with the girl,' he said, with a kind of twang to his accent that Madden couldn't place, the damned bricks of the man. As he climbed the steps, he was aware of the green-suited chap following him up, but determined to ignore him, forcefully pushing through the doors of the ballroom and neglecting to hold them open for the stranger just behind him, then instantly regretting his rudeness as he heard the hard clack of the door strike something that was distinctly not-door. He immediately turned to see the man bent over, clutching at his face on the other side of the glass. Mortified, Madden went through to him, pulling a linen handkerchief from the breast pocket of his suit.

'Are you all right?' he said, his hand going to the man's back, the other pushing the handkerchief up towards his line of vision. Blood fell in a radial splash pattern on to the marbled flooring, and the man took the handkerchief and pressed it to his face before lifting his head up and back.

'Here, hold your nose at the bridge,' Madden said, knowing from past experience that this was a technique that, like holding your breath for hiccups, sometimes worked and sometimes didn't. But at least it allowed him to feel as though he was in control of the situation and not the cause of it. The man in the green suit held his head back, both hands cupping the hankie to his face, his eyes closed and watery.

'I'm awful sorry, I didn't mean to do that.'

'Yes you bloody well did.'

Madden was horrified, and felt his already red face turn puce.

'Any idea how much this suit cost me?' the man said, and Madden saw for the first time the splashes of red on the lapels, and down the front of his brown shirt, which he wore open at the collar and without a tie. He had never seen a grown man wear a brown shirt and a green suit before in his life. The idea was inconceivable in Shakespeare Street. He could probably walk through Maryhill barefoot and have less attention paid to him than if he wore a suit like that himself.

'I'm awful sorry,' Madden said, his voice becoming desperate. 'I'm sure it'll wash out. Was it awful expensive?' Taking the hankie from his face, Madden saw that the man's nose appeared to have stopped bleeding for the moment. The end was bloodied, and a large lump was beginning to swell up by

23

the bridge. The man tentatively felt around the general area with his fingertips.

'Only bloody well gone and broken it, haven't you. Bloody Christ in heaven. Six years trying to avoid a thumping on the rugby pitch, then you come along and *whammo!* All for nothing.'

His nose began to drip again.

'Hold your head back,' Madden said. 'It's the best way.'

From under the hankie, the man said, what was he, a bloody doctor or what?

'Not yet,' Madden said. 'First-year medicine. The next best thing.'

Madden remembered how the green-suited man had laughed, a loud splutter that gargled a deal of blood back with it. An infectious laugh.

'Well, well,' he said. 'Likewise, I'm sure. You'll make a fortune if you carry on the way you are at the moment. Christ.'

'I'm awful sorry,' Madden said, 'I really am. If you want to get your suit cleaned, you can send me the bill for it. My name's Hugh, by the way.' He stuck out a distressingly formal hand. The fellow with the bloodied nose eyed it cautiously, head still tilted back. 'Owen,' he said. 'But everyone calls me Gaskell.' He shook Madden's hand limply. 'I can't honestly say I'm pleased to make your acquaintance, not right this minute anyway.'

'Are you studying here as well?' Madden asked, rummaging in his inside jacket pocket for something to write his address on.

Gaskell let out a long sigh, again snorting back the blood in his nose. '*Yessssss*,' he gurgled, then spat a bloody clot into the hankie. 'I *am* a student here, I *do* study . . .'

Madden didn't know how best to respond to Gaskell's tone, so carried on being what he'd thought was responsible and doctorly, the way he'd imagined in those days how he might be when fully qualified. Ah, youth, ah, dreams. 'That's it. That's right. Hold it above your head.'

Gaskell waved a hand at him in irritation.

'For fuck's *sake*,' he said. 'It doesn't fucking well *work* half the time anyway. I'm a fucking medic too, you know.'

Madden thought he'd seen him somewhere before, but had just assumed he was one of the many anonymous faces here that he didn't know but saw on a daily basis. Lectures or lab, that must be it.

'I'm in your fucking tutorials, for fuck's sake! You know, Kincaid's group? Anatomy? I see you there every other week!'

Again, Madden had no idea what to say.

'Well,' he offered, after a suitably painful period had passed, 'very pleased to meet you.' And he had stuck out his hand once more.

Three

The sixties happened elsewhere. For Madden they were in newspapers and on the radio, somewhere south, London, Carnaby Street, 'I Wanna Hold Your Hand'. His sixties were different, as his hair-thinned sixties were now. It had been enough in those days simply to take the morning walk – why waste the bus fare – down across the Kelvin and on to the bright lights, such as the times permitted, of the West End. How might he have described himself then: eighteen going on fifty? It was fair to say that part of him had always been the age he was now. Was it the dormant part or the wide-awake part that he was defined by? Certainly his memories of the time weren't connected to any great sense of liberation, or momentous possibilities just around the corner. Before Gaskell he'd hardly spoken to another student during that whole first semester, and instead had flung himself into his studies with an enthusiasm he'd later reserve for the mortuary. Gaskell it was who had described Madden as a 'young fogey'. He was the sort of person, he'd said, who had leather elbow patches sewn into the tweed lining of his elderly soul.

Yet, at the same time, Madden had been half aware of the lopsidedness of his devotions, that he should be making an effort with folk of his own age, as his mother would tell him without much conviction. His father rarely deigned to offer an opinion: the very fact his only child had chosen to go to university and not to Colville's steel yards and earn a living was a source of neither pride nor disappointment; he'd often spoken of the benefits of an education he lacked himself and in the same breath of the necessity of being able to earn a wage, of being able to put a roof above the heads of the family, of being a man's man in a man's world. He believed in the revolutionary power of socialism, yet despised wage strikes as union manipulation and strikers themselves as ingrates, unworthy of the job they'd been given. Kick the buggers out and let someone else have a shot, see how they like it, he'd say. If he had his way he'd sling the bloody lot of them out on their arse. He hated scabs even more, they were dupes of the bosses, but saw no contradiction in this. Madden felt no political allegiances at all, but instead would adopt whatever was the prevailing attitude among his university peers on the few occasions he was quizzed on such subjects. The issue itself did not matter, only how he responded. That was the way to be included. That was the way to be absorbed as part of something, part of the cause. And he would have liked to have a cause, some worthy ideal to grab him by the throat, to demand of him *Fight! Fight or die!*

Some kind of companionship would have been a start, but it seemed he lacked social graces, the ability to put others at their ease in his company. Something about him was missing. Something in him didn't fit. Instead, he would watch the other students in the lecture halls with the eye of a practised anthropologist. Imagining there must be some clue in their mannerisms and gestures, the cadence of their voice, the way they dressed, he felt he was in some way absorbing something he could cultivate in himself, into his own personality.

Days or weeks passed when he had been so completely (what was the word?) *possessed* he was hardly aware of his own existence, had become much less real to himself than *that other*, the group, the set, the *I'm-in-with-the-in-crowd*. People like Dizzy Newlands, Hector Fain, Carmen Alexander; a rectangle with himself as the invisible fourth side. Carmen, bottle-blonde devotee of Tommy Steele (already old hat) keeping the suitors perpetually in competition, though it was obvious she'd eventually choose the knitwear-catalogue looks of army cadet Dizzy over Hector, since he at least had the good sense to flirt with her and laugh at her jokes. Meanwhile Hector the radical chuntered on with his eternal monologue; Marx, Hölderlin, the non-existence of the soul, the existence of the soul, the fight against the petit-bourgeois liberal democracy, the effectiveness of ju-jitsu. Soon the times they would be a-changin'. It would be time to man the barricades, ration the bread, dig a bomb shelter before Kennedy and Khrushchev blew everything out of the water.

Dizzy and Carmen walking so close their arms occasionally brushing each other, benignly giggling while Hector squinted. *What? What are you laughing at?*

You, Dizzy would say. *The man who's going to shoot the capitalist running dogs from behind the pulpit.*

And Carmen would burst into a fresh round of giggling, her hand covering her mouth discreetly because actually her gums were so expansive that if Dizzy ever got a good clear view of them then he'd drop her like a hot stone and find himself a new Diana Dors. Poor Hector, crushed again, strutting off in humiliation, unable to reconcile his God and his Cause. Dizzy shouting after, *Hector, wait. I didn't mean it.*

But you did, didn't you, Dizzy, of course you did. All's fair in love and war and all's equal in the class struggle, a man's a man for a' that. Get the other guy before he gets you, so sayeth Marlon Brando. Dizzy, calculating, feigning dumbo for Fain. He and Carmen sharing complicit looks of sympathy for their departed friend, their hands momentarily touching. A guilty smile on Carmen's lips but no laugh. Giggling isn't appropriate, and she couldn't possibly give old Diz a flash of those terrible gums. He'll never marry her that way.

Madden listened in, breathed their air. He might have been any one of them. He might be Dizzy with the camera that his father bought him for his nineteenth birthday casually looped over one shoulder and a cigarette dangling from those handsome lips. Say cheese. Or Carmen, worrying whether her roots show, about the Christmas prelims, whether Dizzy has told everyone he calls her Ham-bones because of her skinny legs. Smile, please, everybody, that's right. Best of all would be Hector. Wee Eck, as he hated to be known, all socialism and sulphur, keen player of chess but no strategist and unable to *finish*. Snap snap.

None of them paid Madden any mind, beyond a civil nod when passing. They were not those kinds of friends. They were not friends at all. Dizzy and Carmen started going out, and Hector slunk off to find a girl who was less of a challenge, though Madden wasn't convinced he hadn't caught a glimpse of those gums. He'd bumped into him once, literally, crossing the quadrangles at a quick trot to get out of the rain, his revolutionary arms pressing a pile of books against his chest, the same put-upon look on his face. He careened into Madden and the books fell on the ground. Madden, as usual with apologies primed, bent to help him pick them up, Sorry, sorry. Could he help?

No he blooming well couldn't, silly bugger. Was he blind or something?

Madden was stung. Forgetting himself he snarled, *He's fucking her, you know. Good old Dizzy. All the time you had your head in* Das Kapital *and he was fucking her right in front of you. You thought Dizzy was your friend, didn't you. Perhaps you'd better stick to Sunday school.*

If Hector ever did have to fire on the enemy from behind his pulpit, he'd have the same look of horror on his face. When he stood up his eyes were filled with hurt incomprehension as Madden walked away. But it was Hector who won in the end.

And who the hell might you be? he shouted after, to which Madden had no reply.

*

There were others that Madden had observed too. For a while it had been the very few foreigners studying at the university. People like the industrious Aduman, about whom it was difficult to know anything except for superficial things. His country of origin was Senegal and he was so shy it precluded speech. He kept entirely to himself, even in company, standing awkwardly on the outskirts of any group of people he had the misfortune to be invited to join, a pleasure rarely bestowed on Madden. The pockets hung shapelessly at the sides of his oversized sports jacket and he kept his hands stuffed in there wherever he walked. There was not a single button remaining on the jacket. Hands buried, he'd pull the two sides together when it was cold, an impossibly long woollen scarf of indiscriminate colour permanently twined about his neck. Aduman lived in a crumbling tenement house broken up into bedsits in Cecil Street, just over the brow of the hill, two minutes from the campus, and Madden would watch him stoop in the street to pick up lost change, half-smoked cigarette ends, discarded chip-pokes, a forlorn figure one step from destitution and likely the only Senegalese, never mind black, in the whole of the west of Scotland. Madden admired the way he had isolated himself, the way he relied on nobody except himself. There were no hangers-on, no group or set, with Aduman. He seemed to want or need no one, in fact had designed his life so it could be that way. It was an admirable ability, Madden decided. He was absolutely and completely alone. Yet, unlike himself, Aduman did not seem to care or crave other human contact, the necessary evil of companionship. Madden knew his own failures were the poisonous and diseased attachments he despised himself desiring, but was unable to prevent himself longing. The need to exist at the peripheral edge of another's life and somehow take succour from it, bleed it without the other's knowledge like a vampire bat hanging from the neck of a cow. And Gaskell, it seemed, had filled that need better than anyone.

He hadn't wanted to leave the ceilidh that evening, despite his bloodied shirt. The night, he was fond of saying, was young. And youth had to be honoured, youth and the young had to elbow the old aside to make room for themselves. Wouldn't Madden agree with those sentiments?

Oh, yes, Madden said, though he found the sentiments in question to be trite, the sort of thing that people of that generation were always saying in those days. But, blood splashed on his lapels, and his nose swollen, Gaskell had cut a fine impression – not least with himself – of tragic rebellion, the kind of figure Madden supposed he must have always wanted to be. A James Dean awaiting his moment to go up in flames in a burning wreck, an Elvis shaking up the jailhouse. A Che Guevara or a Kennedy – not yet the icons they would later become, but soon to be. And in a way he got what he wanted later, followed the attitudes and the posturing through despite himself. The hail of bullets beckoned, the young death, the good death.

Yet Madden could never believe that there was any truth in any of these poses for this new . . . *what?* Again he found himself wondering whether friends was what they had been, in the beginning at least. Friendships were few and far between; they were elusive and could not always be trusted. If anything, his unconnected connectedness with Gaskell had taught him as much. Contact, a symbiosis of one soul with another, *love*. The ever-fixed mark, the parasite that devoured you from within. But Madden had never been in love, not then. Gaskell, he believed, would only ever be capable of loving himself.

When they had returned to the ceilidh, Gaskell forced him to drink a toast. 'To Jacobites,' he said. 'To Bonnie Prince Charlie,' he said. 'To the miniskirt. To old acquaintances never being forgot. To this uncouth brawling that you Jocks call dancing!'

The ceilidh band were squashed into a corner at the far end

of the great oak-panelled galleon of a room, two hundred people or more each engaged in the closed combat that was known as Strip the Willow. Brylcreem-quiffed and skinny-suited young men, ruddy faced with booze, hurled helpless girls in staggered footwear about in broken-glass arabesques, the band long since having given up any attempt at guiding the tempo. The accordion player was staring grimly into the middle distance and the fiddler flagellated his instrument with a bow that was so frayed it looked more like a cat-o'-nine-tails. Both were in their fifties at least, and despite the energy they gave to the performance, there was an exhausted desperation to it. The accordion player stared into the void of the crowd, indifferent to the carnage that was occurring on the dance floor. Several young women had come crashing into the seated tables that lined the hall, and more than one young man had reeled dizzily off to the relative safety of the bar. Over on the far side of the hallway, Madden could make out the familiar face of Kincaid, sitting at a table, throwing his head back every now and again in laughter. He appeared to be holding court with some of the other academics and their spouses. Madden wondered whether the woman on his left was his wife. She was exchanging mock-put-upon looks with the wives or girlfriends of the others.

Gaskell tapped his foot along, pointed and snorted with laughter at the whole shambolic scene. He gulped down his whisky and ordered more, grimacing and shaking his head as he downed them. The dim lighting camouflaged the blood spots on his clothes; besides, in this place he could be the terrorist he really wished he had been, the anarchist with the bomb in his pocket.

'Hieronymus Bosch couldn't do better!' he shouted at Madden over the rammy. 'Now I know where you Jocks learn to fight!' He clapped his hands and ordered more whisky for Madden, refusing to take his refusal at face value.

'Look,' he said, 'you don't have to worry. I've got money, so

I'll stand you a round. Generosity is the better part of valour, or something. You can buy me a drink next time.'

Madden wondered when that might be. He had little or no money all of the time. His father had told him he could get him work at Colville's, but Madden had allowed the offer to die stillborn. *More cut out for a mortician anyway, if you ask me*, his father had added. Prophetic words indeed.

'Why did you follow me out earlier?' Madden asked Gaskell.

'Saw you were on your own, didn't I?' Gaskell said, wiping his hair back from his face, his angular cheekbones and white pallor giving him an oddly insubstantial look. Someone not there, or someone who had ceased to become real. A dead man, a ghost.

'There's lots of people here on their own. Why follow me?'

'I watched you run away from that poor girl. All she wanted was to dance, and you ran away. I couldn't stand it. I wanted to grab you by the scruff of the neck and drag you back up there. I was going to say, "Look, mister, dance with this girl . . . she's taken a lot of trouble to walk over that dance floor to ask you to dance, and you've embarrassed her. You've made her look a fool. And a man should never make a lady look like a fool, especially not in a public place." Her friends are probably sitting with her right now. They probably watched the whole thing.'

Gaskell didn't look at Madden, staring instead at the dance floor. The band had moved on to a slower number, and the casualties of the last dance limped or crawled back to their tables to tend to their injuries. The floor thinned out and was mainly populated by sedate couples gently birling round the room to the waltz that the now seated musicians scraped out in a fair impression of 2/4 timing.

'It made me angry to see that,' Gaskell said. 'I felt you owed the girl an apology. Or at least a dance, don't you think?' He turned to look at Madden. Madden sipped from his half-pint.

'Yes. You're right,' he said. 'She must have been upset by that. I should apologise.'

'Bugger your apologies, man. Go and dance with her!'

'I don't know where she is,' Madden said. 'Besides, she'd only say no. I ran away from her, why on earth would she want to dance with me now?'

Gaskell sighed through his nose inaudibly, but a fleck of dried blood twitched at the corner of his nostril, then flew out and pinged off Madden's cheek. He wiped himself with distaste, but neglected to mention it to Gaskell. He seemed tightly wound. Possibly, he was capable of violence.

'You know what, Madman? You're absolutely right. Why would she want to dance with you. Why would anyone want to dance with you. It just doesn't stand up to reason, does it?'

He knocked back his whisky and placed his glass back down on the counter.

'Will you just look at that *marvellous* creature . . .' he said, and Madden peered across the room, trying to glimpse whoever or whatever it was that Gaskell was so taken by. Of course. There she was, across the other side of the room, momentarily abandoned by her worshippers. She seemed at a loss as to what to do and edged a cigarette stub away from herself with her shoe. It was an extraordinary sight: Madden might have put it down to powers of the mind, voodoo or something. Carmen raised her head as if searching the crowd on the dance floor, then stilled her gaze, seeing Gaskell but not seeing him. Madden glanced at Gaskell, saw Gaskell smile effortlessly at her. She looked away, caught, then looked up again. Madden didn't quite believe things could actually happen like this.

Wiping his mouth with his sleeve, Gaskell said, 'Well, I think I shall have a go, even if you won't. Besides, it doesn't look as though the band will be much longer for this world. I fully expect to see all of them again on Monday morning.'

Madden was puzzled. 'Where are you expecting to see

34

them?' he asked. He could see Dizzy Newlands wave at the girl, but she was already moving towards the floor. He could see Hector staring at Carmen, then at Dizzy, and put a pint to his lips, his face opaque, vague.

Gaskell tipped an invisible hat to Madden before backing into the crowd, feet itching in a boss-nova shuffle. 'On the slabs, Madman! We'll be opening them up soon if they're not careful . . .' He sidled underneath the linked arms of a drunken couple who, ignoring the etiquette of the waltz, were attempting the Twist instead, their enthusiasm not matched by their execution. It was more assassination attempt than elimination dance. Madden stood on his tiptoes to try to catch sight of Gaskell, but he had already found himself a partner and was cavorting about in wholehearted fashion to 'Step We Gaily On We Go'. That tall, slender girl, with blonde hair and strangely conservative knee-length white pleated dress. A great expanse of gum. For a moment he stood, fixated on the arm Gaskell had placed on Carmen's back, their other hands with fingers intertwined. He could see the connection between them, the way their eyes were locked. Madden had to look away. He knew that she would be completely taken with Gaskell, that they made the perfect couple. He knew that they would embark on a long liaison that would teeter precariously between his highs and her lows, between frantic pleas from one to the other, between remorseful acceptances and vicious rejections. He knew all this because he was imagining what sort of girl Carmen ought to be, and now because he knew Gaskell too. They were perfect for each other. Even bloodied and half drunk, Gaskell was perfect for her. As she was for him: her sweet-natured enthusiasm, the slightly gauche candour of her spiritedness; these would be irresistible to someone like Gaskell. At the very least, Madden could see that much.

He turned and stood once more by the bar – actually a Formica table tended by one of the Union dinner ladies, a woman of early middle age with a convincingly Caledonian hostility to custom. Putting his glass down, he attempted to catch her eye with a gesture of his head, but she gazed doggedly past him and said 'What can I get ye?' to the person behind him instead. He jerked around and glowered at the offender, a man, feeling it almost within his power to punch him for his rudeness. But not quite: the chap was a good three inches taller than him – though Madden considered himself of above average stature for a Glaswegian male of that time. He lowered his eyes quickly and swirled the dregs of his drink around his glass.

'I know you, do I not?' the man said.

Madden raised his eyes to meet the taller man's gaze, but found he could not.

'Yes. You're Gaskell, aren't you? From anatomy?'

Madden finally brought his head up, the weight of his skull complicit with gravity in their desire to keep him staring at the floor. Dr Kincaid was staring past him at the Union dinner lady, his hand raised to present her with his money. He flicked a glance occasionally in Madden's direction, talking with his pipe jutting from his jaw.

'No, I'm Madden,' he said, some part of him regretting he hadn't answered in the affirmative. It would have been something, to have been someone else, to have another man's life, even if it was just for a moment. A second.

'Of course, of course,' Kincaid said. 'But I know you from anatomy, do I not?' He nodded a thank you at the dinner lady, then smiled at her. Madden was unsurprised to see her smile back, toy briefly with her caterer's cap, then hand over two glasses to the doctor, who downed one immediately before raising the glass to the woman, who topped it up again from a bottle of Laphroaig.

Madden said yes, he knew him from anatomy. He was in the doctor's anatomy tutorial group. The words fell out of his mouth, a drunken wooziness taking their edge away so that they sounded to him as if they had been read from a page rather than spoken by a living person.

'I remember. Yes,' the doctor said, savouring the taste of the whisky. 'Could do with some more effort from you, Mr Madden,' he said. 'A wee tate more of an effort, aye. Tell me, what made you decide to read medicine?' Kincaid angled his head towards Madden, looking at him out of the corner of his eye, not worthy of full engagement.

Madden felt suddenly very drunk. 'I . . . want to become a doctor,' he said.

Kincaid pressed his face close to Madden's, his breath a mixture of pungent iodine and tobacco, the vague aroma of formalin, the fragrance of university corridors. Madden pulled back slightly, but not so much as to give offence.

'Ah! A *doctor*, he says. A *physick*. A quack. A faith healer. A shaman. A *sham*, even.' Kincaid winked. 'Well, which is it, boy? Out with it!'

The doctor swayed slightly, his face pushing closer to Madden's, one hand resting on his shoulder. Madden was aware of the sensation of his own face, the weighty flabbiness the booze had lent it, and Kincaid's hand gripping his collarbone.

'A doctor,' Madden managed to say. 'I want to be a . . . *good* doctor.'

Kincaid grinned at him with spittle-flecked lips, He moved his hand on the back of Madden's neck, pulling him gently towards him so that their foreheads touched.

'A good doctor. Very noble of you, Mr Gaskell, a fine ambition. Very fine. Very noble,' he said, his demeanour altering perceptibly. This time Madden did not correct the doctor's mistake. He was too drunk. 'And a fine saw-doctor you'd make too. A fine shaman. But it takes effort, Mr Gaskell. It takes a lot of hard work and late nights. Many sacrifices. Blood, sir, it will take blood. The *red sweat*! And one has to undertake this aforementioned hard work and these latterly described sacrifices for the right reasons. The right reasons, Mr Gaskell. Otherwise—'

Madden waited for the otherwise to put in an appearance, raising his empty glass to his mouth and then letting it hang to his side once again.

Kincaid again patted his cheek, and stood upright. He smiled as if at some private joke then tapped his nose with a forefinger.

'The right reasons?' Madden said.

'Excuse me,' Kincaid said. 'I'm being rude: let us not talk shop. A drink! Tonight is a night for the celebration of that too brief thing.'

Madden watched the doctor turn to the bar once again, his height a distinct advantage as he waved a pound note at the woman behind it. It occurred to him that the too brief thing to which the doctor referred might be licensing hours. He briefly eyed his watch: it was already gone nine; the pubs on Byres Road would have called time already; his father would have already begun the trudge home.

Kincaid was still holding the other drink in his hand, and had not touched a drop of it. He collected two whiskies with the other hand and waved away the change. The woman looked delighted, even as she tried to push the change back into the doctor's hand. Madden was swaying on the spot, his nerves now pleasantly jingling, as though he were able to observe himself detachedly from behind an opaque window, unconcerned and immune. Because for the moment he was Gaskell, not Hugh Madden. And there was respite in that. There was relief in it.

'Here,' Kincaid said, handing him the glass. 'Wha's like us.'

The doctor sipped a few drops from his own, and Madden did the same, savouring the richness of the malt. He was used to the blended stuff.

'That's the damned bricks,' the doctor said. Madden was aware for the first time that Kincaid's pipe had never left the side of his mouth the entire time they had been speaking, sticking out from his salt-and-pepper whiskers like a narwhal's tusk. He was turned out in a green kilt and knee-length wool socks, a skean-dhu – or perhaps a scalpel – jutting from the cuff. A distinctly *square* look, for any male under the age of forty at any rate. But he carried it off well. He wondered whether the kilt was Kincaid's own tartan, then if *he* had a tartan. Probably the Maddens were subsidiaries of some more powerful clan. More likely they were just Irish.

'Tell me, lad, why you're not out there giving it laldy with the rest of them. Not here on your own, are you?' Kincaid was bobbing on his toes to the music, his fist keeping time with the imagined skirl of pipe bands instead of the wheezy elbowing of the player who sat at the end of the hall battering out 'Speed Bonny Boat' on a chipped accordion.

'No, sir, I'm—'

'That's the spirit,' Kincaid said, engrossed in the music. 'Should be out there on that floor engaging the enemy. Speaking of which . . .'

'Sir?'

Kincaid furrowed his brow, following something Madden wasn't tall enough to see.

'Enough with the "sirs",' Kincaid muttered. 'Tonight you find me in my informal capacity. My night off, so to speak. Call me *Mr* Kincaid.'

Madden breathed easier. A certain external stiffness, a constricting collar of deference, prevented him from dissolving into the usual tics of discomfort that he failingly had assumed would pass for amiability in company. That collar was all that kept him from diving under the nearest hedge when forced to 'converse' with someone like Kincaid. He gazed like a drugged goldfish at the cufflinks on the doctor's shirt, his bow tie black and unstrung around his neck. Perspiration speckled his forehead.

Madden mopped his own brow, aware that Kincaid's

moisture would be mingling with his own: their mutually perspiring skins, their inhaling and exhaling lungs, producing invisible cloudlets of excess. Chemical compounds, monoxides, micro-organisms. Life's wastes. It was repulsively intimate. They were invading each other's bodies without consent, each unthinkingly subjecting the other to a kind of chemical and bacterial rape. In fact, the entire hall. The entire building. The whole bloody world, if you wanted to look at it like that, was just one huge seething mass of microscopic sodomy. He felt a bit giddy at that, and took a sip of his whisky. It instantly induced the required level of stupefaction. He calmed down slightly, looking up to see an elegant woman, possibly in her mid-thirties – younger than Kincaid anyway – join him at his side. She placed a protective hand on his back, as if gently applied pressure could goad him in the right direction without the good doctor realising he was actually being led.

The doctor smiled indulgently and kissed the woman on the cheek, which she presented to him with feigned affectation.

'Mwah!' Kincaid said, doubling her affectation with his own. 'There you are, lighthouse of my life, wrecker of the clipper that is my heart . . . I was about to come looking for you.'

'Of course you were,' the woman said, laying a slim and angular spread of manicured nails around the glass that he still carried. 'Absolutely you were. But then you got distracted, didn't you? This *is* for me, isn't it?' She was very good looking, pale skinned and dark haired, a rosiness to her cheeks that might have been a result of the heat, or drink. Whatever the reason, it suited her and gave her a youthful shine, an appearance of vitality. She struck Madden as possessed of a very Scottish look. But in a good way.

'It is, it is,' Kincaid said, presenting the glass to her as if surrendering a drawn blade, over an outstretched arm and bowing his head to her.

She took it and sipped, then frowned. 'I said gin and tonic. This is gin and lemonade.'

The doctor threw up his hands. 'There was no tonic, beloved. This is a student union: all they drink in student unions is lemonade and orange squash. That not right, Mr Gaskell?'

Madden harrumphed into his own glass and felt his ears go red.

'I'm awful sorry, it's actually Madden,' he said after a pause. 'It's Hugh Madden I'm called.'

'Don't apologise on my account, Hugh,' the woman said. 'You'll find my husband terrible with names. By the end of tonight I doubt he'll remember his own. He rarely remembers mine.' She smiled drily at Kincaid, and he returned the compliment.

'Mr Madden, allow me to introduce my wife, Maisie,' the doctor said. 'Maisie, this is Mr Madden.' Again, he smirked at his wife.

'Rosemary,' she said to Madden, offering her hand. 'Just ignore him. He thinks he's funny. I believe I've had the pleasure of meeting our friend Owen already.'

It took Madden a moment to realise she was referring to Gaskell, but he nodded stupidly anyway. Kincaid was glowering at his wife, and attempting to light up his pipe with a match, but couldn't manage to strike it effectively while still holding his glass. Madden and Rosemary Kincaid waited for him, his brow growing increasingly furrowed until finally he acknowledged defeat and handed his glass to Madden, who took it without protest. His wife continued to stare at him with something akin to pity on her face.

'Bright lad, Mr Madden here,' Kincaid said between blue puffs of smoke. 'Needs to buckle under, though, heh? Put a bit of thought into what he's about.'

Rosemary Kincaid sighed. 'Can we not talk about this at the moment, please?' she said, taking her husband's arm. 'All they're doing over at the table is gossiping like a shower of fishwives about students and teachers and all whatnot. I swear this is the last time you're getting me to one of these . . . *events.*' She smiled at Madden, who didn't know what to do. It occurred to him he ought maybe to smile back, but Kincaid's wife wasn't looking in his direction any more.

'Come back and rescue me,' she was saying to Kincaid. 'I'm sure Hugh has other people he wants to talk to.' Again, she smiled at Madden, and this time he smiled back punctually, aware of showing too many teeth.

'What *other* people?' Kincaid demanded. 'Other *people*! Never heard of such a thing. Can't have it. Won't have it. Send for the police!' He shook his head, and Madden and Rosemary Kincaid laughed indulgently for his benefit.

'You know, those other people you're always talking about. *That brief thing . . .*'

'What was that? You mentioned it earlier, Dr Kincaid,' Madden found himself saying, perhaps a little too shrilly, a little too suddenly. Both Kincaid and his wife were staring at him as if he had just unzipped his fly and shown them his penis. He felt his ears turn puce, and he lowered his voice.

'You said this night was a celebration of it. I wondered what it was. What the brief thing was that we were celebrating, I mean . . .'

It was Rosemary Kincaid who leaned over and whispered the answer in his ear, their cheeks touching.

'*Youth*, Hugh,' she said. 'Tonight is a celebration of youth. And my advice to you is to go and find one of them to dance with. Preferably of the female variety.'

She turned to Kincaid. 'And we oldies will do the same. Come on, Lawrence. You're going to dance with me . . .'

Kincaid shook his head, but his wife was already easing him towards the dance floor, the vibrations from which Madden could feel in his sternum.

'For pity's sake, Maisie, it's trench warfare out there . . . can you not wait for a waltz . . . ?'

'Then fix your bayonet, doll, and let's go over the top . . .'

They made their way into the throng, but not before Kincaid turned his head over his shoulder and tossed Madden a wink. Then he couldn't see them any more.

'Quite a couple they make, eh, Madman?'

Gaskell was standing at his side, wiping sweat from his eyes with his sleeve.

'You've met them before?'

'Oh, here and there,' he said, making a very big show of tapping his nose with a forefinger as Kincaid had done. 'Out and about,' he added. 'I didn't much feel like conversation – not with the old boy anyway. He irritates me.' Madden nodded, watching Gaskell tuck in his brown shirt, the upper half darkened by sweat. 'A drink?' he asked, but didn't wait for a reply before waving to the woman behind the bar. Madden was powerless in here, among these people: it wouldn't matter if he said, No, actually, I'm fine at the moment; it would be ignored anyway. He had ceased to be. He was evaporating into the ether. He wasn't Hugh Madden, son of Hugh Madden and Patricia Madden, née – née what? He couldn't recall. Ran . . . Randall . . . Ramsay? Beginning with R anyway. Naturally, his mother had never existed before her marriage either, and as her only son he could only have the life sparked into him when he became absorbed in some other process too, another coupling, a pairing. The one could feed and nourish the other, and the other could sustain and sacrifice for the one. Maybe such a union could bear its own fruit, the natural offspring: a new Hugh. He shivered. His whole body must suppurate and ooze with infection. He was repulsive, he revolted folk so much that he was barely able to look them in the eye for fear of seeing that same repulsion reflected back at himself. And there were so many people. So many who must be avoided. They were like a plague, a pestilence, all with eyes that watched and faces that looked. Madden closed his own eyes and breathed in through his nose, attempting to dull his brain somehow, clear his stifling thoughts. There was only one thing for it—

'Cheers, Madman,' Gaskell said, staring at him with studied curiosity. He passed him a glass filled with whisky. 'You all right?'

Madden took the drink and swallowed it down, screwing up his face. The soothing balm reached down into his stomach and upwards into his thoughts, cauterising them and squatting in their place. The beautiful god of sleep and dreams. Morpheus.

Gaskell put a hand on his shoulder, and he flinched. 'Don't,' he said, pulling back.

Gaskell put his hands up. 'Hey, not me.'

Madden slouched to the bar and waved his hand at the woman behind it, trying to get her attention, but she was serving someone else. He waved again and told her to give him whisky, but she told him he'd had enough, go home to bed, sonny Jim. Gaskell was pulling at his sleeve, saying calm down, calm down. He would get one for him, it was no problem. Madden shrugged him away and began to shout at the woman, elbowing some room for himself, some small place at the bar where he could stake a claim and call it his own. This, he would say, is the property of Hugh Madden. May he rest in peace. Gaskell was pulling him backwards by his blazer and he found himself spun round and held by the lapels.

'What's the matter with you?'

'You have to lance me,' Madden said.

'What?'

'You have to lance me,' he said again.

'Why do I have to lance you?' Gaskell asked, laughing.

'Because I'm a boil,' Madden said, giggling. 'I'm a boil and I need a good lancing.'

'A boil, are you?' Gaskell said. 'Well, in that case we have to do the right thing and go find a lance.' He snorted another laugh, and his nose began to drip blood. 'Buggeration,' he said. Dragging Madden by the arm to the corner of the room, he wiped his nose with the blood-smeared square of handkerchief he had been using all night.

'I'll get a lance all right,' he said. 'I know the kind of lance you need. Now sit down over here and get yourself nice and calm and lanced, and I'll get you a nice clean alcohol swab to mop up with. And don't move.'

Gaskell pushed him down on to a long wooden bench, the kind they used in school gymnasiums, and he sat for several long minutes staring at his feet in an attempt to get the two pairs of shoes he was wearing on his left foot to divide into four. Someone came over and tapped him on the shoulder. He looked up and there was a two-headed girl standing in front of him asking him for a light. He didn't have a light, he said, he didn't smoke. The girl quickly put her hand down by her side and seemed on the verge of tears. He hoped she wouldn't burst out weeping with all eight eyes at once otherwise everyone might drown.

'Can I sit down?' she asked him. Madden waved a hand towards the bench and she sat, smoothing her red woollen skirt under her legs as she did so. Madden half turned and looked at her so that she gradually began to shift uncomfortably about, unsure of where to put her hands and crossing and uncrossing her legs.

'Do I know you?' he asked, in a too loud voice.

She glanced nervously over, shook her head vigorously and wondered at the four pairs of fidgeting hands in her lap. He was obviously behaving boorishly, exactly the sort of behaviour he normally despised, and it was enough to instil in him a sense of his own self.

'I'm awful sorry,' he said. 'I was sure we met somewhere, that was all.'

She looked up, her expression difficult for him to make out.

'Ehm, we did. We did meet earlier. I asked you if you'd like to dance. You said to excuse you then you never came back.'

'Ah,' he said. 'I . . . was . . . needed somewhere else.'

'Oh,' she said, then was quiet.

'I think I can get you a light, if you want . . . ?' He was desperate to get out of this, but her expression was as sharp as cold steel. 'Go if you want,' she said. 'I suppose that's what you always do.'

'No,' he said. 'It isn't. I mean, I don't.' Something in his look had revealed his intentions.

'I'm sorry,' he said once more. He paused, then with great effort of will he said: 'D'you want to dance now?'

She nodded with a kind of baleful acceptance, and they both stood up. Gaskell appeared with the drinks. Madden could make out the figure of Dizzy striding purposefully towards Gaskell, dragging Carmen Alexander along by the wrist.

'Thank you, Madman!' Gaskell said, as Madden veered across the floor. 'At long bloody last. Chin-chin!' Madden reached out and caught the proffered drink and downed it as the girl tossed him before her, into the back of another couple. He struggled with her for control of the movements – he'd had as many years of country dancing leathered into him by his schoolteachers as anyone else in the room – but she insisted on leading. Ladies' choice.

His steps were confounded by drink, and the girl giggled at his efforts while he struggled to keep abreast of the others around him. Couples crashed against him as they went round, Madden feeling the nausea rise with each successive turn. He caught sight of Gaskell and Dizzy, lost them for a moment, and then saw them once more, this time joined by Hector. Carmen stood between them, Dizzy's posture aggressive, Hector no doubt talking good sense. Carmen silently thrilled by it all. Only Gaskell, it seemed, was unfathomable, couldn't be read. And then Dizzy was being pulled away, Hector had pinioned his arms, presumably stronger than his physique indicated. Dizzy was shouting something and Gaskell was nodding and smiling, Carmen's expression sharp, disgusted, looking now to Gaskell. Dizzy made a rush forward, but was halted again by Hector, who lifted him bodily around the waist and swung him away. Definitely, he was stronger than he looked.

The band paused between tunes, allowing Madden to catch his breath. The girl was thanking him. He was apologising for his two left feet. She nodded, refusing to let go of his hand, and he noticed for the first time a large mole above her left eye, dark brown. He allowed himself to concentrate on this flaw, let its steadying throb mute his sickness. It was no use. He was about to excuse himself when the music started again and he was dragged along, hopelessly out of time, pitched around by the girl, making no attempt to fight her lead. Couples moved away in irritation and he didn't care. There was no fighting her. At last, the music came to a stop and he began clapping along with all the others, some with hands raised high above their heads.

The girl was thanking *him* this time, and it was his turn to nod, which he did, panting.

'Shall we take a seat?' he asked, not caring whether she joined him or not, but she followed him back to the benches, docile now the music was all over.

'Shame we couldn't have another try,' Madden said, in as sober a voice as possible. 'Looks like they're knocking it on the head for tonight.'

'Oh no,' she said, shaking her head cheerily. 'They're just having a break. They'll be back on in half an hour. We can dance then.'

Madden felt the dumb, forced, redundant smile fall from his face.

'Right,' he said. 'That's good. I'll look forward to that.'

A look of knowing hurt flashed across her eyes. Her mole seemed to be pulsing at him. 'You don't have to if you don't want to. If you'd rather be left alone then you only need to say.'

'No, it's not that, really,' he said. But it *was* that. He wanted her to go away and let him return to his seat, which he would not move from for the rest of the evening if at all possible. Ugly thoughts were crowding his mind; the only way to deal with them more alcohol.

'What's your name anyway?' he was asking her, but didn't quite catch it as Gaskell intervened, leading his – what was she anyway? – *girl* over by the arm.

'Have a good time out there?' Gaskell asked Madden's partner, the fracas with Dizzy conveniently forgotten. 'Should think so too. This,' he said, turning her away from Madden, 'is Carmen. You two will likely get along famously.'

Carmen nodded a greeting, smiling, her hand coming up automatically to conceal her gums. Again, Madden failed to catch the other girl's name. Carol, Caroline? Something like that.

'I've just rescued poor Carmen from an unhappy relationship, haven't I, darling?' Carmen smiled again, pensive this time, glancing briefly over at Madden with vague recognition. 'Would you like me to do the same for you?' Gaskell added, deliberately keeping his back to him. ''Course you would. Can't have you stuck with the Madman here, can we?' He turned and beamed at Madden, as though he was meant to agree that, yes, the poor girl absolutely needed rescuing from him.

'That's not fair,' Madden began to protest, but Gaskell tutted and led Carmen and Carol or Caroline or whatever her name was away into a clique, an arm around the waist of each. Madden followed after, ashamed and guilty at the same time. He stood around foolishly on the edge of the group, waiting for Gaskell to throw some crumb of conversation in his direction, but he was murmuring into each woman's ear, first Carmen, now Madden's dance partner. He fixed his look on Madden even as he spoke, as if to say: *This is what happens. Get used to it.*

'Come over here, Hugh, join us!' he said, raising his voice, and Madden went, despising himself.

'Now, what d'you two lovely ladies make of this sorry-looking sort? Not much, eh? Carmen? Not very prepossessing, is he?'

Madden decided to leave, and turned in the direction of the door.

'No, wait!' someone said. 'Wait a minute!'

He felt himself pulled back by the sleeve of his coat. He refused to turn around, and stood instead with his eyes closed, wobbling a bit on his feet.

'Don't mind him,' Carmen was telling him, her voice with a slight Ayrshire taint, grit in the ice cream of an otherwise appealing confection. As were her gums. 'He doesn't mean it. He's just trying to be provocative.' She turned Madden around, grasping him by the jaw, forcing him to look into her eyes. 'He should be careful who he provokes sometimes, shouldn't he? One day he'll provoke the wrong person. Maybe he's already done it.'

Madden mumbled something in agreement, but could see she hadn't heard, that her gaze was off somewhere beyond his shoulder, fixed on Gaskell, he presumed. He took the opportunity to wipe his eyes with the sleeve of his jacket, adjusting his glasses self-consciously when she turned back to look at him. He could see that he ought to find her beautiful, that her slightly asymmetrical features ought to, together, transcend themselves, and he wished that he could will them to, that he could make them add up to something more, become something other than just features, body parts. But he couldn't.

'All right now?' she said. 'Come back and talk to us? Don't

mind Owen. He just wants to be the centre of attention, that's all. Come.'

She gave Madden her hand: it was cool. His own was sweaty and sticky with spilled drink and he was ashamed of it. It would have been unbearable to him to have her touch it if he hadn't convinced himself it belonged not to him but to someone else. She led him back to the other two, Gaskell amusing the girl Madden had danced with – if it was possible to call it dancing. She threw her head back and laughed and he felt Carmen squeeze his hand tightly for a second.

'But maybe we shouldn't provoke him. Maybe we're the ones who should be careful,' she said, and glanced up at Madden with tight lips. She squeezed his hand again. 'You shouldn't get too close to some people,' she said. 'It's like looking at the sun: you can be blinded.'

Yes, Madden silently agreed. He could see how that might happen. One day, someone would get burned.

Gaskell was watching them come over, listening to and laughing at what the girl was saying. But not really there. Not really there at all.

'Hugh, I'm sorry, I didn't mean it. Scout's honour. I was just pulling your leg. Need another lancing? Really, I was just a bit put out, you know. Bit of trouble with the ex-boyfriend earlier, while you were strutting your stuff. I shouldn't have taken it out on you. That was cruel.'

'Yes,' Carmen said in clipped tones. 'It was.'

The other girl looked blankly at Madden and Carmen, and he was reminded that he had been none too polite himself. He smiled submissively at her, and she seemed to accept it, smiling in return.

'All friends again? Good,' Gaskell said, drawing Carmen over to him. She allowed him to put his arm around her waist, and he bent over and whispered something in her ear that brought a flush of colour to her cheeks. She slapped him playfully on the chest. But then her expression changed and she stood up straight, pulling away from Gaskell. He followed her gaze and then dropped his head, shaking it and muttering something to himself.

Dizzy Newlands faced Gaskell and Carmen, his features taut. Behind him, Hector hovered, unable to do anything.

'I just wanted to say all the best,' Dizzy said. 'I just wanted to wish you good luck with everything.'

He seemed to have steeled himself for this moment, but even as he spoke his voice began to crack. He raised a glass up to them and then drank it down. Hector shaded his eyes with his hand and looked at the ground.

'Dizzy, please,' Carmen said. Gaskell was eyeing him warily.

'No, it's all right,' Dizzy said. 'I mean it. I wish you all the best, Carm. In everything you do. I'm sorry if I gave you a fright earlier.'

She dismissed the notion with a shrug of her shoulders. 'Nothing to forgive,' she said.

Gaskell straightened up.

'Of course there's nothing to forgive!' he said, smiling.

'I wasn't talking to *you*,' Dizzy said. 'And if you know what's good for you, you'll keep your fucking trap *shut*.'

Gaskell shrunk back against the wall.

'That's enough, Dizzy,' Carmen said. 'Please go now. You've said your piece.'

There was an awful moment, a kind of teetering stillness that descended for a fraction of a second. To Madden, it was the moment when anything, any cataclysm, seemed possible. He had known a few such moments since then.

'Dizzy . . . ?' Hector said, appealing to his friend. 'Diz?'

He gently placed his hand on the other man's jacket. Dizzy began to walk away, then turned and said, 'I'm sorry, Carm. I really am. Let me buy you two a drink.'

Carmen shook her head.

'Please,' he said. 'I'd like to be friends with you. I want to be friends with you. Let me buy you a drink. Please.'

'OK,' Carmen said, relaxing, 'All right. One drink.'

Dizzy sighed. 'Great,' he said. 'I'll get a round in for everyone.'

Madden let out his breath in silent relief, and offered to help Dizzy with the drinks. Dizzy nodded blankly, and they went, Madden noting with some pleasure the way Gaskell gazed after them.

His money was all used up. All gone. There were lights dancing around the edges of his eyeballs. Fireflies. Had there been a conversation with Dizzy? Yes, Dizzy. Good old Dizzy, good old Diz. Parp parp on the saxophone, they'd had a good blow together. Or was it the trumpet. A good old chinwag about something. Yes. About end-of-term papers, an exchange of lecture notes. Had it been lecture notes? He thought so, yes. Essays. They could help each other, Dizzy was saying, You scratch my back and I'll scratch yours . . . What a laugh, Madden said. Help each other. It was ridiculous. Buy him a drink and he'd help, Madden told him. He was stony. Absolutely dead drunk stony broke. Whisky, he said. Dizzy frowned. Perhaps Madden shouldn't, he was telling him. He looked pretty well done in. No, Madden said. A drink. A whisky. Then he'd do anything Dizzy wanted. Anything he asked. He'd kiss his bare backside for a drink. That wouldn't be necessary, Dizzy said. Oh, but it would be, Madden told him. Completely and absolutely. Absolutely and completely necessary.

There were a heap of them on the floor of the dance hall. Faces looked down from the walls, faces and lists. Dux. Luminaries framed in gilted frames. Guilty frames, guilty graduates. He was laughing, crawling on his hands and knees to the edge of the floor. He was trying to stand up, there were hands helping him. There was music playing. He could see Carmen Alexander. What was her teeth doing. What was her gums doing. Someone pulled him over into a chair, but there was someone already in it. They pushed him off and he was on the floor again, laughing. The lights were bright and he was leaning on an elbow. He was trying to get up off the ground. He saw Gaskell raising an arm and then there was shouting. A fight, someone throwing a punch, people kicking. Gaskell. Of course Gaskell. Always Gaskell. There was yelling and someone trampling over him. Duxes, luminaries. They were all trampling over him. He hunched into a ball.

He was drinking water, a lot of water. Heap big water, he said to the girl next to him. What? she was saying, What did he say? Did she read the Beano? *he was asking. What about the* Dandy? *He was Desperate Dan, he said, he could eat a cow pie out of an ashet. He could eat her cow pie, he said. Out of an ashtray. Then she got up and walked away and he was on his own. The lights were dimming at the edge of his eyeballs, and Gaskell had his arm. His nose was bleeding again. Gaskell's nose was bleeding again, he told him. Had he been fighting with the Bash Street Kids? Yes, Gaskell told him, it was the Bash Street Kids . . . Dizzy and Bashful and Sleepy and it was over Snow White, he said. Carmen, Gaskell said. He was waving a finger in front of him. Carmen was what it was over, he was telling him. Had he woken her up with a magic kiss? Madden asked, laughing. That was right, Gaskell said. A magic kiss, and then he'd got her to bite his poisoned apple. It had nearly killed him, he said. Such is life, he said. Such is life. He was wiping his nose with a piece of toilet paper. A girl was holding Madden's other arm. He had seen her somewhere before. She was smiling at him. She was all smiles, he said. All teeth. She was all smiles and teeth and Gaskell was all nose and blood. They were walking. Where were they walking, Madden was asking. Then giggled. Where the mood took them, Gaskell told him. Wherever the wind should fetch them up . . . That was nice, Madden said. That was really very nice.*

There were four of them, not three. How had that happened? Where had the other one come from? Madden couldn't remember. Gaskell was with her, they were both smoking white cigarettes, their teeth chattering. He felt the cold himself now, sitting on the tenement steps. His head was sore. What was her name, he was asking the girl next to him. The smaller one. Did she have a name? She'd told him her name already, she said. Three times she'd told him. Minnie the Minx, he said. Now he remembered. Beryl the Peril, she said, and then they were laughing. It was still cold, he said, and she put her arm around him. Don't do that, he said. Please. Don't do that. He felt dizzy. I feel Dizzy! Gaskell said, but Carmen wasn't laughing. I really feel Dizzy, Gaskell was saying, and then he was kissing her on the mouth.

Madden groaned and rubbed his ears. He had a terrible thirst now, and his headache showed no signs of easing off. He and the girl – he was too embarrassed to ask her name again, so had simply stopped saying anything – had walked to her place, the end of Alexandria Parade. It had taken them two hours already. It was his own fault for offering. A gentleman through and through, no doubt about it. Neither had a penny on them, but they held hands anyway and walked along in silence, Madden concentrating on the sound of his thinly soled brogues scraping the pavement. The girl had already apologised for the walk, but Madden bit his lip, because for him it was not even halfway over yet – he would still have to walk all the way back to the west again. And he could find nothing very appealing about her: she seemed practically mute. He was minded to chap on her head a couple of times, to see if there was anybody home. All he could remember of what she had said was that she stayed in the accommodation for nurses at the hospital up there, in a room with another girl. From this, he had concluded that she was a nurse. It seemed the most likely explanation. Meanwhile he had formulated hypotheses on how he might get her to reveal her name to him once more, without having to ask again outright. But thus far he hadn't come up with any promising abstract. He would have to trust to contingency.

The night of the young, that was a joke. From the pressure behind his eyes it felt more like the night of the living dead. And there was the Necropolis not far from here, just behind the hospital. Perhaps the pair of them could bed down for the night in one of the plots, duck down into a vacant crypt with the rest of the ceilidh zombies, the assorted refuse of the evening's revellers. But Gaskell probably had the pick of the place already, no doubt lying with Carmen beneath consecrated soil.

He couldn't come up to her room, the girl told him when they got to the hospital and chewing on a strand of lank hair. Her face was puffy and flustered, foundation covering an array of subterranean plooks. He told her it was all right, he didn't mind, and they stood for a while, with awkward hands clasped, and she told him that actually, it was all right, they could go up if he didn't mind ducking under the window of the night porter's office. They weren't meant to have boys in. He asked about her room-mate, and she shrugged but said nothing, so they walked in through the main entrance and he hunched over as they passed the porter, who offered no objections. The girl led him along passageways that opened out into bigger passageways, then closed again into darkened ones where black shapes sat and which she told him to be careful of. They were moving silently, both treading as quietly as possible through the halls, and he tightened his grip on her hand, as they turned left, then left again, climbing dingy stairwells with the smell of carbolic illness stiflingly present. Madden was convinced he would never find his way back out again, there were so many stairwells and corridors, and allowed himself to trust instead in the girl's sense of direction.

'Here,' she said, stopping in a dim subway of darkened wards. 'Take your shoes off now. Everyone's sleeping.'

At the end of the hall, she stopped again, and let them into her room, leaving the light off.

'I can't see a thing,' he said, and she slapped his shoulder, then began to unbuckle his trousers and pull his shirt up over them. He felt helpless but offered no resistance, allowing himself to be pushed down on to a bed in the dark. 'Get under,' she whispered, so he did. She climbed in beside and they began fumbling with each other and he felt her mouth on his, the sour taste of stale alcohol on her breath. Her breasts felt chilled and flaccid, not like he had imagined them to feel at all, and she made glottal noises with her breath as he pushed his hand up under her skirt and tugged at her nylons, the vague thought of childhood meat rations disturbing his concentration. He had expected to be overcome with terror, but instead was calm and unhurried as the nylons came out from under her and he searched the lower belly and pubis, while she stroked and tugged at his crotch, coaxing his penis to rise, and at last – to his mild relief – rigor set in. A proud moment, literally so. Her tongue wriggled in his mouth and she pulled him quietly on top of her.

After, he remembered how he had tried to put it inside her, but couldn't seem to find the specific point of entry, and had at last to be guided in by her hand after several failed attempts. She let out a stiffer gasp when he pushed it in, again cut short by a glottal stop, and it was only the two hands on his hips that reminded him there was more work to be done. He supposed he had half expected to labour away there until she gave birth, but it must surely have been quicker than that.

'*Meat rations*,' he said, without meaning to.

'What?'

'Nothing. Sssh.'

'You said meat rations,' she said.

'No I didn't. I didn't say anything.' He thrust deeply,

hoping she would be distracted by unquenchable sexual arousal. Or pain, at the very least.

'Ow. Be careful.'

'Sorry.'

'What did you say?'

'I told you. Nothing. Keep still.'

'You said meat rations. You think I'm just some lump of meat!'

'I said sweet Kathleen, I was thinking of the song!'

She seemed satisfied with that, and he thrust again with renewed enthusiasm: it was the quickest way out of his plight, the path of least resistance, so to speak.

'Don't do it inside me,' she said, 'please . . .'

But then he was shoving it hard and those seconds occupied a space that was the same space in which there was occurring chiefly a sense of arousal in the so called branch-block the pallor often varying to a degree unseen basically a disease a stress condition a measure of clotting a blood magnetism filling an otherwise flaccid pallor in the organ radiating over the left arm similar to the heart region angina chiefly but it was never possible to rule one thing out entirely given that a) leads to b) not necessarily proving that b) follows from a) mutual exclusivity is entirely possible likely even and inflammation actually germs growing in the heart which ventricle? any ventricle? and it was said that pig hearts might be used half-man all porcine squeal squeal couldn't treat that with antibiotics, no, not likely with the belly pork ticker possibly a rise even in nervous tension the what ifs? crowding around now the what ifs? a) leads to b) must inevitably produce c) although the patient may be incapacitated of course they would with the pig ticker and the tail curling around at the end like a corkscrew the pig sticker surely would require surgery the fear of, no, the dread of septal defects the growth of trotters an abnormality non-existent one auricle leading to another but one auricle not necessarily leading from another congenital mechanics of the heart the mechanical pig sticker simply a pump then breathlessness swelling simply a breathless swelling of the ankles the toes cleaving together the hoofs cleaving together oxygenation inadequacies that led to, that led to, no, leading to tetralogy of fallot then a blue baby not a pink one and there it was insufficient oxygenation a serious condition an operation, yes, an operation or the blue cyanosis and at the other extreme that curly tail oink oink those trotters this little pig went to market this little pig stayed at home this little piggy ate roast beef they would eat anything wouldn't they, eat anything not pay attention to the cholesterol although they liked acorns best certainly no instances of cannibalism or even nephritis stroke fibrosis of the tissues uraemia hypertension primarily a psychosomatic disorder, yes, except in pigs it was related to suppression of emotions overcontrolling of the emotions automatic fear of the emotions a west of Scotland a Scottish condition let it all come out let it all rise bubbling to the surface they say except to the piggywinkles extremely expressive beasts hardly likely to be too strait-laced the man with the pig's valve pumping away the pig sticker of course this is just speculation since a) overflowing emotions lead to b) lowering of the blood pressure yet b) lowering of the blood pressure does not necessarily follow from a) overflowing emotions unless it is a very sensitive pig—

—hard to see what all the fuss was about pigs were decent animals why not let them hibernate within the thorax the organs could be swapped over sympathetic nerve fibres could relax the pressure the spasm as well as drugs, there were plenty of drugs alcohol being chief among them though there were also e.g. rauwolfia veratrum methonium compounds to render the pig sticker insensate others too transvacilcodex narcicalzine erythrometalermia to name but three though there is a possibility of the organ rejecting these possibly and in such a scenario the recommended dosage would have to be altered reduced increased 1) depending on the pig and further 2) whether it was using any alternative not in the sense of new age they called it but alternative in the sense of emotional problems emotional in the sense of irritant treatments taken in compliment in contingency as also as part of a calorie controlled diet not a controlled substance as in a controlled substance per se but to have the substance under control i.e. not to affect or effect change or unnatural stimuli acorns ought to be enough for God's sake, not to engorge or otherwise induce contradictory urges or at worst a rise in unknown instabilities the heart performing in an uninhibited and thoroughgoing fashion? function? in sympathy in harmony with all the other organs proteins mitochondria each operating as in its natural propensity no anaesthesia of any limb no inhibited part nothing worse, far from it, certainly not in the case of pigs there have been no recorded instances of successful animal magnetism Mesmer termed it odylic force or state induced in pigs at all doubtful if they would respond at all unless some sort of emotional rapport were developed some animals indeed susceptible not pigs though a man with a human brain a pig's heart and b) a pig with a human brain or c) any other variation of time for another small libation alcohol always being the drug of choice except for pigs such sweet animals intelligent affectionate delicious they liked apples too so that was another thing in common not just their organs but tastes too, appetites, forbidden appetites was it possible for a pig to taste with a grafted human tongue? an irritant it might act as an independent organ they were pink in colour but a pig's? forever jabbering jab-jabbing away never giving the host a moment's peace the poor creature trotting about is that my apple over there? wiggle wiggle goes the pig sticker of course there was another organ that might be exchanged the redundant sticker that he had never used on anyone except this one time, oh what was the name of the girl? it was Kathleen oh absolutely it was Kathleen oh he was choking, he was being strangled, there was the rigor pulsing oh oh I will take you home Kath-leen—

It was perhaps a full ten minutes before he ejaculated inside her and withdrew, his headache pounding, the futility of it too shaming for words. Momentarily, he had no idea where he was.

' "I Will Take You Home Kathleen"? Was that the song you thought of?' she was asking him. He said yes, only just able to make out the edge of the bed in the dark as his eyes became accustomed. But there wasn't any song. He had made it up.

To his horror, she began singing softly to herself.

'Oh, I will take you home Kathleen . . . That's lovely. Did you mean it?'

Madden was nonplussed. Mean what?

'That you'd take me home . . . that you'd take care of me. If . . . you know.'

'Know what?'

'You did it inside me. Spunked up. I asked you not to, but you did anyway. It's OK, I don't mind now. I might be in love with you now.'

'I'm sorry,' Madden said.

'Don't worry,' she said. 'It doesn't matter.'

'Shut up,' he said.

The light clicked on and Madden squinted. There was another girl staring at them from across on the opposite bed. The room-mate.

'Jesus Christ almighty, Kathleen, can you both not shut up! I've got a shift starting at seven!' She slammed her head back down on the pillow and pulled the blankets down over her head. The bedside lamp revealed a grey cell of spartan decor; two beds on iron frames, two bedside tables, two lamps. One dresser, one wardrobe. No decorations except for a single blacks-and-white photograph cut from a magazine on the wall above the other girl's bed. It was a picture of the Eiffel Tower. And a wooden crucifix.

Madden was pleased, though. He had remembered the girl's name, and was no longer a virgin into the bargain. And it was also how he met Rose.

Four

He never saw Kathleen again, and it was some time before Rose proposed to him. Gaskell was a different story. Three days after the faculty ball, his mother had knocked on the door to his room, and he'd quickly slid his journal under the pillow. When he'd told her it was all right to come in, she found him sitting leafing through case studies of Glaister's from *Medical Jurisprudence and Toxicology*. His mother looked drawn and ruddy faced, her hands and forearms blackened from lugging coal up three flights of stairs, the apron she wore smeared with the dust. She was wringing her hands together and she brought an atmosphere of late autumn into the room with her from outside. For a minute, she seemed not to have the words for what she wanted to say. After long seconds Madden said, 'What is it, Ma?' She looked to her feet then to his face, then back to her feet again.

'You've a visitor, son,' she said.

He gawped at her. 'Who?' he said, eventually.

His mother made way, holding the door of his room open for the guest. It was Gaskell, in his green suit. He stood at the door and smiled, then thanked Mrs Madden for bringing him through. Madden's mother allowed a brief smile, more akin to a wince of pain, to flash across her face, then ducked away, pulling the door closed behind her so that Gaskell and Madden were left with only each other.

Oh, don't bother to get up or anything, Gaskell told him, he'd been in the area and remembered Madden had given him his address. Madden had said to bill him for the suit if it needed cleaning, wasn't that right? Madden nodded, reaching for the jar on the bedside table he kept his money in – the little he had. No, no, Gaskell said, waving him to put the jar back. There wasn't any need for that, it had been taken care of. Was it all right if he sat down? Madden nodded, clearing the books off the only chair in his room, but instead of sitting Gaskell went to the window and looked out, the sun beginning to bleed into the horizon and the sound of weans playing in the street outside. Nice view here, he said. Just about see over to the river, if those tenements weren't in the way. Madden shrugged. It was just a view to him, he said. He'd grown up with it, so never noticed it any more than a farmer would notice a sheep. Gaskell laughed. What a thing to say. A view of a sheep! What a thing. What was it they said? Red sky at night, shepherd's delight or something? That was right, Madden replied, red sky in the morning . . . shepherd's something or other. He didn't know, really. Gaskell turned round to him. Was he doing anything in particular at the moment? he asked, looking around the walls of Madden's room, taking in the amateurish figure drawings that hung from the walls, the anatomical sketches by Leonardo da Vinci that he'd meticulously copied from prints found in the library at the university, the yellowing map of the globe from the perspective of Siam.

Interesting, that, Gaskell said, and Madden was about to say something about it, yes, it was interesting to see the world from the other side . . . yes, the Siamese thought their country the largest, grandest, most accomplished in the world, yes . . . but in the end he kept quiet, as though waiting for approval, fearing Gaskell's judgement too greatly to venture any explanation.

Gaskell noticed the glass cage on the floor behind the door, sat on top of opened-up newspaper. What was that he had in there? he asked. Madden felt himself blush. Rats, he said.

Rattus norvericus, to be precise. Norwegian rats. He kept them. Like pets? Gaskell asked, kneeling down and tapping the case. Yes, like pets, Madden said. They were very easy to keep, except they had expensive tastes in food. Gaskell laughed again, easily, seemingly unaware of Madden's own discomfort. This was his room and he wasn't used to having it scrutinised by others, least of all strangers in green corduroy. He noticed that Gaskell was also wearing a crimson and gold paisley-pattern cravat, and that his nose was still a bit swollen, his eyes somewhat purple. He was carrying a set of large gauntlet-style leather gloves and a pair of goggles. Doesn't look like much fun, he said. What doesn't? Madden asked. Being a rat. They don't get out much, do they. Madden shrugged. Then Gaskell said if he wasn't doing anything, did he fancy going for a ride? Madden looked at him, perplexed. A ride? A ride where? In what? Gaskell laughed again. Anywhere, he said, anywhere at all. The bike's outside. Come on! He reached over and grabbed Madden by the arm and began dragging him towards the door. Come on, Gaskell said, put these on. He handed Madden the goggles. Can get a bit windy, you know. Madden was speechless. He let himself be dragged along the hall, past his sullen mother, and on to the landing, then down the stairs of the close. At the bottom, they met his father returning from work. As they passed he flattened himself against the tiles of the wall to let them by. Where you going? he was asking. Out, Madden said. Out where? he asked, following the pair of them to the mouth of the close. Just out! Gaskell shouted, swinging his leg astride the black Norton motorcycle parked outside, the sidecar gleaming like new. Get in, he said to Madden, pointing to it. So Madden got in. Right, Gaskell said, up, up and away!

Later, Madden was never sure whether they had really been close, or not. Were they friends? He'd had few friends before, so it was difficult to compare. He recalled once when he'd been very small, looking up the word 'solitary' in a dictionary given to him by his father for that specific purpose, and not understanding why. He'd been much too young to use a dictionary, the whole thing had been ridiculous. It means to be alone, his father told him. That's what you are in this world. He had to understand that he couldn't rely on anyone. He had to understand that he would get by only with his own gumption. Then, he'd told him to think about the word, understand what it meant. Madden sat staring at the letters, the words, and tried to understand. Solitary. Alone. Every time he'd tried to turn the page his father had grabbed him by the back of the head and forced his face down to the page, as though he were a dog that had messed the carpet. Solitary. Alone. He remembered refusing to cry, though the tears had been close. He'd wondered where his mother was, why she didn't come and rescue him. His father sat in the big chair, the one only he was allowed to sit in, staring down at the boy, rolling cigarette after cigarette. Madden had no idea how long he'd been made to sit there with the dictionary, only that it had been an immense distance of time.

When he was with Gaskell, he sometimes had that feeling of time slowing down like that, of being afraid to speak for fear he would commit some crime for which the punishment would be exile once more. In fact, he had never realised that his condition had a name until he'd met Gaskell. And after, it couldn't have been more obvious to him, as though the words were spelled out on paper for him. He was stateless, a refugee. He was in exile.

That first time on the motorbike, they had driven out of the city, as far as the waterworks, and he'd felt like never coming back, just to keep going a bit farther, then a bit farther again, letting momentum carry the two of them as far as it would. It had almost been a relief to come to a halt, though; such exhilaration could never last for long. The world made its own demands, and they had to be heeded. They'd strolled and Gaskell had talked and Madden listened.

'So what d'you want to be when you grow up?' he said.

'A doctor. What else?'

'A doctor. That's not an ambition, that's what you told your parents when you were ten. What do you really want to be?'

'A doctor. A surgeon.'

'"A doctor. A surgeon." Sounds to me like you've been telling yourself that for a long time, yes siree.'

'Well, it's true. I've wanted to be a surgeon ever since I was old enough to understand what it was.'

Gaskell snorted. 'You what! Bloody hell. What ten-year-old wants to be a surgeon? I don't believe it. Not a bit of it.'

Madden was irritated. Who was this beatnik anyway to tell him he was a liar.

'Well, what do *you* want to be, then, if not a physician?'

'*Physician!* You've got it bad, right enough, Madden. You really have. Not only do you want to be a doctor, but you want to be a physician too. Well I never.'

'So why study medicine if you don't want to be a doctor, then?'

'Simple. This is what dearest Daddy will pay for me to do. If I don't study in the medical facility, then no allowance. The family is too well off by your standards for me to get any kind of funding. So if I want to study anything, then I can take my pick: medicine, law, engineering, physics. The world is my oyster.'

'What do you want to do instead?'

'Good question.' Gaskell squinted at the sun, leaking red and orange into a low bank of horizontal cloud. It was getting dark.

'We should go,' he said. 'The lights on this machine are a bit suspect. It'd be best to head back soon.'

From the little Madden knew of this stranger, it was an oddly measured thing to say, though it hadn't struck him until later how much closer to Gaskell's true nature the remark was.

Of course, he was always striking attitudes. Even in his days-long depressive bouts there was an element in him that perceived himself to be *performing*, that without Madden as audience he was terrified he might simply cease to be. *Without you, there's nothing to reveal, Hugh.*

'So what do you want to do?'

'What? Sorry, old man, I was miles away. What to do, what to do, what to do. Good question, very good question. First I think we should return to the fair city of your birth – you were *born* there, weren't you? – ditch the Covenanter, and then retire to a suitable hostelry for the evening. What say you?'

'I don't have much money.'

'Ah, money. Don't worry about a thing. Providence will . . . well, *provide*, I suppose.' Gaskell reached into the inner pocket of his corduroy jacket and produced a five-pound note. 'See? I only have to speak, and it is done!'

Madden didn't know what to say. He had never seen so large a sum in the hand of a fellow student, nor equally any adult.

'Fine dining, low women, and liquor to match! What d'you say, Madman?'

'Don't call me that, please.'

'Sorry, old man. Just joking.'

The Hillhead Raskolnikov, Gaskell called Aduman, when Madden was describing him wandering the streets hoping to avoid the landlady, trying to beg, borrow or steal enough money for the electric meter.

'He's already pawned the buttons off his coat,' Gaskell said. He and Madden would have to do something for him, deliver an anonymous parcel to his room. Bread and sausage, all wrapped up in a new scarf.

'Don't forget some spare buttons,' Madden added, and Gaskell had laughed.

'Who else?' he asked.

'Who else what?'

'You know . . . who else did you spy on?'

'It wasn't spying.'

'What was it, then?'

'It wasn't seedy or dirty. You've got that on the brain.'

'Who else?'

'Beth Tripp, Port George, Saudi Mehmet, a few others. Beth Tripp was best. She'd a voice like a foghorn, typical Yank. Chewed gum constantly.'

Did she really chew gum? He wasn't sure. But it was the sixties. She must have chewed gum if she was an American. Madden may have made that bit up, but he could see how he would have told it to Gaskell. He'd known even then that these embellishments were what he enjoyed most. He interrupted constantly, lighting cigarette after cigarette, blowing smoke at Madden in that dingy room of his, paperback novels strewn about the floor, piles of medical notes everywhere. Battered guitar with no strings on it in the corner, Dansette record player on the mildewed sideboard. The same LPs always on since Gaskell only owned three, none of them hit parade: Ella Fitzgerald, Billie Holiday and someone called Varese. They were part of his stance, the Gaskell disdain for anything he considered to be merely modish.

Clothes in heaps on the bed and stuffed into the tops of the floorboards to keep out mice and keep heat in. Neither had worked. Gaskell always sprawled, never sat, and seemed to take pleasure in making Madden physically uncomfortable. There was nowhere else but the bed to sit on, so Gaskell harangued Madden about how *square* he was for wanting to sit on a chair and the bloody Chinks and the Japs never bothered with them and they were quite capable of sitting on the floor for hours, even days at a time, and Madden could bloody well learn a thing or two from them, so he could. Then he'd burst out laughing and call Madden a bourgeois and an intellectual and tell him to knock on next door and get a lend of a chair off the chap in the next room, he wouldn't mind, he'd run off without paying his rent anyway, sensible chap. Madden would frown and feel still more uncomfortable until Gaskell relented, sighing, and went next door for the chair himself. Only when seated would he be able to relax in any way, and his temperament improved after a couple of jiggers of Grouse.

'So who else, then?' Gaskell goaded, never content to let a subject alone. Madden already regretted the little he had given away.

'No one, just them.'

'You're a very strange man, Madman, did you know that?' he said, emptying the tin plate that served as an ashtray on to a newspaper.

Madden let the remark pass, but the idea excited him.

'What're you doing?' he said, shifting in next door's chair, crammed into a corner by the eaves of Gaskell's cupboard of a room in Wilton Street.

'I'm out of smokes,' Gaskell said, sifting through the cigarette ends and ash.

'Haven't you any money?' Madden asked.

Gaskell harrumphed. 'I'm like Billy Bunter at the moment.'

'What's that?'

'Expecting a postal order. The one that never comes.'

'You had money up till the other week. I saw you. What happened to it?'

Gaskell looked up, his fingernails black from squeezing the strands of unsmoked tobacco out of the fags on the paper. 'I gave it away,' he said, winking.

'You gave it away? Who to?'

Gaskell shook his head. 'Property is theft, Hugh.'

'Money isn't property. What'll you do for food? For heat?'

'I told you, I'm expecting a postal order.'

'From who?'

'My mysterious benefactor, who else.' He sprinkled some of the tobacco on to a piece of newsprint torn from the corner of the paper, rolled it and put it to his lips. As he did so, he was unaware of the tobacco pouring out of the end on to the floor. He lit the roll-up, inhaled, and the entire thing burned as far as his fingertips so that he had to drop it quickly on the carpet. 'Shit,' he said.

He looked up at Madden, flicking his filthy fingers through his too-long hair. Madden felt a disturbingly *paternal* urge come over him, and tried to push it from his mind.

Gaskell wore the same suit until it was filthy, saved coppers from returned ginger beer bottles and ate only sporadically. He was painfully thin and pale and would sit semi-clothed in a pair of ancient dungarees and a semmit with a donkey jacket over it while the suit went round and round in the launderette. It would have been unbearable for Madden to live the way his friend did, but Gaskell was inexplicably ignorant of the stares they received when Madden forced him to take his one change of clothes to the wash. He would sit willing the other waiting customers to keep their attention on their own machines for fear they associated him with the tramp in the donkey jacket. More often than not, it was he who supplied Gaskell with the money in the first place, and he would sit in some great sulk of resentment while his clothes got washed. Madden couldn't understand him at all. The money orders seemed to come and go and Gaskell had discouraged Madden from ever asking about his family. All he would say was that they were 'establishment' and that he wanted nothing to do with them. All Madden could get from him was that he'd grown up near Wales, in the south, and had come north to irritate them.

'So. There weren't any others after this Aduman character,' he said. 'You sure about that? You sure you weren't following me around before that ball?'

'For God's sake. It was you that followed me.'

'That's true.' Gaskell nodded, reaching for the Grouse bottle. He poured himself a couple of fingers and passed the bottle to Madden. 'You must have put the evil eye on me. And the lovely Kathleen. What happened with her?'

'Nothing happened. Nothing happened with any of them.' He neglected to mention Rose. 'What happened with your parents? What's happening with Carmen Alexander?'

That would shut him up. But perhaps that was being too optimistic. It certainly seemed that way lately.

A chance encounter over a chance act of congress, was that how it could have been described? Hello, yes, pleased to make your acquaintance, oink oink. Oh, Rose you say? Why, charmed, I'm sure. Simply charmed. Likewise.

Kathleen had left the room to go to the toilets to see to *women's private things*. Madden supposed she was referring to vaginal ablutions, and in the meantime her room-mate locked her out. Couldn't stand her snivelling, she told him. They both listened to Kathleen scratching at the door, wanting let back in, it was cold out there and the shapes in the corridor frightened her. The girl in the other bed had clicked her bed-side lamp back on and both she and Madden stared studiedly away from each other at mysteriously attractive bumps and swellings in the wallpaper.

After a while Kathleen stopped asking to be let in, and Madden wondered vaguely whether she was still alive out there, and why the girl on the iron bed frame opposite him disliked her so much.

Rose. He'd liked the name, even then. But the curious personality in possession of it he wasn't quite so sure of. Yet, there was something.

So, was he going to look after Kathleen? she asked him, leaning upright on one elbow and looking at him. Was he going to *take care of her*?

And of course, he was excruciatingly embarrassed. He had never imagined that he would have an audience for his first performance in a professional capacity. Until tonight he had specialised in solo arrangements only, and even those with infrequency. It had been an odd experience, the ultimate moments not quite as sweet as he had been led to believe, and the penultimates anything but savoury. What Kathleen had gained from it he had no idea. A splash of fluid, a teaspoon or so of his infecting ink. A million contaminating spermatozoa. He was glad, despite the callousness of the act, that Rose had closed the door on her. It was unpleasant to have to listen to the grunted couplings of others. Unpleasant and base.

She couldn't abide the girl, she said. And Madden should be careful of her – she'd convinced herself of three pregnancies this year alone.

Madden. That was his name, wasn't it? Funny name that. Madden. He had a first name surely?

'Hugh,' he said. 'But everyone calls me Madden.'

They hadn't spent the night talking. The hours had not flown by in the shared stories of their lives, anything but. Rose felt even less like a potential lover than Kathleen, certainly no *soulmate*. Still, they had been drawn together: perhaps by complicity, perhaps by a mutual sense of safety in their parallel exclusion. That was it, really. They were companions in exile.

Madden, deny it though he might, had probably seen something of an open door in Gaskell, a way back in, but with Rose the attraction had been entirely different. A way to stare through the window at the company warming beside the hearth, and not at the same time feel the cold without. Her exclusion was comfortable for her: she had exiled herself, but could return at any moment. Even the way she had locked out her room-mate seemed to spell out her independence. Madden regretted he couldn't be as original as Rose, that he couldn't see past the Dizzys and the Carmens and all the others in the world; he wanted her detachment for himself. It was always easier to be alone, always easier to trust the learned behaviour, especially if that behaviour had never been optional in the first place.

Solitary. His father had shown him the meaning of the word, even while he had lain awake listening to animal noises coming from next door, a pilfered slice of canned meat in his hand under the covers, still cold from the plate. He ate it slowly with the strangest sensation building inside him, the noises infrequent and guttural. *Oorgh. Uuurgh. Oink . . .*

He chewed the meat slowly, savouring every tiny piece, crushing it into a paste with his endless masticating. When it was all finished, he would wipe his hand on the mattress and listen to the sounds and wonder at their significance. It sounded as though his father was in great pain. If his mother was too, then she suffered in silence, transformed into the sound of rocking springs.

Squeak. Squeak. Squeak.

Dammit! his father shouted from the room next door. *These fucking mice!* The exclamation was inevitably followed by the sound of his heavy steel-toecapped boots being flung across the floor at the offending rodent.

In the morning, probably an hour later at the most and still dingy outside, he was awoken by a generously proportioned girl of roughly his own age. She had stabbed him in the chest with a finger, pressed it next to her lips and told him to move over while she slid in under the covers next to him. That's better, she said. Nice and cosy now.

'I have to get up for my shift in a minute or two,' she told him, her face pressed worryingly close to his. 'D'you want to give it another try with me?'

'Give what another try?'

'You know, what you were doing before. With Kathleen.'

'Not really,' he said. 'Sorry.'

'Something wrong with me?' she asked, poking him again. 'I've got nicer legs than her. Nobody says so, but I know.'

Madden laughed, and she leaned up on one elbow and smiled at him.

'D'you want to know how I know?' she asked.

Madden observed with detachment the bulges in the ceiling.

'Not especially,' he said, wondering where his specs had gone.

'Are you a poofter?'

'No,' he said, giving up on the glasses. 'I'm a doctor.'

Rose groaned, and lay back on the pillow. 'Kathleen found a doctor. How wonderful. She works in a hospital and she goes out and finds herself a nice skinny, glaikit doctor-student. Wonders will never cease. Well, Mr Dr Madden, so very pleased to make your acquaintance. Don't you want to know how I know my legs are so nice?'

She raised one naked limb up from under the cover and stretched it upwards, pointing the toes of a rather dainty foot. Madden pretended not to be interested, searched under the cover for his missing spectacles.

'I have *verrry* nice legs, Hugh. Vy don't you vont to look at zem?'

She was affecting the accent of a Dietrich or a Garbo, waving her leg about in the air and pouting at him.

'Yes,' he said, 'you have nice legs. I get the point. I suppose *this* is how you know you have nice legs?'

Rose had shot him a glance of sudden violence, then rolled her island bulk on top of him. He felt the air being crushed out from his lungs. She glared down at him.

'Are you saying I'm some sort of *cheap woman*? Are you trying to tell me that I'm some sort of tart?'

Madden oozed a negative, his breath wheezing out in gurgling clots.

Rose rolled off again, a look coming into her eye that was like a light being switched back on. She laughed.

Madden caught his breath again, sitting upright to let the air in a bit more easily.

'So,' Rose said, a smile playing about her lips. 'Do you want to know how I know my legs are so nice . . . ?' She stroked the limb in question with the cupped palm of her hand to her calf.

Madden nodded. 'Pray tell,' he said.

'Because the Lord told me.' Madden looked at her and she smiled, as if recounting a compliment from a teacher at school. 'The Good Lord came to me one night and said, Rose, you have got a smashing pair of pins on you, no doubt about it!'

Madden had no reply to this statement.

'Want to know what else he told me?' Rose said.

He nodded, slowly.

'He told me to use them wisely.'

'Use them wisely?'

'Uh-huh. Use them wisely. Didn't say what for, though.'

Rose threw her head back and laughed loudly. 'Come on, then,' she said. 'Upsadaisy. I need to get going and I can't be leaving you here all day. Get dressed. I'll show you the way out.'

So he had got dressed and they followed the long corridors out past the wards, the lights flickering on in them erratically, shuffling forms beginning to muster. Some areas lit, some still darkened, Madden had followed Rose down the interminable stairwells, trying to appear nonchalant as they passed orderlies and trance-like nurses, prematurely wizened by sleep, their faces not yet elastic for the day ahead. It was a good thing she had shown him the way too. He didn't doubt he'd still be wandering those corridors if it hadn't been for Rose. He hoped they wouldn't encounter Kathleen somewhere along the way, but Rose seemed unconcerned at the prospect. Of course, like Gaskell's, that same unconcern was part of *her* stance against the world. It defied challenging. If they had met Kathleen, she would simply have shirked the embarrassment aside and carried on as before, her Good Lord at her side to protect her. He had never known back then whether she was entirely serious about her faith, whether it was some sort of joke she was conducting at the expense of the world, himself included. And if it had been, it had become real enough with time.

'I have to get back now,' she said, once they were at the main entrance. He stood dumbly at the edge of the road he was about to walk down once more, then turned to her.

'Could you possibly lend me some money?' he asked. 'Just the bus fare,' he added as her look glowered. 'I'll give it back, I promise.'

She crossed her arms across her chest and then nodded. 'Sure thing, Doc,' she said. 'How much d'you need?'

Madden shrugged non-committally. 'I don't know. Whatever you can spare will be fine.'

Rose tapped a foot and searched about in her skirt pocket. He remembered later that she had looked, well, quite *matronly* in her nurse's uniform. He supposed he had found her attractive, in a perverse way.

She handed him a handful of coppers. 'That'll have to do you, Madden,' she said. 'If it's not enough, you can always resort to Shanks's pony.'

He said thank you in his most polite voice, and turned towards the street.

'Just a minute!'

He looked back. 'What?'

'If you want to pay me back, you can take me out. To the pictures. Or the zoo. Yes, the zoo. I like the animals in zoos.'

'All right,' he said. A strange turn of phrase, that one. *I like the animals in zoos.* 'What animals d'you like the best?'

Rose tapped her foot again, considering. 'I like giraffes. Giraffes are the best animals for me. Yes.'

'Why giraffes?' he asked, because it seemed like the correct thing to do.

'Because, Madden, they've got the nicest legs!' She grinned at him. He the wildebeest: she the lioness. It was ever thus, he told himself.

Gaskell was always a mass of bumps and bruises: Madden couldn't fathom how he managed to contract these injuries with such regularity. He was an ongoing work of art, a canvas that metamorphosed from day to day and week to week, yet Madden was never comfortable asking how he'd received these wounds, since it would involve confronting his own culpability. The incident with the door was never mentioned by Gaskell, but Madden felt keenly guilty of his carelessness. Occasionally, when Gaskell opened his bedsit door, Madden had to stifle a gasp at the state of his features, always compellingly malnourished, yet still striking, or should that have been *struck*?

Gaskell simply grunted and claimed to have always been spectacularly clumsy, and laughed the matter off. It occurred to Madden that it was no accident his clumsiness had increased dramatically since his involvement with Carmen.

'Quite a girl, isn't she, Madman? A catch, you might say.'

'I wish you wouldn't call me that,' Madden said. There had been a brief respite in the rain, and Gaskell had insisted on dragging him down along to the banks of the Kelvin, all the while constructing infantile limericks which he was trying out on Madden. It was difficult for him to say which irritated him more: Gaskell's deliberate goading, or the walking itself. He'd never had much of a liking for either fresh air or rhymes.

'She's awful nice,' Madden said without conviction.

'You don't find her attractive? Bloody hell, what kind of a man are you?' Gaskell flicked his cigarette into the river, the water level much higher than it had been a few weeks before and silt brown in colour.

Madden shrugged. 'I don't think about looks much,' he said.

'Agreed. Looks aren't everything, are they? Only the part that shows. But she is a looker, just the same. You'd have to admit that much.'

'She's very pretty, yes.' Madden dragged his collar around him: it was chilly. The sky was overcast and seemed to start about a foot above their heads. Perhaps it was falling in, right enough.

Gaskell punched him on the arm playfully.

'And what about your lady friend, eh? I must say, I didn't think you'd be her type.'

'I don't know what you mean,' Madden said, embarrassed.

'Kathleen. You went home with her, didn't you? I saw you . . . dammit, what's that word you use here? Winching! That's it. I saw you winching with her. That's a great word, isn't it, Hugh?'

Madden was miserable. 'It's a wonderful word. You should keep it.'

'I will, I will! I'll write a poem with winching in it.' Gaskell was grinning through a cracked lip at Madden. The two large knuckles on the index and middle fingers of his right hand were skinned: Madden didn't bother to ask why.

'Anyway,' Madden said, 'she's *not* my lady friend. I have no intention of ever seeing her again.'

Gaskell paused. 'Now, that seems to me a very strange thing to say, Madman. Nice girl like that and you're not seeing her again. I'd no idea you were so disdainful of the ladies.' He leaned against the railings and began to roll another cigarette, glancing up at Madden as if trying to make his mind up about something.

'I'm not disdainful,' Madden said, exasperated. 'I'm seeing someone else, if you must know.'

Gaskell perked up immediately, stuffing his cigarette between his lips.

'Well, well,' he said. 'Another lady . . . you're a dark horse indeed, Hugh. So who is this mystery girl? It *is* a girl you're talking about, I assume?'

'As opposed to what?' Madden said sharply.

He picked up the pace again, leaving Gaskell to light his smoke.

'I don't know, do I? A Christian Scientist. A Turkish chef. How should I know what sorts of thing you get up to when I'm not around to chaperone you?' Gaskell said when he caught up. He threw an arm over Madden's shoulder, and chummed him along. He smelt of ash and stale alcohol. His suit was missing today: again, it was the dungarees and donkey jacket he wore. From this Madden deduced that Gaskell wouldn't be seeing Carmen Alexander today: the dungarees seemed to be reserved for Madden's benefit, while Gaskell had the suit cleaned for more important occasions.

'I don't get up to anything,' Madden said more or less truthfully.

'So who is she? Come on, out with it!'

Madden sighed. 'She's just someone I met, that's all. At the infirmary. I'm supposed to take her out somewhere this week. I've been putting it off for the last week or so. I'm flat broke as usual. As you can probably tell, I'm not much of a romantic.'

Gaskell clapped his hands and laughed, and Madden cringed inwardly at this affectation. Gaskell slipped his arm through Madden's, and sighed.

'Ah love, ah me,' he said. 'First the delectable Kathleen – who I liked by the way, even if you decided it was better to play the field – and now this infinitely superior filly. Wonders will never cease. What's her name? She does have a name, doesn't she?' He puffed on his cigarette and the breeze licked the smoke from out of his mouth before he could inhale it.

''Course she's got a name.'

'So what is it, then, or is it a secret?'

'It's not a secret.'

'So tell me, then!'

Madden broke his arm free and pushed his glasses back up against the bridge of his nose. 'You wouldn't like her,' he said.

Gaskell dropped the cigarette and ground it underfoot.

'And why wouldn't I like her?' he said, feigning hurt, and with a spread hand placed against his chest.

'She's not beautiful. She's not like Carmen.'

Gaskell snorted. 'So Carmen *is* beautiful, is she?' he said, as if Madden's words confirmed what had hitherto been a mere suspicion. It struck Madden as uncharacteristic of his friend – he wasn't at all sure that this was what he was – that he should need Madden's seal of approval in order to convince himself. A small wave of elation washed over him, and then was gone.

'Yes,' Gaskell said thoughtfully, 'she is, isn't she.'

They walked along in silence for a while. Then Gaskell stopped.

'So when do I get to meet this girl of yours?' he said, his introspection suddenly vanished.

'Her name's Rose,' Madden said. 'And I don't know that you do.'

'Do what?'

'Get to meet her,' he said.

'Rose. A good name, that. I like it. A Rose by any other name . . .'

'No, not by any other name, just Rose.'

'And you don't want me to meet her. Very nice that, I must say. After everything I've done for you.'

Madden harrumphed. 'I don't know exactly what that might be.'

Gaskell laughed again. 'I'm your confidant, Hugh! I'm your conscience! Everyone needs a conscience. Happy to oblige.' He made a show of curtsying. Madden looked away.

'I'm sure I'll like her just fine,' Gaskell said. 'And she'll like me. We'll be bosom pals.'

'I don't doubt it. That's why I'm not sure if you'll meet her.'

'What, afraid I'll steal her away from you, is that it? Fear not. I've enough on my plate with the charming Carmen. And Newlands. I couldn't cope with any more.'

Madden could see that he meant it.

Gaskell flicked a hand through his greasy hair. 'So where will you take her on your date?' There was a note of genuine curiosity in his voice.

'Maybe the zoo. She likes animals. Not the pictures anyway,' Madden said. 'I don't understand how anyone can get to know anyone else if they're both staring at a screen in the dark.'

'Oh, I think you'll find there are ways, Madman. Picture houses can be very intimate places, if you give them half a chance.' He winked good-naturedly at Madden, staring over at the brown river water swirling not far from where they were standing. An uprooted tree floated past them.

'Now I'm going to have to love you and leave you,' he said.

'Why?' Madden asked, his disappointment obvious. 'Can I not come with you?'

Gaskell shook his head and tutted. ''Fraid not, old man. Where I go, you cannot follow. Private matter and all that. You don't mind, do you?'

Madden shrugged his shoulders. 'I suppose not,' he said.

'Good, good,' Gaskell said, rubbing his hands together and blowing on them. 'But we'll catch up soon, eh? You can tell me who you've been spying on this week!'

'It's not spying,' Madden said, annoyed. 'It's . . . *observing.*'

'Of course, of course. Behavioural research. Anthropology. Science. I quite understand.' He beamed broadly at Madden.

'Well, perhaps it is. What of it?'

'Nothing whatever. Everyone should have *diversions.*'

'And what are yours?' Madden asked. 'Poetry and puerility, as far as I can tell.'

Gaskell suddenly lunged towards him, the smile gone, his face pressed close to Madden's.

'None of your fucking business what I do, all right?'

Madden automatically drew himself inwards, his eyelids flickering as if fearing a blow. Would Gaskell have struck him? He couldn't believe that.

Gaskell dusted Madden's lapels and straightened him up, his mood altered as soon as he had made his point.

'Now,' he said, 'as for first dates, a public house is my personal recommendation. If it's intimacy you're after, then alcohol will speed the way. And if not, it'll get you drunk, which may be just as good.'

He smiled and turned back the way they had come. Madden was a little shaky, his pulse still racing.

'Cheerio, then,' he said, trying to sound sarcastic. But it didn't come out right, the tone of his voice vulnerable and pathetic. He watched Gaskell walk away, then he turned and gazed instead at the churning river.

Farther down, he could see the black boughs of the tree that had passed them before trapped against some rocks, its leafless branches clamouring desolately against the massed water.

A first date at the zoo. Rain drizzling into his eyes from the fringe he was attempting not to cut, Rose to one side of him chewing on a toffee apple like a six-year-old. The sun shone intermittently between stupefyingly dark clouds and then disappeared again. He should undoubtedly have gone with Gaskell's suggestion: alcohol and shelter, fine conversation. Rose seemed to like it, though, and gazed with the pleasure of a simpleton at the assorted reptiles in their algae-darkened tanks, nothing but other reptiles and too-hot light bulbs for company. Had she really been eating a toffee apple? Maybe not. Likely a trick of the memory. More probably it had been a banana. They were bound to have bananas in zoos. The whole place was depressing to him. It seemed to be dissolving slowly into the mire it had been raised up on. They daundered past the elephants, which eyed them with apparent disdain, their flanks darkened by rain and mud. No giraffes. No orang-utans. No lions. They was a bear in a manufactured cave which refused to come out: they could see its brown flank next to the entrance. It couldn't have been particularly dangerous: there was a guard walking about with a hose spraying bear excrement off the ground. Rose made faces at him as though he were the exhibit. Now she was a monkey, her mouth a round O; next a big cat with talons extended. It was all hilarious. Madden walked despondently, head downturned against the sky and insufferably conscious of the hole in his right brogue which let the water in, despite the piece of linoleum he had carved an insole from and stuffed down there.

And so, he reflected over the years, their relationship proceeded, and he was never quite sure why. The zoo, the circus, the movies. The carnival, Rio de Janeiro. The moon, the stars. Endless questions from Rose, endless answers from Madden. He never took his turn, she said, never asked her anything. Was he not interested in her at all?

'No,' he said. But she just laughed. Their first kiss was shared at the bus stop, like so many others of that time. Madden, again, didn't know why he went along with the whole thing, and Rose didn't seem to mind. She was immune to him. She spent long hours examining her body in her room: her legs and ankles. She would look at her tongue in the mirror and say, Ah. He should have realised then that she was certifiable. What was she looking for? he wanted to ask her, but never did. He wouldn't have been surprised to find her rifling through her own stools.

Gaskell steered clear of her after two or three stilted encoun-ters, Gaskell working his charm and Rose immune, aloof, distinctly unimpressed. Her tongue was too sharp. Madden told her that. Your tongue is too sharp by far. But she had spotted something only just beyond the horizon and said that God had given her this tongue. Doubtless he had told her to use it wisely into the bargain.

'She,' Rose told him. 'The Almighty is a woman.'

Madden kept silent.

She had wanted to become a nun once, she told him as they sat in the Men's Union waiting for something, anything, to happen. She had wanted to join an order somewhere, she told him, and live out her days exclusively for the Lord. Yes, she believed. What was so strange about that?

He had shrugged. Nothing, he supposed, and let her continue talking while he observed Gaskell and Carmen Alexander caught up in yet another argument, one of the many. She had, apparently, taken some time away from her studies to visit a relative in England. On her return she seemed different somehow, as though she had come to some painful realisation. Perhaps that any attachment to Gaskell made her vulnerable, weakened. Easy meat.

Was Madden listening to her? Rose snapped. Was he paying any attention to what she was saying at all?

Madden nodded as always and sipped his tea, the Union canteen half empty. It bothered him that Gaskell always sat alone with Carmen, that he was never allowed to join them. It was silently understood that they separated into their respective romantic units, yet Madden always found that his attention was never fully with anyone but Gaskell and Carmen. An absent Gaskell was more of a conundrum for him than a present Rose. There were mysteries with Gaskell, puzzles. His full attention was, as Carmen had said, too blinding, but Madden still needed it, even if in recent days it was only half as bright and now dimming. Vaguely, he was aware of his friend – were they? – losing interest in him, and with that he seemed to cling nearer to Rose, sought a balm in her maternal folds. She was not by any stretch of the imagination beautiful, but neither was she ugly, and their relationship had gradually blossomed from grudging affection to occasional bouts of French-kissing, which revolted him. Rose seemed keen to explore the inside of his mouth as though her tongue was a pin with which to extract the last whelk from the shell. Sometimes he feared she might peel his face back around his skull like the skin of some fleshy banana, then set about sucking on his exposed meats, so excessive did her cannibalistic impulses become. These attacks would last ten, twenty minutes at a time, and in the most public places. At her bus stop outside his mother and father's flat; at the gates of the university or the entrance to the hospital; in queues at the chip shop or even there, sat in the canteen of the Men's Union. All of which was a horror for him to endure, but which he did, for reasons he had never explained to himself with much satisfaction. She was just *there*, in the end. And in those days there was so *much* of her too: once she was settled, she was *settled*.

And she could talk. It was something which didn't come easily to Madden, and he was happy to let her words wash over him. It wasn't strictly necessary to listen to every word. He was so unused to talking. It was painful to reflect on the interminable silences he endured at home. The enforced soundlessness of his childhood, the unending periods of absolute focus they had involved. Only his father was allowed to make a noise. His mother was there to acquiesce, to agree and defer. Her face was a mask which betrayed nothing except subservience, and occasionally fear. He couldn't recall a single incident which had brought anything to her lips but the most fleeting of inflections – indicating what he was never sure. Anger? Joy? Irritation? And at the same time, there would be his father shouting, *What, woman? Spit the damned thing out, why don't you? D'you want that lassie of a boy to grow up thinking his mother's a bloody mute?*

'Dumb,' she had said once.

'What did you say?' his father asked.

But the mask had already slipped back down, and she shook her head and went to the scullery and began washing and drying crockery with the fanaticism of a convert. Madden had sat, a forkful of stewed sausage in his hand, waiting for the inevitable cataclysm, but there had been none. His father watched his mother's back, his face reddening. But he said nothing. Very quietly, he folded his newspaper in front of him on the table, stood up and went out, closing the front door behind him with a barely audible click. He had returned after closing time and taken every plate in the scullery and thrown them out of the window while Madden and his mother glowered stupidly at the floor, in silence. When he was finished he had stood upright, straightened his shirt and jacket and sat down in his chair. *Not so dumb now, eh?* he said. *No, not so dumb as all that, eh?* And he'd winked at Madden.

In that house, talking was noise gone mad. Talking was a stream of broken plates, or a glass slammed down hard on the table. But with Rose, it was different. What violence there was in it was not directed at Madden, but sought his complicity. It was a voice that treated him as a *significant other*, and he was unused to that. For Gaskell, he played straight man and audience, but only when there was no better audience to be found. Madden was excluded from his *other* company, their paths crossing only coincidentally. Gaskell kept them separate from one another, but still somehow in competition. At least, that was how Madden saw it.

On the other side of the Men's Union, Gaskell, green-suited for Carmen's benefit, toyed with her hair and she pulled away sharply, yet he persisted. Madden didn't doubt that she would soon surrender once more, as she always seemed to. Gaskell was one of those people with too great an abundance of charm, and too little of shame: it allowed him the liberties denied to mere mortals like Madden, or even Carmen. It disgusted Rose, but more likely through jealousy than any more noble motive. On the few occasions they deigned to speak to one another she kept her words short and clipped, as if afraid that to allow herself to be more expansive would be to be drawn in, the way all the others seemed to be. Madden didn't doubt that either, but wasn't sure whether he was grateful that Gaskell showed no interest in her or not. He had vaguely wanted him to be jealous, but it didn't seem to be working. So here they were, sitting in a half-empty Union canteen during the Christmas break, waiting for the rain to go off outside. It was so miserable a day that Madden allowed Rose to hold his hand for a full five minutes before he simply *had* to free it.

Gaskell winked at Madden, beckoning him to come over. Rose had seen too, and reached again for his hand.

'Stay here, Madden,' she said. 'With me.'

Madden was surprised she could even imagine he might, and he knew that he would go over. It may have been in Gaskell's, but it was not in his own nature to be rude. He considered it to be a flaw in his character sometimes, an aberration that had him at its mercy. Yet, it was ingrained.

'I have to,' he said, standing up and edging himself around their table. Rose shrugged, and then opened her handbag and began touching up her lipstick, observing herself in a small compact.

'Fine,' she told him. 'Do what you want. Just don't expect me to sit here on my own all night, that's all.'

Madden groaned. 'I'll only be gone a minute or two,' he said.

'Suit yourself.'

As he made his way over to the canteen bar, he could see from the way she held her body that Carmen had drunk too much. Gaskell was talking into her ear and pointing a finger in Madden's direction. Carmen guffawed suddenly, and Gaskell shrugged.

'To what do we owe the honour?' Carmen said, as he joined

them. Her voice was slurred, and her eyes opaque. 'We thought you didn't care for our company.'

He was nonplussed, and stuttered out a reply.

'Madman here is an observer of men,' Gaskell said coldly. 'And of women too. Isn't that right, Hugh?'

Carmen snorted again, putting her drink to her lips. He'd never seen her drunk before: had, in fact, rarely seen her touch alcohol at all. He didn't think it suited her.

'Yes,' she said. 'I heard you liked to spy on people. I heard you liked to make up stories about them.'

Madden shook his head, unable to find the right words. He was mortally embarrassed.

'That's right, darling. He makes up stories, makes *people* up. Not very nice, is it?'

She shook her head, staring glassily at the barman polishing tumblers behind the counter. 'No,' she said. 'It isn't.'

'Perhaps he's made up a nice story about us,' Gaskell said, still staring pointedly at him.

'If you've just called me over here to humiliate me then . . . I'd better go,' Madden said.

Gaskell ignored him. 'Perhaps, Carmen dearest, he's even made up a story about *you*.'

This time, she turned her attention to Gaskell, her mouth open slightly, and something passed between them.

'Perhaps,' Gaskell continued, 'our Mr Madden has observed *you* and knows *your* secrets. Perhaps he knows everything about us. It's possible, isn't it, dear? Perhaps he's made up a little story for himself regarding your trip. But what could he possibly know about what you might have done there? Nothing, eh, dearest? Why, he'd have to have heard about it from someone . . . tittle-tattle, gossip. No one would *ever* tell tales about you, Carmen, would they. No, of course they wouldn't. And God forbid anyone would ever tell tales about *me*. That wouldn't do at all. Not at all.'

Carmen said nothing. Instead she stood, picked up her

glass and poured the contents into the lap of Gaskell's green suit.

'I'll say whatever I like to whoever I like,' she said through clenched teeth. 'And, yes, that includes you. Why shouldn't I? It's not as if you even care . . .'

He grimaced in discomfort as the ice from her drink leaked over him. 'Thanks, darling, thank you very much,' he said, peeling the wet material away from his skin.

'You are a shit, aren't you? You really *are* a shit.'

'Of course, dear. Whatever you say, dear. I'm a shit, isn't that right, Madden? I'm a shit of the highest order. A *shite*, even!' He began to laugh.

Carmen turned to Madden, who backed away slightly.

'You'd better leave, Hugh. I don't think I want to have to look at you.'

Madden needed no further encouragement.

'What was all that about?' Rose asked him when he returned to their table.

'No idea,' he said. 'No idea at all.'

Rose shrugged and went on reapplying her mascara.

'I think we should go somewhere else,' Madden said.

'Like where?'

'I don't know,' he said, buttoning up his jacket. 'Just . . . somewhere *else*.'

As they left the building, they met Dizzy and Hector going inside. Hector nodded at Madden, his dislike of him apparent, but Dizzy stopped him.

'Off somewhere a bit more lively, eh? I don't blame you. Dead as a dodo round here at the moment. And this perpetual bloody rain doesn't help either!'

His catalogue-model looks were somewhat deflated, and he looked as if he had been drinking. His eyes were like Carmen's, glassy and opaque. He also had a purplish welt on the right-hand side of his chin and a slight swelling. Madden shrugged, not knowing what to add. He would never master small talk, he felt.

'Listen,' Dizzy said, 'how about we swap some of those papers like we agreed? I've missed that many anatomy labs . . . I really need to catch up. That's your speciality, isn't it?'

Rose snorted, but said nothing, and Hector shuffled about on his feet, obviously impatient to get inside.

'I suppose so,' Madden said, embarrassed by the flattery. 'I could maybe use some of your tutorial notes too. I never seem to catch everything that's said. My pen isn't up to the job. Too slow.'

Again Rose snorted and this time Hector grinned too. Madden ignored them.

'Well, that's settled, then. Here . . .' He began ruffling through papers in a cracked leather briefcase until he found the ones he was looking for and handed them to Madden.

'I don't have my papers with me at the moment,' Madden said. 'Perhaps I could drop them off to you another time?'

Dizzy appeared not to hear: there was the sound of a familiar laugh coming from downstairs in the canteen. Gaskell.

'That's fine,' he said, after a pause. 'Any time you can get them to me will be fine.'

He looked at Hector, who shook his head. 'Maybe we should go somewhere else?' he asked Dizzy. It was too late. Dizzy was already striding down the stone steps to the Union.

'Em, goodbye, then,' Madden said as he went past.

'Yes, goodbye,' Hector said, hurrying after his friend. 'Excuse me . . .'

Madden felt Rose's hand take his.

'Well,' she said, 'where are you taking me now? It's early still.'

Madden felt like another drink and led her outside without pausing to answer her question.

*

Rose swung herself free of their clinch against the wall they were leaning on. They had finally elected to go to a pub – on her money as usual. On the way out of the Doublet, Rose had grabbed him lustfully and pinned him using her superior upper-body strength. She then went at him with her tongue, and he, having not the power to escape, endured.

He didn't quite know what to do about sex with Rose. He knew that it was inevitable that they would have to do it, but he desired no repetition of his encounter with Kathleen. Thus far, he had been conveniently saved the bother since they had nowhere private to go. Rose had attempted to drag him into the park after leaving the Union, but he had resisted.

'It's cold and wet in there, it'd be horrible,' he said. The prospect made him shiver.

'It's warm and wet in here,' Rose said, guiding his reluctant hand between her legs. 'Wouldn't that be nice?'

'You told me you were Catholic,' he said, using his best jocular voice.

'Ye*sss*. I a*mmm*. But I want to do it. We've not done it yet and I don't want to get married to someone I haven't done it with yet.'

'You think we're going to get married?'

'I don't know. I just know I don't want to rule anything out. If we were going to get married, I'd have to do it to make sure you were all right.'

'I don't know what you mean by that. If you don't think I'm all right, why keep on seeing me?'

'I just want something to happen!'

Madden straightened himself up and fixed his glasses. It was getting dark now.

'Like . . . doing *it* . . . on the wet grass?'

'No,' she said. 'We can sit on a bloody bench or something!'

He stooped, hands in his pockets. 'That'd be wet too. All the benches will be.'

'Well, if you'd rather do it with *Owen* . . .'

He felt stung, as if he she had slapped him.

'I bet you'd prefer that, wouldn't you? You and your little English bit on the side.' There was a sneer in her voice that he found hurtful, that he was used to hearing directed at others rather than himself.

'You like the boys, don't you, Madden,' she said. 'Owen's your favourite, your vewy vewy favouwite.'

The affecting of the baby voice was horrible.

'Shut up,' he said. 'I don't like that.'

'Well, let's do something . . . I mean *anything*. We don't have to do *it*. I mean let's just do *something*. You've not even introduced me to your parents yet!'

Rose wobbled a bit as she spoke, her jowls reddened and her dark hair swinging and damp in the smirr.

Madden shook his head. 'You don't want to meet them, believe me.'

'Why not? Are they cannibals?' She wiped her hair away from her forehead and looked momentarily very pretty in the dimming light. His parents were undoubtedly many things – none of them very pleasing – but they weren't cannibals. Not next to Rose, at any rate.

'Will they eat me alive?' she went on, poking him with one of her tiny childlike fingers.

'No, they won't eat you,' he said.

'Why not? Why won't they gobble me up? Gobble gobble gobble!'

'Stop that, please,' he said, deflecting her jabbing finger away.

'Why wouldn't they eat me all up, like Chicken Licken, Hugh?'

Poke, poke.

'I said stop. Stop it.'

'Chicken Licken and Henny Penny and Turkey Lurkey. Why wouldn't they eat me all up?'

Poke, poke, poke.

'Because there's too fucking much of you!' he said.

Rose slapped him so hard his glasses fell off.

Madden's apology finally accepted and his face still stinging, they went to the pictures – a phenomenon Rose insisted on calling 'the flicks'. The Americanism annoyed Madden intensely, but under the circumstances he decided that mutual silence in a darkened picture theatre would be an ideal way to end their evening together. Rose was still annoyed too, but Madden refused point blank to take her to his parents' home. None of which amused Rose overmuch: she was convinced he was ashamed of her, that his parents couldn't be allowed to meet her. Why? Her weight? Because she was a nurse? Was she not good enough for their blue-eyed boy? Madden denied every charge, but wouldn't elaborate on his reasons. There was nothing wrong with her weight. He had told her that, why wouldn't she believe him?

Rose became morose. 'It's true,' she said, 'I'm too fat.'

Nonsense, he'd said. There was no such thing. He liked her size just fine.

'My legs are nice, though, aren't they, Madden?'

'Your legs are fine,' he told her. 'Not too fat, not too thin: just right.'

She seemed to perk up at that, then complained of a pain in her chest.

'What might that mean?' she said.

'Nothing. It doesn't mean anything. It's just a pain. People get pains all the time. It doesn't mean anything. They're just pains.'

He shuffled along the road. He no more wanted to go to the pictures than she did. But of course, he would never say that. If he did, the possibility that she might pester him into some vile carnal act might arise. Or worse, she might insist he take her home with him. His father would have been unbearable if they did. His mother no help at all.

'They can't just be pains for no reason,' she said. Her hair was hanging down over her face, giving her a forlorn appearance. The sky must be falling down.

'Yes they can. What do you want to go and see?'

'How can things hurt for no reason? There has to be a reason for things. That's what these things mean.'

'Mean?'

'Things hurt because something's wrong inside. They hurt for a reason. If I get a pain in my stomach, it might be because I've got an ulcer. Or a twisted intestine. Or because I've bumped myself when I'm expecting a baby.'

'Or because you ate too much,' he said, then quickly added, 'There's a cowboy picture on. Bang bang, get them injun varmints! Fancy that?'

Rose frowned. 'I don't mind. As long as it isn't too long. I'm hungry.'

Madden sighed, and reached into his sodden jacket pocket. One day, he would own an umbrella, he decided. No self-respecting gentleman could live in a city like this without owning such a necessary implement.

'Here,' he said, 'have a Victory V.' He handed her a sweet, and watched her very carefully place the lozenge in her mouth. She began sucking slowly on it, as though she expected it to have to last many days, but gave up and began to crunch on it more or less immediately. Madden smiled to himself.

There were no people in the queue for the movie, only one man coming out, though the previous showing was still running: the sounds of whoo-whooing and gunshots audible from the grubby foyer. Terrible dive, the Rio Locarno, but the only cinema with anything even halfway decent on near by. The odour in the place was stifling, a mixture of stale cigarette and pipe smoke enlivened by the reek of unwashed bedclothes. They walked in and the man in the booth stopped them.

'Show's nearly done,' he said. 'Not want to wait for the next one?' His nose was very red and bloated. It was almost purple.

'We'll just go in and wait,' Madden said, flicking his hair back over his face. 'If that's all right. We're pretty soaked.' He raised his arms to let the man get a look at him, but he wasn't paying attention, so Madden handed over a couple of coins and waited for the machine to spout out his tickets.

'What's the picture?' Rose asked. There had been a poster outside, but neither of them had paid it any mind, only wanting to get into the warmth. She wrung the cuffs of her blouse and sneezed.

'That probably means a cold, see?' she said.

Madden blew on his hands.

'Cowboy thing,' the man said. 'It's got that fella in it. You know the one.'

'Which fella?' Madden asked.

'The one with the face. You know the one I mean.'

'Oh, yes,' Rose said. 'Him with the face? Wears a hat, doesn't he? I know him.'

The man in the booth winked at her. 'That's the chap,' he said. 'The one that wears the hat. With the face. He's the one inside, on the picture. *All Guns West* or something. *All Guns East*. Lot of pish, if you ask me. Sure yous don't want to wait till the next show?'

'Thanks, we'll just keep our eyes shut till it's over,' Madden said.

'He dies at the end. The man with the hat. Best bit, I reckon. Eejit. Gets scalped.'

'The one with the face?' Madden said, irritated. 'Surely not. Well, we'd better get in there. Don't want to miss the beginning. Now that we know the end.'

Rose took his hand and he didn't object, then they headed along the red corridor, a thousand cigarette burns on the carpet. It looked like a map of the Milky Way. They pushed through the red curtain into the theatre. An usherette with a pinched and sunken look tore their tickets for them and gave them their stubs, and they went and took seats near the back, on the aisle, so Madden could stick one leg out into it.

The seats in front of them were punctuated with solitary sitters, occasionally couples lit up in silhouette when the screen brightened, now and then someone standing to move along a bit, or let someone pass. The man with the face and the hat was blasting away at some distinctly non-aboriginals; they fell and died from rooftops, or tumbled to their knees, hatchets raised. The man with the face was mortally wounded, it seemed, but was fighting on. Madden's interest was aroused. It was strange that a man with a face like a hard-boiled egg could come to such a sorry pass. The beginning was looking more and more worthwhile.

Five

Madden stood up from the headless corpse of one Eugenio Bustamente, late of Fastgo designs over in the East End. A place that dealt in sheets of glass. Cut, laminated, bevelled and bullet-proofed as well, so far as Madden knew. He was wringing his hands and rubbing at the palm heels. Slowly, the life began to return to them, however temporarily. Would that Mr Bustamente were so fortunate.

Eugenio.

Spanish name, was that? Portuguese? He didn't look it. White as any Scotsman he'd ever seen. Freckles to boot. From what he could see of them, through the chap's partially opened mouth, he had green teeth too. That settled the matter. His mother or father was Spanish/Portuguese, had married a Scot, sought a better life with him/her, resettled, and had been blessed with a son – perhaps an only child as Madden was himself – the hapless Eugenio. Birthed here, in the dear green-toothed place. Madden felt sorry for him, sad for his imagined past.

Poor Eugenio had already folded, laid down his hand and left the table. And so young too, only thirty-six years old. Still, it wasn't exactly true to say he was headless: half of it hung on by a sinewy piece of meat and gristle, though the spinal column itself had been cleanly cut through. The lesser half of Eugenio's face was sitting on a stainless-steel tray next to the electric kettle and teacups. Caldwell & Caldwell's kept their espresso machine upstairs in the Welcome Room so that the guests could get a look at it, though Joe Jnr insisted staff use the cheaper stuff that sat on a heated plate, restricting the quality coffee to clients. Madden couldn't quite remember whether Joe's father had been as stingy, but he didn't think so. No. Not old Smokin' Joe. There was some expression he was fond of trotting out, something about eyeballs. What had it been?

'Don't suppose you're familiar with it, are you?' he said to half of Eugenio Bustamente's head. His hair was very fine and sandy-brown, like, he decided apropos of nothing, a Russian wig. 'Thought not.'

Madden knitted his fingers together and with a virtuoso flexing stretched his arms out in front of him, palms outwards, cracking the knuckles. He'd rattle out a quick prelude or fugue on this Bustamente chap as soon as he got the sensation back. He was wondering whether maybe those fingerless gloves cyclists wore might help. It was pressure on the ulnar nerve, causing all this grief. He needed a coffee, a decent cup, not this powdered stuff down here. He was jangling today all right: blame it on that selfish swine Kincaid. Not forgetting his imminent wife, though of course it was Madden expecting her, rather than she expecting. Acting the midwife to an eighty-year-old was more than he could cope with today.

'Ah, but you don't have to worry, my sleeping beauties,' he said, stepping back from the body and surveying the two shrouded others on either side, Kincaid and a serene-looking woman, her diabetes having taken her off unexpectedly in the night. *Sleeping* was precisely the wrong word, though. It implied that a *waking* would – if not inevitably, then probably – take place at some indeterminate point in the future. Not a chance. These poor buggers were *dead*. This Eugenio Bustamente chap was decidedly *not* getting up again. *Ever*. Not if you scratched your nails down a blackboard or poured boiling water in his ear. Though he looked as if he might have been something of a shifty character at one time. Unpredictable, perhaps. A chancer. He was staring at Madden with eyes at least four feet apart. Very dark eyebrows, he noticed for the first time. Might have been what he'd heard Joe Jnr call a *monobrow* if there hadn't been such clear blue kettle between them, one half of Eugenio's head in a Tupperware dish next to it, the rest of it on a slab on the other side of the machine.

Still, it had proved a very serviceable kettle over the last three years or so. Indeed, life down here in the bowels would have been twice, nay, *thrice* the poorer had it not been for the humble ministrations it provided. Even if it was only soluble coffee it had to minister *with*. Small mercies like this were what made the day bearable.

Eyeballs.

That was it: 'There's folk in the world that'd take your eyeballs then come back for the sockets.' One of Joe Caldwell Snr's more considered opinions, Madden recalled. A cynical view of human nature, but not one that warranted dismissal out of hand. There were all sorts of people in the world. Some took the eyes, and some came back for the sockets as well. Not least Joe himself, who wasn't averse to the occasional act of sadism when working over a corpse. As if death wasn't indignity enough. He was a capable mortician; not showy or overly talented, but capable: probably by virtue of the deadened pace with which he prosecuted his business. It had taken Madden a long time before he had realised that he should never underestimate the old bugger, and simply because he proceeded with all the haste of a defrosting fowl that was no reason to think that he was slow *himself*. He was not stupid or vain, which was more than could be said for Joe Jnr.

Madden unrolled his rubber gloves and snapped them into the sink. They were meant to have disposable ones – Madden had specifically requested them on more than one occasion, even Catherine the Phantom Assistant had requested them – but Joe Jnr had decreed from on high that they could boil the ones they had and use them again. That had beaten everything. Even Catherine was flabbergasted.

Boil rubber gloves? Are ye joking? she'd said in her nasal whine. Madden had gritted his teeth and kept quiet, not wanting to give her the excuse she was doubtless looking for to vent her spleen at him. *What fanny boils rubber gloves? Eh? Tell him, Madden. Tell the prick nae cunt does. Nae cunt!*

He'd declined, and left the room. The possibility that he might stick a haemostat through her ear was too dangerously close to the surface of his thoughts for her well-being.

Anyway, now Madden was beyond caring. The place was haemorrhaging clients and there was little he could do about it except get on with things and hope to die anywhere but on the job. He'd have been considerably the riper before Catherine the Useless deigned to get him under the ground. He decided on a break and a sit-down upstairs in the light of the Welcome Room before continuing.

Before he went up, he took his flask from the black medical bag and poured a jigger into the Glasgow 800 mug, swirling it around and inhaling its vapour before taking a drink. Then he threw a cover over Eugenio's body and took the tray with the other half of his face on it and put it into a Tupperware container. It was already labelled with his name. There wasn't much likelihood of getting it mixed up with anyone else's head, but he moved it anyway because he had a piece of Madeira cake in a tub just like it that he was going to have a slice of with his coffee. Satisfied, he climbed the stairs up to the ground floor rather than take the lift. It was better to stay as active as possible when you got to this age.

Joe Jnr returned, the ardour of his Tintinesque comb slightly dampened this late in the afternoon, with the temperature in the Welcome Room up to the ceiling. Madden was sitting in one of the leather armchairs with his hands clasped over his chest and a damp cloth over his eyes. The radio was on loudly so he could hear it from reception, but even so he must have dozed off. He stirred and sat upright, staring about him in a vague hallucinatory way. He had been dreaming about ration coupons again, the sudden availability of canned meat, Spam and corned beef. The voice on the radio was gabbling ecstatically about the body discovered in Loch Ardinning.

He listened with vague interest to the details, but found he couldn't commit to the report fully. He changed the channel to Radio 2. He'd discovered that the sedative qualities of Radio 2 deejays' voices were second to none, particularly that of the Irish fellow, Whatsisname. It'd come to him eventually. Once he'd woken up.

'Having a lie-down on the job?' Joe Jnr said, nodding with open contempt. Madden ignored it.

'Some heat, eh?' Joe Jnr went on. 'Murder out there, so it is. I got the flowers, but they're already looking a bit peeliewallie. Maybe we should start buying fakes. Plastic's the way forward. Never wilts!'

He reached a hand up under his shirt and scratched at his oxter. The coolness of the cold room, and simply climbing the stairs, had brought Madden out in a sweat, so much so that it had given him quite a worry. He wondered whether it meant he still had warm blood in his veins: surely the about-to-become-elderly were meant to feel the cold more. He was always seeing ancient grizzled old girls in the streets with overcoats and cardigans on regardless of the weather. He looked quickly away as Joe sniffed his fingers, feigning the rubbing of an itch at the end of his nose. The man was an unreconstructed finger-sniffer. It pained Madden to have to be around this kind of a sanitation catastrophe, so in Joe's company he permanently kept his head turned into a two o'clock profile, one where he would never actually have to set eyes on the horrors of Joe's scratch-and-sniff hygiene. Unfortunately when the weather was like today's it left him perfectly angled to savour the truculent hum of his sweat instead.

Madden went through to reception with Joe Jnr trailing after. He fiddled with the radio aerial, following the static leaps of geography and wavelength, adjusting the volume when he found someone whose voice didn't annoy him overmuch. Finally he settled on a local channel in the distracted hope that there might be some announcement about Kincaid on it. Unlikely, he knew – he'd have to look for the obituaries in the *Herald*. Still. There might be something. Joe wouldn't approve, of course. At one time it had given Madden a great deal of barely suppressed pleasure to tune into the muezzins calling the faithful to prayer during Ramadan, not through any sudden conversion, but because Joe Jnr hated it. One morning, letting him into the building, Joe Jnr had turned beetroot with inarticulate fuming simply because Madden greeted him with '*Salaam aleikum*'.

Joe Jnr told him to stick his Paki talk up his arse.

Still, there was nothing that could induce Madden to say a bad word to anyone about his employer. He would not be caught gossiping, not even with Catherine the Invisible, even though she prattled on inanely for the entirety of every shift.

I was like that, she was always saying. *I was like that. I says to him, I'm no coming in here every morning sticking tubes up deid folks' arses if you're gonnae speak to us like that, so I'm no . . .*

Madden always surprised himself by defending Joe Jnr's actions to her. Simply to shut her up. Joe Jnr is a reasonable man, he would say. Yes, he was a touch on the stingy side, yes, he didn't have the soundest of business acumen, yes, but he was well-meaning and reliable three days out of most weeks, thank the Prophet, peace be upon him. Unlike poor Catherine, who was now an apparently permanent absentee, may God destroy her home. For a while he had taken up the idea of studying Arabic in his spare time, just to have some idea of what the muezzin was actually saying, but he never got round to it. He was either too busy at work, or he was tending to Rose.

Allahu akhbar.

Madden squinted through the window into the street, the

desire to spot Maisie Kincaid – though he doubted he'd recognise her – before she set foot inside Caldwell's foremost in his mind. It would be less unsettling to see her first: he could prepare himself mentally, even if he had only a few seconds' warning; take deep breaths and so on. But there was no one out there, only a few workmen at a cement mixer across the other side of the road. Perhaps they had known this Eugenio Bustamente chap.

'Didn't manage to get a hold of Catherine,' Joe said, biting his fingernails.

'Not picking up the phone, is she?' Madden said, familiar with the routine.

Joe sighed loudly. 'Just the answer machine. Reckon I'll have to try her maw. No been very busy round here, have you? Place is a pure state, so it is. Have you heard from her?'

It was pointless to argue. Their hopeless dynamic – employer/employee versus upstart boss/idiot – had remained cryogenically static for a long time now. Madden understood his role of designated fool, his status that of a new-start despite his long years in the business, and Joe approached everything from the indignant position of a teenager who'd been caught in the act of pilfering his father's wallet. He seemed to feel it necessary to wrong-foot his employees whenever possible, blame them for things that were neither their fault nor could be helped. Things just didn't go right sometimes. His father had known that. He'd have turned in his grave at Joe's behaviour, if he hadn't been cremated. Turned in his urn, then. Except his ashes had been scattered.

'No . . . I haven't spoken to her.'

'Right. Well, I suppose I'll have to speak to her, then, won't I?' He went over to the reception desk and picked up the phone.

Madden sprayed the flowers of the plants and wiped the leaves of the others for dust, though he'd done it already, and when he looked up there was a young oriental woman coming in the door, so he held it open for her. Not a tall woman, wearing large, rose-tinted sunglasses and with a pinched and artificial look to her face, though that might have been as a result of the over-application of unsuitably Western make-up. Her lips were heavily rouged – he shuddered to think of the stains she would leave on glasses and teacups – and her narrow cheekbones were too pink for her darker skin. He sneaked a glance at Joe, but he was already talking on the phone, presumably to Catherine's mother, and waving his hands about animatedly.

'Can I help you?' Madden asked the woman, talking to people never his strong suit. He was staring over her shoulder out of the window too noticeably; the woman began to speak, then looked to see what it was that had caught his attention. Madden checked himself.

'Excuse me,' he said, 'I . . . we were expecting someone. I didn't mean to be rude.' He'd never conquer that habit now: at this time of life there was hardly any point trying. Years of struggling to keep it under control had failed to make any difference at all. He was always staring over someone's shoulder, or drifting off while they talked. His life was a series of encounters in which he was always nodding in the wrong places while staring expectantly out of windows.

The woman flicked her long black hair over her shoulder and pressed a palm to her chest.

'I come here to see someone,' she said, with a strong accent. 'I have to make some arrangement for them.'

'I see,' Madden said, regaining his professional composure. 'And what sort of arrangement might that be, could I ask?'

She looked at him as though he were a cretin.

'What sort of arrangement you think? The final arrangement.'

Madden wondered whether she was perhaps proposing he have someone killed.

'The final arrangement? Ah, yes. Of course.' He waited for

her to elaborate, but this was obviously the wrong tack. The woman was inexplicable behind her sunglasses. Inscrutable even.

'What . . . sort . . . of *arrangement* . . . did you have in mind?' Madden asked, in a barely fluid stodge. The feeling had begun to creep over him that they were both now embarked on some sort of coded cold war exchange.

'I want to make the final arrangement,' she said, beginning to get annoyed. 'For my husband. He's dead. The family say he in here. I have to find out through his executioner.'

'Oh,' Madden said, snapping out of it. 'Your husband's executor? I understand. Of course, of course.' He was disappointed to find out she wasn't Spanish too. Somehow he'd pictured poor Eugenio as having a petite señorita at home frying up tortillas, a slender frame nestled atop generously proportioned buttocks. This woman sounded Filipina, or maybe Thai.

'My husband family don't like,' she said, shaking her head. 'They don't want me to come to the . . . when you put him under the ground . . .'

'Funeral,' he said. 'They don't want you to come to the funeral? I'm very sorry to hear that, but I don't believe that – as his wife – they can have any legal right to stop you from attending . . .' He tried to shut up. He might be talking himself into a spot of bother with Joe if he overheard. But Joe was still talking on the phone, his gestures wilder than ever.

'Excuse me, but if you want to come next door into our Welcome Room we can have some privacy: it's a bit noisy in here.' He smiled the usual forced effort and extended a hand in the direction of the room, guiding her into the leather armchair he'd only recently vacated. Her apparel struck him as slightly unsuitable for the weather they were having, especially the mink stole. He assumed it was mink, though he'd no idea really. Possibly not. Whatever luckless creature she was wearing, it must be murderously hot. She crossed her pink-satin-leopard-print-skirted legs to reveal long slender feet. They were surprisingly large, almost licentious in their pink PVC high heels. She wore gold rings on two of the toes on her right foot, the index and the middle one. She leaned forward in her chair and took a long white cigarette from a packet in her handbag, a small patched-brown leather affair, and lit it without asking permission.

'Yes,' she said, 'they don't want me to come. But I want to go. He was my husband. So I ask his lawyer what to do and he says come here and you can see him before the final arrangements.' She took a deep drag of her cigarette and exhaled. Madden was surprised to see her blow a smoke ring. 'I want to see him,' she said. 'He was my husband. His daughter don't like me. None of his daughter like me.'

Madden hoped she wouldn't cry. If she cried he would – he would – he—

Nothing. He would sit there and do his job. He extended a cupped hand for her to tip her ash into. She smiled winningly at him.

'Thank you. My name is Tess,' she said. 'I want to see him again, you know? Kiss him before they daughter stop me. There will be *soooo* many people at the . . .'

'Funeral?'

'Yes! *Sooo* many people. My husband had so many friend. When I go, I won't get alone with him. So I want to see him now. Can you help me, Mr . . . ?'

He cleared his throat. 'It's Mr Madden.'

'Mr Madman, can you help—'

'Madd*en*,' he said, irritably, 'Mr Madd*en* . . .'

'I want to see my husband, Mr Madden. Can you help me to see him? His daughter hate me. But I hate those old woman bitch too.' She took another long drag, her right foot jigging up and down over the other.

'We can help you, yes. Of course. But your husband, Tess, is not in a good way.'

'He dead.'

Madden nodded. 'Quite. What I mean is, you may find it upsetting to look at him now. Many people want to see their loved ones after they've passed on no matter their condition, and often they find the experience upsetting. And your husband in particular is not pleasant to look at.'

'*Noooo*,' Tess said. 'He was *verry* good looking. He was *verry* kind.'

'That's correct, Tess. He *was* very good looking. Not now.'

Madden saw a tear begin to leak out from under one of her tinted lenses and he inhaled silently through his nose. She took another drag from her cigarette.

'Those daughter won't let me . . .' She began to sniff.

'Very well, Tess,' Madden said. 'If you wish to see him, then see him you must.' She smiled at him again. A beautiful smile. So full of teeth.

She tipped her ash into Madden's cupped hand.

'Thank you,' she said. 'You're kind too.'

'Not at all,' he said, parting the curtain to check on Joe. He was still on the phone, this time favouring a beseeching tone so horrible that it sent the hairs standing up on the back of Madden's neck. He turned to Tess. It occurred to him that she had more of that peninsular colouring, with the darkness of the Indian subcontinent within reach, a more Thai shape of face. But he was no expert. She might have been Korean for all he knew. But he was damn sure that she had a name that didn't trip off the Western tongue with quite so much ease as 'Tess'. No matter. It was none of his business what she wanted to call herself.

'If you'd like to come this way we'll go down to the cold room now. But . . .' He turned and frowned at her. 'I'm warning you again that you may find it distressing.'

Tess nodded, but showed no signs of being discouraged. He led the way down, using the stairs. They were properly carpeted and the wallpaper was of a reassuringly abstract motif for just such rare occasions. The lift was a bit too – how would he have put it? Industrial? Mechanical? – *inhuman* for clients. They climbed down the stairs: Madden let her go into the mortuary first. She looked around and nodded her head, as if she approved of the way the place was set up.

'If you'd like to step over here . . .' Madden said, leading the way. He went to the bodies in the corner. Tess took an audibly deep breath and waited. Madden lifted back the cover of the sheet. Tess scrunched her face up in disgust.

'I did say your husband wasn't a pleasant sight,' Madden said. 'I did warn you.'

Kincaid's wife nodded her head, stunned and pale despite her colouring.

'What is this? I understand he don't look so good as before,' she said. 'But this not my husband.'

'Ah,' Madden said, stunned. He'd shown her Eugenio Bustamente's corpse.

He'd assumed she'd been married to the younger man. Stupid.

Tess was visibly shaken, her hands crossed on her chest and her mouth open. 'You want me to die too?' she yelled, looking away from the corpse. 'You want I drop down on the floor too? I speak to you boss man about this! I speak to law!'

'I do apologise,' he said, quickly letting the linen sheet fall back over the body. 'A misunderstanding, that's all.' His hands were shaking: he flexed them several times. Had Maisie died, then? Divorced Kincaid? Tired of living with his dirty little secrets? Madden's mouth was dry: he needed a drink.

'Please calm down, Mrs Kincaid,' he said, not at all hopeful.

'I calm down when you show my husband to me! Not this . . . *thing*!'

Composing himself, he went to the adjacent gurney and placed his hand on the sheet that covered it. He could see that her hands were shaking too. He took a breath.

'As I say, I do apologise. Please don't be upset. This is your husband here, Mrs Kincaid.'

He drew the sheet away from Kincaid's face and let her look. She seemed genuinely upset. How strange. Perhaps she had really loved him.

'He look so peaceful,' she said, 'like only sleeping.'

'Indeed, Mrs Kincaid. He sleeps eternally now. Your husband has earned rightfully the eternal repose that awaits us all.'

'I come back and see him when you make him up? Those bitch daughter don't let me come to the final arrangements.'

'Funeral,' Madden corrected.

She nodded irritably and said, 'Yes. I know. Funeral. Those bitch daughter don't let me come.'

Madden agreed that she could. 'Good,' she said. 'Then I come back soon. Two days or I speak to law.' He had been about to protest, but she was already on her way back up the stairs. Halfway up, she turned and said: 'You do him good, Mr Madman. You make him beautiful. Not for his bitch daughter. For me.'

Then she was gone.

'*Madden*,' he said to no one in particular. 'My name is *Madden*.'

He turned his attention to the head of Eugenio Bustamente, lying partially uncovered. A dead man. Head sliced in two. One half inside a Tupperware container. Everything as normal. Proceed.

A simple misunderstanding was all it was. He supposed Maisie must have left him long ago, or perhaps she had died, right enough. Madden couldn't ever imagine Kincaid as having been *lonely*, though. Not enough to remarry, not at his age. He presumed, from his new wife's youth, that their nuptials had been a *recent* development. Why, then? He had his daughters, his many friends and colleagues. The Lodge. And he was comfortably off, too. That big house out in –

where was it? – Bearsden or Milngavie? It must be worth a fortune. Madden supposed it would go to the daughters, along with everything else. Or maybe *Tess* – that surely was not her real name – had got her claws into it. Yes. That must be why the daughters despised her. Well, good luck to her. Kincaid's daughters would have to be getting on themselves these days – what was it he used to say? Something about youth, the beauty of youth. Or was that Gaskell?

He flicked the sheet from Kincaid's face and looked at it, waiting for something, he wasn't sure what, perhaps that old look of disdain, the furrowed brow of disapproval. He noticed moisture around the eyes – the body was crying? No. Madden was surprised to find it was liquid that had fallen from his own eyes on to the good doctor's face. He wiped his eyes under his spectacles, marvelling at the wetness on his fingertips. He took a deep breath, chuckling to himself.

'Tell me,' he said, 'what's it like there?'

Where? Kincaid said, his lips moving but his eyes firmly shut.

'You know. The other side. Death.'

There isn't any other side, laddie boy. You know that.

'There must be.' Madden laughed. 'You're talking to me from it.'

You're mistaken, Mr Madden. No one's talking to you from anywhere. You're talking to yourself. Bad sign that.

'So what d'you advise, then, Doctor? I don't know the disease for this particular set of symptoms.' Madden was chuckling to himself, his arms crossed over his chest. It really was very funny.

I'd advise you to pour yourself a stiff drink and take the rest of the day off. And stop talking to dead people. They're terrible conversationalists.

Madden sighed and wiped his eyes again. 'Worse than Jehovah's Witnesses?' he said, almost doubled up with laughter. The doctor's lips moved again.

Much worse. No sense of humour, you see. Fatal for con-versation, that.

Madden snorted. 'Fatal,' he repeated. 'That's priceless,' he said. 'That's absolutely priceless.'

'What's priceless?' Joe Jnr said, staring at Madden with a worried look. 'Who're you talking to?'

Maisie Kincaid had died from peritonitis, Joe Jnr told Madden, frowning and irritable, leafing through a brochure of imitation plants. Three years ago, he said. Three years. Madden had no right to be showing anybody's dead body to anybody. Except in mitigating circumstances, Madden pointed out. No, Joe Jnr told him, not in mitigating circum-stances, not in any circumstances . . . unless Joe said it was all right. Was this not such an occasion? Madden asked. The woman was his wife, after all. Even if it wasn't quite the wife he had been expecting. He wasn't wrong there, Joe said. Not only was she not the right wife but it wasn't the right body either. Congratulations, Joe told him. Well done. Played a blinder there, Hugh. No, really, two–nil to you. He sat shaking his head and looking at the flowers. Madden stirred his coffee. They were both drinking the good stuff for a change. Madden supposed it was something of a special occasion. He was staring out of the window and nodding, the radio interfering with his concentration. Maisie Kincaid was dead of peritonitis, he said to himself. What? Joe asked. What was that? Nothing, Madden said. No it wasn't, Joe Jnr said. It wasn't nothing. He had said something. What was it? *Maisie Kincaid died of peritonitis*, Madden repeated, closing his eyes and rubbing the thumb and forefinger of his left hand into the corners underneath his glasses. The men across the road were finished up for the day, the cement on the lip of the mixer hard and set. Not too many days like today in the world. No. A dearth of days like this. Was he listening? Joe Jnr was asking. Was he paying any attention at all? Madden thought about the question for long seconds, then sipped his coffee. He had, very publicly, poured a tot of whisky into his, uninterested in whether Joe noticed or not.

'There was me on the blower to Catherine's maw for a good half an hour,' he was saying. 'A good half an hour . . . and when I turn my back you're showing complete strangers the goodies in the deli. Fuck's sake.'

Madden winced at his language, but said nothing.

'Aye, you better enjoy that drink. Here, where's the bottle? I could do with one myself.'

Madden reached into his lab coat pocket and handed Joe the pewter flask. He unscrewed the top and took a swig.

'It would have been very painful,' Madden said wistfully. 'Ugly. Do you know what happens when someone dies from peritonitis?'

He was still staring out of the window, watching clouds begin to form in the early evening. Perhaps there'd be rain tomorrow, and the earth would give in to the sky and reach towards it, green would stretch long arms upwards and the world would once again be young. Vaguely, he was aware of Joe Jnr looking at him, but didn't care.

'Naw, maybe you better tell me, eh? You're giving me a perforated ulcer, so you are . . .'

Madden smiled at him. 'Joe,' he said, 'if I'm giving you anything it's an *ulcer*. The perforation you'll have to take care of yourself.'

Joe Jnr shook his head. 'Yeah, whatever,' he said. 'Peritonitis, peptic ulcer. You're giving me the lot!'

Madden stood up and went to top up his coffee from the espresso machine, the burbling of the machine a balm to him. The radio chattered indifferently, the news again.

'Help yourself,' Joe was saying. He swirled his own coffee with a spoon.

'We'll be lucky if she doesn't sue us for mental distress or something,' he said, after sipping.

'Who?' Madden asked, then remembered. 'She won't sue,' he said. 'She wants to see him. Why would she sue if she wants to see him?'

'How do I know?' Joe said. 'Because she could get herself a nice fat settlement out of court? Because she'd have us bang to rights? It's a blame culture, man.'

The coffee was delicious: bitter like the darkest chocolate. Of course, it was meant to have carcinogenic qualities, and otherwise be very bad for the insides. Possibly a contributing factor in peptic ulcers. He could envisage a hole forming in Joe's own stomach with each successive sip and an infection setting in. An abscess, a cyst. Swelling like a tiny inverted contraceptive cap.

Joe rubbed his stomach and placed his cup on the glass table top, and with it the imitation-flower brochure.

Was it happening now? An unpleasantness in the stomach, an acid sensation?

'She won't do that,' Madden said again. 'She's got Kincaid's daughters against her already. She went to his executor because she'd no idea whether she could come here legally or not. And, come to think of it, she may not be legal herself.'

'Aye, well . . .' Joe said, rubbing his belly in semicircular motions. Next, there would be tenderness all over as well as signs of gas and fluid. The balloon ready to pop. Would he have the good grace to die instantly, Madden wondered, or would he drag it out, make a mess with his vomiting and bleeding? The latter, he decided, was more likely.

Rapid pulse, high temperature, state of shock. Distension, diarrhoea, constipation . . . it would take a keen scalpel to let the fluids escape. Madden could do that for him. If he begged. It would be a kindness. If he pleaded.

He wondered how Joe Jnr would look on the slab. Well. He was young, and the young always made the best corpses. There was something so effortlessly *vital* about them. They seemed to gleam. Their bodies lit up a mortuary. Even Eugenio

Bustamente, with his tongueless head. Half a pomegranate, the seeds scattered. And he would surely be in the underworld now. Sleep and dreams, Eugenio. Sleep and dreams. Peace be upon you. *Salaam.*

'You know what you have to do, don't you?' Joe Jnr was saying. Madden looked at him, the Tintin comb now sadly detumescent, a limp shadow of its former glory.

Madden stiffened slightly, bracing himself. 'Yes,' he said. 'Could I at least stay till the end of the month? I'd like to be the one to see Mr Kincaid off in reasonable shape . . .'

Joe scrunched his face in distaste, or at some invisible fist squeezing his insides. 'What are you talking about? I'm not giving you your cards!'

Madden was nonplussed. 'What, then?'

'Christ's sake, Hugh . . . what would I sack you for? You're the only guy I've got! Catherine's maw says she's not coming back. She's going back to college, she says. She sent her maw a note from somewhere out on the coast, says she's taking a wee holiday to herself. Just like that! Her maw says she's never done anything like it before. She says that the note said she was thinking about going back to finish her course.'

'What course was that?' Madden asked, feigning curiosity. Of course, he knew all this stuff already.

'Dental nurse. She used to say teeth are healthier to be around than corpses.'

'So what do you want me to do?'

'Fix Kincaid up proper. It's got to be good, though. No corner-cutting. I need that body up and running by the day after tomorrow at the latest. If you do a decent work-up on him, we can give Mrs Kincaid her preview before the funeral. That might go some way to smoothing things over . . .'

'Of course,' Madden said. 'I'll get right on it.'

'Hugh, I want you to work on him exclusively until then, OK? Forget the other two. The diabetic hardly needs any work and, well, I'm pretty sure there'll be a closed coffin for the decapitation.'

'You mean Eugenio?'

'First-name terms now, are we? You've been here too long, pal. Maybe you should have got out sooner, like Catherine. Bitch.'

Madden nodded again, and finished his coffee. Very good stuff. Colombian, so it said on the empty sachet. Dashed fine, if he said so himself.

'And Hugh?'

Madden looked at Joe. 'Yes?'

'Try not to get into too many long discussions down there. You're paid to work, not to chat.' He grinned and raised his cup to Madden.

Madden blushed deeply and walked quickly through the Welcome Room towards the stairs leading below, only just catching the news item about the dead body in the loch. It was worrying, but then again people were always turning up dead. All over the place.

Six

He arrived home late that evening to find the front door left open, his wife Rose slumped on the living-room sofa, and the stink of carbon in the hallway. He'd been going to tell Rose, Guess who came to the office that morning, finding himself uncharacteristically upbeat at the prospect, but all that had been forgotten as he'd taken in the new situation and had moved through it as though directed by some *higher power*. Those were the words he'd use later – as though guided by an invisible force, a voice telling him exactly what to do and where to go. He hardly had the words for it: he had simply reacted to the circumstances, taken aboard what mattered immediately and allowed to wait what could afford to wait. Wasn't that funny, Rose had said to him when she was well enough to hear the story of how he'd come to her rescue, wasn't it strange how he had gone straight to the kitchen?

Madden had shrugged. He had simply wanted to see what was causing the smell. It might have been a chip pan on fire, or the iron left sitting on a pile of shirts. What was funny about that?

'Nothing,' Rose said, 'just the way you describe it, that's all.'

'What?'

'You *allowed to wait what could afford to wait*.'

'I don't follow.'

'You went to the kitchen first. To see where the fire was. I might have been dead, but you went to the kitchen first.'

'Don't be silly, *dear*,' he said, taking her hand. 'If you'd been dead, it'd have benefited nobody to have the house burn down as well.'

Rose had forced a smile at the joke, and he'd stroked the back of her hand, turning it over to examine the whitened lines of her palm. It was still surprising to him how pale her palms were when she had such a dark complexion.

'I suppose nobody means you,' she said, nodding to herself. 'There wasn't even any fire, was there?'

Madden made a clicking noise with his tongue. He had come back and the door had been open, he said. Mrs Spivey was nowhere to be seen. He had come in and could smell a smell. What had he been meant to think? He could see she was unconscious on the sofa. What had he been meant to do? Suppose she'd been poisoned with smoke inhalation? If he'd gone to her aid he might have succumbed too. Then where would they be. Nowhere, that was where.

'There wasn't any smoke, you said,' Rose said. 'You said there was only a smell. A smell like a pillow burning, you said.'

But when he had got into the kitchen he'd found no pillow burning, or iron left turned on. He'd found two pieces of blackened toast sitting smoking in the toaster, cindered, the way Rose liked it; the way he'd forbid her to have it if he were around to stop her. He knew that Mrs Spivey would give in to her, though, unable to resist Rose's lamentations. Oh, she never got to eat what she liked any more, oh, Hugh would never allow her to enjoy her food like in the old days, he said that carbon was a cancer agent, that butter gave you heart disease, that the butchers didn't sell trotters any more and she used to love a good trotter.

'I wasn't unconscious, I was asleep,' Rose said. Madden nodded. He hadn't assumed she was unconscious, but he neglected to mention this to her. She would only think ill of him. 'I was watching TV and I dozed off,' Rose said.

'I've terminated Mrs Spivey's employment,' Madden said suddenly. Rose recoiled at the information, her look a mixture of fear and upset, as though it were somehow her own fault that this was happening. She protested that the blame lay not with Mrs Spivey, but with herself for falling asleep like that, that she wouldn't let it happen again, that she would pay attention, but Madden simply raised his hand to silence her, and dutifully she became calm again.

'The woman was incompetent,' he said. 'She was neglectful, she was lazy . . .' He let the words trail off, restricting his charges to ones he knew could justifiably be answered. Rose looked at him. 'Ellen is my friend,' she said simply, turning her eyes down to stare at her hands clasped in her lap. Madden found this kind of attitude most difficult to deal with. If she threw a tantrum he could silence her with a raised hand, or defeat her noise with his silence. Rose had once told him he was the most patient man she'd ever met, that sometimes it made her want to tear her hair out, but that she'd realised it was a virtue eventually, that it was a gift from God. That was his one great talent, she said, unending tolerance, a willingness to wait just that little bit longer than the other person. She was wrong, though, it wasn't patience. He was no more tolerant than she, he simply couldn't abide to give that much of himself away. To lose his temper would have been like being caught spying on a neighbour through a net curtain. The idea of such a compromise was almost as much as he could bear to think about.

'We'll find you new friends,' Madden said, getting up from the arm of the couch and going to the window. He looked out over the rooftops, the cranes of the shipyard visible over the slates of the opposing tenements. He'd been born not far from here; indeed, he'd lived his entire life within what could surely not amount to more than a few square miles. Rose too, though she had lived in England for a while before they had met. Until this evening, it had never occurred to him that he would very likely die within this same tightly circumscribed area. It seemed to him afterwards that the voice that had guided him, the invisible force that had removed him to the kitchen, hadn't been simply the fear of fire, or the fear of the destruction of his property, or the fear of the sudden demise of his wife. It had been more than that. It was the primal knowledge that he too would die one day. The instinct to survive at all costs had possessed him. That overwhelming realisation of the importance and order instinctively placed on things had left him reeling slightly. Life, property, wife: he felt as if some kind of corner had been turned, that some kind of undercurrent that had always run just below the surface of his existence was about to sweep him off to somewhere he'd never be able to get back from. That two slices of burnt toast should be the cause of all this turmoil made him feel completely ridiculous.

Madden struggled hard to hide his sense of incontinence from Rose. He'd taken the bread from the machine and thrown it into the bin and opened a window, where he'd stood gulping in the air as if it would save his life. Several thoughts were fighting for oxygen and he had to flood them with it, let them swallow it down. When he felt able to come back inside he'd crumpled on the linoleum.

'I don't want any new friends, I want Ellen,' Rose said. Madden nodded and let the curtain hang back down again. 'She probably only went out for a loaf or something. She often does.' Rose still had the same expression of mousy sub-servience on her face, and Madden sensed her momentary alienness, as though his real wife had been replaced by this monstrous facsimile, like his wife in every respect, yet some-how inexpressibly different. He felt like grabbing her by the shoulders and shaking her, he felt like shouting, *Where's my wife? What have you done with her? Where's the real Rose?*

'She often went out? She was meant to be looking after you. How could she have done that if she wasn't here?'

Rose shook her head and twisted her wedding ring about her finger. Madden had already told Mrs Spivey that her services would no longer be required. It had been a fraught exchange: she had sworn at him and demanded payment up to and including the end of the month. As soon as she had raised her voice he'd felt the urge to stove in her skull with some heavy object: a crystal ashtray, a frying pan, the iron sitting cold upon its shelf next to the ironing board.

In the version he'd given Rose, Mrs Spivey was the villain, abandoning her helpless charge to her fate. Mrs Spivey, too late up the stairs to stop his own dear Rose succumbing to the smoke. Mrs Spivey, leaving the door open so that vandals and thieves could lay waste to their home. Mrs Spivey, practically snatching the money from his hands when he'd finally given it to her, calling him a *thug* and a *poltroon* and a *bodysnatcher* and *a damned Bashi-Bazouk*!

'We'll get the agency to send someone over tomorrow,' Madden said.

Rose nodded. 'Hugh?' she said. 'Did she really call you a Bashi-Bazouk?'

Madden clicked his tongue. Perhaps not a Bashi-Bazouk, exactly. Perhaps not a thug either. She'd used coarser words than those. By the time she'd come back from the grocer's or wherever it was she'd been, he'd recovered himself sufficiently to get up and pour some cold water from the tap. It was only then, as he sipped from the chipped brown Glasgow 800 mug, that he remembered Rose, and went through to see how she was. It was difficult to explain what had happened next. He was standing over her, gazing at her slack-jawed face slumped against her chest, when Mrs Spivey came in from the shops. She'd gawped at him as if at a burglar, as if ready to scream, and he had put up his hand to her in the hope of stemming her accusations before they left her mouth. Mrs Spivey wasn't as dutiful a subject as Rose, though. She'd dropped her carrier bag on the floor and made towards the phone on the occasional table next to the sofa and he'd found himself backing away, towards the window. He stammered and kept his hand raised between them, but Mrs Spivey would not be deterred. I want you to leave, Mrs Spivey, he said to her. I want you to collect your things and go right this instant, Mrs Spivey. I was doing no such thing, Mrs Spivey, he said. You are being ridiculous, he told her. Please put the phone down. No, I insist, please put the receiver down. There's a quite obvious explanation if you'll just allow me to . . .

It was true he'd had his hand around Rose's throat but it wasn't what Mrs Spivey was thinking. It had been quite the opposite. Rose, her head lolling, permed black hair still as thick as ever. What the hell did he think he was playing at? Mrs Spivey said, her Portadown accent becoming strained. She had her hands folded across her chest. She was a formidable woman, her face and hands red and her hair pulled back tightly into a bun. She looked as if she might easily clobber him one, if that was the right word. Yes, Mrs Spivey was just the sort of woman to clobber a man. He wondered whether the police might find him lying dead on his own living-room floor, a frying pan next to his head. Done in by his wife's carer for checking her pulse. At the same time, he had a tune going round his brain. Oh, I will take you home Kathleen . . .

'So what was it you were doing with your hand about her neck?'

'I was checking for the absence of pulsation in the principal arteries. I was checking for the cessation of blood circulation. But there wasn't any.'

'Any what?' Mrs Spivey looked as if she might clobber him yet. Or worse, *batter* him.

'Any cessation of blood circulation.'

Mrs Spivey fixed him with a squint. 'Are you trying to say . . . What is it you're trying to say?'

'That Rose is still alive. She's got a pulse. She's breathing.'

'Of course she's still alive. Why wouldn't she be alive? I was only gone a minute for a pint of milk.'

Madden hadn't immediately seen the connection between the milk and cessation of function in the respiratory and circulatory system, but came to the conclusion later that Mrs Spivey had a far greater grasp of somatic death than he had given her credit for. It stood to reason that if Mrs Spivey had only been *gone a minute* then it was unlikely Rose could reasonably be pronounced dead within the timescale were the primary cause of death asphyxia, in this case through the probable inhalation of smoke. It was entirely possible – likely even – that the heart could continue to beat for several minutes even after respiration had stopped. Later, after he had paid Mrs Spivey what he owed her and sent her on her way, he'd come to the conclusion that her reasoning had been, though not said in so many words, to wait for a period of roughly twenty minutes before pronouncing Rose deceased.

Neither of them had to wait that long, though, since Rose had awoken groggy from her medication about fifteen minutes later and had wanted to know where Mrs Spivey was.

'I was having a lovely dream,' she said. Madden was still somewhat shaken.

'What did you dream?' he asked, not really caring.

'I dreamt I was at the theatre, and I saved Abraham Lincoln from getting shot. I was the hero.'

'Mmm,' Madden murmured, remembering he had some news for her. 'Guess who dropped by work today?'

Rose was still groggy. She'd be whining for chocolate shortly. 'Who?' she said, rubbing her face.

'Lawrence Kincaid. The good doctor himself.' He didn't mention anything else. Not Tess, not the news that Maisie had died, not even the mention on the news about the woman's body being discovered so close by. Close enough to drop by of an afternoon, close enough for Sunday afternoon picnicking. He'd lost count of the number of times he'd taken Rose up to the banks of the loch and let her roll the eggs their baby might have had, had he lived long enough.

Rose had another difficult night. Madden had administered to her, seen that she was comfortable enough, and was in the process of taking what his father used to refer to in the rare highs of the low-pressure front that was his normal humour as *a small libation*. The habit had been passed to Madden, and it bothered him, though he could never quite seem to shake the expression, or its impetus, at its source. He sat heavily on the armchair next to Rose, whisky in hand, and observed the loosely arranged limbs of his wife asleep again on the bed. Her breath came in shallow puffs that lifted a curl from the side of her face and held it wavering for a second or two, then lowered it back down again. As every night, he sipped his drink silently until he was absolutely sure she was too deeply under to wake before he moved about or made any undue noise. Rose slept with difficulty. It would be a good half an hour before he could feel comfortable enough to leave her alone. Sometimes he had only to stretch his legs out in the chair he sat in for her to rouse, whimpering, and begin pleading with him not to leave her alone in there with just the light of the table lamp. At other times she woke and didn't recognise him at all for a few seconds before he raised his palm for silence and she calmed again.

Often, her condition was so poor that sleep was an impossibility, and on those occasions she couldn't stand him to be anywhere near her. And it was preferable too for him not to be around: he spent far longer at work than either Joe Jnr or Catherine, even though the financial gain was negligible and there was often little to do. Still, it meant he could relax somewhat, read a little, drink a little from his bottle in the black bag, live a little in the company of the ex-living, his sleeping charges. He could catch up with the latest technological leaps being made or work a little more on whoever had come in that day. Sometimes he got a little drunk and a little maudlin too. He felt, not without some degree of guilt, that the mortuary was his real home, and his actual home was a mortuary. These days, he found they were both easy concepts to confuse.

Rose lay as still as any corpse on the embalming table, a good woman, with a heart of gold, but an organ that was only infrequently up to the job her body demanded of it. She herself was only intermittently aware of the gravity of her condition, being so graspingly possessive of so many *other* conditions, not one of which she could bear to let go of. Over the years he had tried countless times to convince her that these disorders were part of a larger, greater disorder, the nebulousness of which constantly escaped her, and yet was the dark matter that held her suffering intact.

The truth was that chronic sickness had become for her a way of life: it was the concentrated and clarifying focus of her existence. In a sense, it defined her. She maintained that no one who had not suffered as she was suffering could have any possible comprehension of what it meant to live life as a perpetual, losing war of attrition with disability and disease. And slowly, Madden had come to realise that the disease with which she was afflicted was the morbid fear of disease itself. Nothing could have convinced Rose that this was the case, though. Any real symptoms, any genuine sickness, could instantly be marshalled to her cause, be made to demonstrate how she had been right all along. There. You see? Didn't I tell you there was something wrong? The irony of the situation was that when she had, finally, been diagnosed with a heart condition, she had felt all her years of obsession were vindi-cated, that the countless consultations with doctors and physicians from every stratum of the medical spectrum had been justified. And it was a painful irony, literally so, for her angina brought with it severe incapacity and discomfort much of the time.

But all those years, Madden couldn't help but think, all those years searching for the one piece of evidence that would confirm her suspicions to her, had taken it out of him too. And the illness persisted, carried on as if an entity in itself. For Rose, the heart condition had never been the point. The symptoms she searched so obsessively for were phantasmal: even now he could not convince her otherwise. Her night terrors were not justified fear of arrhythmia, or pulmonary embolism, of cardiac failure or respiratory attack. No one could convince her that these were anything other than side effects of her as yet undiagnosed host condition to which her parasite existence clung, but which never revealed itself.

Madden watched her sleep, sipping his drink quietly. He watched her determinedly, his attention focused on the minutiae of her facial features, the tic-like twitch of her curl, spontaneously hung in the air above her face; the position of her hands, one tucked under the pillow beneath her head, the other thrust down and clenched at her side in an affectingly infantile fist. Gradually, over many minutes, he waited for that hand to slowly loosen, to allow the fingers to spread out and relieve their grip on whatever phantasmal throat her sleep placed at her bedside night after night. Perhaps it was the fear of disease, perhaps it was this spectre which attended to her dreaming self. Only the loosening of that fist could signal to Madden that she was safe now until morning, that she could be left unattended. In the meantime, he watched and waited and sipped his drink. Then the door buzzer sounded.

Mrs Spivey came back again trailing one huge brute of a son – an effort to extort money from Madden that afterwards he supposed must have succeeded far in excess of her ambition. By this time it was past midnight and she refused to stop ringing the door-entry buzzer until he let her in. When he went to the front door and looked through the spyhole she was standing there with arms folded in all her fish-eye-lens grotesquery, hatchet-face reminding him of his mother's. He opened the door, finding himself immediately pushed back into the room by the son, who must have been standing out of view next to the door. Mrs Spivey strode in, arms folded across her chest and tucked into her armpits in a way that made Madden resolve never again to purchase supermarket fowl. He was about to speak when the son put one great simian mitt on his shoulder and gripped his clavicle tightly. Madden winced and curved his neck, shoulder and head into the pain.

'All right, Mr Madden, how's tricks?' the son said. His accent was Glaswegian, but that was little consolation. There was something of the Orangeman about him, the stubbled red crew cut and the bomber jacket. Madden couldn't recall his name right now and it didn't seem imperative.

'Time to open up the tills,' the son said. 'My ma reckons she's a bit short on change for the parking meter.'

'I've paid you adequately already,' Madden said, directing his words towards Mrs Spivey. 'Get this gorilla off of me.' He felt the son give his collarbone another twist.

'Adequate isn't enough. Reckon that fucking agency'll sack me for getting fucking sacked, so as far as I'm concerned you fucking owe me fucking compensation, cunt. I looked after that fucking eejit of a wife of yours for six fucking months, feeding her, giving her those fucking injections, listening to her fucking moaning on the whole time, so I did. Changing her fucking nappies and wiping her fucking arse. D'ye think I'd fucking put up with that day in and day out for what you fucking pay me unless I fucking needed the fucking money? I could go back to fucking cleaning toilets for a living but I reckon yous owe me a wee bit more than that, don't ye now.'

'Shshh! Rose is asleep, I don't want you to wake her.'

Mrs Spivey uncrossed her arms and then crossed them again. Raising her voice, she said: 'Did you not fucking hear me? I said you *fucking owe me!*'

'I paid you till the end of the month, what more d'you

want? I can't afford to give you more than I've already given you.' Madden was twisted up around the source of the pain, almost on his tiptoes. He noticed the son's filthy boots had left track marks over the carpet.

'I could go to a fucking industrial tribunal for unfair fucking dismissal.'

Madden twisted on his tiptoes, trying to discover a way of standing that loosened the boy's grip enough for him to rest back on the soles of his feet.

'I would strongly advise against that. You're not in a position to threaten me with legal action. You went missing from the workplace!' He noted a tone of desperation creep into his voice even as he said the words. He had no idea whether that was true or not. Did temporary carers have the same rights as normal full-time carers? What rights did full-time carers have? He'd never considered the matter before.

'Brido, break this oul' eejit's arm,' she said.

'All right!' Madden said. 'How much d'you want?'

'Another month's pay. After that we'll see.'

'What? You can't do that, I'll go to the police.'

Brido twisted his collarbone again and he winced in pain. He was sure this must be happening to someone else. He was a middle-aged man, almost elderly! Just then Rose came through from their room, rubbing her eyes. She had her dressing gown draped over her shoulder and limped along on two crutches, her greyish nightie showing. Madden could hardly conceive of a more shameful sight and blushed deeply.

'Hugh? Ellen? What's going on?'

Mrs Spivey nodded to Brido, and he released his grip, dropping his arm to his side. Rose rubbed her eyes, oblivious.

'What's going on is I want what I'm owed,' Mrs Spivey said. 'And I'm not fucking leaving before I get it. Or *he* gets it.'

Rose looked shocked and swayed a little on her crutches.

'Don't worry, dear,' Madden said, 'we're just having a little dispute about what we owe Ellen. Go back to your room and lie down, everything's fine.'

Rose looked from Madden to Brido to Mrs Spivey.

'I thought we were friends,' she said to her ex-carer. 'Friends don't do things like this to each other.'

'No, you're not fucking wrong there,' Mrs Spivey said. 'So if we all want to remain friends we'll just have to come to some sort of agreement, won't we.' She nodded at Brido, who placed his hand on Madden's shoulder again but didn't grip him as before: instead he patted Madden, as though they were old buddies catching up on the good times.

Rose gazed at Mrs Spivey with vague hurt and then back at Madden. 'Please sort this out, Hugh. If we owe Mrs Spivey anything then pay her whatever she asks. It's very late, you know.'

'Bri, you and Mr Madden sort this out between you, and I'll see that Rose gets back to bed all right.'

Her son nodded, and Mrs Spivey went over to Rose and helped her back towards the bedroom. Then she turned to look over her shoulder and winked at Madden. 'I'm sure it'll work out just fine, won't it, Hugh,' she said with a nastiness to her voice that made Madden shiver.

Madden said, 'I'll get my wallet,' and immediately the hand disappeared from his shoulder. Brido turned and grinned at him, smoothing down his collar for him and then standing hands on hips.

'That's another fine mess you've gotten yourself out of, in'tit, Mr Madden?' he said, smiling affably and making a sort of breathy whistling noise. Madden rubbed his shoulder, deliberately exaggerating his discomfort in the hope that he might engender some future restraint from this overgrown teenager with the hands like steel traps. He could see that he was relieved not to have to act further, but also that he would do exactly what was required of him should his mother demand it. It wasn't a comforting thought.

Mrs Spivey's son looked around the room, wandering over to pick up ornaments from the mantelpiece above the fire, examine behind the curtains, nod and cluck to himself like a nosy mother hen: Madden was half expecting him to run a finger over the skirting boards to check for dust. From behind, he appeared too large to be seemly in a flat of this size, his big bap of a head only a few inches below the ceiling. He was particularly taken with a photograph of Madden and Rose standing outside Nardini's in Largs, his hair blown inanely across his face, exposing a tuppence-worth of the baldness that would eventually overtake most of his skull. In the photograph, Rose held her skirt down against her legs so that the wind couldn't lift it up, and held a large and curlicued ice-cream cone in her hand, raspberry sauce running down over her fingers, apparendy in hysterics over the actions of either the photographer or someone else behind the camera. Madden hated the photograph: Rose kept it there purely to irritate him and years of feigning indifference to it had finally paid off. He could stare at it with what he was sure must be some sort of passive/aggressive impunity. Not at the moment, though. Precisely now, it was a source of utter humiliation for him.

'Nice picture,' Brido said. Madden stood completely still, staring at the boy with barely concealed hatred. 'Nice place. Yous keep it nice, so yous do. Nice home.'

'Thank you,' Madden said, suppressing himself. 'Rose does – did – the decorating. I've little talent for that sort of thing.'

Brido sat down in Madden's armchair. He motioned for him to sit down too.

'My ma's a good woman, Mr Madden,' the son said. 'Works hard, worked hard all her days to see me and ma brothers had everything we wanted, know what I mean?'

Madden neither spoke nor moved.

'Sit *down*, Hugh. All right if I call you that? Call me Brido, by the way. Every other cunt does, 'scuse my French.'

'Brido, I—'

'Nah, fuck it, I cannae fucking stand that. Call me Brian. My name's Brian. Listen to Muggings here, cannae make up his fucking mind what his fucking name is!'

Madden was sure the word he meant was *muggins*. On second thoughts, perhaps *muggings* was more appropriate to the situation.

Brido – Brian – was kneading one fist into the palm of his other hand, leaning forward in his chair in a way that was extremely unsettling. Madden decided to sit after all.

'Like folk think you're some sort of numptie, being called Brido, man. Brian's my fucking name man, call me Brian. You know, my ma even calls us it? That gets to me, man, so it does. Don't say anything but. Like she knows how I feel about it. I'm always saying, Don't call us that, Ma, call me my name, but she's no hearing. Like she's brilliant and everything but fuck, man. Don't say anything. I mean, I love my ma, she done brilliant by me and ma brothers, worked hard for us and that, looked eftir us when the old boy fucked off, but man, can ye not call us wir fucking *name*? Fuck, I could go a drink. Ye got anything to drink? No, better not. The thing is, Hugh, I need some money. I know you've gie'd my ma money, but she disnae know I need it an' all. Private matter. Nuff said. So the thing of it is this, I'm gaunnae be back.'

Brido had sat back in the armchair and was watching Madden, crossing one leg over his knee.

Madden didn't know what to say. Was he being black-mailed? Again? Twice in one night? His life was slipping away from him. The days before now had been an illusion. He'd believed his life had been shuffling slowly along, that things would carry on in much the same way from one day to the next, that there would be work and rest and eating and drinking, and that he would bother no one and no one would bother him, or Rose would stabilise, or get better, or get worse, and Joe Caldwell would turn over the reins of the business to him, would finally see the logic of it, he'd use the money he'd put by and buy him out, Kincaid would take his place in the ground and let him be finally, and the toast would no longer get burnt and they would find another carer for Rose and then *this*. He was being threatened and extorted from and blackmailed and called an *oul' eejit* and perhaps even a *damned Bashi-Bazouk* and a *fucker* and now the sky was falling down. Mouth dry, he fanned his collar, airing his neck. What was Mrs Spivey doing in the bedroom to Rose? What were these track marks doing on his carpet? None of it made any sense. He forced his voice into a semblance of regularity, mentally willing the tremors in it to steady. Come on now, he was telling himself, steady now. Steady.

'What do you want, Brian? I don't have a lot of money. I've some savings, but we're not wealthy. You can see that, can't you? That we're not wealthy people?' And surely it was a mistake to try to appeal to the boy's better nature. He had no better nature. A son like that would kill you eventually. A son like that would be like living with an infectious disease. A misdiagnosis: you had believed that he could understand you but he could not. Not you, not his mother, not anyone. Madden was convinced he was talking to a monster, that he was at the mercy of a monster crept to the light and staring enviously in through the window. His hands were shaking a little.

'Listen, Hugh. I'm going to come back the morra, so you better have something for me. I need money. I've seen your wife. I know your home. It's nice, a nice place. A nice home. Yous are nice people. Not a word to my ma, eh? Brido this and fucking Brido that. You won't call me that, will you, Hugh. Naw. Brian's my name. I prefer it.'

He knew he had to resist this. If there was anything sure, it was that he had to speak up now and stop this going any farther.

'Brian, listen to me. This has gone far enough. I've given

you money, all I can afford. Twice today I'll have given you money. Rose and myself, we need money too. You can see how she is. We have to look after her.' He paused, waiting for the words to have an effect, but Brido remained still. 'We have to make sure she's all right. My wife, well, she's an invalid, isn't she. She has a few problems, but we can't just let her suffer on her own. She's not capable. To tell you the truth, Brian, often I find it difficult. I understand you had a hard time growing up, you and your brothers. I understand your mother did all she could for you. I understand how hard she worked, what she went through. But the important thing is that you had each other. You had a family around you. There were people there who could help. That's all anyone can ask, isn't it?' Again, he paused. Brian was slowly nodding.

'All we have is each other,' he went on. 'All we've got is ourselves. If we don't look after each other, then where would we be? Rose and myself, we don't have any children. There's only us. To tell you the truth, it never happened for us. Who can anyone blame for that? It's not anyone's fault. It was God's will. Nobody can argue with God's will. You and your ma, you're different. You're the lucky ones. I can see how much your mother means to you, and how much you mean to her. You have to appreciate that. You might think she doesn't care about you, but it's just not true. She thinks the world of you, I can see that. She just has her own way of showing it. Don't be discouraged, your mother's a proud woman. She has difficulty saying just how she feels. But I'm certain that she's proud of you. She'd do anything for you, Brian, you know that. Deep down, you know that's true.'

The light in the room was dim, cast only by a single table lamp, so that it was difficult to make out Brido's expression, though his head continued to nod slowly. Madden waited for some sort of a reaction. It was possible he'd laid it on a bit thick. Brian was still nodding. Madden felt he had to add something else, that the silence was becoming too oppressive.

He remembered that same feeling from tutorials with Kincaid, how he'd been in awe of Kincaid's effortless ability to smooth over the silences between the slowly formulating answers of the students. There, in the stultifying atmosphere of tutorials and in the funeral home, was where Madden had learned the same skills. 'Speak softly and use a sympathetic tongue, that's all you need to do,' Joe Caldwell Snr had taught him. Bereavement counselling, they would probably call it these days, though Madden wasn't up on the current buzz-words. Even the phrase 'buzz-word' had wrong-footed him for a time. He still associated it with glue-sniffing.

'Nah, fuck that shite,' Brido said, standing suddenly, his knees cracking audibly with the effort. 'I'll be back the morra.'

Madden gripped the arms of the chair, fearing the son was about to strike him. One blow from Brido would undoubtedly cleave his skull; appeasement was the obvious solution to the immediate problem.

'Brian, I've told you we don't have any more money. Is there something else I could help you with instead?' He could feel himself tensed, adrenalin beginning to override lucidity. But the boy was not about to hit him: the distracted look on his face seemed to indicate that some elementary cognitive process was under way. He stood, kneading the knuckles of one hand in the palm of another, but the gesture was, apparently, indicative of contemplation rather than impending violence.

'If I can help you with anything – within the bounds of reason – Brian, I will,' Madden added, doubtful that Brido – Brian – was familiar with the concept.

Mrs Spivey returned to the room. Madden felt sweat come immediately to his brow, back and shoulders, glad not to have to make the choice between fight or flight. Even Rose, in healthier times, had been infinitely more able in the former department than himself. For one thing, she could have crushed a good-sized navvy using her own body weight as a weapon at one time. Not so these days. Sadly, not so at all.

'So,' Mrs Spivey said, her arms assuming their customary position under her oxters, 'where were we?'

Madden sighed. 'I was just about to settle up another month's wages for you, Ellen. Will a cheque be satisfactory? I have no cash here in the house.'

Mrs Spivey looked at Brido, and he glanced back, lips set in a hard man's pout. There was an endless gulf of three or four seconds before he gave the nod back to his mother.

'We'll take a cheque, yes, thank you,' she said, her condescending tone yet another indignity for Madden to endure.

'Then if you'll excuse me a minute, I'll just get my cheque book and we can settle up.'

Mrs Spivey looked suspicious.

'It's in the other room,' Madden said, breathing more easily now. 'With Rose.'

After he had written out the cheque and Mrs Spivey had insisted he sign the back of it, Madden had ushered them to the door as quickly as he was able to do without seeming like a poor host. As he opened it to let Mrs Spivey out, she had fixed him with a look, then continued out on to the landing. Following her out, Brido jammed his foot in the door and turned to Madden.

'I know about you, Hugh,' he said. 'I know what you did. It'd be a shame for that to get around, wouldn't it?'

Madden stood almost able to hear the sound of the blood in his veins. Seconds passed, then he said, 'What d'you mean?'

The son tutted. 'I think you know,' he said.

'Know what?' Madden asked. It would not have done to panic. Not then, not yet.

'The score, Hugh. You know the score.' Brido winked at him. At close range Madden could see that his entire face was dotted with tiny red speckles, as if he'd been too long on a sunbed.

'Just you think about that, and we can have a wee chat the morra.'

He winked once more, and pulled the door closed behind him.

Madden paced the room, his mouth and throat dry. It would be impossible. Of course, impossible. No one could know. He was referring to something else, obviously. Yes. Obviously. Whatever had been discovered, wherever it had been discovered, Brido could know nothing about any connection Madden might have had with it. There was no connection to be made. He'd been talking about something else. What, then? What? There was nothing else. There was nothing else in his life now, there was nothing else to connect. Therefore no connection. Therefore nothing.

Obviously, nothing.

Seven

It was a strange time, Madden recalled. It might have been the thirties or the twenties for all the impact it made on him. He had simply been uninvolved in the era, had not been part of a *generation*. He knew that on the evening they had seen *All Guns West* he hadn't waited for the final credits to roll so he could read all the names of the extras because movies in those days had put the credits before the start of the picture. Once finished, a title reading simply THE END was flashed on-screen, and the curtains had rolled. In any event, he hadn't yet developed his obsession for scrutinising every single actor's name as it scrolled up, poring over the billing for names who had later gone on to become stars, male leads, famous character actors. Even in a classic dud like *All Guns West*, there might have been one or two faces that had played 'Indian with scar # 3', and then gone on to have a long career in B-movies playing more diverse characters, more demanding roles.

Mobster with knuckle-duster # 17.

Corpse with grim look # 21.

His memory wasn't always exact. Had *All Guns West* really been called *All Guns West*? He wasn't convinced. It may very well have been *Six Guns West*. Possibly not. Six guns didn't seem a very substantial force to stem the tide of ruthless Apache imperialism. Even the Magnificent Seven had that one extra man – Steve McQueen. Stole the show and went on to become a major star in his own right.

These days it gave him pause for thought, the meaning of those lives on the cast list, the nobodies who might become somebodies, the somebodies who went back to being nobodies. The ones who made the big time; the ones who stayed at the bottom of the ladder and never moved. The ones who lived and died on-screen, then lived and died again on-screen, and then again on-screen, and then just died. Where was their camera? Staring at someone else, only other nobodies to remember their passing, other nobodies who soon forgot as they were forgotten themselves. Tombstones, really, those cast credits. Lists of the dead. Madden felt some kinship with them: he had been a nobody too, and would remain one, whatever happened. His potential had always remained unfulfilled; it had been killed off in its prime and had lain on the slab uninterred ever since. He smiled at that.

He didn't pay too much attention to *All Guns West* at the time, the intricacies of plot and character. There were too many other things of dim fascination occurring in the theatre, a great deal of them within the confines of his own thinly upholstered chair, then later upon his own body. At first it was only the discomfort of sitting awkwardly in the too-narrow seat that bothered him. Angles and spears jutted into him, his buttocks sagged too deeply into the seat itself. Nails poked and jabbed; he found patches of wear on the armrests to pick at, traces of aged patterning to be outlined with a finger, the fraying undergarments of some old gal who had been around the block more than once. The screen he watched bulged and sagged with the weight of the film it was showing, the action crackling with what looked like a million lost hairs and bits and pieces of fluff and dead skin. Momentarily, the players would be jarred with these myriad dusty disturbances, and the action of the plot become secondary to the interplay of minutiae, the leftover silt of the many hands that must have handled the reel previously, fed it into the projector, coiled it between the spooling of a hundred or more showings.

All Guns West. Not a new picture, certainly not younger than himself. He wondered why anybody ever came to see films – flicks – like this, duffers to begin with and featuring an actor chiefly celebrated for his resemblance to a hard-boiled egg.

He vacantly watched the movie, not taking it in, aware of Rose munching on the salted nuts he'd got her from the usherette. There was still an orchestra pit in this cinema – but no orchestra to fill it, and the dialogue tannoyed out from a tinny speaker somewhere, drowned frequently by the sudden bursts of music that over-dramatised every inane line. Even the colour was gaudy beyond belief, but apt for such an aged tart of a film.

The smell of the theatre bothered him: he would have had the place swabbed down with disinfectant. It was wholly rank. Madden felt it seep through his pores, leaving him tainted and unclean. He shifted periodically in his seat, Rose holding on to his hand, her mouth full of nuts. Sense told him not to shift it. He had been bashed once already today. Further failures of etiquette would probably not be tolerated. He imagined her capable of scalping him, the lid taken off the top of his skull to reveal the ductile contents. The yolk.

Put that tomahawk down, why doncha?
Tomahawk must taste white man's blood once it is raised.
Put it down, I tellya!
Pow! Pow!

No use trying to save him now. He was a goner.

Madden's skin felt itchy; he wasn't sure whether it was his imagination or whether the chairs were infested. Glancing at Rose then back to the action, he wondered whether it was perhaps *she* that was infested. But no, likely not. She was a nurse, and he hadn't detected any fondness for lice, despite their large number of very adequate limbs. It had to be the theatre itself, the ancient red-velvet upholstery, a breeding ground for any number of biting fauna. He should have brought her here instead of the zoo on that first date.

Men on horses sallied forth across the same area of brush-land repeatedly; this time cowboys, now the Indians. As a boy, he'd preferred the cowboys, but the Indians were more compelling in this particular tragedy. They seemed to be a rather paunchy, jowly bunch, not much given to rising quickly from their wigwams, he supposed. Somewhat palefaced as well; they looked disconcertingly like middle-aged white men in make-up. Were there no real Indians left, then?

Rose placed her hand on his leg, and leaned her head over on to his shoulder, her damp hair rubbing against his cheek. She smelled of talcum powder and peanuts.

'Enjoying this?' he asked in a low voice, though it seemed unnecessary to whisper. There were murmurings and curt remarks being exchanged from a few rows down, familiar voices, but he couldn't place them. Possibly some other student he knew, attempting to enrich their cultural horizons, or failing that, get in out of the rain.

Rose nodded against his shoulder and crunched on. 'I need to go pee in a minute,' she said. 'D'you know where the Ladies is?'

He muttered of course not, then told her to ssh. He was watching the movie, he told her. The good bit was about to come up, but in his mind he was already picturing her squatting with her nylons around her knees. He shifted so that she pressed less heavily against him.

There was some minor activity below in the orchestra pit, human shapes walking down towards it intermittently, then coming back again, returning to their seats, or leaving the auditorium entirely. It was too dark to see what the attraction was; he could make out only the occasional movement, the recognisable shape of a torso or head. He looked about the theatre at the other rows, none with more than two or three people in them, a consequence of it being this time of year, he decided. A solitary man sitting in the row in front and a few seats to the left turned and stared back at him, glanced at

Rose, and turned quickly back to the film again, the flickering light from the screen glancing off his face briefly. He looked familiar, but Madden couldn't place him either. It was too dark for that.

A Red Indian came whooping and bounding down off his horse, tomahawk slashing for the scalp of a screaming woman who cowered over an infant. Blam. Big Chief Egg-on-His-Face shoots him dead, turns and shoots another, his hide jacket waving its fetlocks in the wind. Blam. Pow. Blam blam blam.

He strides towards another Injun. Bullets zing past. A terrible cry. An Injun whooping. Dead on the ground. No blood at all. Remarkable really, when you considered the slaughter going on, that there wasn't blood everywhere. Factually inaccurate. Shoot a man in the heart from point-blank range: he'll bleed. Undoubtedly. Vigorously. Bleed till the longhorns come home. And this a colour picture too. By rights the blood should be leaping all over the place. The Injuns were winning, despite them mainly being the ones getting done in, despite the random heaps of paleface corpses. And they were using bows and arrows and tomahawks and all whatnot. That had to have been a messy business. Madden wondered what tribe they were. Blackfoot? Pawnee? Apache?

'I really have to go to the toilet,' Rose said, tugging at his sleeve. 'Where is it?'

He shook his arm free. 'I have no earthly clue,' he said.

Someone behind said shush. Madden concentrated on the movie, scratching his arm and trying not to think about fleas.

'If you see the usherette, ask her,' he told her, trying not to raise his voice.

'Where is she?'

'Maybe down there, in the orchestra pit. I think there's a queue, though.'

Rose snorted inexplicably.

'What was that for?' he asked her.

'Nothing. Just because.'

'Because what?'

Rose was sitting upright now, staring at the screen, her munching at an end, and Madden squinted at her in the dark.

'You tell me, Doc Holliday,' she said, not looking at him.

Madden resigned himself to not getting a satisfactory answer.

'Who's winning?' Rose asked, squirming in her seat. 'The goodies or the baddies?'

Madden wasn't sure. A suede-clad cowboy and one of the few athletic-looking Indians circled each other with Bowie knives drawn, though he had no idea if that was what they were. The Indian was stripped to the waist, a slash of red running diagonally across his chest. Muscles taut, he looked very much like Burt Lancaster, agile switches of the blade from one hand to another. The moves didn't fool the cowboy, who kept his own knife fisted in one hand, his stance unmoving, reddish sideburns penetrating far along his big block of a jaw.

The Injun began to sing as he weaved an ellipsis round the other chap, carving initialled arabesques in the air in front of him, then dived at the blond cowboy, who sidestepped nimbly and slashed in return, drawing a cut along the other's shoulder.

'Oooh!' Rose said.

They were on one another, free hands gripping opposing knife hands, tumbling to the ground, the Indian chap on top, then flung off, the other leaping to his feet and kicking sand in his face. Another tussle, a feint. The cowboy marked across the cheek, pausing to taste his own fluid. The Indian smiled grimly. A final blood-curdling howl and he dived, blade extended towards the goody, the hero, simultaneously withering, curling like black smoke into himself, a sound like water thrown on to hot fat—

The lights slowly came up, the people in the orchestra pit scattering. They must have thought there was a fire in the building.

'What happened there?' Rose said.

Madden shook his head. 'The bloody reel's melted, that's what. They've let the projector get too hot.'

Madden looked up, the lights on at a dull glow, the withered cornicing of the ceiling reminding him of Miss Havisham's wedding cake. When he returned his gaze to the theatre, he actually did see a large rodent of some kind scurry off down the side of the wall, into the comfort of darkness again, on legs too short to be nice.

'Get the fucking picture back on!' someone shouted, doubtless an aficionado of the genre. 'He was gonnae scalp him!'

Someone else said, 'And then dip his soldier in the yolk . . .' but it was impossible to identify who. It occurred to Madden that the cinemagoers were largely men, though there were one or two couples giggling in various corners.

The projectionist shouted, 'Gie's peace! I'll get the other reel on as soon's the machine's cooled down enough. We'll stick on an extra cartoon for yese at the end.'

The lights began to dim again, returning the theatre to the accustomed level of dinginess, Madden more than ever aware of the smell in the building, now made even more unpleasant by the reek of singed celluloid. No one was left in the orchestra pit, and no sign of the usherette with her arse-sooked fag-end of a face.

'If you want to go to the lavatory,' he said, 'now might be the ideal opportunity.'

Rose harrumphed, her usual mood settled back down upon her again. Madden was almost relieved. Self-pity was abhorrent. He tolerated only himself to indulge in it.

'Ideal,' he added, as if passing judgement, then feeling foolish.

'Whatever you say, Doc,' she said, and straightened out of her seat. He shifted his legs to one side to let her pass, then realised it wouldn't be enough and stood out in the aisle. Rose shuffled past, looked down the aisle, turned, looked up towards the back of the auditorium, looked at Madden and frowned.

'Down, I think,' he said. 'Toilets are usually down. Aren't they?'

Rose huffed. 'I don't know if there are any kind of regulations regarding the matter.'

Madden put his hands in his pockets, but they were still damp, and he took them out again. He could picture Kincaid saying something like, *Regulations be damned*, but he contented himself with silence.

'Cleanliness is next to godliness,' Rose said. 'Wouldn't that mean the toilets should be upstairs?'

'It's worth a try,' he said.

'Well,' Rose said, 'be good. And don't go anywhere without me.'

'Wouldn't dream of it.'

He sat down again and let the darkness swallow him up. He had only been there a few moments when he felt a presence beside him, a disembodied something pressing close, his shoulders stiffening with the realisation that there was someone else's hand touching his leg. Rose playing a joke on him. She must have come back in through another door and sneaked along the row of seats. Except there was something wrong about the hand, something not right. Not Rose. The hand squeezed his leg and he pulled sharply away, leaving the hand dangling. *Calm down, dear boy*, a man whose face he couldn't quite make out said. *No need to get all hot and bothered. Unless you want to.*

He stood up. 'I'll report you to the police,' he said, suddenly calm. 'I'll have you arrested.' The man quickly got up too, and shuffled along a few chairs. He was middle-aged, possibly. There was something in his slouch that gave him away, a heaviness of the breathing. An irregularity. *What did you come here for, then?* the man was saying as he retreated backwards. Madden wasn't sure whether it was the lighting or fright which gave the man's pallor its brief, ghostly intensity. *Working for the polis, are you? Well, you can sod off!* The man raised a fist at him, but seemed less real than any physical threat he might make. *Go back where you came from! Informer!*

Even in the dark he could feel the heat from his cheeks, and sat back down in the row behind the one he and Rose had previously been in. The heavy drapes that were partially drawn across the screen absorbed him, allowed him a surface on to which he was able to displace his sense of himself. He felt degraded, but was unsure why, of what had just occurred. Perhaps the man had mistaken him for someone, his overtures intended for someone else entirely; a friend, an acquaintance. The dimness of the lighting favoured this hypothesis. Two friends arranging to meet in a cinema at the end of a perform-ance, the next beginning presently. And it was very wet outside, they would both have wanted in out of the rain. Of course, as a theory, it couldn't be faulted. Yet there were gaps, holes to be filled.

He had even heard of such clandestine meeting places, covens of deviation and effeminacy. His own father had warned him of their existence. He wished Rose would hurry up: he wanted to leave now. Someone else would be bound to spot him, sidle up alongside with his *dear boy's* and his *are-you-sitting-comfortably-then-I'll-begins*. The smell of soiled bedclothes was intoxicating, like meat three days on the hook. It took your breath away. So this was how it was done. Three rows in front, he could see the back of a plural entity, moving in almost imperceptible rhythm with itself; it sep-arated and reabsorbed itself, joined at the two heads, made a low moaning sound. He watched in fascination, adrenalin thumping through his body, as if he might suddenly gasp along with them, die with a little yelp at the same time as they did. When the being finally divided into two distinct halves, he exhaled long and deep and settled back in the chair as though part of it. He needed a spot of air. He longed for it; cool and clear, a smirr to rinse his filthy face with. But he couldn't leave, not without Rose. One half of the couple stood and fumbled with himself, his jacket or trousers, then shuffled precariously back along the row of seats and sat down again farther away. The red eye of a cigarette winked on, blinking open and shut with the inhalation. After a moment or two, the shape got up and left. The other silhouette continued sitting where it was, perhaps awaiting the arrival of another friend. Or perhaps the usherette with a choc ice. He was quite parched himself. Yes, definitely very dry.

Rose returned and sat once again, searching briefly for him before he poked her to let her know he was sitting in the row behind.

'You've shifted,' she said. 'Are they putting the picture back on?'

'Maybe in a minute,' he said. 'Once they've loaded the other reel.'

She had put some make-up and perfume on when she was away: he could smell it, sickly and overpowering. It left him feeling a little nauseous and strangely ashamed.

'Let's go,' he said, 'I can't be bothered waiting any longer.'

'I was wanting to see the end,' Rose said gruffly. 'I wanted to find out who gets scalped.'

'We've seen the end already, remember? When we came in?'

'I know that, I'm not daft. I meant the run-up to the climax.'

He started to stand up, but she pulled him back down into his seat by the sleeve of his jacket, and he came down with a bump, something sharp sticking into his buttock. Adjusting his position, he settled back again and looked balefully ahead as the drapes drew backwards again, and two or three lack-lustre cheers went up. Abruptly the action commenced, at a completely new and inexplicable juncture, the music jarring in its sudden loudness.

Woo-hoo, the Injuns went. *Hey-ya hey-ya, hey-ya hey-ya* . . .

Over and over again the few surviving cowboys – reduced to riding bareback on thieved Injun Mustangs across that same bit of scarred Hollywood back lot – came and went. Soon, they all lay dead on the ground, pincushioned with arrows.

They slunk out into the foyer, the first to leave. Madden had leapt from his chair the moment the film came to a conclusion and walked towards the door not even bothering to see whether Rose would follow. The usherette stood there smoking a roll-up, her face almost a part of the fag. She nodded at Madden and he acknowledged it with a curt movement of the head, then went out leaving the door to swing behind him. There was a thump and he stopped mid-stride, a sense of déjà vu overwhelming him.

And there *he* was again, pushing the door to with one hand, another cupped against his mouth. A few people filed out past him, all men. Nobody asked how this character was, though he was obviously in no small degree of discomfort.

He hadn't seen Madden, whose inert panic held him still on the spot, but who wanted to walk briskly out the front door more badly than anything. He couldn't, though. The green suit was already getting drips of fresh blood on it. Gaskell looked up through watery eyes and seemed to diminish and shrink before Madden.

'*You*,' he said, spitting blood in horse-like slabbers. 'I might've known.'

Madden didn't know what to say, his humiliation at Gaskell's hands in the Men's Union too fresh to allow his anger articulacy. No doubt later he would come up with some barbed comment of his own, too late for it to be of any practical use.

'What're you doing here anyway?' Gaskell said. He reached for his handkerchief and was about to place it over his burst lip, then for a reason Madden didn't wish to consider put it back in his trouser pocket again.

'I was with Rose,' he said. 'She wanted to see the picture. I'm awful sorry. D'you want a lend of mine?' He reached for his own hankie and proffered it, but Gaskell shook his head.

'For fuck's sake,' he said. 'I wish you could find it in your heart to stop hurling furniture in my direction . . . now I've got the gob to match the nose.'

There was a large hump on Gaskell's nose from their first encounter: it would always look like that now. It afforded a more Romanesque quality, an air of Latin nobility. Certainly not unattractive.

'Making a bit of a habit of this, aren't you, Madman?' Gaskell leaned back against a greasy area of wall, the paper on it peeling. 'Beginning to think you've got something against me. Did I do something to you in a previous life? I must have. Yes, I definitely must have done something.'

'I'm sorry,' Madden said. 'I really am. It's just I was in a bit of a rush to get out.'

Gaskell looked up. 'A bit of a rush? I thought there was a "we" involved.'

'I beg your pardon?' Madden said.

'You said you were here with Rose,' Gaskell said, straightened up now and dabbing at his lip. 'I don't see her . . . you sure you weren't with some other, ah, company . . . ?' He reached into his pocket and took out a tin of tobacco, then began rolling a cigarette. Lighting up, he discarded the match without extinguishing it, and it lay burning on the carpet, creating a small black impression around itself. Madden tutted and stamped it out with his foot, remembering to use the shoe that didn't have a hole in it.

'My turn to say sorry. And about what I said to you in the Union too. So there it is. Sorry,' Gaskell told him without any apparent conviction. 'Look, I don't care if you're with Rose or not. I don't care why you're here or who you're with. Truth be told, I'm in a bit of a hurry myself.' He dragged on the roll-up. Madden nodded: there seemed to be no further words necessary, but still he felt he had to speak, dispel from his mind whatever misconceived idea his friend (were they?) was beginning to formulate.

'I was here with Rose,' he said, still with the handkerchief held in his hand. 'She was here a minute ago . . . I don't know where she's got to . . . She . . . I can't recall where she went.' He looked up through the circular porthole in the door into the blackness of the theatre. There were still a few people in there heading towards it.

Gaskell nodded, dragging Madden by the crook of the arm.

'Yes, I was with Carmen too, but she left. We had a fight. You saw that, of course. Well. Now I want to go home.'

Madden recalled the slurred spite she had used on him, and then Gaskell too. Her lips had been too tightly drawn to reveal the ugliness of her gums.

'You were in there on your own, then?'

Gaskell glanced around him. A number of men and one or two women stood at the entrance of the theatre, waiting for a gap in the rain to make a dash for it, and they disappeared among them. Madden was surprised at the number of people there were. Far more, it seemed, than had been actually sat inside watching the film. But then they were likely just passers-by wanting shelter from the weather.

'Yes. Exactly. In and out on my own. Like yourself, Madman,' Gaskell said, puffing and grinning humourlessly at the same time.

'I wasn't on my own,' Madden said, pushing the hankie back into his own trouser pocket.

'Anyway, I have to get going,' Gaskell said. 'See a man about a dog, so to speak. I'll catch up with you soon, will I?'

It seemed less of a question than a statement, some sort of veiled command. A threat perhaps. With Gaskell, he was never entirely sure.

Gaskell leaned out of the way, as the small crowd jostled for space. He relit his roll-up, and again threw the match unextinguished on to the floor, where it sizzled out on the damp carpet.

'Look, I'm off,' he said, then, '*Shit*,' and bowed his head towards the floor, his face unknowable. Madden looked about to see what it was that had caused his unusual edginess.

A tall figure pushed towards them, evidently not recognising Madden, his eyes searching the hunched figure in the green corduroy suit.

'Ah. There you are. Run off, have you?'

The good doctor's breath smelled strongly of whisky. If he was perturbed by Madden's presence, Kincaid did not show it. He squeezed up beside them.

Gaskell peered sharply up. 'Why don't you fuck off, Hugh,' he said.

'Aye, bonnie lad,' Kincaid said, 'fuck off. There are private matters needing attended here, eh? Private, personal matters.'

The doctor was looking flushed, his eyes bleary, as if on the edge of tears. He gazed imploringly at Gaskell, the bluster of his manner empty.

'And you can fuck off too,' Gaskell said. His look was one of undisguised contempt, and the doctor was wilting under it.

'Owen . . .' he began to say, a nervous hand reaching up to his moustache.

'I've told you,' Gaskell said. 'I'm not interested. Why can't you get that through your ugly old skull?'

The rain had lessened now, and the sheltered crowd had begun to drift off in twos and threes into the night. The good doctor turned to Madden, but his eyes were on Gaskell.

'What? *This* is all you could *manage* instead, is it?'

Madden shrank inwardly at the salt of the older man's words, tried to think himself free of the situation, but couldn't. Not until Rose caught up with him, hating her for forcing him to endure this.

'I'm awful sorry,' he said. 'I think someone's looking for me . . .'

'Looks to me like they've found you,' Kincaid said, he and Gaskell staring at each other.

Gaskell flung his cigarette out into the street. 'I've had enough of this,' he said. 'I'm going. You can both get to buggery.' He strode off into the street, stopping only to take a kick at the door of a car parked next to a slickly polished Morris Minor.

Kincaid stepped down too, his tweed jacket open and shirt dishevelled, both arms down at his side, the palms out beseechingly. He watched Gaskell stride off, two men standing in an entrance across the street wolf-whistling piercingly at him.

'Owen!' he shouted. 'Gaskell!'

But Gaskell strode on.

Kincaid turned to stare dully at Madden, then walked over and placed a gentle hand on the collar of his jacket, smoothing it down as though stroking a beloved dog. His eyes were heavy and sad and still seemed not to recognise Madden. He swayed noticeably as he stood, reaching into the inside pocket of his jacket and producing his pipe. He sighed, and tamped tobacco down into the bowl.

'Have you a light, boy?' he said to Madden, who shook his head.

'Don't blame you. Nasty habit. Very bad for one, they say. Like so many things.' He looked around, but there was no one left to ask, so he shook the contents of the pipe out into the gutter, and gazed at the burn that ran down it carrying the tobacco away.

'Some things . . .' he said. 'Some things can be very bad for one. Weaknesses, predispositions.' He glanced over his shoulder at Madden, then back to the river in the gutter. 'Predilections. All sorts of things. Bad. All of them bad. Fatal, some. Here endeth the lesson.'

Turning to face Madden, he smiled with something of the old assurance and Madden felt glad for him.

Kincaid stepped over and placed a hand on Madden's shoulder once more.

'Ready to come home now?' someone said. Madden saw Maisie Kincaid leaning out from the window of the Morris Minor. 'Had enough fun and games for this evening?'

Her hair was different, she'd done something with it, and her face was very pink and flushed.

'I suppose you enjoyed the movie, did you?' She directed her question to Kincaid, who appeared to cower at the sight of his wife. 'Cowboys and Indians,' she said. 'Which did you want to be when you were a boy, Lawrence?'

'Maisie . . .' was all he could say.

'Don't,' she said, 'just don't.'

'Maisie, I didn't mean to—'

'I said *don't*!' she said, sitting upright in the driver's seat of the car. 'I don't want to *hear* it! Just get in!'

Kincaid stood where he was, swaying. He looked at Madden and then back to his wife, but still did not move.

'No, your new friend is staying where he is. Hugh, isn't it? Yes, I remember the face. Definitely, I remember the face well.' She nodded an acknowledgement at him, but Madden did not return it.

'Maisie, I . . .'

She slammed her hand down hard on the horn and kept it there, the sudden explosion of noise sparking Kincaid to life as though an electric switch had been hit. He tottered drunkenly over to the car, and got in the already unlocked passenger door, slamming it shut on his own jacket, opening it again, pulling the garment in and slamming it shut again.

Maisie took her hand off the horn and started the engine before glancing sharply at Madden.

'I really wish this was goodbye, Hugh,' she said, 'but something gives me the feeling it's only au revoir.'

She slammed the car into reverse, gunned forward, arcing out into the street Madden watched the car, its tyre treads rippling the orange reflections of the street lights on the oil-black surface of the road.

Rose was standing beside him. 'And where the hell have you been?' she said. She pulled at his sleeve, and he pulled back, sickened with people jerking him one way and another, asking him one thing and another then answering their own questions for him one way and another. He was tired of all of it.

'I was right here,' he said. 'Right here on this step. Where have *you* been?'

Rose huffed. 'I lost you in the dark. I was waiting over at the ticket office. Could you not see me?'

'No, I couldn't see you.'

'Well,' she said. 'You couldn't have been looking very hard, could you? All these old perverts staring at me as if they wanted to rape me.'

It was Madden's turn to guffaw. He noticed spots of Gaskell's blood on one of his shoes.

'What?' she said.

'Give it a rest, will you,' he said. 'Let's get out of here before the rain comes on again.'

Rose perked up. 'Madden, d'you think there'll be anywhere open just now?'

'No. Why?'

'I'm hungry. I want you to buy me a bag of chips.'

And Madden, for the first time, raised his palm to silence her: the first silencing of many. He was just too exhausted to speak. Too, too tired for words.

Eight

'It is a fact rarely noted, except by worthies such as my good self, that there is little these days in the way of disputation over cadaver *ownership* – legally speaking – since most anatomy departments – generally speaking – now have an adequate supply of bodies available for freshmen medical students, a situation vastly preferable to the use – prevalent in previous decades – of indigent or unclaimed bodies. Of course, a few notorious examples seek to give the lie to our otherwise spotless reputations as high-minded and selfless seekers after medical truth. The cases of Burke and Hare spring to mind.'

Kincaid's voice boomed when in command of a hostage audience: whether through excessive alcohol intake or overweening ego it was hard to tell. In any case it produced the desired result: the full attention of both the post-doctoral research graduate and the transplanted surplus of other departments. There was, in tutorial groups, a prevalence of failed mathematicians and engineers who had switched subject rather than continue to struggle with their initial preferences. Some vindictive urge in Kincaid himself seemed to enjoy needling these unfortunates, presumably for not having the *damned bricks* to choose his own worthier discipline in the first place.

It had been clear from early on that he regarded Gaskell as potentially worth the effort, though Madden could never quite predict in what way this might manifest itself: some goading remark on the contingency of ethics or a haughty dismissal of current trends in popular medical thinking might be enough for either Gaskell or Kincaid to rise to the bait. Perhaps Gaskell's background in philosophy had something to do with it. Perhaps Kincaid's dismissive and often alcohol-fuelled rhetoric was provocation enough. Either way, both were as bad as each other for relishing the combat.

Madden himself was content to take a back seat in such situations, partly through the proprietary sense he felt for Gaskell, and partly because, despite himself, he enjoyed their little run-ins, the occasional head-to-head that was so much a characteristic of their relationship. The fact was that Gaskell could get away with baiting the good doctor, something that Madden felt with some security might get *him* run off the course entirely should he attempt the same.

'I thought the universities turned a blind eye to that,' Gaskell said, not looking up at Kincaid, but maintaining a quiet scratch of pen against notepaper. His suit was in the usual between-washes state of rumpled grubbiness, and his face and hair both had a lank, creased look about them. A large, dark ink stain bloomed on his right earlobe.

'Indeed, Mr Gaskell. The want of bodies was great in those days, and the supply small.' Madden looked sidelong at the other handful of souls captive in Kincaid's crypt of an office. Only Gaskell was taking notes.

'So, might you say you support that collusion?'

Kincaid sighed, dusting irritably at the lapel of his tweed jacket. His crimson bow tie was jauntily conspicuous. It wouldn't have surprised Madden if he turned up to work wearing a beret. 'Support, I think, is the wrong word.'

'But collusion is the right one?' Gaskell continued with his note-taking, never once looking up at Kincaid, who sat in a wooden swivel chair with his back to the single, narrowly arched window that was the only source of light in the room today. The cramped shelves on either side of him were piled high with stacks of notes in a kind of dishevelled flourish which obviously appealed to someone of his bullishly Luddite sensibilities. Or perhaps to Gaskell's, though Madden was convinced both men would deny such an obvious mindset, but each would be quick to point out such a failure in the other.

'I suppose "collusion" might be close to the point. But collusion, I think, isn't far off.'

Gaskell looked up for the first time. 'Why not murder? That's what was going on, wasn't it?'

'Murder it may have been, Mr Gaskell, but not on the part of the faculties. They simply neglected to research their sources thoroughly!'

There was a murmur of low laughter, and Gaskell looked back to his notebook and began scratching away again, waiting for Kincaid's small victory to subside.

'But medical students and anatomists themselves were involved in grave-robbing and other . . . *methods*, were they not? How can that be justified?'

Kincaid darted a thumb and forefinger over the hair of his upper lip and stated drily: 'Sadly necessary to the cause of anatomical advancement, I believe. In London and Edinburgh, between 1805 and 1820 – during those fifteen years there were roughly two thousand medical students and a scanty seventy-five executions. Hardly enough to satisfy even the humblest cravings of, say, our Mr Madden here.'

Again there was a murmur of laughter. Madden shrank inwards into his chair, coughing quietly into his open palm. Gaskell glanced at him sharply, as though *he* had offered the offending remark. Madden shrugged and looked at his knees.

'Now, gentlemen – *ladies* – if you will, I'd like to point out a few simple facts to Mr Gaskell, ones that may have escaped his attention. Everything we know about the body today – about anatomy – can be traced back to professional resurrectionists like Mr Burke and Mr Hare. We could go back farther, much farther, but even Galen required a few corpses to wield a scalpel with, and all he could practise his dissections on were animals. Animals, mind you! Then nothing. Nothing till the fifteenth century. The fact is that we need dead people. We need dead people to help living people live. If that seems an unappealing reality to some of us, then I would suggest that we find ourselves another discipline to study. Perhaps the engineering of dams, or the pursuit of epistemology. Both worthwhile endeavours, we are assured by our colleagues over in the faculties of engineering and philosophy, and yet both activities that are not without inherent risk to the individuals involved in them. Particularly the latter. And, I'm sure, many of whose unfortunate casualties have been opened up here on the surgical tables of our own dear green institutional premises. The way of the world, Mr Gaskell, I'm afraid. You don't agree?'

'No, Mr Kincaid . . .'

'*Doctor* Kincaid, please.'

'No, *Doctor* Kincaid, I don't agree.' Gaskell, staring straight at Kincaid, tapped his pen – a very attractive gold-nibbed Parker – on his notepad, unaware of the jolts of ink that bled from the tip on to his scribblings. 'It seems to me that any knowledge, any advancement, can't be made legitimately if it justifies the killing of people. How can it?'

'Ah, *legitimacy*. Well, you might have a point there too, I'll admit. But legitimately – by which *I* mean by due process of law – was how most of those corpses arrived at our tables. It may be distasteful, but it remains a fact that the body-snatchers and sack-'em-ups were put out of business by the passing of laws which allowed the unclaimed and indigent specimen to be used for dissection purposes. And in more modern times it has become more or less the norm for individuals to donate their own bodies for the purposes of anatomical dissection. And the practices of previous centuries, and previous cultures, though unpleasant and undoubtedly dubious, had also their part to play in this. Because, as Mr

Madden will no doubt tell you, we still need specimens. Isn't that right, Mr Madden?'

Madden avoided Gaskell's gaze.

'Yes, I think so,' he said.

Kincaid gazed airily over at him. 'Yes what, Mr Madden?'

'Yes, Dr Kincaid.'

'And can you explain why that's right? In words of few syllables, if you please.'

Madden flipped mentally through his learned-by-rote medical epigrams, his anatomical verb tables and stock replies.

'Because no one dies of old age,' he said.

'Precisely. No one dies of old age. Now you, I, Mr Gaskell and all the rest of us here know that to be a nonsense, but it is nonetheless a fact *legal*. And if we are talking legitimacy' – he glanced sharply over at Gaskell, who was furiously blotting at his jotters – 'then we must accept the pronouncement of the law. The law defines death, not doctors or surgeons. The true biological mechanisms of dying – of death – have nothing to do with how we mere physicians define it. Death requires a name. It requires a disease. It requires a cardiac failure, a stroke, a pneumonia all of its own. It requires an accident; it requires a deliberate act either of the self or the intention of another. Suicide, murder, misadventure, disease. No one dies of old age. It's the law.'

The bell for the end of the session came clatteringly to life and caused Madden to flinch to attention. Automatically, the tutorial group scraped their chairs behind them and gathered their things up. He noticed Aduman slipping out of the door before everyone else, as though he'd been gradually edging it open the quicker to get away, the perennial scarf following after like some antediluvian tail. Four or five others followed him out, among them Hector Fain, an enormous blotch spreading callously on the left-hand side of his neck. If he'd keeled over there and then, it wouldn't have taken a medical genius to see from the wound that he'd been necking the night before. It was the single most unlikely event Madden could imagine happening to a revolutionary God-fearer like him. Better he did die now, perhaps. Lightning could surely never strike twice in such inhospitable soil. Was it possible that he'd been given the love-bite by Carmen? As a badge of honour, for loyal service, so to speak? No. Such a thought would never cross her mind. It must have been someone more Hector's *speed*. She must undoubtedly have been committed to the cause.

'A word, Hugh,' Kincaid said, as Madden was stepping out of the door. He turned to glance at Gaskell, who edged stiffly past him, not acknowledging his look. Madden stood where he was, unsure of whether to sit down again or remain standing.

'Close the door behind you, Mr Gaskell, if you would be so good.' Madden watched the door close after him and shifted on his feet, unsure of what protocol desired of him.

'There's a matter I'd like to discuss with you.'

It was Carmen Alexander that Kincaid wished to discuss. A girl of *a quite striking pulchritude*, to use one of Gaskell's favourite coinages. Someone whom Madden had observed the day after their run-in at the Union, sitting on a bench in the Botanic Gardens: her last afternoon alive.

She must have just finished her lectures for the day, was completely alone, and feeding the pigeons. Unseen, he had been oddly affected by her unselfconsciously miserable look, her eyes red as if she had been crying. She tore at a bread roll, scattering the crumbs on the ground. There was a new hardness in her gestures since Madden had seen her with Gaskell in the Union. Once, he supposed she must have been a nice kiss-me-quick postcard picture from Largs or Dunoon, a nice Italian girl, first generation to be born in Scotland, didn't want to work behind the counter of a café all her life as her parents had. He could practically smell the chip grease off her, real dripping in the fryers, just the way they made them back home in Barga, somewhere up in the hills just far enough away from Mussolini to give them half a chance. Until she had met Gaskell, Madden imagined for her easy, shallow friendships, casual meetings in cafés and trips to the pictures, chaste dancing on Saturday nights at the Cosmo and furtive fumblings in closes on the way home, to be back in her lodgings by half past eleven, not a minute later, mind. How the other half lived. And died. There would have been a freedom for her in those banalities, the way there never was for plainer girls. Her quite striking pulchritude made all the difference in the world. She knew it, of course. The Carmen Alexanders always knew such things.

When she got up to leave he had made his way after her, maintaining a loping distance as she walked up past the Kibble Palace and on over the hill to the Kirklee gate, her posture an exclamation mark of propriety, of *not-that-kind-of-girlness* . . .

When he'd reached the top himself he was unable to see her on the other side. There were few other people on the path; a young couple cooing over an infant in a pram, an old lady with hair like a chaffinch's nest, two kids grappling noisily with each other on the grass near the trees. Then he'd seen her, momentarily obscured by the wrought-iron gates at the bottom of the hill, taking *his* hand.

And here she was again today, up west, in the city, the big time. Dead as they come.

'It's just routine, of course,' Kincaid said, an odd choice of word for the occasion. But of course, dead bodies were utterly routine for him. He just happened to have known this one when it still walked and talked. He flared his nostrils and took a small mahogany box, no bigger than a mussel shell, decorated with mother-of-pearl, from inside his waistcoat pocket, flicking the lid open and offering the contents to Madden.

'Snuff?' he asked. Madden shook his head, and the good doctor frowned, obviously disappointed in him.

'I prefer it the frontier way myself,' Kincaid said. He took a pinch of the black dust and pressed it into a plug in one palm, then pushed it up under his upper lip. 'They say it can give a fellow cancer. You don't believe a word of it, do you, lad. Young chap like yourself, why should you. You'll never die. I expect she believed that too.'

'You mean Carmen?'

'Carmen, that's right. Her family are Italian, I think. *Alessandro*. Altered the spelling herself, I'm informed.' The doctor tucked a finger inside his lip, adjusting the plug. 'Care for a dram, Hugh?'

He shook his head, embarrassed by Kincaid's use of his first name: a deferential hangover from his schooling. He was rarely addressed by anything other than just 'Madden'. Only his mother used it with any regularity. Rose used it in much the same way as she had, a smack of the maternal about it, as though he were about to be punished for something, or called to sit at the table. If Kincaid had asked, *Call me Lawrence, please*, it would have been more excruciating than if he had asked Madden to sing.

'Well. I believe I shall indulge.' Kincaid opened a drawer in his desk and took out a pewter flask and unscrewed the cap. He gulped quickly, without the sucking of teeth displayed by the inexperienced imbiber.

'The police were here yesterday,' he said. 'They found her body in the Kelvin, not too far from here. Not a word to anyone, mind. The constabulary have asked if we can keep it under our hats for the moment. Don't want every Tom, Dick and Harry nosying about. I trust you can be . . . discreet regarding the matter?'

Madden nodded.

'Said she'd been there for three or four days.' He looked at Madden, waiting for a response.

'Did you know her?' he asked.

Madden shook his head, his thinking not clear. No, he

wanted to say. He had never known her, he had no idea who she was.

'But you knew of her? She was a student here at the faculty. You must have seen her around.' He shook his head. 'I can't believe there'd be many chaps around here who wouldn't have noticed a girl like that.'

'I knew who she was. I mean, I didn't personally know her, but I did know who she was.'

Kincaid nodded. He tilted the flask, and took another gulp. 'That's the damn bricks,' he said.

Madden felt under some considerable pressure to say something more.

'Parents are distraught, of course. Absolutely devastated. She was Italian, did I mention that?' Kincaid, nodding at his own words, picked a sheaf of papers from his overcrowded table top, leafing distractedly through them.

'Did she drown?' Madden asked into the gloom. He felt sick.

'Well, let's see. Your papers are very good, you know,' Kincaid said, fanning them at shoulder height. 'We have a corpse. A girl. Nineteen years old. Three days in the Kelvin, possibly longer. What sort of state would you say the body would be in on recovery?'

Madden shrugged. 'Depending on the temperature and condition of the water it would be . . . unrecognisable.'

'*Unrecognisable?* Come on, boy! It'd be bloated with gas! It'd be putrefying! Where's your damn bricks?'

Madden flinched at the doctor's outburst, felt his hands twitch upwards as if to fend off a blow.

'The girl *drowned* all right. But not in the Kelvin.'

'I don't follow . . .'

'She was *asphyxiated* all right. But there was almost no water in the body cavities. Someone done the lassie in then took her dooking for apples afterwards. She was strangled.'

Nausea was rising in Madden, and he asked for a glass of

water from the doctor's sink, set in the wall opposite his desk, underneath a high shelf of undisciplined case notes. Kincaid ran the tap for a few seconds, then passed him a porcelain teacup-full. He drank it down in one mouthful, and handed the cup back to Kincaid.

'Not like our Mr Madden to be squeamish, is it,' Kincaid said, a vague contempt wrinkled on his forehead. 'Come on now, laddie boy. I've seen you in that dissection room. Hardly a fish out of water in there, are you. What's the matter with you?'

'Nothing, Mr Kincaid . . .'

Kincaid let the slip pass.

'No one's interested in *you*, particularly, Mr Madden. But we've a problem here, obviously. The police have requested that all the departmental heads – in all faculties, mind – do a bit of . . . *investigating* . . . on their behalf. So we lowly academics are merely putting out some feelers. A regular Pinkerton's we are here in Medicine. We'll get round to everyone in due course. I'm asking what you knew about this girl now because you have shared lectures, laboratories and even the occasional tutorial with her. Your work is improving, you know. You're a lad with potential. But there are many others too who have shared classes and perhaps more intimate relations with this young lady, so if you know anything – anything at all . . .'

Madden nodded, a detachedness beginning to thaw his seasickness. It irked him slightly the way Kincaid had automatically assumed that there was no way he might have had *intimate relations* with a girl of Carmen *Alessandro*'s obvious qualities. But he was right. She was not quite his *speed*. She was made for the Gaskells of the world.

'Then we'd be very grateful if you could keep us informed. It can only reflect well on you.'

'Yes, Dr Kincaid,' he said.

'Very well, then. That's all for now. You may go.'

Madden nodded and was about to leave, but then turned to ask Kincaid something. He was already unscrewing the neck of his pewter flask again. Before drinking he leaned over his sink to hawk an excremental streak of tobacco juice into it.

'What is it?' Kincaid said, wiping his mouth with a square of white handkerchief and returning it to his trouser pocket. He was as usual immaculately, if eccentrically, turned out with a matching tweed waistcoat under his jacket, his crimson bow tie somewhat indecent against his chicken-white neck. As ever, Madden felt self-conscious around such a peacock of a man.

'Might I be allowed to view the body at some point?' he asked.

Kincaid tutted.

'I doubt that, Mr Madden, I doubt that very much. This one's not for the public table. You understand, I'm sure.' His look was forceful enough to tilt Madden backwards slightly on his heels. 'She was molested, by the way. I think to have one of her peers view her now might be to add insult to injury.'

'Yes, of course,' Madden said. 'I'm sorry. I shouldn't have asked.'

'We don't have her anyway. She's with the police coroner at the moment. Arrangements will be made for the burial later.'

Madden turned to go once again.

'Do you know if she was seeing anyone, Hugh?' Kincaid crossed his arms across his chest. 'A boy, perhaps?'

A boy. Of course there was a boy. There were always boys.

He had watched her walk through the gate, taking the downturn to the Kelvin Way, a childlike swing to her hand, her step almost a child's skip. He himself was only a boy back then, as Rose was constantly reminding him. A glaikit, gangling and none-too-appealing one at that.

He wasn't Carmen Alexander's *speed*. He'd found a park bench and sat down, closing his eyes, and had felt himself nothing more than the slow drip of bodily loathing, a well of cellular disgust. He didn't wish to dwell on it. The rain had begun to come down in earnest. He watched her open a clear plastic umbrella above her head and stood up from his bench.

'A boy, Dr Kincaid?' he said.

Kincaid nodded. 'Indeed, Mr Madden, that's what I said, is it not? Specifically a boy*friend*.'

Madden ran a hand across the back of his neck.

'No one that I knew of, sir.'

Kincaid nodded. 'Very well, Hugh. But if anything comes to that forensic attention of yours, you will let us know, won't you?'

'Of course, Doctor. Anything.'

'Then that will be all for now. Off with you, then. Can't be having you late for your next lecture, can we?'

Nine

Madden left Kincaid's office and turned right on University Avenue, then cut back in through the blocked spires of the old building with the intention of crossing through the quadrangles, but was met by a crush of students exiting through the Lion and the Unicorn Staircase, so he continued straight on through the gate to the right of it, then left up the brow of the hill towards the flagpole, not knowing where he was headed, but then knowing too that this was not the case, that he knew exactly where he was going and that to go there was pointless, would settle nothing, would leave him no nearer what he was actually looking for. He had some sort of a fever; he was perspiring and his throat hurt. He had felt it earlier in the day. Perhaps he had felt it the previous night too. He didn't know. Everything was different now.

The afternoon light had soured, and the flag itself snapped ravenously at the sky, so he stood for a while at its base because to pause was not to proceed, though he knew he would proceed in the end, that he would go there again anyway, no matter what measures he might take against himself in the interim. Nothing short of lashing himself to the mast of the flagpole. The red ziggurat of the Kelvin Hall Art Gallery squatted below, beneath a sweep of cloud shadow, the gardens themselves a well-groomed patchwork of bruised green, through which the Kelvin was flowing and where it had kept the body of Carmen Alexander secret for three days, caught in the shoals by the bank. It was the fever making him go there, he knew that. If he had been well, he would never have gone again. Never.

He stumbled down the hillside in a straight line, either ignoring the more straightforward access route of the path to the far side of the old building or forgetting it was there entirely. The feeling of fever wrapped itself around him, enveloping him in its welcome aura, and he was halfway over the fence when he became aware of what he was doing, and was then surprised to find that he was stuck.

One railing had pierced the pre-existing hole in the sole of his right brogue while he gripped the railings on either side of his body, the other leg clamped tightly in the space where he had swung it over. He waggled his left leg uselessly like a trodden-on insect, but could neither work it up to a halfway position on the crossbar of the fence, nor heave himself over the other side using the strength of his right leg without seriously injuring his foot on the railing's spike. On the other side of the fence was only a thickly wooded area, though he knew that the path towards the Way was only a matter of forty or fifty yards distant at worst.

A stupor came over him; some kind of endorphin-induced seizure in the temporal lobes of the brain, the influence of some malign opiate, a narcotic dullness. For a while he hung on, doing nothing and experiencing no particular urge to remedy the situation, simply hanging, his weight balanced evenly so that he was, for the time being, reasonably comfortable. A rigor tightened: he felt himself crouch in the corner of his room, his mother watching as his father told him that if he wanted to act like a bloody lassie then he could damned well use the chanty like a bloody lassie. Madden had begun to cry as he strained over the porcelain bowl, his thighs seizing up from his enforced squat. All he could remember of these incidents themselves was the crouching, the pain of his thighs, and the admonitions of his mother. Not there, Hugh, she'd said to him, you're missing the bowl. And then his father's rages, forcing his face down on to the carpet and into the pooling urine around his feet. And the sudden lack of fear, or of disgrace; a strange drifting serenity as though being cushioned by warm air. Like morphine. The god of sleep and dreams. Stuck on the railings, he felt as lucid as at any time in his life. Of course, there was no magic to it. Of course, it was simply science in effect. The hypothalamus, responding to stress. And he *was* stressed. Who wouldn't be? Someone had died: he might well be a suspect in her killing. Or if not he, then likely someone he knew. Good old peri-aqueductal grey matter. Good old ACTH hormone, good old adrenal glands. They had saved the day again.

Except for Carmen Alexander. She'd have experienced exactly this sensation just before she had the life throttled out of her. It was then, thinking of her, that Madden felt the first stabs of a cramp in his right leg which informed him that the world was coming rightways up again, and in no uncertain terms. At the same moment he became aware of the pain, the rain began again, as it had every day for the last week.

His humiliation was complete. The water came down in thick droplets, and he was groaning with the pain in his leg and the impossibility of moving it. He began bleating like a sheep with its foot in a snare, shaking the water from his eyes with violent jerks of his head. There could be no more miserable way to end your days than like this, crucified atop a rusty fence. Not Carmen Alexander's going nor that of any other could equal this; pronged through the arse on a fence! *Help!* he began shouting, *help! I'm stuck like a lassie!*, but at the same time he wanted no one to discover him here like this, in ignominy, and he let out a wail of grief for himself, waggling his speared shoe frantically, trying to ease the cramp in his leg and simultaneously loosen the grip the railing had on his sole. After repeated bursts of waggling, and by inching his other leg forward between the two railings that clamped it – it had more or less lost all sensation from the groin down – he dangled panting for breath. Soaked through, he began shivering uncontrollably. Again, he shouted for help, but could see no one through the darkened trees ahead, nor turn his head so that anyone up by the flagpole might stand more chance of hearing him. Then, with one great spasm of action, he jerked his foot so hard that it slipped out of the shoe and at the same time he used the actual muscles of his groin to launch himself forward and slipped off the fence, landing heavily on his left shoulder.

Despite the pain in his legs and the throb of his upper left side, in that second of falling to earth his gratitude knew no limits and he squelched bodily on to his knees, crossed himself, thanked the God of the Christians, the God of the Jews, the Allah of the Mohammedans, Buddha, Vishnu, John F. Kennedy and Her Majesty the Queen, all in their infinite mercy and wisdom, in a single breath that evaporated as soon as he tried to stand upright, and collapsed on his backside once again. Burning pins and needles danced in flux between the foot of the left leg that wasn't there any more and a groin that had ceased to exist. His shoulder ached punishingly; he began shivering all over again. His stomach hurt from the pressing of the fleur-de-lis points that had been prevented from impaling by his supporting his own weight against them, and the palms of his hands were sore and rust stained. The cold of the rain had left the top of his head feeling like lead. His shoe was still stuck on top of the railings like some outlandish fruit. From here on the downward side of the slope, the fence was far too high for him to have any hope of retrieving it. Now he cursed the God of the Christians, the God of the Jews, the Allah of the Mohammedans, Buddha, Vishnu, John F. Kennedy, Her Majesty the Queen and the Duke of Edinburgh, in all their limitless corruption, with a single stream of polished bile that surprised even himself, and that partially restored his will to continue with his pathetic and thankless existence, for the time being at least.

Thunder rumbled in the distance. The rain was still coming down in ballistic volleys, lightening momentarily only to then batter down on him again with renewed vigour. Christ, he was cold now, the shivering a St Vitus's dance of tics that flickered over every major muscle group in the body, and gripping the iron railings for support, he began dragging himself to his feet. When fully upright, he caught his breath momentarily and then began hobbling tentatively down through the long grass of the slope, lurching from one tree trunk to the next. Every time he reached another tree, he would shelter from the rain, stamp his feet and rub his hands together in an attempt to introduce some sensation into his extremities before plunging stiffly forward once again, more in hope than expectation.

When he could clearly see the path to the Way ahead, he began crying again. The most appalling prospect would be to be recognised in the street by every passing stranger as the hapless, hopeless and helpless eejit he knew he must look. It was right that he should be despised for it, as he would doubtless despise such failure of dignity in another were the situation reversed. So, dragging his sodden collar tighter around his neck, and pushing his hair back out of his eyes as best he could, he attempted to stand upright and affect the noble bearing of a destitute gentleman, rather than a demobbed cripple in the habit of soiling his clothes when the worse for drink.

Reaching the verge, he limped along with his shoeless foot on the grassy side, mire oozing between his toes, the other on the stony path, squinting through the squalid light and wiping the rain from his face. It wasn't far to the main road now, a matter of a few hundred feet, and when he finally came to it he sagged against a tree for a few minutes, bracing himself for the long and laboured mortification of the trudge home.

His legs had almost returned to life now, and he was just about able to walk normally, but his shivering had become relentless even as he was forced to deport himself with some semblance of dignity. He began to proceed along the tree-lined avenue, back in the direction of the university he had left so long ago this afternoon. No one passed him; everyone had taken cover from the sudden storm. That was a mercy.

At the junction there was no traffic, and he crossed over to the other side without looking either left or right, indifferent to his fate so long as it was private. The lights from the Men's Union pulled him towards them and up the stone steps, and when he reached the doors, he found he hadn't the strength left to draw them open. He knocked twice on the door, then sat down on the steps in the pouring rain, still shivering, and burst into a fresh round of tears.

This was it all over now, he had nothing left to give. Instead, he would die here on the steps of the Union, a few heroic feet from sanctuary.

A voice behind him enquired what it was that he wanted. He half turned and looked pleadingly at the man, the concierge, in white shirt and black cap, a swallow tattooed on the back of one hand.

Everyone in this town had the plague, Madden told him. No one was immune, no one was uninfected. Carmen Alexander had died of a disease, she had brought the infection on herself. It was her fault. She had asked for it. He couldn't quite recall what it was that actually killed her, syphilis perhaps. Or gingivitis. Gum disease had seen her off.

Everyone in this town was diseased. The concierge was diseased too. He had Swallow's lymphoma, a variant of the plague in question. Didn't he know that? Did he not understand? No point in going to a doctor about it. Madden was a doctor, and he couldn't cure him.

What plague was that? the concierge asked him. What the hell was he talking about?

That plague, Madden said, pointing inanely at the man's tattoo. The Ink Plague.

Ink plague?

That was right, Madden was saying, the Ink Plague. Everyone had it. There was Gaskell with his blots, and Fain with his spills. He had it himself, Madden was saying, he spurted deadly condemning ink, no one was safe.

The concierge told him to beat it, he was drunk.

No, Madden said, he wasn't drunk. He was a member of the Union, and he was here for a drink. A hot one. Tea would do, but he preferred hot chocolate, my good man.

If he was a member of this Union, why was he only wearing one shoe? the concierge said. Go on, clear off . . .

He produced his Union card from his jacket pocket, and handed it to the man, trying to stand up, falling forwards so that the concierge was forced to catch him. Here, he said, what're you shivering like that for? You're drunk.

Madden began sniffling again. No, he said, he wasn't. He really was *not well at all.*

Then he vomited down the front of the man's trousers.

There, he said triumphantly, ink!

Get away from me, the man said, pushing him bodily backwards so that he stumbled, his shoeless foot sliding away from him. He slid sharply rearward, the step disappearing from under, flapping at the air with both arms in an attempt to balance himself before finding the ground with him once more, three steps down and back on the road again.

Go on, get lost, the man was saying, get out of here, before I call the police.

Madden gawped at him, strings of fluid and matter trailing from his open mouth, the unannounced spew startling him into a kind of unsober dread, though he was sure that he had not taken a drop that day.

Go on! the man shouted. I'll call the police!

Madden put up two plaintive hands, caught bang to rights. He could expect no shelter here, unless it was that of a police cell. He was baffled at what he had said to give such offence. The violence of the concierge seemed unnecessary, he was only trying to get in out of the rain. Everyone deserved to be in out of the rain. Had he been a down-on-his-luck gentleman, suffice to say that his place beside the fire would have been guaranteed. The concierge would have tipped his hat to him and said, Damn good to see you, sir, excuse my language. He would have brought hot victuals and stoked the coals. There would have been broth, a damper of bread, meat from the pot. I'm afraid it's just the below-stairs leftovers, sir, but you're more than welcome to it. No, no, don't thank us. Glad of the company is what we are, sir, glad of it. Chance to do a Christian deed by one such as yourself. A toff, sir, that's what you are, a toff.

He would have been brought woollen blankets, given a change of clothes. His suit and his single shoe would be hung up to dry by the fire, and he could have watched the steam rise from them and doze till he was brought his toddy and a pipe. It was not to be, though. He had been cast out again, into the wilderness where he would sicken and lay down and be stepped on by the whole world until he was completely flattened and could finally be rolled up like papyrus and his dried skin used to clothe the weans of paupers. It was too much to bear. Too much, too, too much. And the man responsible for this outrage against decency, this crime against the human race – this swine of the Glasgow University Men's Union who stood before him now would be hailed as a public hero and very likely be made rector. *Gaudiamus igitur, juven es dum sumus*. Well done, my good man, jolly good show. *That's the damned bricks*.

He gave the concierge a final, baleful look and then began to walk again, placing one hand on the low Union wall for support. Exhaustion drained the power from his sudden lurches of stomach, and the shivering seemed to have passed for the moment. His foot was raw and tender now, and he winced every time he placed it down on the ground in front of him, but there was some hope left: the rain seemed to be weakening finally; and with that he could make out a few souls walking along Bank Street ahead of him and hear the sound of traffic; cars or buses. Where he was now, the road divided and he had a choice, but he was unsure what the right one would be. He might continue on down the hill, where he knew there was a telephone in one of the public houses there, and then call someone with the few coins he had; or he could keep straight on for another few hundred yards and turn left into the main artery of Great Western Road.

Neither prospect had much appeal. He had no idea who he should telephone; his father did not own one. He was against them, in the same way that he was against perfumed soaps and women who smoked publicly. *They bloody things*, he said, *effeminate is what they are. Talking, talking, talking . . . only a race of bloody effeminates would spend their time talking to a dashed machine.*

The list of effeminate things was a long and unhappy one. He despised the National Health Service as the invention of effeminates. Only effeminates couldn't, after all, take care of themselves.

Telephones, perfumed soap, and women smoking in public – even those who were *not* guilty of smoking in pub-lic – all had effeminacy in common. Accordingly, with the exception of Madden's mother, he avoided any contact with them. Once, he had come home from the pub in a spit-ting rage because there'd been an unaccompanied woman standing in the public bar. *The public bar!* he shouted. *What was she doing in the public bar? The lounge bar is the place for women!*

There were inventions, institutions, people – regardless of gender – that might randomly be considered effeminate, and no qualification ever offered. All despised with the exception of the motor car, the want of which he felt keenly, but couldn't afford. Madden's mother had offered to help with the payments on one, but the suggestion was met with a forbidding silence which neither she nor Madden had felt inclined to break.

Carrying on into Great Western Road seemed a likelier bet. From there he could make it as far as Byres Road, and use his money for a bus: there was no nearer stop serving the right route. The trudge was a daunting one and he would have to pass a lot of people on the way, with the prospect of another downpour impending, but there was nothing else for it.

Unless he went to Gaskell's lodgings instead. The landlady might let him in to wait even if Gaskell wasn't there: she knew his face, though he sensed she disliked it. It was not an appealing face, by all accounts, but at least it was a familiar one, and she would let it in the door. If not, he would plead with her. Although he had no real idea of the time, the night didn't feel late. Yes. It was feasible he could walk that far, and there would be fewer people around if he avoided Great Western Road. It was possibly further to Wilton Street than Byres Road, with a tedious uphill climb along Belmont Street and over the bridge. But it seemed worth it. He wondered why he hadn't thought of it before. But then again, he knew why: Gaskell had been in the undercurrent of his thoughts, along with Carmen Alexander, all day. Now he wanted to sleep so badly that it was immaterial what might have passed between them at the Rio.

Buoyed up, he moved onwards along Bank Street, a growing warmth he took to be encroaching hypothermia cheering his overworked limbs. But perhaps he was being melodramatic; certainly he felt none of the delirium of only a short while before, only a pleasant warmth that disregarded the sodden state of his clothes, and made his uncontrollable shivering seem a distant memory. It was possible he would lapse again, but he was certain this would not be the case; he would make it now to Gaskell's lodgings without passing out. His foot no longer stung as he pressed it to the pavement, and all pain had disappeared from the rest of his battered body.

The heat had spread as far as his ears, and it was they that were most warmed; in fact, they seemed to tingle with heat, burn even.

The only thing that bothered him slightly was thirst. He walked – not *limped* or *shuffled* but actually *walked* – for the first time in an impossibly long while, and in what must have been only an impossibly short one reached the main road. The speed he moved at was impressive, he had to admit. It was doubtful he could move any faster without breaking into a sprint. He would have liked his mother to have seen him move like that. He had never been much of a one for sports at school. She would have been proud of him, his father too! His mouth would have been wide open with pride at the athleticism of his only boy, instead of with his habitual abuse. *Well done, son*, he'd say. *Well done*.

Still, he couldn't believe that in all that rushing inundation of water he had never simply opened his mouth and accepted it. And of course, now he had begun to sweat, so that by the time he was crossing the main road, a sparse flow of traffic between himself and Gaskell's side of the road, it was fairly lashing off him. He paused, waiting for a space, but the lights remained a static red, determinedly avoiding the possibility of change. He wiped his brow with the sleeve of his soaked jacket, and felt its warmth. It was amazing how much it had heated up in so short a time. An elderly woman was standing next to him giving him a queer look, so he smiled at her and said he'd lost his shoe in the park. She edged away from him under her umbrella, and he shrugged to himself as he stepped into the traffic, all the while licking his lips and swallowing, trying to introduce some wetness into his mouth.

The sky was clearing now, he could see the light increase, and he laughed as the thought struck him that he had been out all night, and how fast the hours had passed, he couldn't *believe* the rate the hours had flown by at. No time had passed at all and here it was, the dawn on its way and he was still here, still on the streets, only a ten-minute walk from the university he had left a lifetime ago. And he was well, it was going to be all right if he could only find something to drink, a glass of cold water, or beer, anything. He sucked at his mouth. He could hear bird sounds from far off, likely swallows returning from Africa, rested after a night's sleep and now singing for the dawn. They would know where to find water, they could lead him to it. No, it wasn't birdsong at all, but people on the other side of the road: they were waving to him, egging him forwards, and one face he recognised, a figure resplendent in emerald suit, one arm waving wildly at him. He smiled warmly and waved back, and then he knew: he could feel it between the toes of his shoeless foot. A small puddle trapped in a pothole in the road. He stooped to scoop some water into the palm of his hand, and drank it down, then took another palmful. It was gritty and tasted vaguely of ash, but he was beyond caring, his thirst overcoming him. As he bent over a third time, he saw that the water was red. Blood was leaking from his foot into it. He stood upright and felt the colour drain from him, and stepped straight ahead into the oncoming traffic. He was only half conscious of the screeching brakes and horn as he crossed over, and of the panicked eyes of Gaskell before he collapsed in the gutter on the other side.

For a long time he tried hard to convince the voice in his head to tell him the truth, which was that he was dying, and later that he was already dead. He pointed out the evidence in favour of his argument, but the voice cross-examined him, and would not let the matter drop, even when he pleaded with it to let him be, to leave him alone, to put him in the ground where he was meant to be right now if only the voice would listen. A voice can't listen, the voice told him, a voice has no ears to hear or eyes to see. All a voice can do is talk, and all anyone who hears the voice can do is listen. And a voice that cannot listen is a voice that cannot reason, so stop wasting your breath in idle argument.

That was when he gave up fighting the voice, and let it continue with its monologue uninterrupted. The voice was the voice of his father, then of his mother, then of Gaskell, then of Kincaid. Finally, when it became the voice of Carmen Alexander, he stopped listening too, so that the voice began to lose its temper with him and hurled insults at him, calling him a *bourgeois pig*, and shouting, *Where's your damned bricks*, but he didn't hear the insults, only the voice. It began then to whine, to implore, to plead and then at last to cry in long, airless gasps, as if being throttled into silence by his silence. Listen to me, it said, you have to listen to me, but Madden ignored it, which was simple because it was only a voice. Finally, the voice stopped altogether and he was left in silence. He must have won the argument, then, he decided. So this must be death after all.

'Madman, are you awake?'

Madden felt someone touch his shoulder.

'I'm dead,' he said, 'leave me alone.'

The voice laughed.

'You're not dead, old fellow. Not by a good bit yet.'

Madden opened his eyes with some difficulty: they were heavily crusted with sleep. There was a single bare light bulb hanging directly above him; the plaster on the ceiling was peeling and a large bubble of the stuff looked ready to come bursting down on top of his head. It was Gaskell's room: he was in Gaskell's bed. With growing alarm, he pulled himself into an upright position against the pillow. Gaskell was sitting on the chair he got Madden to borrow from the lodger next door. He obviously had no intention of returning it.

'Nasty wound you've got there,' Gaskell said. His expression was blank behind his long white cigarette, sitting cross-legged, wearing his dungarees and donkey jacket. Ella Fitzgerald was playing on his Dansette, her voice muffled by scratches and the crackle of dust. The necrosis of the room had crawled farther down the faded wallpaper, as though it were dying, inch by rotten inch, of Dutch elm disease or a slow impetigo. The state of the place revolted Madden more with each successive visit. It would be better if the whole building collapsed into the ground.

Gaskell frowned. 'How did you manage it?' he asked.

Madden rubbed his eyes, felt his chest clammy with sweat, and realised he had been undressed by someone.

'Manage what?'

'To gouge that hole in your foot,' Gaskell said. 'It's the size of a half-crown.'

Madden peeled back the bedclothes and exposed his foot. It had been bandaged up: the work of a professional. He wondered whether it had been Gaskell.

'I don't remember,' he said. 'I climbed a fence, I think. How long have I been asleep?'

'Asleep? That was no sleep, Madman. That was a *swoon*. That was a *dead faint*. That was a bloody *fever*, that was. You've been out of it for two days. Delirious, you were, a lot of the time. Talking in your sleep and all sorts. You were lucky not to catch pneumonia out in that rain, wandering about with no bloody shoes on and a great chunk out of your foot.'

Madden saw now that the floor was covered in spread-out sheets of newspaper. Some of them were stained red, he presumed with blood from his foot. Gaskell noticed him stare and stood up, walking to the centre of the room. He pirouetted, losing his balance slightly on the spin, and stamped out a leather-booted foot to stop himself keeling over. His eyes were bloodshot and his hair matted, his face covered in smudged ink. It was decorated by a thin stubble, blond at the sideburns but very strong, almost ginger, around the chin.

'The fauna in the carpet were getting to be a problem,' he explained. 'You've never seen the like of the creatures that live in it. I sit here, on my chair, waiting for the big game, my pea-shooter primed. I tell you, Madman, I fear for my life in here sometimes, I really do.'

'I fear for your sanity,' Madden said quietly, leaning over on one elbow.

Gaskell was over at the bed in one stride. He grabbed Madden by the hair and yanked it roughly.

'Don't fucking let me hear you say that again, all right?'

Madden nodded violently, both hands splayed out by his ears, the fingers spasmed in defence.

'Never. Do you hear me?'

'All right,' Madden said, 'I'm sorry, I didn't mean it.'

Gaskell let go of his hair and pushed his head roughly back, jamming his cigarette aggressively back into his mouth. 'Anyway,' he said, sitting down on the edge of the bed, his tone instantly calm again, 'I'm not the one Kincaid wants to talk to about dead Italian girls, am I?'

Madden smoothed his hair back down. It felt greasy.

'What d'you mean?' he said defensively. 'Don't they want to speak to you about her too?'

Gaskell harrumphed, then began coughing violently into the sleeve of his donkey jacket. 'Oh, they're speaking to everyone. I expect they'll get round to me soon. But I've nothing to tell. Everything's above board with me.' He turned and looked pointedly at Madden. 'Isn't that right, Madman?' he said.

Madden looked down at his pale ribcage above the bed-clothes, pinching abstractedly at the spareness of the flesh there. 'I wish you wouldn't call me that,' Madden said.

'Of course, it's just routine,' Gaskell went on. 'I expect it'll all blow over after a while. Whoever did it was obviously an amateur anyway, and amateurs always make mistakes. Amateurs get caught in the end. Don't they?'

Madden nodded. 'Yes,' he said, 'they do.'

Gaskell leapt up from the bed and placed a finger over his upper lip in parody of a moustache, and began to mimic

Kinkaid. 'And why, Mr Madden, is this the case?' he said. 'In as few words as possible.'

The impersonation was a passable one, and Madden began to laugh nervously. 'Because there's no such thing as the perfect crime.'

'Precisely, Mr Madden. Because there is no such thing as the perfect crime. And an amateur is the one thing a murderer cannot afford to be.' Gaskell made a sweeping bow, and stood affectedly puffing at his cigarette. 'They always leave something behind at the scene, don't they? Some tiny detail overlooked. A footprint, a tear of clothing. Even a shoe.'

Madden began to get up from the bed, self-conscious in his nakedness, but his legs would only support him shakily, and he sat down in a heap once again.

'Uh-uh,' Gaskell said, 'our Mr Madman won't be going anywhere for a while. Get back into bed.' He walked over and placed his hand under Madden's legs and lifted them sideways and up on to the bed again, pulling the covers over them. Madden eyed him questioningly. Gaskell put both hands up, and backed away slightly.

'You should be in bed. You're too weak. Stay there and I'll go and see if I can't get something for us to eat.'

'But I have to go home. My parents . . .'

'I'll call them.'

'You can't. They don't have a telephone.'

'Then I'll go round. Either way you're not well enough to move just yet. Don't worry about it. I'm sure they'll understand.'

Madden doubted that was the case, but knew he wasn't in a position to argue about it at the moment. The voice had spoken and all he could do was listen. Silence would eventually triumph.

Gaskell buttoned his donkey jacket and pulled the collar up around his neck. 'All right, then, that's settled. You'll stay here and I'll find us the victuals. Probably be able to get catch the

Co-op if I hurry.' The expression on his face was a rare mixture of fear and pleading, and it unsettled Madden. He nodded slowly, and settled back down into the bed.

'All right,' he said. 'Perhaps I'll just sleep a while longer. What time is it, by the way?'

Gaskell flicked up his wrist, feigning to read a non-existent watch.

'The time is half past five on a Thursday evening.'

'So it was Wednesday you found me. It was light, I remember that. I'd been out all night, and the dawn had come up.'

Gaskell snorted in derision.

'The dawn had done no such thing. It was Tuesday evening.' Madden frowned.

'But I remember distinctly the dawn. I heard the birds . . .'

'You might have heard birds, but that doesn't mean they were singing for the dawn. The storm had cleared, and it got light again. What is it you call it up here in your bumpkin language? Ah, yes. It was the gloaming. You were roaming in the gloaming. There wasn't any lassie by your side, though.'

Madden was quietly stunned. 'So . . . ?'

Gaskell tipped an invisible hat to him. 'That's right, old fellow, old bean. You were last seen leaving the university at the grand old hour of two thirty. I found you at five. That's . . . my arithmetic is not good, Madman, but it's hardly forty days and forty nights you were in the wilderness. Two and a half hours, wouldn't you say?' He ducked his head under the eaves, and opened the door. He looked back as he was closing it, and Madden looked away, momentarily afraid to meet his gaze.

Gaskell had been wrong about one thing, though. There had been a lassie with him that night, or afternoon, or whatever it was. A memory, a ghost. Her name was Carmen Alexander.

*

He listened to Gaskell's steps receding down the stairwell, heard him stop and murmur something to someone and then pass on. Other footsteps came and went. The landlady? Another lodger? Impossible to say. When he was sure Gaskell had left the building, he got up and, leaning on the bed for support, began to look for his clothes. His jacket hung across the back of the chair, still damp, his trousers and underwear beneath it. All damp. He laughed at Gaskell's thoughtlessness, the way he'd given up his bed for his friend, if that's what they were – *friends* – but it had never occurred to him that this same, ill, friend might need dry clothes to wear once he had recovered. Madden went over to the single cupboard – a door that opened directly on to the stone outside wall of this frayed attic room, and which contained a single item of clothing: Gaskell's green corduroy suit, washed and pressed, slung from a coat hanger. Madden lifted the sleeve of the jacket to his nose and sniffed. Mildew.

Ella Fitzgerald sang, 'Gimme a Pig Foot and a Bottle of Beer', the recording clicking repeatedly over the final gravelly strains. Madden went over to the Dansette and placed the needle at the beginning of the song again. He opened the top drawer of the dresser and peered inside. A handful of coins, a pound note, and the keys to the Norton. Three pairs of socks in various states of ill health. His own foot throbbed slightly when he placed weight on it, but not disconcertingly so. Whoever had mended it had done a good job. He reached into the back of the drawer and rummaged around, but could find nothing of interest, then drew his hand back sharply as he felt something live touch it, then scurry away. Gaskell had not been understating when he said he was in fear for his life up here. It wasn't only the carpet which was infested. He sighed and sat down on the single chair. There were medical notes and abandoned novels piled everywhere, so he began to browse through them, hoping to find something to distract himself with: the idea of rats or mice didn't disturb him, but being alone in this hovel did. Especially the knowledge that he had slept in Gaskell's filthy bed for two days.

Some of the notes had infantile doodles on them, spaceships and racing cars. Others depicted erect and ejaculating penises; there was a very graphic and elaborately drawn picture of a man penetrating another man using a mechanical contraption, intricately detailed with spikes and spines and all manner of impaling and chopping mechanisms jutting from every conceivable corner. There was also a list of groceries next to a name and a question mark. The name was 'Dizzy'.

Madden stood up and went again to the cupboard under the eaves with the suit in it. He reached into the outside left pocket but discovered only a packet of chewing gum and the crumbled remains of a cigarette or two. In the inside pocket there was a label with a number on it: the receipt from the service wash at the launderette. There was also a black-and-white picture of a man, his head cut off at the top of the frame, hugging two figures, one on either side of him, a boy and a girl. The boy was cut off just below the mouth. And the girl was smiling; it was the same gummy smile he had seen somewhere before, the smile of a nineteen-year-old Italian girl now deceased. Her hair stood in a lacquered contortion, bottle-blonde, her eyes heavily mascara'd and her lips with some kind of pale, possibly white lipstick applied. She reminded Madden of someone he couldn't quite place. Yes, that was it. Priscilla Presley. She looked like a blonde Priscilla Presley.

The three posed, their backs to some sort of plush, expensive-looking curtain. It was a very poor sort of a picture, no more than a snap really. Madden turned it over, but there was nothing written on the back. He replaced it in the pocket of Gaskell's jacket and closed the door.

Putting on his damp clothes, he left the record to trundle around in crunching circles and took a piece of paper from the pile of notes and wrote a note to Gaskell on it with the pen in the pocket of his wet jacket. Then he scooped the pound note from the top drawer of the dresser and closed it once again.

He placed the note next to the record player and let himself out of the tiny room and went down the stairs.

The light in the corridor was dim: only the landing three floors down was lit. Madden could make out movement down there. Human shadows slanted from one end to another, so he waited in the dark for a moment, unsure of whether to proceed or not. If it was Gaskell, he had no desire to meet him on the way back in. If it was Gaskell's landlady, likewise. After a while, the light snapped off below, and he would have had to grope for a light switch here on this landing had the skylight itself not provided a diffuse etching of the stairwell, enough at least that he wouldn't trip and break his neck. Squinting, he made his way down, taking the weight off his bad foot by hanging on to the banister.

Reaching the front door, he glimpsed the landlady on the stairs above him and quickly opened the door. He stepped outside and into Wilton Street. Limping off in the direction of Maryhill Road brought on a shivering pain right through his entire right leg. He stood in the middle of the street waving desperately at the first taxi to pass his way. It was with no regrets at all that he gave the driver his address and told him to take him home quickly.

'Where have you been?' his mother said to him, shining a plate with a dish towel. Her face had the usual stung look, and hair came down in wisps from the tight bun she wore it in, mousy with grey streaks. Madden limped past, and into the kitchen, running himself a glass of water from the tap. He drank it in cool sips, not gulping but pausing between each small mouthful as if to remind himself of its taste.

'I had an accident,' he said, cradling the glass in one hand. 'I hurt my foot.' He raised his bandaged extremity a fraction of an inch, aware of how foolish it must look with its padded white bandage, his toes sticking out the end. His mother nodded.

'Where's Da?' he asked her.

'Gone out.'

'Looking for me?'

'The pub.'

'Oh.'

'He decided you must have murdered someone and had to go into hiding,' she said, continuing to squeak her towel around the plate.

Madden sipped his water.

'He decided that. After the police came.'

Madden stood still, waiting for a solution to present itself. The towel continued to squeak around the plate.

'Did you murder someone, son?' she asked him.

'No. I had an accident. I told you.'

'You hurt your foot, yes. I see that. How did it happen?'

'When were the police here?' he said, putting his glass down. 'What did they want?'

His mother picked up another plate from the draining board.

'They said they wanted to talk to you. In connection with a very serious matter. Did you stand on a nail?'

'What matter?' Madden could feel a vague tightening in his chest; the palpable beat of his heart. 'What did they want to discuss?'

'Did you go somewhere you shouldn't have, Hugh? That's dangerous. You know that. You shouldn't go places with strangers. It was one of the things we taught you when you were wee.' His mother giggled suddenly, covering her black-ened teeth with her hand. 'You know,' she said. 'Knickerless girls shouldn't climb trees . . . Were you up a tree, Hugh. Were you k.i.s.s.i.n.g?'

The tightening was getting worse; it was spreading to his lips, his facial muscles.

His mother swayed slightly as she replaced the plate on the draining board.

Madden took a step towards her and grabbed her by the lapel, shaking her hard. 'Where is it?' he said, his mother sagging to the ground beneath him. He refused to search her: he would stand here until she gave the bottle up. 'Give me it!' he said, and she began to giggle again. 'Give me it, Ma.' He could feel the throb of his foot now, the pulse in it. 'Look,' he said, as calmly as he could. 'Give me the bottle before Da comes in. You know what'll happen if he finds you like this. You know.'

She sat in a heap on the floor, her knees uncovered. 'Your father was right, you know,' she said, not listening to him. 'You are . . . *effeminate* . . .'

He felt the anger leap up into his forehead. He looked at her and let go of her apron so that she slid farther down on to the floor. He was shaking. He picked up a plate from the draining board and held it over her head.

She saw the plate and began giggling again. 'Go on,' she said, suddenly sober. 'I dare you!'

He was trembling; the dish was trembling too. He held it above her head and she fixed him with her eyes, ignoring it, her eyes challenging him. He could do it; he could bring it down. It would have been one solution. Instead, he lowered it slowly, until it hung at his side.

'*Wait* till your father gets home,' his mother said, quite calmly. 'Just *wait*.'

He turned away from her and went over to the window above the sink, something within him reaching out towards the darkness, not seeing anything.

'What did the police want?' he asked, leaning his weight on the porcelain. 'Why did they want to see me?'

She began to get up, bracing herself against the sideboard with one hand, one leg reaching out and pushing up. Madden saw how small the room had become: once it had seemed the size of the world to him. It had been a vast cavern, the biggest room. There was the recess that had once been his playground, behind his mother. It was so small, almost dwarfed by the huge table that filled it, donated by the death of a neighbour in this very close. So generous, the dead, so thoughtful. He wondered whether all the furniture in the house had come to them this way. Probably. His mother had gone round to borrow a cup of milk and come back with a mahogany table. A bargain. The milk, however, was off. The rest of the neighbours must have taken what was left of the pickings.

'They wanted to speak to you,' another voice said. He turned round. His father. He stood, his bunnet still on, larger than anything else in the kitchen, despite his stature. Madden's mother began to fuss around nervously.

'They wanted to talk to you about a police matter,' he said. 'The disappearance of somebody.'

'Here, let me get your jacket off,' Madden's mother was saying, her face gone very flushed. 'Oh, it's sodden . . .'

Madden's father glowered at her, pushing her hand away from him as she tried to get the buttons open. 'Leave it!' he said.

Madden found he had nothing to say. His father turned his gaze to him and he could do nothing but lower his own eyes to the ground and stare at his wounded foot.

His father looked at Madden with barely suppressed rage.

'Something funny, is there?' he said. 'It amuses you that the polis come to my house – *my own house*, mind! – wanting to ask me questions about my son – *my bloody son!* – in my own home?'

Madden had no answer. He was picturing a shoe, planted like a flag on a stick in the ground, losing his attention in the dotted pincushion designs of the leather.

'Tell me!' his father said, slamming a palm flat against his own leg, his body stiff and straight like a drill sergeant on parade.

'Oh, Daddy, it's all right . . .' his mother said.

'*SHUT UP!*' he shouted not three inches from her face, so that both she and Madden jumped slightly. She was instantly silent. His father reached over suddenly and grabbed at her, pulling at her apron, and she retracted her arms protectively, wrestling with him for control of the object she was hiding, but he was too strong. He discovered the snub little bottle. There was barely more than an inch of gin left in it. His mother's face sagged in defeat. She put her hands up to her face and covered it, as though she were a child playing peek-a-boo. She did not cry.

'Go to bed, Mammy,' Madden's father said. 'Go to bed now.'

She turned and walked out of the room, closing the door quietly behind her. Madden's father watched him, breathing heavily through his nose. For a long time, he simply stood there breathing before speaking again, but when he did his voice was even and unhurried.

'I don't care what you've done, or where you've been, d'you understand me, son? I don't care. But I will not have you bringing the polis up to my door. I will not. D'you understand?'

Madden nodded.

'This was the first and only time it will happen. So I'm giving you one month.' He was waiting, apparently, to see the effect his words were having on Madden.

'One month?' he echoed, perplexed.

'One month,' his father said, only now taking his bunnet off and beginning to unbutton his coat. 'After that, I want you out of here.'

Madden was stunned. 'But I don't have any money,' he said.

'Then you've a month to find work. There's always Colville's. Or if that's not to your *taste*, then you can find something else.'

He hung his coat on the back of the kitchen door, and leaned down to take his whisky bottle from the cupboard.

'And if you're not out by then, I'll throw you out myself.'

He poured the contents of the bottle into a glass from the draining board, so clean it almost dazzled when it caught the light. Then he raised it to his lips and sipped. 'Have a dram yourself if you want, son,' he said. Madden focused forlornly on the bottle. 'You're over eighteen now. You're a man. Go on. Have a dram with your old da.'

He seemed quite cheerful as Madden lifted the bottle and took a glass for himself.

Ten

News of Carmen Alexander's death had done something to the campus. Madden had avoided Gaskell, as he felt the other to be avoiding him, searching instead the windows of hardware stores and grocers' shops for TO LET notices, forgoing both library and revision, a blank period when he often found that hours had passed without register. It was an interminable task, one that would apparently cost him what little remaining shoe leather he possessed and likely a speedier deterioration of his bad foot into the bargain. The direness of the weather increased incrementally with the number of – like himself – similarly dispossessed students who morosely trudged the streets in the relentless downpour. On more than one occasion he saw Aduman jotting details from a window on to a sodden notepad, the limp scarf wound high around his neck and hanging forlorn at either side, one hand dragging his buttonless lapels together on the dingy streets at the dingy hour of one or two in the afternoon of some dingy Sunday when there was no hope of a roast beef dinner for either of them, especially now that he was avoiding Rose. He felt himself to be outside of everything, and supposed that some sort of kinship existed between Aduman and himself, but the Senegalese obviously thought different.

Not so much as a nod from he to Madden, as though they hadn't shared a single tutorial or lab the whole year. If he hadn't known better, Madden might have perceived himself as having been *cut*. Surely not. There was no reason for it at all.

Certainly no reason for Aduman not to give him a perfunctory nod, a brief flexing of the eyebrows, just to remind Madden that, yes, he did exist. He had half a mind to stride right up to the fellow and say, *Now look here, I know you recognise me. What's all this about?*

Then again, perhaps he had heard rumours. Well. As far as he knew, rumours were all they would be. The police had not expressed *particular interest* (to use Kincaid's coinage) in him; nor had they suggested he might have had anything to do with the dead girl other than a passing acquaintance. And that was literally all it was; a *passing* acquaintance. Her relationship with Gaskell was of more pressing interest. Madden had been left with a number to call if he remembered anything he regarded as important. Day or night, the officer had said to his father. No clue was too insignificant, no detail to be left unconsidered. That Aduman character had really the bloodiest of cheek in believing any nonsense he might have heard around the half-empty campus. Damned bricks of the man.

Of course, he made no admonishments to Aduman. Instead, he scribbled on his own damp notepad with his — bloody foolish in these conditions — damned fountain pen, the sorry splats of which ran and stained, leaving him none the wiser as to which address he had to look up next. No blotter, no brains. Unable to think ahead. And as yet he had no means of funding this terrifying enterprise. He wondered vaguely about what he would eat and how he might carbonise it to the required standard, but put the thought out of his mind, telling himself that since he was unable to think ahead there was little to be gained by thinking ahead. He would eat or starve as the case may be.

At the moment he was starving, since in his pique he was refusing to sit with his mother and father at the table. When his father went out for a pint, he would pocket something while his mother's back was turned and quickly exit himself, thence to waste another evening treading the streets in search of alternative accommodation. He half suspected that his mother had taken pity on him and kept her back turned deliberately while he scavenged, leaving convenient lumps of chilling fat and gristle, the occasional cold cut, easily to hand. Hunger had forced him to consider going to see Rose, but he felt strangely proud of his abstinence, his body a kind of physical taunt to hers. As a result he was wasting away into nothing, his skinny-waisted trousers already hanging off him like the hand-me-downs of an older sibling. The fact that the trousers *were* hand-me-downs in the first place only confirmed as much. It was hard to envisage a more shiny-arsed pair of breeks ever having been passed from one generation to the next: he doubted he would ever fully appreciate his father's generosity in the matter. He'd invested in them so as to have at least one decent spare pair, but they'd proved too tight for his more robustly muscular build. Still, it had taken Madden's own near-naked destitution for his father to grudgingly give him the pair. The silent pleading his mother had done on Madden's behalf had finally driven him to it. They already had one patch of a not-quite-matching colour sewn roughly inside the seat. The telltale sign of the artisan-style stitching could be spied only by an observer of purpose and deliberation when Madden bent to sit. Still, he didn't suppose his colleagues in the Department of Medicine were over-keen on discovering his shameful secret. Half of them dressed similarly and called it *fashion*; ill-matching suits and trousers, bizarre combinations of beard and headwear. The sixties had not then quite washed the beatniks out of their hair, and when they did, they would only grow it long and with another disgrace of facial sprouting again a few short years later.

In Gaskell's case, he could carry on wearing exactly what he was at the moment; if it went out of style, he had only to hang in there and his attire would be back in again in a month or two. Dizzy and his eejit's nickname – a trumpeter, for Christ's sake! (or was it a saxophonist? Madden could never recall) –

and his comfy sweaters and jealous hurt. Gaskell with his affectations and pulp novels and his bloody *limericks*. Hector Fain, socialism and the Soviet Union's a great place really, if only they were all Presbyterian as well . . .

Carmen *Alessandro* with her nothing much at all, now.

Even Aduman had his scarf. A man in possession of a decent scarf could rightly expect to put less in the gas meter: a matter of crucial importance to a Senegalese in the west of Scotland with probably another three winters to endure before he graduated.

Madden would trail down the road behind his father at a distance, the idea of the pair of them sharing their respective journeys abhorrent, at least to Madden. His father seemed to favour the public houses of Byres Road, the Curlers and Tennents. Possibly he liked the walk, or perhaps the proximity of the university, the education he had never had, never needed, nor wanted, but thought was a good thing, or perhaps a bad thing depending on how effeminate he considered the place that day.

There were innumerable bedsitting rooms to see, some of them little more than cupboards containing damp mattresses and the odour of mould. He had, he realised, been somewhat naive in going to see the places with the very lowest rents first. He miscalculated in this regard, losing the slightly more upmarket rooms to savvier students. It couldn't be helped, though. He had never lived anywhere but home. Even so, the cheapest places had appalled him. Those rooms were not dwelling places; no one could have achieved anything resembling a life in such conditions. They might achieve tuberculosis, or bronchial pneumonia; it was conceivable they could achieve diarrhoea or the mange. He didn't doubt that a reasonably quick death was attainable if one were indiscriminate – as one would have to be – regarding basic nutritional hygiene, and pest control. He fully believed there were new strains of cold-adapted tropical disease that might joyously flourish in such decompositional graveyards. That the land-lords and ladies of these manors had the damned bricks to promote them publicly without fear of the law was hard to credit.

After a short while Madden began to read the notices in the shop windows with more care. Yet he still encountered such bedsits with alarming frequency, despite the growing number of checks and balances he applied to every listing he saw, the first check being the amount asked for tenancy.

He had no idea why he bothered with such a rule, really, since he had no job and no means of paying for anything until he found one, but he fancied he'd have greater luck with employment than rooms. So it turned out to be. An evening with Rose, now chaste once more since it was what God would want for her, had given Madden some better ideas regarding the matter. Colville's was out of the question, she told him.

'Steel yards? You? It'd kill you!' And she laughed caustically, not even bothering to conceal her contempt.

'My father works there . . .' he said. 'If he can do it, so can I.' Even Madden wasn't convinced by this reasoning. 'He says it'd toughen me up.'

'Toughen you up? You really think?'

'Um. It toughened him up, why shouldn't it toughen me up too?'

'Are you used to physical exercise, Madden?' Rose gawped at him over her crossed arms as they sat in a café sipping watery coffee. He wondered whether she was going off him. He hoped not: he almost enjoyed having someone to talk to, even if they never did talk about anything he was interested in. If he were honest with himself, he would have said she was his first proper friend. Discounting Gaskell. Of whom he wasn't sure and was afraid for no clearly definable reason. Gaskell seemed to fill up his thoughts a lot. There were images that dropped into his mind: flames, the cinema ablaze, a kind of hell. Writhing bodies twisting and melting into each other. Gaskell. Kincaid. Others. Carmen.

'I can get used to it,' he said, raising his coffee cup to his mouth and poking the crumbs of his Empire biscuit round the Formica table top.

'You can get used to it if you've done it all your life, maybe,' Rose said. She glanced occasionally at his dish with the half-eaten biscuit on it, so Madden made a point of picking the glazed cherry off the top and footering with it in an unconcerned manner, deliberately not putting it into his mouth. Then he placed it carefully back on top of the sweetmeat.

'Not that keen on glazed cherries,' he said. 'D'you fancy it?'

Rose looked over his shoulder. 'Now that you've played with it with your corpsey-fingers, no.'

'Whose corpsey-fingers? What does that mean?'

'Nothing. Just. You know.'

Madden didn't know. Had she heard something he wasn't aware of? Had somebody said something to her? It wasn't impossible.

'I don't know,' he said. 'I have no idea.'

'Well, just the . . . bodies and that. You know what I mean. Makes me think of poor Gaskell.'

'Poor Gaskell?'

'You know . . . Carmen. How she died. Gives me the creeps thinking about dead bodies, knowing hers is on some table somewhere, all cold and with people poking about it.'

Relief broke in a small wave over him: he hoped it didn't show. Still, he was surprised she could be so squeamish. She was a nurse, after all.

'I've not handled any bodies for a week,' he said. 'It's a holiday. There's nothing cold to handle until term starts again.'

'I just don't like the idea, that's all. It's off-putting. I can't bear the thought of you touching me after you've been touching *them*.'

'It's never bothered you before,' he said, sulking.

'You've never touched me before,' she said, staring at him flatly.

'Of course I have. I'm always touching you.'

'That's right,' she said, picking the cherry off the biscuit and pointedly dropping it into the round hole of her mouth. 'You touch me. Keep telling yourself that. I doubt you even touch *yourself.*'

That sort of talk made him feel queasy. Of course he didn't touch himself. The idea was so silly. Why would he touch himself?

He felt a shoeless foot push up between his legs under the table, and press his crotch with its warmth. He tried to pull gently away, but could get no farther than the back of the seat. Rose was sliding gradually under the table as she chased him, uncaring of who might see.

'And you *never* touch me with *that,*' Rose said, chewing on the cherry with her mouth open, as if it were a stick of gum.

He pushed her foot away with a leg, and she drew back up in her seat. He half expected her to start blowing bubbles. She leaned over and said, 'Are you going to eat this or not, corpsey-fingers?'

He shook his head and she picked the Empire biscuit up and crammed it whole into her mouth. She would regret that, he decided. An Empire biscuit was a very dry confection. All the while, Rose defiantly chewed, her mouth covered in floury crumbs and bits of icing sugar.

'Tho,' she lisped. 'Noh' Cowviwwth. Wheawh ewth then?'

'Here,' he said, passing her his now cooled coffee. 'We can start again when you speak my language.'

Rose slurped and chewed for a few more minutes and then wiped her mouth with a serviette from the tin dispenser.

'Ah,' she said. 'Where else if not Colville's, then?'

'I've no idea. The knacker's yard?'

'Funny. As if you'd be capable of doing in another creature. You haven't even got the wrist strength to do *yourself*.'

He let the remark pass.

'What about funeral services?' Rose said. 'Your corpsey-fingers'd be ideal for that.'

'Funeral services?'

'Funeral services. You're used to handling dead folk. Why not get paid for it? Might even be useful revision for you.'

He thought for a few seconds, nodding quietly to himself.

'Well?'

'Funeral services. It's an idea,' he said. 'Certainly, it's an idea . . . But I don't know anything about the trade . . .'

Rose sighed. 'Fucking hell, what's to know? You get the bodies in and give their arses a wipe and stick them back out again!'

'I'm sure there's more to it than that . . .' he said. He smirked at her as knowingly as was possible.

'Not much more,' Rose said, ignoring it. 'You just give them a lick of warpaint. You dress them in their Sunday best. You have wee chats with them about their love lives. Anything else, I'm sure you could pick up. There,' she went on, 'go and ask the man behind the counter for a phone book. You can look them up, see if anybody wants an assistant.'

Madden was again nodding, beginning to come round to the idea. He was, if anything, more qualified for such a position than most casual prospectors. It might even be fun.

'Need a special interest in the deceased to work in a place like this,' Joe Caldwell Snr had said to him after the interview. His slow manner was off-putting. It was as if he were always waiting for something more important to happen. Perhaps he was waiting for people to die, but later on Madden revised this opinion. He was measuring out time in the minutes that passed between his skinny, hand-rolled cigarettes. It was almost possible to see the slow seconds tick through his head, the consciousness of how long the day took to pass, wearing him ever down, his heavy brow permanently braced for yet another painful second to pass on the clock he had no need of, such were his timekeeping abilities.

Madden, he said, had passed the interview with flying colours. The best interviewee he'd had, and also the only.

'Most folk can't be bothered with this kind of work,' he said. 'Got a bit of a bad reputation. I've had apprentices in here take the boak. You're no squeamish, are ye?'

He glanced furtively at Madden, who shook his head in the negative.

'Aye, well. We'll see about that, heh?' Caldwell Snr pushed up the sleeves of his oversized director's blazer, then let them fall down his tattooed arms again.

Madden was still getting over the brevity of the interview. It had gone something like, *You the boy wants to apprentice. Aye? When can you start?*

Formalities over, Caldwell took him on a grand tour of what was now called the cold room. It was pretty old stuff, but functional, he said. Besides, the job was money for old rope. 'Just get them in, wipe their arse and stick them back out again,' he said. 'That's it. Ye get some bad ones in, but. I've been in here sewing and stitching for a couple of days, so I have. Folk are ayeways selfish like that.'

Madden didn't know what he meant.

'Like what?' he'd asked.

'Acht. The best they can manage is to drop deid in their own scratcher, or in the infirmary. Usually in the one piece then. But there's all these bams that come off the scaffolds, so there is.' He winked at Madden. 'Lost count of the yins that come off the scaffolds,' he added, balefully pushing his sleeves up, and once again letting them fall. He had a full head of grey hair, with a kind of tuft at the front, though Madden couldn't say what age he might be.

'Burns are bad as well,' he said. 'A bloody liberty it is.

Expecting me to deal with that. Know what my motto is, son? Naw, you widnae . . . My motto is: if the bam's already been cremated, be best cremate the bam.' He laughed a slow wheeze, as though he never tired of hearing himself say that, and Madden noticed his upper dentures slip a bit when he did, so that he had to make a twitch of the jaw to realign them.

Madden smiled, as usual too late.

'Might as well cremate them if they're burnt, heh?'

Madden smiled again, not entirely convinced he should. He was wondering whether there was anything else this old lunatic had to impart by way of wisdom. Likely plenty.

'Right,' Caldwell said. 'There's another part-timer comes in, Teuchter fella, student like yourself, so there's the three of us. Important thing is this.' He held up an old tin for keeping loose tea in. 'This is the tea money tin. We've all tae chip in. This week's my week, so I'm treating. What ye fancy?'

'To drink?'

'That's what I says, in'tit?'

'Ehm, tea, please. If you're making a cup.'

'I'm no making anything. You're the new-start. Start with the kettle.'

He gave Madden another long look. 'Just kidding.' He winked. 'Here,' he said, producing a quarter-bottle from his jacket pocket. 'This'll settle the stomach.' He took a swig and passed the bottle to Madden, and he drank too, not keen on the idea of sharing lip-space with this manky character.

'Here's tae us,' Caldwell said, taking the bottle back again and putting it to his lips. 'Damn few, and they're aw deid.'

Joe Caldwell Snr was a veritable wealth of dubious information, opinions, conjectures, myth and fact. He had some sort of genius as a receptacle for the apocryphal and plain nonsense. He was entertaining, in small doses, and administered his wisdom only in nugget-sized quantities over many years.

Madden put on an overall and joined Caldwell immediately after the interview, having no reasonable excuses to hand as to why he wasn't able to begin work there and then. Caldwell had kept his silence in the cold room that first day, treading with hushed reverence, all casual brutalities in his speech and actions concentrated by the temple-like atmosphere of the place. He showed Madden around the room, quietly indicating the location of the instrument cabinets, the standard domestic and hand sinks, the autopsy table – a fine custom-made piece of stainless steel, and the most state-of-the-art bit of equipment in the building. Caldwell seemed to need to lay hands on it, and glanced up at Madden with a sort of guilty smile, as if he had been caught stealing his own cash from the tea-money tin. There were four common features to such tables, he said, his voice low, hands fluttering over the pristine surface, reaching out as if to pick a particularly generous peach from a tree in a neighbour's garden, then drawing back.

'Now, lad, there's dimensions. Every table's the same dimensions: seven feet long by three feet and – guess what – three feet and *six inches* wide. *Six inches*, imagine that. Any idea why?' Caldwell scratched at his ruff of hair, pushed his sleeves up, exposing the faded blue of naval tattooing.

Madden said, 'No. Why six inches? Is that special?'

'Nae fucking idea,' Caldwell said. 'Thought you might be able to tell me being a uni fella and everything.'

Madden shook his head. There was nothing in his limited knowledge of the faculty syllabus that explained why these tables were the dimensions they were. Seven feet at the head and foot was plenty for your average Scot. If they got any Norwegians in, he supposed there might be problems.

'Reckon it's for fat lassies,' Caldwell said. 'Birds with a bit of extra girth and that. Hanging over the side. Mind you, I like a well-fed yin myself.' He frowned and dug around for his bottle, Madden declining his offer. 'That wife of mine was a good fat yin. Plump and that . . . you know . . .'

He made a kind of outline in the air, searching for just the right word or phrase.

'Generous?' Madden offered.

'That's the very dab. Generous. I like them generous. Plenty to go round, heh?'

Madden concurred. Not only did it seem to be the right thing to do, but it was a not dissimilar opinion to the one he held himself. A woman should be fat, or at least not thin. A malnourished woman might be susceptible to disease or exhaustion, might sicken and die, and then who would look after the children? He wasn't sure how much actual truth there was in his beliefs, but they had the benefit of a basis in logic and science. Besides, it was what his father believed, and no matter what else he might feel about the female of the species, Madden felt him to be correct in this one area. Skinny women, his father said, were effeminate. They looked like boys. *Masculine*, Madden had neglected to point out. *Skinny women looked masculine . . .*

'All the tables have got a horizontal false top, for lying the bodies on,' Caldwell carried on, his false teeth obviously uncomfortable. He kept massaging his jaw with a thoughtful look, and Madden wondered whether they were a new set just settling in.

'And they've a true top, incline-recessed for drainage. Handy things as well,' he added. 'Folk don't just stop pishing and shiteing themselves just cause they're brown breid! With this thing, just hose it doon. Hey presto, good as new. A marvel is what it is, I'm telling ye. A wonder of the twentieth century.

'Now, all tables have a drain as well – either in the centre, or at the foot. Another handy implement, if you ask me. Nae cunt ever does, but if they did say, "Mr Caldwell, in your experience what would you say had made the mortician's job a sight easier than it used to be?", well, I'd tell him just what I told you.'

Madden wasn't sure what he had told him, he spoke so quietly down here.

'I'd say, "The modern, stainless-steel, centre- or bottom-drained autopsy table into which water and gas can be piped, and within easy reach of an electrical outlet.". And I might go on to recommend certain instruments too. If I was to be asked, that is.'

He looked at Madden and paused. After a silence Madden said: 'And what . . . instruments . . . do you find most useful, in your profession . . . ?'

Caldwell was pleased with the question, because he raised his voice slightly and leaned back against the table, stroking it unconsciously with his hand.

'Well, there's many and varied instruments we use here. There's all manner, and they've all got their uses. The best of all possible instruments in the best of all possible surgeries: that's the mortuary to you.'

He went to the cabinet at the wall, opened it and began placing tools on a mobile instrument table, and with a jerk of the head indicated that Madden should join him in surveying their glories.

'These,' he said, picking up a trowel-like tool, 'are brain knives. Smashing things, so they are. Handy for stripping wallpaper as well. But,' he added with a lugubrious wink, 'we would never use them for such a purpose. Would we, heh?'

Madden shook his head.

Most of the equipment Madden was familiar with, and had at least seen if not handled, though there were the sorts of specialist instruments here that were always found in businesses dedicated solely to a single pursuit.

There were gleaming scissors (straight, curved and double-blunted) and straight scissors (pointed) in neat rows on their simple linen dress, now exposed in all their burnished naked-ness. There were bone-cutting forceps like scorpion's pincers, and rib-shears with blunted scarab heads. There were saws and bone gouges, periosteal elevators and autopsy needles. There were chisels and haemostats and double rachiotome Luer saws. Caldwell spoke their names in vaguely reverential tones, lifting them up to the light as a high priest might before opening up the chest of an Inca, before placing them once more in their sacrificial robes and closing the cabinet door.

'We've had these for years,' he said. 'Most of it. I mean, obviously the worn-out stuff gets replaced. But if an amputating knife gets blunted, you've just got to sharpen it up. 'Course, stuff gets chipped and broken all the time. That's the single biggest outlay. Broken tools. And it's a shame as well, 'cause they're things of beauty and that.'

Caldwell had a slightly foolish look on his slab of a face, and massaged his jaw self-consciously.

'I mean, somebody went to some trouble to produce they things. Craftsmanship, that's what they are. I'd rather look at they tools than the Mona Lisa. I mean, what is she? Some lassie with a toothache.'

'A toothache?'

'Aye. How else d'ye explain it? She's no grinning, she's girning. She's had a bit of root-canal work done. Either that or it's a gumboil. Oil of cloves is what she needs, I reckon.'

Caldwell seemed quite serious. 'That's no art to me,' he said. 'It's just paint. Now, the man that made *these* . . .' He opened the cabinet door again and lifted out a pair of rib-shears and held them up to the light. 'He was an artist.' He turned the shears so that their teeth caught the light and glinted cold and clear. 'What d'ye think?' he said to Madden. 'All right, it's not your samurai sword, no one's claiming that. It's maybe no gaunnae change the course of history. Neither are the rest of them in that cabinet. But, see, it's like your common man, your working man.'

Madden nodded, not following the older man's train of thought.

'You don't get it?'

Madden didn't.

'Well, you've got your samurai swords and you've got your surgical instruments. The one is forged and folded and hammered and forged and folded again, over and over. It takes months just to get the blade right, to get the decoration and that single edge ready. And they cost a lot to produce. So only the noblemen can possess them, and they're forbidden to the commoner and that. Their blades are so sharp they can cut through chain mail, and when they used to get into scrapes with Europeans with their foils and rapiers and *en garde* and whatnot guess what happened?'

'I don't know. They all got shot?'

Caldwell laughed. 'Well, aye, maybe. But that's another story. Naw, what happened was that your Europeans with their rapiers and foils could poke holes in your samurai, perforate him like a teabag.'

Caldwell paused to take a swig from his bottle and run a hand over his ruff of hair. 'Your samurai chap might have got himself stabbed five, six, seven times and still live. 'Course, he'd likely be laid up for a while, or die later, but the point is he might live, or even continue fighting. But your Europeans, Portuguese or whoever, Dutch . . . well, if the samurai gets one good clean cut in – just the one – well, that's it. The game's a bogey. His sword might take off an arm or cut you clean through the belly to the spine in one stroke. Just the one blow is all it would take and his man would be incapacitated. Now *that's* a decisive bit of kit, that. And to your samurai, it wasn't simply a work of art or a piece of fine craftsmanship: the sword was his *soul*, the essence of the man, the warrior. See what I mean?'

Madden still didn't, but nodded anyway.

'Naw you don't. Don't blame you either. It's a tricky one. But it's like this. The sword is the soul of the samurai, and all his honour is bound up with it. If a peasant brushes against it, then the noble is expected to cut him down on the spot. It's a work of art, that sword. But it's a device for the murder and oppression of one caste of people over another. So the sword represents a caste, or a class of folk. It's the samurai sword that is the bit of history that's remembered. Naebody remembers all the commoners what got stitched up – if they were lucky – by the doctors with their mass-produced tools. It's those same tools and instruments that stitch up the samurai and the Portuguese and Dutch sailors poked full of holes. Fair enough, you might say, I bet not too many peasants or workers felt the benefit of those tools, and you'd maybe be right to say it. But it would be the workers and artisans that produced them. It would be the workers and artisans that tempered their blades and made them as cheaply as they could. 'Course, it would be another class of folk – doctors and surgeons – that would use them. But the point is that, no matter what else, these tools might be said to represent the worker, the common man and the peasant, in the same way that the sword represents the nobility, a whole feudal system. A backwards and oppressive regime!'

Madden looked at him, wondering whether he was expected to say something or not, and judged that he was.

'So you're saying that these instruments are . . . *what*?'

'Simple,' Caldwell said softly. 'These tools, whatever their usage in the past, are egalitarian tools. They're a lost history. Where your nobles kill and maim, these tools are used to mend and repair. Even after death, they're used to good cause – in the name of learning and science they benefit all. Whether they feel it or no: and it is my opinion that they *do not*. And, though they're rude instruments compared to the samurai sword, they are infinitely more precious and beautiful for their simplicity. They aren't engraved, they aren't decorated: they're made in their thousands these days . . . But still . . . but still . . .'

Caldwell looked thoughtfully at the shears, then replaced them in their cabinet. 'These things are a treasure. And that's a fact.'

He sighed, and surveyed the room, though whether his look was one of pride in the trappings of the business he had founded – called simply 'Caldwell's Funeral Services' in those days, there being no Joe Jnr in the picture yet – or of a vague dissatisfaction at his lot in life, was impossible to tell. Madden wondered whether this extraordinary lecture was a sort of justification he needed to make to himself, a litany he repeated to whoever would spare an ear: a speech that more precisely meant, I'm not what you think I am. The wisecracks and spurious jokes were maybe his manner of dealing with the gloomy trade in which he was involved; and the icons of the cold room were elevated to new significance by his desire to make his job, and therefore his existence, more meaningful. Madden knew then that Joe Snr, despite his ways, had the soul of a romantic. Albeit a blue-collar one. As for himself, Madden didn't know whether he agreed with Joe Snr or not. Was funeral services a middle-class occupation? Surely not: the job was so hands-on. It was manual labour a lot of the time, he was convinced. So Joe was right.

'Right,' Joe said. 'So this is where we do the autopsies, the embalmings, though there's not so much call for that as you'd think. Most folk want the coffin closed. Now and again, though, you get someone that wants to have a keek at their deid. Wives and that, sons and daughters. So you'll need to pay attention about that bit. Where we keep the bodies is in that storage room at the back.' He motioned Madden over and opened the heavy, locked door.

'Needs to be kept between a thirty-eight- and a forty-two-degree Fahrenheit range. That's the limit, and I'd recommend that you don't forget to lock the door when you're done in there. I had this assistant a year or two back and he left the thing open a couple of nights. Some of the corpses got a bit, eh, *infested* . . .'

'Infested with what?' Madden asked.

Caldwell scratched his head and waggled his jaw. 'Maggots,' he said. 'Mostly maggots.'

'Oh.'

'The bodies have to be laid horizontally on the shelves,' he went on quietly. 'With a wooden block under the heid. After that, you just fling a clean sheet ower them. One above the other.'

Madden could see a couple of cadavers in there at the moment.

'Never gets too busy, though,' Caldwell said. 'As I say, wipe their arses and stick them back out. Got one in for autopsy the now, though. Care to take a look?'

'Oh yes,' Madden said, his interest picking up. 'Who do you have?'

Caldwell went over to a drawer in the cabinet and withdrew a clipboard. He flicked over the pages, stuck his pencil behind his ear and hummed.

'Recent one,' he said. 'Been in a couple of days. There, upon the shelf there. That's it, you can just slide it out. Aye. Pull the sheet back.'

Madden did as he was bidden.

Caldwell came over and they both looked at the washed-out face of the corpse.

'Aye. Someone done this one in,' Caldwell said. 'Polis had her for a good while, forensics and that. Usually that only takes an afternoon or so, but this yin was done in. They keep the bodies till they're about fit tae burst sometimes. Bit skinny for my tastes. Good-looking lassie, though. Sweet dreams, hen,' he said, then looked at Madden. 'Thought you could handle this stuff,' Caldwell said. 'You getting the boak or something?'

Madden shook his head. 'I'm fine,' he said. 'It's just . . . I knew her.'

'Oh aye?' Caldwell said, raising his eyebrows and pushing his sleeves up again.

Madden nodded, but declined to add anything else. The body on the shelf belonged to a second-generation Italian girl, her family possibly from the Barga area, migrants who owned a café down on the West Coast. Ayr, Troon, somewhere like that.

Caldwell said he would talk Madden through some of the basics: he was welcome to have a look with him at this asphyxiation. He meant, obviously, Carmen Alexander. Of course, the police pathologist had given her the once-over already, he told Madden, who listened in queasy admiration to Joe Caldwell's autopsy explanation. Carmen wore the kind of grimace that Madden had often heard described but had seen for himself only once before.

She was not pretty to behold. Not any more. The gums she'd been so self-conscious about had turned a darkish hue, and the lips were drawn tightly back, the tongue not protruding in the manner of, say, a garrotting or hanging, but tucked neatly inside the mouth, shyly out of sight. There was some kind of lingering beauty to her, though. A ghost of a beauty lost now, only its shadow somewhere near the eyes, the forehead. The pitiful way her fists were clenched across her chest.

She was naked. Madden looked at her breasts, the large pink aureoles of her nipples, their pointed tips. Beneath the surface of her skin wandered pale blue veins like underground rivers. Madden began to sweat, trying not to see it. But the image was already there:

Taking her arms, her wailing and grunting for breath over now, eternally.

Madden couldn't help but look at her pubic hair, surprised that it wasn't brown or blonde, or even ginger. But of course. She got her colour out of a bottle. The hair between her legs gave away her Mediterranean ancestry as surely as her surname. Yet she had altered hers to Alexander. Surprising, then, that she hadn't bothered to match collars and cuffs.

'See where they make the incision?' Caldwell was saying. He'd not bothered to dress for the occasion: the autopsy had been done. He was just talking Madden through it. This one would get embalmed and the coffin would be open – she'd been a good-looking girl. Her ma and da would want to say their last goodbyes. Plus, they were Catholics, he said. Catholics were more inclined to have open coffins and public viewings. And, because she was only a lassie, they were having some special sort of service for her up at the university where she'd studied. A terrible shame, really. Caldwell wouldn't have been surprised if there were hundreds of folk there, people she'd never even met when she was alive. That happens, he said. When a youngster cops it, every cunt turns up. That was part of the reason she hadnae been interred yet: these things had to be arranged properly, gie everyone a chance to come along for a shufti. Well, that and the police coroner.

'We sometimes – like the police surgeon has done here – have to do a total, complete autopsy. Know what that means?'

'Examine the body inside and out?'

'That's it, right enough. Inside and out. Thorax, neck, abdomen, pelvis and heid. Check everything's present and correct, heh?' He smiled at Madden. 'This lassie's been stitched up again nice, so she has. I did that bit after she arrived here. See how regular the stitches are? My wife showed us how to sew. Personally, I'd have liked to get a sewing *machine*, but there you go. Nothing doing there. It's not like the stitches you need for the injuries on live folk, by the way. You can just do these – like I've done here – as if you were taking in a pair of troosers.'

Madden followed the line of the cut between Carmen's breasts, and down through the abdomen and into the groin, the symphysis pubis. Below her neck, the stitches ran off to the left and right clavicles.

' 'Course, you have to do the arse and fanny up tight,' Caldwell said.

'Eh?' Madden said. 'The what?'

Caldwell went inexplicably red. 'Acht,' he said, 'you know what I mean.'

Madden realised that the poor man was embarrassed by the medical terminology. 'A ligature for the anal and genito-urinary orifices,' Caldwell went on, eyes on the body, away from Madden's. 'So there's no seepage,' he added. 'I find a four-ply suture good for the job.'

'Oh,' Madden said.

'Aye. This one here – well, we've had the brain out already. You can hardly see where the face came off . . . all we've got to do is set her expression right.'

Madden was impressed with the neatness of the job, and surprised that her last expression had stayed on her face even though that same face had been pulled down over her skull like a polo-neck sweater.

'Will you be able to alter the expression to everyone's, ah, satisfaction?' Madden asked.

Joe Caldwell stood up and scratched the back of his head. 'Well . . . that's a tricky one. Maybe aye and maybe naw. Should be good enough to view in this case, excepting that she was obviously such a good-looking lassie that you're never gaunnae get a really satisfactory job done, know what I'm saying?'

Madden said he did.

'I mean, if it's a lassie, then in some ways you're better off with a real growler,' Joe added, staring intently at the girl's face. 'This yin's a peach but. Could do with a bit mair meat on her, maybe. Too skinny for my tastes. If she was a pure dug, naebody'd be bothered how good a job ye did. Less work, less attention to detail. Stands to reason, doesn't it?'

'In what way?'

'Well, let's face it, no one takes very close notice of ugly folk, do they? No even their maws and paws. Like they're gaunnae come up to me and say, "Right, I know my wee

Marie was kind of rough, but d'ye not think ye could have done a better job with her nose than that?" See what I mean? The details gets lost if your client's got a face like a rhino's bawbag.'

'I see,' said Madden.

'For one thing, if it's a close relative, they're quite likely to be nae looker themselves. And they don't want to draw attention to that. This one here, she should be all right. Depends.' Caldwell Snr tapped Carmen on the nose with a forefinger and then leaned down against the autopsy table, resting his chin on his forearms. He sighed slowly.

'She was strangled, this one,' he said. 'A murder. Throttled and then dumped in the river to fool the polis.'

Madden was by the Kelvin banks once again, the hard thump of his own hoarse breathing in his ears, the steady pattering of the rain on the leaves of the trees.

'No fooling anybody, but. She was asphyxiated, not drowned. Take a look at her, hardly waterlogged at all. Hardly any gas in the tissues.' He shook his head slowly. Madden said nothing. 'The thing is,' Caldwell went on, 'whoever did this either knew nothing about how a body behaves after death, or wants everyone to think they know nothing about it. This lassie was a medical student as well. That makes me kind of suspicious. Doesn't it make you suspicious yourself?' He glanced over at Madden, who felt damp under his shirt.

'I suppose so,' he said, picturing her nylons torn and hanging free of one leg, her lips drawn back in the death grimace. Undergrowth and the weather always a constant. Her killer making sure they were alone. The gloom of the dankness, the relentless foliage. Mud, bracken, putting one foot in front of another. Shale and shingle and lapping water. A weir not too far away, the bough of a long-fallen tree. Giant hogweed all around.

'Tell you what,' Caldwell said, perking up. 'The bastard that did this knew something about how to do it efficiently. The bruises on the neck there . . .' Madden looked at the bluish marks on either side of her throat, faint and not at all the sort of thing produced by face-to-face manual strangulation.

'That's no really your typical mark. In fact, it's no really an asphyxiation in the regular sense.'

Madden raised his head, listening only vaguely. The body floating, hidden by tree boughs; knee high in water. The body semicircling clockwise, turned by the current.

'What is it, then?' Madden asked, not particularly caring.

'That's pressure on blood flow to the head. Not oxygen. Someone would have to know what they were doing. They'd need to apply a particular kind of choke.'

Madden looked at him. 'And what sort of person might have the knowledge to do that?' he asked.

Caldwell whistled. 'Now you're talking. Loads of folk. Folk with military training. Someone that knew how to wrestle. Maybe even doctors. You know, close combat stuff. I learned a few tricks in the navy myself . . .'

'Show me how you think it was done,' Madden said.

Caldwell looked at him and shrugged in a resigned sort of way.

'Acht, I cannae remember much about it now. There were all sorts of ways. This one would have to be applied from the rear. I think. Like I says, I'm no expert.' He crossed his hands in front of his face in a vague impression of the sort of thing he meant. 'The police fella agreed.'

'How d'you know that it was applied from the rear?'

'Well . . .' Caldwell scratched his head, embarrassed again at having to explain what he meant. He'd have made a useless teacher. 'The position of the bruises, and the way there's no finger marks. In the normal course of a throttling, you'd expect to see bruises around the windpipe, possibly damage to it too. Crushing. There's none of that here . . .'

'Indicating?'

'Indicating that whoever did this probably put it on from behind,' he said. 'Using a kind of choke hold, or a pressure hold to squeeze out the blood flow to the brain. Like I said. Using their forearm maybe. The thing I remember about those kinds of holds was that the victim passes out very quickly. I mean, literally within seconds of the hold getting put on. Bang, that's it, lights out. Not even particularly unpleasant either. If you keep the choke on for long enough—'

'How long?'

'I dunno, twenty or thirty seconds? If you hold it that long, the victim will die. Dead easy. Like I say: good night, Vienna.'

'And you think that's what happened here?'

Caldwell looked uncomfortable, didn't care to be taken too seriously.

'Nae idea really,' he said, rolling his sleeves up once more and scratching at his tuft of hair. 'It's possible. There's other ways too but. What the hell, I'm no a polis! Let them work it out.'

Madden focused on Carmen, thinking. Her hair was lustreless now, matted and caked in some sort of slimy substance, undoubtedly the contents of the stagnant pool by the shoals she'd been discovered in. He had heard there had been an anonymous call to the police.

'Show me the choke,' Madden said. 'Show me how you think it was done.'

Caldwell crossed his forearm into the crook of his other arm, at the elbow. 'I showed you already. Like this,' he said. 'Maybe.'

'No,' Madden said. 'Could you demonstrate it on me? I mean, using me as a dummy?'

Caldwell shrugged and waggled his teeth back into place. 'Sit doon, then, I can give it a go,' he said, motioning Madden to come over. 'It'll be quick, if I do it right,' he said. 'Painless.' He stood behind Madden and placed his left forearm across his windpipe, locking it into the crook of his other elbow.

Madden felt the palm of Joe's right hand against the back of his head, and a constriction, not being able to breathe, and he coughed, reached his hands up towards the choking limb, a sudden recollected horror seizing him. But then black fireflies swam in front of him and there was nothing.

He rubbed his sore throat. The choke had come on so quickly that he'd felt only the most momentary discomfort. Then he had been out cold. It was just like Joe said. Lights out. Bang. Good night, Vienna.

He hadn't any idea of time when it happened. He couldn't remember anything about it.

Joe apologised profusely afterwards, saying he should never have done it, it was dangerous. And it might not even be the way it had happened anyway. Madden, though, knew that it was. He had absolutely no doubt in his mind that this was how it had been done. He could see it happen in front of him. The girl, walking along the path by the river; the assailant stepping out from the bushes, a hand going across her throat. The forearm locking into the crook of the elbow and her eyes glazing over before she had time to make a sound. Then being dragged back into the undergrowth where her dead body was raped, even as it lay still twitching. If such a thing were possible. Could a dead body be raped? Certainly it wasn't likely to offer any great resistance.

It had been a long day. And not yet over, but he decided to forgo the usual bout of food scavenging at his parents' and treat himself. A fish supper would be well earned: he could think of it as a sub from his wages. He crossed back to Dumbarton Road through the tenements and followed the bright lights, letting them lead him to fried potatoes and battered haddock. He was ravenous. The smell of the chippy washed over him like a hot surf, and his stomach groaned in appreciation, it was so long since he'd had a decent meal. No growing man could live on scraps of cold meat and Empire biscuits indefinitely. He was famished. Resurrected men like himself, those lucky enough to get another bite at the apple, needed sustenance. Perhaps more so than those who had yet to die their first time. And as deaths went, it had been better than most. If he ever were given the right to choose the manner of his own execution, that would be the method he would choose. Clean, and quick. Hardly any discomfort at all. A good death.

Eleven

The chips had been limp and stale, and the grease had coagulated on his fingertips in the cold night air as he walked up the steps of his parents' tenement, then stepped back down as two policemen in uniform exited it. One was a good foot taller than Madden, a distinct height advantage, and that without even considering the helmet. He had placed a hand on his shoulder, an action that filled Madden with dread, as if he were about to be walked up the steps and swung from the gibbet there and then.

'Hugh Madden?' he said, his tone brooking no argument. Madden would have felt pity for himself if he were forced to say, No, actually, Officer, you've got the wrong man. Instead he nodded, trying to suppress his urge to scream and limp headlong into the night without looking back. He would simply keep on going until he ran off the edge of the world.

'We'd like a wee word, son,' the officer said. He had a large head, turnip shaped, with a wide, flat boxer's nose and the ears of a rugby player. His height, and a fair degree of corpulence, gave the impression of impressive physical abilities now gone somewhat to seed. An athlete at school, perhaps now too partial to his pie and his pint.

The smaller man with him – obviously the one in charge – leaned against the bonnet of the police car smoking a cigarette. He'd said nothing yet, but was clearly trying to create an impression.

'Yes, Officer,' Madden said, politeness costing nothing. 'How can I help you?'

The smaller man threw down his fag and ground it underfoot.

'Wondered if you'd like to take a ride with us, Hugh,' he said, opening up the back door of the vehicle and gesturing inside. Madden noted the seat to be scattered with empty fag boxes and drained bottles. The label on one read 'India Pale Ale'.

'I've to be at my mother's soon,' Madden said, realising immediately how pathetic he sounded. It wasn't as if he was only ten years old any more.

'Don't you worry yourself about your mammy, son,' the tall officer said, grinning. 'I'm sure she'll not mind you helping us with our enquiries.'

Madden climbed into the back seat of the car, pushing the empty packets and bottles aside with distaste. The big policeman got in the driver's seat, and the smaller one with the nasty-looking scar running from cheek to hinge took the front passenger seat. Madden waited for one of them to say something. The smaller one turned round in his seat awkwardly.

'Now, Hugh,' he said, smiling in a serious but affable way, 'We've been by your mother's place before, but we must have just missed you. As it happens, there was no harm done. You know why we wanted to speak to you, don't you?'

'Who are you?' Madden asked.

'We were investigating the murder of an acquaintance of yours,' the man with the scar said. Madden fidgeted in his seat: his legs and buttocks were itching.

'We're just interested parties, Mr Madden. We have certain leads to follow up, certain information . . .'

The man with the scar looked ill at ease in his police uniform; his hat, before he'd removed it to squeeze in, had sat too low over his ears, and the moustache he had grown in an obvious attempt to disguise his facial disfigurement was patchy and scrub-like.

He leaned towards Madden and glowered at him with intensity. Madden wished for once that he *was* upstairs at home, that he was locked safely in his room with his maps and anatomical drawings and his pet rats, or still being lectured by Caldwell in the safety of his cold room. Where was Gaskell? Where was anyone? He felt like crying out, the noose tightening around his neck.

The scarred man saw his distress and reached over and placed a hand on his knee. 'Now,' he said, 'don't you be getting all worked up just yet, Mr Madden. We're not here to charge you with anything, all right? Just a wee item wants clarifying, that's all. OK?'

Madden breathed unsteadily through his nose.

'Who are you?' he said.

'Who are we, Mr Madden? Well, who'd you think we are?' He looked at his colleague in the driver's seat and they both laughed, as if at a private joke. 'We're working the case. We're the boys that're keeping an eye on things. Who d'you think we are?'

Madden said he didn't know.

'Take a look at these uniforms, Hugh. D'you mind if we call you Hugh? Why, we're about all that stands between civilisation and anarchy out there,' he said, gesturing with a hand. 'You might well say that we are representatives of civilisation. We're the *boot* and the *truncheon*. That no right, Davie?'

'Right enough indeed, chief,' the bigger man said, staring hard at Madden in his rear-view mirror.

'So, as the boot and the truncheon, we're here in our official capacity. That is to say, we wish to ask a few questions, Hugh. *A few questions of you, Hugh,*' he said, giving the words a musical lilt and chuckling to himself. He slapped the bigger man, Davie, playfully on the shoulder.

'What do you want to know?' Madden asked, flexing his fist. His fingertips were slightly numb from the use of the surgical instruments he'd been practising with in Caldwell's.

'Well. Now. What do we want to know, Davie? That's a good question. That's a corker of a question. I mean, what is there to know? In this case, there's so much. First off, there's you, Hugh, there's you . . . You knew *her*, did you not?'

Madden shook his head. 'I never knew her,' he said. 'I knew of her, but I didn't know her.'

The chief frowned. 'You knew *of* her but didn't know her? She was going out with a friend of yours, wasn't she? Owen Gaskell? Yet *another* medical student?'

Gaskell was another medical student, yes. He was a colleague, yes. He had gone out with Carmen Alessandro, yes, it was true. But Madden was now convinced of one thing: Owen Gaskell was *not* his friend.

'He isn't a friend of mine,' he said.

'He sure isn't your friend, Mr Hugh,' the chief said.

Madden shrugged at him, confused.

'No siree, he ain't no friend of your'n. Not no how.'

'No way,' said Davie. 'Friends like that, they'll stab ye in the back, so they will.'

'I believe he already *has* stabbed you in the back,' the chief said, thoughtfully tracing the outline of his scar through his moustache.

Madden's chest tightened; he could feel himself get light headed, the rigor descending.

'What d'you mean?' he said. 'How has he stabbed me in the back?'

'Don't you remember, Hugh? Don't you remember going down to the Kelvin? It was a wet, wet night, Hugh. I'd have remembered. I'd have minded . . .'

But he couldn't remember all of it, that was the trouble. He could see flashes of it in the dark. Glimpses that winked at him like individual lenses in an insect's compound eye. He could see parts, but not the whole.

'I had a fever, then,' he said. 'I don't remember everything.'

'Well. Your friend Owen Gaskell—'

'He's *not* my friend.'

'No. He's not. He's the *boot*, in this case. He's the foot putting the boot into you. He's the truncheon battering your nut.'

Madden was bewildered. 'What are you talking about?' he said, his voice a thin cry. 'What do you mean?'

The chief with the scar looked at him, and reached behind him into the car for something. He produced a large brown envelope with some bulky object inside.

'This,' he said, reaching into the bag, 'is what I mean.'

He held in his hand a plain brown brogue, one finger hooked inside a hole in the sole. At the toe, there was a dark stain.

'Aye,' said Davie, his gaze meeting Madden's in the rear-view mirror, 'he's stabbed you in the back good and proper. Booted you right intae touch, so he has.'

That wasn't good enough, they told him at the station. The shoe was up there for some other reason. Was he seriously trying to tell them he'd decided to climb into the Way? Why would anyone climb into the Way? There was a gate only fifty or sixty feet distant! He could have walked through and saved himself the bother! Now, if someone had wanted out of the Way, they might climb the fence. If someone was in a hurry, if someone needed out fast, or if they had panicked, or if they were afraid of someone else, then they might have lost their reason momentarily, they might have decided to climb rather than look for the gate. And it was a stormy night, too. On a night like that, anyone might have lost the plot. Anyone might have. Because anything was possible on that sort of a night.

Madden shook his head and leaned into his hands. He

couldn't remember, he couldn't recall any of it, he told them. It was later he had gone back, another rainy night, a storm actually, if the truth be told.

Back? He went back? So he had been there before? He had gone down there before . . . ?

Yes, he had gone down there before, he'd been there many times. He'd lived his whole life in the city! Of course he'd been back!

But why go there on that night? Why go there then?

He hadn't gone back there that night, he said. He hadn't gone there then. It was a mistake. He had climbed over the fence because he was sick. He hadn't been well.

Yes, they understood that. They understood that he hadn't been well, they said. He must have been very sick indeed. He must have been very ill. After what he had done, they were sure he must be pretty fucking sick in the head. Wasn't that it? He was a sick fucker, doing that to any lassie. Choking her to death and then shagging her! That was fucking sick, man, that's what that was.

He hadn't choked anyone to death, he said. And she was molested before her asphyxiation. But he did know how it was done.

That was good, they said. That was fucking rich. Of course he knew how it was done 'cause he fucking well done it! He was the sick fucker that had gone down to the Kelvin Way, grabbed the girl and strangled her half to death in the bushes and then fucked her body. That was a joke, that. Of course he fucking well knew how it was done. It would be best if he tried a wee bit harder to remember some more of the fucking details. That might be a fucking idea to start with.

But he couldn't remember, he said. He hadn't been well. His memory was sometimes bad. If something upset him, he said. If he was upset. Sometimes he would forget stuff, kind of shut it out. Not all of it. Just bits and pieces. But he couldn't always remember the details of everything. He didn't know

whether he'd killed the girl. He didn't think so. If Gaskell said
he did, then he was even more sure.

Why more sure?

Because of this.

What?

Being here.

Why being here?

Being here was down to Gaskell. Gaskell put him here.
Gaskell must have told them about the shoe, where to find it.
He must have heard him talk about losing it when he'd been
delirious. He must have gone looking for it.

What about the choke? What about that?

And there's something else.

Tell us.

She didn't deserve it, to die like that.

No one does. Was that the something else?

I didn't do it.

Then they put him in the cell to think things over, they
said, only enough room there for a metal bunk with a wool
blanket on it and a tin bucket in the corner. Let me out! he
screamed. Let me out!

But they wouldn't let him out. They were keeping him
there. And he could see how they might keep him there
for ever. No one knew he was being held captive. He might
simply disappear, they might make him disappear. It was cold
and dirty, the mattress filthy, and he couldn't lie on it, he
simply couldn't. He could see now the thousand other men
who'd lain there, watched them snore and defecate and cry
and moan and suffer fits of delirium tremens and die. And die.
Now they wanted him to die here too, unknown and forgotten. Well, he wouldn't die for them! If they wanted him to
die they would have to give him a fair and decent kangaroo
court, a partial hearing of the first order, and he'd confess then
only if some higher personage such as the Pope demanded it.

So this was where he'd be found guilty. This was where old

Caldwell would have to take him down from the gibbet. The gibbet wasn't quick, the noose wasn't quick. Not always. Sometimes you might dangle there for an hour, slowly suffocating with a neck not quite snapped clean. If you didn't go quick enough they'd swing on your legs! Drag you down!

He couldn't abide the thought, and began to scream and rattle the bars on the door, the steel trap shut on the other side cold and blank and inhuman. No one listening. Let me out! I'm innocent! You can't hang me! I'm innocent!

But no one came to the door and he kicked it violently with his decent foot and then with his bad foot, which hurt immensely, and he shook the bars and screamed himself hoarse. His clothes were soaked through with sweat and suddenly the steel trap opened and a face told him to shut up. Then the trap shut again. He screamed and cried and screamed for he didn't know how long. Hours.

Then he sat in the corner by the tin bucket and cried and rocked back and forth and then finally lay down on the filthy mattress and slept. In his dreams there were spiders spinning webs all around him, slowly winding him up in their nets, and one, fat and squat, crept towards him in infinitesimal move-ments while he struggled to free himself, and yet could not move his paralysed body. He tried screaming but his mouth stayed silent, and the closer the spider got the less mobile he became. It was almost on him when he told himself, This is a dream. Get out of the dream, get out of the dream. But when he woke, sodden with sweat, he was in another net, this one made of bricks and mortar and with the spiders on the other side of the door.

And then he heard it rattle and it swung ajar, the big man with the boxer's nose on the other side, and another stranger. Do you want out now? they asked. He nodded and they beckoned him to stand and when he did they took an arm each and guided him out and he was on the street again.

Go on. You're free. For now.

Free?

For now.

It was morning again. Morning was always turning up these days, even when he least expected it. He was due nowhere, except perhaps at his parents. He had no lectures. Rose was at work.

He walked along, gingerly avoiding putting too much strain on his damaged foot, now aching all over again from kicking the cell door. At first he was disoriented from lack of sleep and the bright incongruousness of daylight, and was not at all sure what police station he'd been let out of, until he recognised the cranes peering over the shoulders of the tenements and knew he was in Patrick. The bottom end. He shivered as the chill air swept through his damp clothes and walked along until he met Caldwell letting himself into the home.

'Up early, are you not?' he said, hardly paying Madden's presence any mind. He wore a long, knee-length herring-bone coat that had seen distinctly better days, but then Madden cut not much of a figure in the sartorial stakes either. Caldwell and he were people who wore what was to hand, and even if they had known how to dress well and had the money to indulge whatever feeble sense of style each possessed, they would neither of them have bothered anyway.

'I spent the night in the cells,' Madden said. There seemed little point in trying to keep it secret.

Caldwell raised his not-young-not-old eyebrows, and continued rattling through the myriad keys he had on his massive brass key chain.

'Nothing *illegal*, I take it?' he said. 'Can't have the staff getting themselves flung in the jail for criminal reasons, heh? Anything else would be fine, you understand. It's purely a matter of principle.'

'I don't know if it's legal or not,' Madden said. 'I don't feel like I've done anything against the law.'

He shivered again and Caldwell stood aside to let him in. It was even colder in the Welcome Room.

'Put the kettle on, then, son,' Caldwell said. 'Ye look as if you could do with a warm-up.'

Madden nodded profusely, blowing on his hands and stamping (very tenderly) with his feet.

When they had their tea, and the two-bar electric was fully warmed up in the office, Caldwell fixed Madden with a look.

'So what's this all about with the polis, then? You no a bit too old to be getting banged up for the night? Never figured you for the type.' He slurped his tea loudly, and let out an audible *aah* after every sip. He was what Madden's mother would have called a *tea jenny*. Every five minutes with a fresh brew.

Madden paused, not sure how to begin, sipping from his own mug.

'Out with it, damned spot,' Caldwell said, putting a rolled cigarette to his lips and inhaling enthusiastically. He leaned back in the worn old armchair with the sagging seat.

'I'm a suspect in that girl's murder,' Madden said, with no other more gentle way to put it. 'The one downstairs.' After speaking, he hung his head in a childish attitude of guilt.

Caldwell cleared his throat loudly. 'You're . . . a . . . *what* are ye? A murder suspect in a murder? Am I hearing right?'

Madden nodded again, but said nothing.

'The polis suspect you put the kibosh on her?'

'Someone volunteered evidence against me.'

'Someone done what? Done the dirty on you! What sort of evidence we talking here?'

'They found my shoe near the murder scene. It was stuck up on a railing. A friend . . . a *colleague* of mine told them it was there. I don't know how he found it.'

Caldwell frowned, stroked his ruff of hair and tapped his cigarette ash into a dirty mug on the draining board beside the sink.

'So this colleague of yours . . . he was sniffing about down there as well, was he? And what was your shoe doing up on that railing?'

Madden shook his head. He didn't know why he was telling Joe this, wasn't at all convinced it was a good idea.

'I went down there to have a look around. After she was already dead. I had a fever, I wasn't all there, I don't think.' He had an urge to talk now, and perhaps that was why he'd come to Joe. Joe, his employer, who expected nothing from him. Who was indifferent. Who didn't care. 'The police think I was involved and I remember some things. But I don't know what they mean, how real they are. It's like I'm not there. Or as if I'm watching myself.' He looked to see what reaction he was getting from Joe, but Caldwell simply smoked, gazing off at some point beyond the corner of the small greasy window that lit the place.

'I feel like I'm watching myself or that there's more than one me, and I don't know which the real one is.' He felt his hands shaking and pushed them into his trouser pockets. 'I've got this girlfriend, you know . . .'

Joe nodded with a grunt, puffed his fag. 'Rose,' he said. 'You said she was nice and plump. That's the way I like 'em myself . . .'

'Yes, Rose. But I don't know what she wants of me. I can't see it. I see myself with her and I don't understand why or how it happened. I can see myself handing in papers at the university and I remember writing them, but the work wasn't my own. D'you know what I mean?'

He looked imploringly at Joe, but his employer only nodded his head.

'I don't remember. My mind's a blank, my life's a blank. I don't know how I got here. I don't remember going from A to B. I know that C should follow, but I don't see the connections. There aren't any connections if I can't see them. Do you see them, Joe? Do you see what it is I'm saying?'

226

He was aware of his teeth chattering, of a kind of intensity that he rarely felt but that he wanted to last just a little bit longer. Some sort of act to take over. Some sort of action. If he had killed Carmen Alessandro, maybe that was why. It was a decision. A choice.

He picked his mug up and took a gulp of the lukewarm contents.

Joe Caldwell shifted in his seat and looked up at Madden.

'Son, I think you need to get some sleep. That's what I think.' He stubbed out his cigarette in the cup, and stood up. 'I don't know how I can help you,' he said. 'But it sounds to me as if you've been shat on by this mate of yours. You didn't kill the lassie. I'd have known it if you had the other day. You're not a killer, so you've nothing to worry about. Maybe you stumbled into something you never expected to stumble into and got a bit of a shock. Maybe that's what happened.'

He clapped Madden on the shoulder and put the kettle back on the hob again. 'Another brew for the pair of us,' he said. 'Then you should get your head down. You can kip here on the couch if you keep out of the road of the customers. How's that sound?'

Madden said it sounded like a good idea, and accepted readily. He wasn't sure whether he would sleep, though, he said.

'I've the very dab for that,' Joe said, and slipped his hand into his inside breast pocket. 'Here,' he said, handing Madden his bottle. 'Compliments of Caldwell's. What you need's to get a hot toddy inside ye. I'll let you see to it yourself.'

Joe Caldwell Snr ambled off to check on downstairs, where Carmen Alessandro was still lying, almost ready for her big send-off. Madden sat down in a sagging armchair and dozed off momentarily till the screaming of the kettle brought him blearily back to consciousness. He wrapped the dirty dishcloth around his hand and picked it off the hob, before remembering to put a tot of whisky in the cup first, with a couple of spoonfuls of caster sugar out of a soiled-looking bag next to the sink. He poured the hot water in, stirring it for a long while before settling back on to the armchair again. He took a sip and felt its pleasing warmth cauterise his senses. He took three or four more sips, savouring the sweetness and the warmth, the way each mouthful could be tracked all the way down his gullet into the pit of his stomach. Then he got up and stretched out on the couch, pulling his jacket over himself. He could hear the wireless in the other room, and felt himself almost at home, almost comfortable. Then he was asleep.

There was a room available on Wilton Street, the same building as Gaskell's, and he decided to go up there and see it, though he knew already what to expect. It was a bleak, soot-blackened place, yellowed in the places that had, for some inexplicable reason, failed to become coated with the stuff like the rest of the building. The yellowed places seemed to exist here and there, strange outcroppings that produced a pitted, uneven appearance on the surface of the building, like a lunar landscape. He stood waiting at the door for the landlady to open it, and would have turned there and then and left, except that he was determined, and he was hungry, and he had no desire to go home or speak to Rose, all of which settled the matter for him. He understood that normal, less effeminate males might spend an hour or two in a public house reading a paper and drinking a pint rather than wander the streets to pass the time, but such options didn't seem to be available to him. So, he waited for the woman to unlock the door.

She seemed unsettled by the sight of him, as though he were a familiar face with no name to put to it. That he understood. He had no name to put to himself either. Who was it that had asked him *what he was*?

Was that even the correct question? *What, why, if he was* . . . any one might have done. He followed her up the darkened stairwell, while she indicated neighbouring rooms on either side of the landings as they passed.

A short woman, stocky, with a poodle-like skullcap of rollers embracing her scalp. She had a net over them, and a face that hung down underneath that was completely round, flat and without discernible features. Madden knew she had a nose – he'd seen her wear it before – but it seemed to have sunk flat into her face. Two black orifices nestled there, where it had been. Her mouth, too, had been absorbed into the mass of spongy flesh. It had ceased to be a mouth at all; it was a sort of grasping muscle.

She plodded upwards, wheezing heavily with each step she took.

These steps would be the death of her, she said, but Madden was distracted by closed doors all around. He felt eyes at the keyholes and peering at him from cracks in the walls. The single hall light bulb wobbled slightly in the air above him, wafted by an imperceptible breeze. It was cold, yet the dampness in the air could be felt in the lungs, the chest.

She aimed a childish hand at a door. 'These used to be flats, but we broke them up intae separate rooms. There's a medical student lives in here, know him, do ye?' she said. 'Strange fella. Wears a green corduroy suit. The idea. Perhaps you'd like to see the room next door? There's two to let. You can see both. Or just the one. Whichever you prefer.'

Madden said he would like to see only one.

She pushed open an outer door that pulled itself shut behind them. There was the row of small rooms with their small doors, and at the end of the small corridor Gaskell's small attic room, up two steps and looking very much like the bolt-hole of some monstrous vermin. There was no light shining under the door. He must be out. Perhaps a matinée at the Rio Locarno.

The landlady flexed the anus in her face at him – he saw one or two lonely teeth inside – and she reached to unlock the door of one of the rooms to the left, opened it and let him step inside before her. She clicked on the main light and he was standing in a room of almost impossible decrepitude.

'Nice wee room here,' she said. 'Smashing for a student, eh? You've got your bed over there – iron frame on it too – your cupboard and wardrobe . . . you've even got a wee Baby Belling to heat up your tea. There's the gas meter down behind the door. Very reasonable too, I might add. What d'ye think?'

Madden looked around at the decor, all a kind of yellowing brown. There was no wallpaper on the walls: they had instead been covered in newspaper pages, and painted over in layers. The headlines had begun to seep through. He supposed, at least, that he wouldn't lack for reading matter if he decided to take the place. He might redecorate himself if it was allowed; medical notes and case studies. Dissections, pathologies.

Except he had no intention of staying. Not for long, anyway.

Neither was there any carpet, only an ill-fitting piece of green linoleum with a fleur-de-lis pattern on it. An entire galaxy of cigarette burns dotted its surface, and here and there were wee dust storms and mould clotting. The room seemed to be at a raised level somehow: the ceiling bisected the single window, and drops of brown condensation formed at spots here and there on its bulbous surface. One of them splashed on to the top of his head while he stood there.

'Rent's paid in advance,' the squat woman said. 'Weekly.'

'So I give you a week in advance?' Madden clarified. He felt like some sort of giant in this room, an effect of the low ceiling, and being on the top floor.

'Two weeks in advance,' the woman said, scratching the back of her leg with a shin. Madden tried not to see the bare flesh of the limbs as they rubbed against each other. 'There's a few house rules, but,' she went on. 'Nae female company after six in the evening. Nae gambling, drinking or gatherings of more than three folk. Nae dugs or cats or other pets of any kind allowed on the premises. That goes the same . . .' she said, staring hard at Madden with watery black eyes, 'for the blind.'

Madden went over and opened a drawer in the cabinet near the bed. There was no bottom to it. He pushed it shut again, and drew open the filthy blind, trying to see down below through glass opaque with dirt. The orange of the street lamps illuminated his face with a diffuse fuzz. It was not necessary to take more than one or two steps to have everything within reach.

'Any other rules?' he asked. The woman hummed and hawed and then said, 'There's a list of the furnishings which tenants are liable to replace if any're damaged, stolen or otherwise . . .' She searched for the right word. '. . . *molested.*'

'Molested?' Madden echoed, letting it slip out before he was able to check himself.

'That's what I says, in'tit?' the woman snapped, jutting her head forward. 'Any molestation will have to be paid for out the tenant's ain poakit. And that's my last word on the matter.' She stood back, arms folded across her chest, her mouth become a tight line that seemed to bend all her features out of shape.

Madden reached up and smeared a palm across the dew drops on the ceiling. 'There's condensation here. It's not good for you.'

The woman stood unmoved.

'It's *watter*, is it no?' she said. 'Watter's *healthy*. Folk *drink* it.'

'If you knocked a few shillings off the rent . . .'

'Take it or leave it,' she said.

'When can I move in?' Madden asked.

'Here's the keys,' she said. 'Gie's the rent and it's yours the now.'

Madden sighed and handed over the money, managing to

persuade her that one week in advance was all he had on him at the moment. Which was true. The landlady, Effie, changed her malign tone as soon as she saw hard cash and offered to bring him a mug of hot tea up, but he declined, saying it was most kind, but that he'd eaten and drunk only an hour or so before. He ushered her out of the room as politely as possible, locked the door and sat down on the bed. Everything in the room felt damp, wet, heavy. He took out Caldwell's bottle and set it on the cabinet beside the bed. Then he took his notepad and pen out, and began to write on it. It read:

I'm next door if you wish to discuss the girl.

When he had finished, he unlocked the door, took the note and pushed it under the door of the neighbouring room.

Twelve

'Who's in there?'

Madden sat up in the dark, pushing his glasses back up his nose. He was holding his breath.

The voice outside knocked quietly on the door.

'Who's in there, I said!'

Madden got up and went over to the door and listened, his breath coming in hard lumps.

'I won't ask again!' Gaskell said. 'I'm warning you.'

Madden braced himself, then put his key in the lock, the darkness of the room only a slight comfort. He opened the door a fraction and looked at Gaskell's squinting face, his nose swollen still, and now with a black eye. With a single movement he yanked the door open, grabbed Gaskell with both hands and spun him into the room. He reeled out of control into the far corner and went crashing into the floor by the bottom of the wardrobe. Madden was in front of him before he had time to register it, and kicked Gaskell hard in the face with his good foot. He felt the dull crunch of something giving way beneath it. Gaskell gave a little moan.

Madden got on top of him and pushed the empty whisky bottle into his ruined mouth.

'What do you want?' Gaskell said, twisting his head away from the bottle. Madden stood up and went over to the door, closing it. Then he switched the light on. He stood over Gaskell.

'Madman . . . ?' Gaskell said, his bloodshot eyes widening. *'You?'*

Madden stamped down on his knee, and Gaskell screamed.

'Better keep it down,' Madden said. 'We don't want Effie coming up here and interrupting us, do we?' He stood, the bottle fisted like a rock in the palm of his hand, ready to swing.

Gaskell's eyes were wet with tears.

'And don't call me that,' Madden said. 'I told you I don't like it.'

Gaskell wiped his eyes on his sleeve. He was wearing his suit, but it looked threadbare and worn, and the knee had a split in it on the left side. There was dried-in blood on the lapels, now joined by fresh spots.

'Look,' Gaskell said, 'I only told them about the shoe to get them off my back. What was I meant to do?'

'You could have told the truth,' Madden said.

'Which was what? What *truth* did you want me to give them? Whatever I said was only going to put me squarely in the picture, don't you think?'

Madden breathed slowly, his limbs alive.

'You should have told them what you saw.'

Gaskell guffawed. 'What? Like you did? I take it you've spoken to those two chaps already yourself?'

'If you mean the police, then yes. I spoke to them.'

'But you didn't tell them the *truth*, did you. No. I didn't think so. Telling the truth wouldn't have done you any good. You told them you'd been down for a walk, got caught in the rain and lost your shoe climbing the fence to get out of it. Is that close enough to the truth for you? Pretty lame story, that. You're a pretty lame story too.'

Madden raised the bottle as if to strike him. Gaskell flinched.

'Look, I had to tell them something. They were never going to send *you* down for it, Hugh. But my case is . . . different . . . as you know.'

He pulled himself up to the wall, and sat with his back to it, his hair greasy and unkempt, face pale and white. He looked small and frightened and done.

'I *don't* know,' Madden said. 'Different how, exactly? In what way is it different? Why don't you tell me.' He sat down on the edge of the bed, the bottle still ready in his hand.

'D'you see this?' Gaskell snapped, pointing a forefinger at his face. 'Do you? You should really take time out from bashing me, Hugh. Really you should. I think I deserve to be spared. But *this* . . .' He indicated his blackened eye. 'This was our mutual friend Dizzy's doing. "For Carmen," he told me. "For what you done to Carmen." It seems he holds me responsible for her sad demise. And there I was thinking it was for something *else* altogether.'

Madden shrugged. 'Something else? Why else would he want to hit you?'

Gaskell let out a pained sigh. 'You remember going to the movies, don't you? You do remember that? That's what makes the difference, you see. That's what makes *me* different.' He gazed pointedly at Madden.

'That's what makes me *here*, in this fucking city, in this fucking country. Far away from the bosom of the family, you see. Can't be an embarrassment to them from here. The university is . . . an excuse, if you like. A handy device to distract from my *true, deviant* nature . . .'

Madden said nothing. He had kept the thought from himself so efficiently that even now he had to strain to sense the truth behind the implication. Gaskell reached into his jacket and withdrew a crumpled cigarette paper, dropping a few strings of tobacco into it, picked loose from the breast pocket.

'The trouble is that like seeks like, doesn't it?' he said. 'So what can one do? One just carries on, despite the prejudices of one's mother and one's father and one's important family. And despite the law of the land as well. One darts from skirting board to the door and back again. One cowers in the darkness and under the bed, waiting for the *boot* to come down and crush one. And in the meantime, like seeks like for a few moments grasped here and there in dangerous places where it's not safe to congregate but which are saf*er*. D'you see what I'm getting at, Hugh? Are you beginning to understand? But of course you do.'

Madden pursed his lips and said nothing, only nodding slowly.

'So,' Gaskell said, taking a match to the cigarette and bringing it to life, 'I go to places where like can – *sometimes* – meet like. And on occasion *dis*like. People who are afraid of poofters like myself and Kincaid lie in wait and kick the shit out of us when we come out. At least, that's what I thought until he enlightened me. Got the situation, Madman?'

Madden raised the bottle again, but Gaskell did not flinch this time. His eyes dared Madden to do it.

'Kincaid?' Madden said, then added: '*Dr* Kincaid?'

Gaskell snorted, choking slightly on the smoke from his cigarette.

'The very same. The *good* doctor.'

'And he's a . . . a . . . *homosexual* as well?' Madden found himself surprised by his own lack of worldliness. Of course, he'd always known. How else could he have written that note?

'Aye, Hugh. He's a poof. He's a bum-boy. He learned it, he says, in the army. Ways and means, eh?'

'And where did you learn it?'

'Me? I always knew. Nobody had to teach *me* anything.'

There was silence for a while. Then Gaskell went on.

'Still. What can you do, eh, Hugh? One needs *cover*, in this society. Folk with tendencies like mine need an alibi. Kincaid as well. Maisie's his alibi, and it used to work quite well for him, I think. Until she decided she actually, genuinely wanted him to herself. Well, that was never going to do, was it?'

'Why not?'

'Can't keep an old poof down, old man. Like will seek like.'

He inhaled on his cigarette and blew a blue ring across the room. A drip of water falling from the ceiling spliced it in two.

'My cover was Carmen. You see how it works? I didn't know or care about her or her boyfriend. I thought she was fun, a good time, someone that I could have a not-too-serious involvement with. The fact that her parents were Italians seemed to me at the time to make this easier. I thought she'd be chaste and Catholic and be satisfied with the pictures and ice creams. Not *my* sort of pictures, you understand.'

Madden sat studying Gaskell's face, as if it were new to him. 'So what happened?'

'She got pregnant,' Gaskell said bluntly. 'I got her pregnant.'

'But . . . how?'

'Oh, fuck's sake Madman, how'd you think? The *usual* way! She was offering and I took her up on it. Mistake, but there you go. Well, she said she loved me, and I'm not a saint. Never claimed to be. She knew about my proclivities, though. I suppose it was her way of staking her claim on me. Maybe she thought she could convert me. But, you know, I take one look at those cute little tits and that round peach of an arse and I think, hmmm. Not for me. Not for long, anyway.'

Madden wiped his forehead. Another big drip had landed on it. 'Go on,' he said.

'She told me about the pregnancy, told Dizzy too. I don't know if she told him it was mine or his. I think she told that creep Fain too. Maybe he believed it was his as well. I didn't care. Dizzy did, I think. She had an abortion anyway. Went down to England for it. When she got back, she was quite angry with me, I believe. Yes, she was quite angry indeed. She threatened me. Said she was going to tell everyone about what I did. Imagine that, eh, Madden? She was going to tell everyone about what I *did*. Do you understand what that would *mean*?'

Madden looked at him, but couldn't read his expression.

'Yes, I believe you do, don't you? Finally. It was always good to be around you, Madman, really a pleasure. You never had a clue, did you? It was so effortlessly *safe* being your friend.'

Madden felt the dryness in his mouth and licked his lips. 'Is that what we were?' he asked. 'Friends? I don't think I ever knew it.'

Gaskell tipped his ash on to the floor. He sighed. 'This is a nice place you've got here,' he said. 'Really the crème de la crème. I believe I still owe this room a chair. Of course, it's yours for the asking.'

Madden spoke slowly and deliberately. 'What would it *mean*, then? Spell it out for me.'

'It would mean,' Gaskell said, 'a jail sentence.'

'That gives you a motive,' Madden said, nodding to himself. 'You might have killed her to keep her quiet.'

Gaskell ignored the remark. 'So,' he said, 'I thought I might buy some thinking time by showing them your shoe on the railing. You can't despise me for that.'

Madden was silent for a long while, and Gaskell sat smoking and dabbing blood from his lip on the back of his sleeve.

'I can't remember everything that happened,' Madden said at last. 'Only fragments, bits and pieces. It's as if it happened to someone else. Tell me,' he said, pleading with Gaskell, 'tell me what happened. Because I'm in it too. And I'm your *friend*.'

Gaskell nodded. 'All right. Might as well be hung for a sheep as a lamb, eh?' He laughed.

'I just . . . I need to have an idea of why she was killed,' Madden said. 'I can't explain it. It means something to me.'

Gaskell eyed him blankly. 'Killed who? Oh, yes. Carmen. I'd forgotten about her. Too busy worrying about myself.'

Gaskell sat thoughtfully rolling another cigarette, then said: 'I told you about my . . . activities, didn't I? You were listening to that bit, weren't you? Well, there are places, and people and like meeting like, and all of it clandestine, you understand. Because no one can know. It's a condition of the society we live in. Public morals and private actions must *concur* . . .

'Well. Mine have had to be seen to concur, at the very least. Of course, what I want to do, and what I can be allowed legitimately to do in my own private time, are not the same thing. Nobody bothered to ask me about it, though. Or Oscar Wilde, the old poof. So there was the ancient story of boy meeting boy, with me not more than fifteen years old and going to a very good school, you understand, really one of the best. My father and mother, bless 'em, felt that I should board. Toughen me up and whatnot. Make a man of me. I suppose my mother recognised it in me from the off. But she was kind, I could always talk to her. I was clingy then, always trying to get her attention. Cried piteously when they sent me off to the school. But of course, a place like that can toughen you up in different ways. Kincaid says the army did it for him: I think he's fooling himself, don't you? All that one does is hide one's nature under the skin, where it can't be wounded so easily. Ever wonder why old schoolboys are so clubbable? It's because they're the only ones they can be who they are with because after a while who they are on the surface and who they are under the skin get confused. Even they don't understand who they are any more. D'you imagine for a second old crooked-cock Kincaid thinks of himself as some sort of queer, some kind of nancy-boy? Not a bit of it he doesn't. He just shrugs off whatever Maisie accuses him of, thinks of himself as just having these rather antisocial habits he can't seem ever to be quite rid off, like taking snuff, or topping up with the Bowmore all day long. And no one would ever dare suggest there was anything unmanly about *that*, would they? Certainly he wouldn't. And he's quite willing to exchange cash for a bit of boy. Charity, he thinks of it as. Doesn't like to talk about it down at the Lodge with all the other old schoolboys, all the other ageing poofs. But he can spot some talent, eh? He can see a nice bit of rough. Every year, when the new students – the *freshmen* – fill the lecture rooms and laboratories of the hallowed Faculty of Medicine, why the old bastard and plenty more like him are just licking their chops, they're drooling over themselves to get hold of a piece. All those innuendoes dropped in labs and tutorials . . . that's the bait for freshmen like me, fresh out of boot camp and fresh out of cash. 'Course I'd do the odd favour for the old duffer. Didn't even disgust me to. I tell you, I've had all the disgust thumped out of me at school. Thumped, thrashed, wanked and spanked, ha ha. So I said I'd do it. Anything he wanted, if he bought me a whisky like the one he was drinking. A good one. A single malt. No money, you see, always a terrible spendthrift. The curse of the upper middle classes . . . when you're used to it, you need more. That's a simple fact of economics. And I always seemed to be needing more. So I started to get him to cough up for it. Him and others. And we could never meet at anyone's home – not with their wives or their children there – and we could never meet anywhere really openly public either.

'So where do you end up? Soliciting strangers in darkened picture houses and public parks. A dangerous game, that. All too easy to pick yourself the wrong gent and end up in a cell somewhere, or kicked to death in a gutter. But where else to go, Madman? Where else can like meet like and get along on their own terms? So that's the situation, as it stands legitimately at the moment. By legitimately *I* mean by the manner in which the law is prosecuted at this time. Bollocks to it, I say. I'm not going on too much, am I?

'Good. Well. So there I was making a few quid off some of these old schoolboys, in cinemas and in parks, anywhere it was possible to get the privacy from the cops for ten minutes. Ten minutes is all! Just long enough to do the job in hand, so to speak. And sometimes, when I've nothing much better to do and things do begin to disgust me, like the affections of the good doctor, I have to get away and find someone that *I* like. You must understand, Madman, even my heart isn't made of stone. I think sometimes of my father, and how he would happily see me flogged through the streets and think after how greatly it had improved my countenance. That's the sort of thing that drives a man to his cups, to use a local idiom. A fellow might hit the bottle! So when I think on these things it used to be refreshing to see old Carmen, you know? And in the beginning it was very refreshing. After all, anyone would have said she was, well, *beautiful*, wouldn't they? Wouldn't you have said that too, Madden, even with *your* dubious sexuality?'

Madden was stung, had no idea what he meant by dubious. There were some things he found it difficult to engage with, that was all.

'If you say so. Go on.'

'I would have said she was beautiful,' Gaskell said. 'A flawed, tragic beauty. I'd have said that she was extraordinary. In so many ways too. Nobody ever speaks of her now, do they? Except to say how she died. I find that extraordinary too. I wonder what became of her after she died. She's not Carmen any more, you know. Now she's ceased to be what she was even in the minds of those that knew her. Except maybe her parents. Even I have difficulty in remembering what she was. And she wasn't perfect. She was no angel. But there were extraordinary things about her that no one'll ever understand now. In years to come, people will hold up photographs of that beautiful face of hers and it'll be impossible for them to imagine her ever having been alive. So.'

He paused to inhale on his cigarette.

'It always surprises me when I read a book or see a film where someone dies. I can't quite get over it. If it's *Anna Karenina*, I think how cruel of Tolstoy to do that. If it's *L'Assomoir*, I blame Zola for Gervais's death. I can't believe he's done it, and I hate him for it. Is that strange? I don't think it is. But I don't want Carmen to be a work of fiction, in the same way that I don't want her aborted foetus to be a fiction, never having existed in some sense. At least, I suppose, Carmen had eighteen or nineteen years. That's how long I imagine she was alive for, because of course, I've already forgotten how old she really was. Already she's dissolving and turning into a never-was.

'Did you ever notice her gums, Madman?' Gaskell asked him. Madden smiled and said that he had.

'They were sort of ugly, I suppose. Too big and wide, and made her teeth seem too small. Kind of odd. If she had never opened her mouth to speak, she would have seemed like an impossible goddess. It was her gums that were her Achilles heel, right enough. Those gums made her a possibility for asinine pricks like Dizzy. Even idiots like Fain! Those gums made her mortal and they might even have killed her in the end. I really believe that. D'you think that's strange, Hugh? I don't. I'm sorry, I'm getting off the point here . . .'

'You were talking about looking for someone you liked.'

'Yes, I was, wasn't I . . . Well, I liked her, up to a point. But sexually, well, you know, it was never going to be my thing. Sometimes when I looked at her body I thought, yes, perhaps . . . It never lasted, though. Even old crooked-cock Kincaid would have been more likely to get a look-in. Another man with *amor* on his mind. But down on the Kelvin Way, I sometimes found what I was after. Often I found it, actually. I can't deny it was exciting. Very, at times. Grappling in the bushes with lorry drivers, what could be better, eh? So I'd go there, after I'd done a bit of business in the pictures, go and clear my head.

'Well, I went down there that night. Me and Carmen weren't talking, and I was worried what Dizzy might do . . . I was worried what she might do, what might happen. The last thing I needed was to get thrown out of another department for *misdemeanours*. I left the university and took a walk, looking to pick up some arse. I thought, why not? There were no other people about, it was wet. But not exclusively so. And why would anyone be put off by wetness anyway, eh, Madman?'

Gaskell winked flirtatiously at Madden, who did not respond.

'I mean, when one has experienced something of a dry spell, wetness is – presumably – to be welcomed, is it not?'

Madden said nothing, and after relighting his roll-up Gaskell spoke again.

'Anyway, the rain was coming and going and I only half expected to meet anyone down there. I came off the Way and went down towards the river, just walking and trying to clear my head. As I said, I was worried. I was worried about Carmen and what she might do or say. A cold, wet evening; dark too. You think perhaps I wanted to keep away from people, and I met her down there so I could do her in? Well, the facts in the case are much more straightforward – if straight is the right word. I wanted to *meet* somebody first. I wanted *company*. You can pick your own euphemism here, Hugh. The truth is that *I desired the furtive companionship of the like-minded in the dampened privacy of the weeds!*

'Kincaid would have described it thus.'

Madden didn't care for Gaskell's sarcastic tone, nor the implication that lay behind it, but he sat unmoving and kept the bottle at his side.

'And of course, it was Kincaid that I met down there. Just my luck, eh? He was looking for boys too. It was a place he normally wouldn't have gone, so close to the university and all. He'd missed me at the cinema, he said. He wanted to *see* me, he said, so he took a chance and came down. That's another euphemism, Hugh. Just in case you don't get it. We *meet*, we *seek company*, we *see* . . . all euphemisms for the unspeakable, the undoable. You've no idea what life is like

243

lived as a strategy of evasion, have you, Madden? None at all.'

Madden, though, did understand what such a life was like. Everything he had ever done, or said, was an evasion of a kind. He smeared a droplet from the ceiling away from his face. It had landed on his forehead cold and hard as a fact.

'Go on,' he said. 'Tell me the rest.'

'Sure I'll tell you,' Gaskell said, tapping his roll-up on the floor. 'We've no secrets from each other, have we? Except how will you know what I'm telling you is the truth? How will you know I'm not just feeding you half-truths, omissions, things I want you to believe because it suits me?'

'Because friends don't do that to each other,' Madden said. 'And I'll smash your face in with this bottle if I think you are.'

Gaskell nodded. 'Yes, you're capable of it, aren't you. You'd do anything necessary. You'd kill, wouldn't you? And then . . .' Gaskell snapped his fingers loudly. 'You'd simply forget it ever happened! Terrifically convenient, that, I have to say. And I always thought you were so hopeless, so – well, excuse me for saying it, but we're speaking plainly here, are we not? – *incapable*.'

Madden felt his jaw muscles tighten at the slight and leaned forward on the bed. 'But I didn't have a reason,' he said. 'I had no motive for doing such a thing.'

Gaskell sneered. 'Motive?' he said. 'Why would a madman need a motive? Let's face it, people all over the world disappear every day, people stab and shoot and poison and kill each other every minute of every day all over the world. What are their motives? *Motive* is a word from a bad detective story. Motive means jealousy or greed or not caring for the colour of another man's tie. Motive means *reason*. The insane don't need reason. The point about lunatics and madmen is that they are by nature *unreasonable*.'

Madden felt hot, his lips dry. 'I'm not mad,' he said, 'I'm not.'

'You mean not *that* mad, don't you? If that's the case, why did I find you delirious, missing a shoe and spouting gibberish about ink that evening? Isn't that the behaviour of a madman?'

'I wasn't well,' Madden said, 'I was sick.'

'Oh yes, *unwell. Sick.* Other euphemisms, other evasions. Isn't unwell another way of saying "unbalanced", or "unstable"? Isn't "sick" a euphemism for a euphemism?'

'Tell me what happened,' Madden said. 'Tell me the rest of your story.'

'Is it my story, Madman? I thought you wanted to hear your story.'

Madden crossed the short space between them and struck Gaskell heavily across the temple with the bottle. He was surprised when it didn't break.

Gaskell's hands went automatically to his head and hovered there, not touching the place where he had received the blow, as if waiting to catch his brains should they tumble from his skull.

Madden sat down again and waited. *Envy, jealousy.* Things he had felt. Words that were closely related, linked in some way. Euphemisms. Evasions. His hands were shaking. It was unacceptable, and he would *never* acknowledge it, would never act on it. Did everyone know except himself? His mother must know. And then there was his father.

Even Rose. It was as though there was another part of him plain and apparent to the entire world, a part that disgusted and appalled him, so much so that he knew, even now, that he didn't even register it consciously as a possibility. For a moment he saw his room, the same one he'd occupied ever since he could remember. For a moment he was feeling the constriction in his throat, the backs of his eyes, the light leaving them, the light being choked out, his useless struggling, his body dissolving into nothingness, the light going out. He had felt himself dead. There was nothing, no oblivion, no awareness,

245

no other light. No state that had a name, no Grace. There were no words for it, there was no name that could be written down that could claim it.

He tried to remember why. Of course, he knew already. Sickness brought out a sweat. He was wiping his temple with his forearm, breathing stiffly through his nose, afraid that if he opened his mouth a scream would come out that would never end, a wail so intense it would obliterate everything.

He stood, walked over to Gaskell and kicked him hard in the ribs. Gaskell did little more than grunt at the blow. He seemed barely conscious. Madden kicked him again, harder.

Gaskell raised his head, his eyes unscrewing slowly. One opened and stared glassily at Madden. There was a swell of purple above the other, still closed. He chuckled and blood fell from his lips.

'*Tell me what happened!*' Madden hissed. He kicked Gaskell again. It was the act of someone he no longer recognised. He stood watched himself carry out these things and saw a creature in possession of his likeness but that was no longer himself, was not a single being but a chimera, two creatures yoked together by violence, a metaphor for a man who was *not*.

Gaskell raised his head and opened the other eye. He seemed fearless now, but only just.

'Tell you what happened,' he said. 'Yes. I'll tell you.'

It was unbearable to Madden, this waiting, but he forced himself into some sort of frame of mind that would permit it. 'Take your time,' he said. Vaguely, it occurred to him how much like his father he sounded.

'I'll tell you,' Gaskell said again, touching a hand tremulously to the burgeoning welt on his head. 'But you know already.' Gaskell grinned at him through a mouthful of shattered teeth, his eyes somehow not there. His head lolled and he seemed to take extraordinary effort over every breath.

'We're not so different, you and me,' he said. 'Not different at all, really. Ha. You knew that, though, didn't you. You've always known. And never known. And this girl . . .'

'Rose,' Madden said. 'Her name is Rose.'

'Yes. Rose,' Gaskell said, a long string of bloody saliva trailing from his lower lip. 'She knows too. But she's like you. She'll never admit it. Maisie Kincaid too. She knows, but won't accept it. Both of them will always fight it, and the fight will crush them eventually.'

Madden had a need to hear his *friend* say the words aloud, and then he would know too. His own breathing took erratic leaps and pulses.

'*Fight what?*' the other being whined, and brought the bottle against Gaskell's head again. He made a low moaning sound, but did not move or otherwise flinch. His head lolled.

'*Like will seek like,*' he said. He lifted his head and fixed a smoky blue eye on Madden.

Madden's head began to throb. ACTH hormone, he told himself, only a drug to drug the drug that was already loose in his thoughts, a fear and abhorrence run away with themselves. He kicked Gaskell in the ribs again, and this time Gaskell yelped. His shirt and lapels were covered in blood.

'I saw *her,*' Gaskell said after a time. His voice was hoarse and barely audible. His eyes opened and closed – sometimes for long periods – and his mouth hung open.

Madden sat waiting, but was not really there any more.

Time passed. His father was on top of him crushing him. His father was behind him, choking him. He could hear the sound of his belt being unbuckled, and gruff, quiet words. And then the pain. It was silenced. It was garrotted into quiet by a pillow, or a hand, or his belt, or his unbearable weight crushing the lungs. All the while the gruff voice saying to be still, saying to keep still, telling him not to move, telling him not to speak. Shush. Quiet. Keep it down. The light disappearing from his mind, everything gone out. And then there was another silence. And when he woke, another silence again, different from before, and not able to recall exactly what had occurred. He was alone, he was solitary. Your own fault, the voice had told him. Your own fault.

He hadn't seen Kincaid. He had followed Carmen as he had done since first he'd seen her take the path from the Kirklee gate, with Gaskell. Except this time she was alone, and something inside him and clicked into negative space. It had been another dead afternoon, that day. Everything about it had been dead. But then he had followed Carmen and now she was dead too. He wasn't himself after the rain had started. Carmen, walking away from Madden. Even then, he hadn't allowed himself to admit it. He wouldn't allow it – not consciously – to manifest itself. What had Gaskell called it? His *true, deviant nature.* All the jealousy and humiliation he had felt. He had been trying so hard as well. He had thought he had perfected invisibility. So he had believed. And then he'd met Gaskell at the ball, and he had lost something of himself to him. And then Gaskell was taken away from him and he was lost, hopelessly and utterly lost. There was no road back from it that he could predict, and he'd had those lapses again, moments disappearing. The past, the future. The present. Where were the fractures? Where were the joins that put it all back together again? Ha. He was laughing silently to himself, eyes fixed on Gaskell's bloodied head. Why had he not loved him back? he wanted to know. Why not?

Because you are a monster, he said to himself. Monsters are unlovable by their very nature.

Your thoughts are already legion. Your thoughts are already epidemic. Your thoughts are a disease for which there is no cure, no saving. The thoughts you know and the thoughts you don't know. Look for yourself. Your thoughts become real even as you sit here doubting them, among another man's blood. You've written them already.

Gaskell breathed softly, like a sleeping infant, a sound like the bursting of a bubble of saliva, a light pop. Madden knew now that he had followed Gaskell down on to the Kelvin banks before. He had, without acknowledging it to himself, brought Rose to the Rio Locarno, as if sleepwalking towards him. Everywhere he went, he could see now, was a kind of extended hunt. For Gaskell, and then for Carmen, because she took him away from Madden and because he hated her.

He had followed Carmen that night, in the drizzle, and found her waiting for him by the bridge. She had seen that he was trailing her, and she had waited, umbrella folded now, fisted like a weapon. When she recognised him, she sneered.

Oh, Madman, she had said, *It's only you*.

And then he was on her and she tried to scream. He was dragging her into the bushes, the damp soil and the grave, and he could remember it, all of it. The other him tried to prove itself a man, a *real* man, and he couldn't, he wasn't able to do it to her. He was ashamed.

And she simply lay there, not moving, silent, like a thing waiting for death. Well. So be it. He would give her that death. It'd be a good one. She hadn't struggled, not even as he bundled her over and got behind her, not even as his left arm had crooked around her throat and the other had locked behind, a technique he had been familiar with since child-hood. Was he not his daddy's boy? Only then, when her hand had flapped at his side, had he become aroused and he was inside her – she didn't even squawk – and thrusting, and choking her, and pushing, and—

It was all over. He knelt panting in the mire, soaking wet, and began to shiver. The other him pulled up its trousers and gaped at the thing face down in the dirt. No one had seen. No one was there. Or so he had thought.

Carmen Alexander lay still.

And then he couldn't remember. Minutes passed, perhaps, or seconds.

He hadn't known about Gaskell's tryst with Kincaid down there. Had the old boy seen? Was he keeping quiet about it to save his own skin? Madden went over to Gaskell and slapped him hard across the face, then again when that had no effect. Slowly, Gaskell raised his head.

'I was just buying some time,' he said slowly, in a voice choked with blood. 'I was afraid. What more do you want from me?' He was sobbing now, not able to look at Madden.

Madden said, 'Why?'

'I told you. I was afraid of what she might do . . . and then I found her dead. I panicked. I'd been down there before, remember? People – *men* – knew my face.'

'Who were you with?'

'Just . . . someone. No one.'

'Kincaid?'

'Earlier. But he was afraid of being seen, so we made it quick, and he left. There was another man too. I'd met him before. I knew he'd have no problem turning me in. Kincaid I don't worry about.' He smiled softly at Madden. 'Kincaid would never let anything come between him and his job. Dead people are just dead people to him. Even if he might know something about how they died. There's some reason to that, though, isn't there? What's the sense in worrying yourself about how they died? It won't help them any . . .'

Madden sat breathing evenly. He still held the bottle in his hand.

'But you never saw me there, did you? How did you know if I had anything to do with her?'

'Who? Oh, Carmen. I'm sorry, my head hurts a bit, Madman.'

Madden kicked him hard in the ribs and Gaskell slumped to one side, crying to himself.

'I told you not to call me that.'

'*Please* don't hurt me any more . . .' Gaskell pleaded.

'All right,' Madden said. 'I'll stop hurting you when you tell me how you knew about me.'

Gaskell's face went pale.

'You *didn't* know it was me?' Madden said. 'You never *saw*?'

'I saw the body. I saw her. It was me who called the police. I just found the shoe later. Obviously I didn't leave a name. You said something about losing your shoe there when you were delirious. I went to see if I could find it. I did it for you!'

'So why did you tell the police about it, then?'

'I told you. To buy some time. For myself.'

'They haven't come back for you yet?'

Gaskell spat blood on to the carpet. 'No, not yet.'

Madden stood up, the bottle ready in his hand. Gaskell began to plead.

'I wouldn't tell anyone, Hugh,' he was saying, 'I didn't know you were there . . . I thought you went to pick up boys, like me, like Kincaid! I thought that was why you'd been down there the night you lost your shoe! That's what I wouldn't tell anyone . . . how *could* I? We're *friends*.'

Madden was shaking his head. 'Friends wouldn't turn each other in to the police.' He raised the bottle up.

'Please, Hugh, don't do it . . . I'm sorry, I'm sorry, I'm sorry.'

Madden brought the bottle down against the palm of his hand.

'No, no, no, no, no, please, Madman, please don't do this, please, I won't tell anyone, Madman, please . . .'

'Don't call me that,' Madden said, 'I don't like it.'

Gaskell's face was a mask of stupid fear and abjection. Madden was disgusted. It was nothing even remotely human. He swung the bottle at Gaskell as hard as he could: it made a cold, nubbed sound, like bone against bone. Gaskell jerked suddenly to his knees, and tried to grab him. Madden brought the bottle down again, and Gaskell fell on to his back, exposing his belly like a dog. He wriggled on the ground, leering up, sticking his tongue out between his teeth, and flicking it around obscenely; Madden kicked him hard under the jaw and his friend growled bloodily, his tongue snapped cleanly off and flopping down his neck to the floor. An odd squealing noise, low and desperate, as he turned back on to his knees and grabbed at the piece of tongue, trying to get a grip of it. The bloodied piece of meat had curled up in some sort of reflex: Madden had heard of, but never seen, such phenomena before – except in the shed tails of lizards. He was transfixed as Gaskell tried fruitlessly to pick it up. Then he remembered himself, and the other Madden brought the bottle down against the back of Gaskell's skull. He dropped flat on to the floor instantly and lay completely still.

Madden leaned over and touched his neck, searching for a pulse. There was one, but it was faint. Sitting down on the bed, he dusted his jacket absent-mindedly. Then he bent down and dragged Gaskell by the armpits up into a semblance of a seated position, holding him upright with his knees. There was almost no blood from the wounds he'd inflicted with the whisky bottle, only an assortment of large purplish lumps and bruises. They were all over his head. Madden wondered how many times the other him must have hit him, but couldn't remember. No matter now.

Madden wiped the excess blood from Gaskell's face with his own handkerchief, then pushed it into his mouth.

With Gaskell facing away from him, he settled his left arm around his neck and across the windpipe, looping his hand into the crook of his right elbow. Lightly, he kissed the top of Gaskell's matted blond hair, still a bit too long, and smelling of cigarette smoke.

'Goodbye, Gaskell,' he said. 'Goodbye, friend.'

He threaded the palm of his right hand into position against the back of Gaskell's skull, and began to squeeze. He held the choke tightly clamped, for a good ten or fifteen minutes – until even through his own excitement he could no longer maintain it. Well over the recommended time needed for brain death to occur. There was no reaction at all from

Gaskell, save an involuntary coarsening of his breathing, and then, after the first minute, a sort of glottal full stop.

Madden let his body slump, and lay back on the bed, breathing hard. He may even have dozed off for a minute. After a while, he became aware of where he was. He sat slowly upright. Gaskell was slumped to one side, his back to Madden, who poked him tentatively on the shoulder a couple of times. Gaskell wasn't moving. A fresh tingle of excitement, a mild nausea and panic, began to take hold of Madden. The blood hummed in his veins. He got up and dusted himself down, aware of his own painful arousal. Distractedly, he wondered what Rose was doing at the moment. He decided to pay her a visit.

Thirteen

It was a long time before anyone discovered Owen Gaskell's body. And in the meantime something had slipped out from somewhere in the back of his mind and acted. Now he was waiting for it to catch up with him and string its noose around his own neck.

At the time, he had waited expectantly for the knock on the door, listening to the sound of the voice whispering constantly in his ear. Carried on with his studies, his papers, the blanks of which the day was made up. And always the same day, starting again and again. He never went back to the Wilton Street flat. There was the perpetual horror of being discovered, but it was a horror of being *outed* for what he was, whatever that might be. He couldn't abide the possibility. It was a kind of limbo he was in. It wasn't possible, he knew, to get away with what he had done. He could recall it quite clearly in infinitesimal detail, and his mind would graze the minutiae, sifting through the particulars, searching for the reason, and the unreason, but everything had become fused; there was no separating one thing from another. So he sat in his room and scribbled on his papers and went in to classes and waited. He sat in tutorials and avoided Kincaid's look, sure too that the good doctor also avoided his. He distracted himself with the others that were left, the Dizzys and the Hectors and the Adumans.

Hector Fain had a girlfriend of his own now. A blowsy sort, who bore a vague resemblance to Carmen in every way except that she was – naturally – unspeakably ordinary and plain. Far too thin, to boot. He imagined she would break when Hector – a sturdy, bespectacled cricket bat of a man whose block of a head barely reached her sparse bosom – climbed on top of her in begrimed Y-fronts. An appalling image.

Then, too, poor bereft Dizzy. Hardly there any more, grief having stunted his catalogue looks, weighed down on him so greatly that it was difficult to recognise him as the same man, or boy, he had been. It was a guilty grief too, and seemed to inspire no pity: he was shunned; even Madden ignored him, despite the beseeching looks he occasionally threw in his direction, a painful, longing glance, as if he wanted desperately to be seen to exist. He made some remark to Madden about wanting to exchange more essays, so that they could revise from each other's. Madden agreed, his own blankness making the transaction easier. He took the essay Dizzy thrust at him, promising to give him the one he requested later. But, of course, he didn't.

Even his nickname seemed to have fallen off him with a clunk. Nobody called him Dizzy any more. He was simply 'him', or 'her ex-boyfriend', or occasionally elevated to a desultory 'Newlands'. That there could be anyone on the face of the planet less like a jazz trombone player (or was it trumpet?) was not difficult to fathom. He had come to embody a different kind of dizziness entirely, more stricken moan than unabashed high notes.

Aduman carried on his usual fashion: Madden knew as little about him as he had ever done, except that his scarf dragged in a more bedraggled state, thin to the point of transparency. It was doubtful that any sort of comfort could be gained from it against the cold, and since it seemed to rain most of the time, it acted instead like a sort of sponge. Presumably, Madden decided, that was where it came into its own. Useless in cold, dry weather, but with the added moisture, and coiled tightly enough around the vulnerable throat of its host, it would likely afford a sort of second-hand heat.

Madden pushed his thoughts onwards: they had to be kept moving these days or they would stick, like dead branches cut off from the flowing current of the river. The sticking bothered him.

It was impossible to sit still for any length of time. He would stand quiet and absent in the cold room at Caldwell's, then suddenly his mind would be impelled into a terrible, desperate kind of motion. In the single room he now rented, anonymous and alone, far from Shakespeare and Wilton Streets, he would stare at his hands, the shoes on his feet, a corner, at nothing. Or he would put the kettle on to boil and be unable to bear waiting for it, and pour out half the water and set it back on the hob again.

'Troubled, are we, Mr Madden?' the good doctor had said to him once after a tutorial. Madden had said nothing. The doctor studied him, but it wasn't clear to Madden what he expected him to say. His look was that of a man gauging the situation, of suspicion but no clear understanding as to what to be suspicious of. 'Preoccupied, are we?'

'No, sir,' Madden said, then corrected himself. 'No, *Doctor.*'

Kincaid smoothed his fingers over the hair on his upper lip. 'I don't wish to give you a poor mark for this . . . *effort*, Mr Madden, but I can't help but get the feeling that everything is not quite right with you. Am I incorrect?'

Madden felt removed from the situation, as if he might very well stand up and urinate in a corner and it would have the same effect as if he opened his mouth.

'This, I'm afraid, is not the sort of work we usually expect from you,' Kincaid went on. He was wearing some sort of velvet beret, and smoking a pipe. Also, a matching velvet bow tie. Both were lime green. Damned bricks of the man. He looked wholly ludicrous. If he had been teaching fine art up in Garnethill at the art school, he would still have looked an oaf.

It was completely like him to be unaware of having committed such a fashion gaffe.

'It's just so much ink on paper. Your work seems to be on the slide, laddie boy. What d'you say to that?'

Madden shrugged, peering over Kincaid's shoulder and out of the window. Another grey day, a steady drizzle pattering the gutters of the slated turret just outside the room. He wondered what was kept in there. Maybe the doctor's fashion sense, or some other closeted manifestation of his psyche.

'Well, I've been having a bit of trouble sleeping lately,' Madden offered feebly.

'Trouble sleeping, you say? Dashed difficult business that. Need to get that sorted out, quick smart, I say. Aye. The quicker and smarter the better too! Unless you want to be doing the whole course again from scratch. Now, I'd suggest that, whatever is bothering you, be it lack of sleep or any other matter, you get a good strong grip on it now, eh? Before you slip any farther from grace.'

Madden nodded and stood to leave, taking the paper that Kincaid brandished across the desk at him, and substituting another he'd been working on the previous week. He didn't bother to look at the mark in the margin, assuming, as had been the case lately, that it was somewhere in the low fifties.

Kincaid harrumphed.

'By the way,' he said, keeping a measured glare on Madden, daring him to make something of it, 'have you seen hide or hair of our Mr Gaskell? Been gone for some time, hasn't he? I know you're his . . . *friend*. That's why I ask.'

Madden stood still, and shook his head.

'You're sure? It's just that we've been missing him – we've not seen him, in lectures or tutorials, for quite a while. No. We've just not . . .' The doctor lowered his gaze. '. . . seen him.'

Madden was about to say something, but then they were interrupted by a forceful chap on the door.

Kincaid glanced irritably at the door and barked at it.

'Wait outside! I'll be with you shortly.'

Madden winced. Kincaid coughed a robust lump of something brown into his sink. He waved a hand at Madden while he wiped his mouth with an unusually grubby-looking pocket handkerchief, a once white square, now rather more yellow in colour.

The door creaked open tentatively and a familiarly scarred chin poked around it, hat off to disclose a shameful abundance of Brylcreemed hair, black and lustrous, with a cow's lick at the front.

'I'm afraid this cannae wait, Mr Kincaid,' the chin said. He stood in the doorway. Strange that he should shut out the dim light of the hall with his slight stature, Madden thought, then realised that the bigger man was there too, dwarfing him from behind.

'Ah,' Kincaid said, a slight tremor to his voice, 'you'd better come in. News on the Alessandro front, I shouldn't wonder. And it's *Doctor* Kincaid, by the way.'

Madden stood, his mouth slightly open, aware he must look foolish, if not guilty.

'You've met our Mr Madden already, I take it?'

The policeman with the scarred chin stared at Madden, then nodded a greeting to which Madden was slightly too slow in responding. The officer's armchair-stuffing hair obeyed no earthly laws of comportment; no amount of Brylcreem, regardless of generosity, would ever hold it completely fast to the bone deck of his skull. It was as thick and springy as it was shiny, and Madden knew, just knew, that the man would be irrationally sensitive about it. He concentrated on the hair.

'Alice who?' the officer said. 'Naw, we're no here about any Alice. We're here about a . . . what's his name again, big yin?'

The bigger officer stepped forwards and produced a notebook. He hadn't taken his hat off, and had to bow slightly to get in under the door frame. Once inside, he raised himself to his full height, and swelled out a prodigious chest. He produced a notebook, and made a show of flicking through the pages.

'I was referring to the dead girl – Carmen Alexander.'

'Oh, that Alice. How'd ye not say, Professor?' the other with the scar said, not without a hint of aggression in his voice.

'Aye. Here it is,' the bigger man said. He paused, eyeing both Madden and Kincaid, then cleared his throat impressively. Madden concentrated on the hair. 'We're here vis-à-vis the discovery of a deceased person or persons—'

'There's just the *one* person,' the officer with the scarred chin interrupted irritably. 'Quit reading fae my notes.'

The bigger chap frowned without looking up. 'Vis-à-vis the discovery of a deceased *person* believed to be one Owen Gaskell, penultimately a student at this establishment.'

He flipped the notebook closed and pocketed it. Madden wondered whether 'ultimately' wouldn't have been more appropriate. Poor Gaskell.

Kincaid had regained control of his voice. The speed with which he took control of the situation was adroit.

'Owen Gaskell, you say. My. My, my, goodness me. This is a shock. This is a surprise. Tell me, Officer, are you at liberty to say what befell him?'

There was no concern in his voice, only his usual academic curiosity.

The bigger officer appeared uncomfortable and moved about inside his uniform. It seemed as if he was trying to scratch an itch without using his hands. The smaller one with the scar wiped his forehead, hat in hand.

'Befell him? He never befell nothing,' the latter said. 'Someone behashed his befucking berains in is what befell him. That do ye?' The officer seemed to be sweating somewhat: Madden convinced himself that it was his own stare which had accomplished this.

Kincaid mumbled something about not wanting to get up the backs of Justice's myrmidons, but entirely misjudged the effect his tone was having on the two men, and instead began to backtrack hopelessly from what the smaller policeman seemed to have taken as an insult. 'Nothing of the sort, Officer. I merely intended to bring a moment of levity to the situation.'

The man was pointing at Kincaid, his accomplice reining him back with a strategically placed hand on the shoulder, so that Madden began to wonder whether he'd read the whole situation wrong: perhaps it was the taller man who was the senior of the two. Perhaps he was staring at the wrong hair.

'Levity *whit*? Can ye fly? Listen up, Professor, this is a serious situation we've got here. Right? We ask the questions and you give us answers. *Straight* fucking answers. Ye're no addressing a coupla bowling balls here! There's a bloke round the corner with his heid stove in. Throttled as well. And he's missing maist of his tongue! Used to be one of your fucking pets, did he no?'

Kincaid was ruffled, took his ridiculous beret off and used it to mop his forehead.

He stammered slightly, began to say something, then stopped.

'Right. Davey, the principal details *if you will.*' This last spat sarcastically, a parody of Kincaid.

The big man flipped out the notebook once again, tilting his helmet back on his head as he did so.

'Owen Gaskell,' he said, 'injuries to the nut, the kidneys and the ribs. Two broke. Um, heid mashed in using a blunt instrument. Also several broken teeth, broken nose, a fractured cheekbone, broken orbital, and – if he had lived – he'd have needed stitches to a cut running from eyebrow to nose. And he was suffocated as well. No pleasant.'

'Asphyxiated,' the scarred man corrected, nodding intensely, eyes closed and arms crossed across his chest, as if listening to a poem being recited. 'Someone must have had a real dislike for the boy.'

'Ah,' Kincaid said, drawing himself up in his chair, 'asphyxiated. Like the Alexander girl. Carmen. When did this happen?'

'Can't say at the moment. The landlady went to collect his rent, but he wasn't in his own room. He was in the one next door. She says she rented it to another young man who paid a week's rent and then never returned. Says she got the horrors just thinking about it: that she'd harboured a murderer beneath her roof! Says he fair gave her the creeps. Couldn't identify anyone in the first line-up, but. Blind as a bat, and stupit wae it. So this deid chappie must have known the fellow that took the huff with him. It's believed the deceased, this Owen Gaskell, had intimate relations with the Alexander girl. So there's your motive.'

He had calmed down somewhat, and the bigger officer removed the staying hand from his shoulder and instead began nodding at everything his friend – were they friends? – said.

'Motive?' Kincaid said, as if he'd never heard the word uttered before. 'I always thought that motives were for trashy novels. Would that it were so,' he went on, shaking his head and returning his beret to its mount. 'I can't believe anyone would want to kill that boy. A very bright lad, he was. Could have gone far.' He continued shaking his head.

'Aye, well, he's gone as far as he's ever going to go now,' the officer said. 'As for why anyone would want him done in, that Alexander lassie might have had something to do with that.'

Madden held his breath, felt as if he might faint.

Kincaid took up his pipe, tapping the ash out into a cup on his desk. He was staring at Madden again. 'What *can* you mean?'

'We mean,' interrupted the bigger officer, 'that we have our chief suspect in custody. We shuffled the line-up around a bit, gave the old biddy a couple of tries. She picked him out after a few goes. Guess we'll just skirt over that wee bit of information when we have to testify at the court, eh?'

The officer with the scarred chin told him to shut his face, which he did with an apologetic look.

'What my *colleague* means to say is that, of course, we'll tell the truth up on the witness stand.'

Kincaid nodded, puffed on his pipe. 'And what, if you don't mind me asking,' he said, 'is the truth?'

The officer with the scar scratched the top of his head and attempted to smooth down his errant hair.

'Her ex-boyfriend done it, most likely. Out of jealousy. Probably. She aborted his wean as well. So there you go. He done in the lassie because of the abortion, and he done in Gaskell because he thought the wean was his own and they got rid of it. Case closed.'

'Ex-boyfriend? You mean that harmless-looking chap Newlands? The one they call "Dizzy"? Surely not.' Kincaid tapped his pipe again, and glanced casually at Madden. The room was shrinking around him, darkening. He felt stifled, choked.

'Aye, well, they always look harmless. The harmless ones are the ones to watch. But the lad done her in, that's for sure. He's a cold-blooded one, right enough. Been seen acting up with the girl and the Gaskell chap. There's witnesses to say they saw him take a pop at him in the Men's Union. What an act he puts on! All that greetin' and saying he loved her. Naw, we reckon he done it. A psychopath is what he is.'

Kincaid and the two officers all shook their heads silently.

Sweat blossomed from Madden's skin; he was swaying slightly.

'No,' he said, 'you've got it wrong. You've got it all wrong. It couldn't have been Dizzy. It couldn't have been.'

'You all right, son?' he heard Kincaid say, the room shrunk tight around his face, puffing smoke and fire. He looked like a devil. He was a devil. Nonsense. Absolute nonsense. Madden didn't believe in devils. There weren't any devils. They'd all been made extinct. Reason, the Age of Enlightenment, economics, medicine, physics, the Industrial Revolution, all of these things had made all the devils extinct. Devils existed only in foreign lands, among the ignorant and the savage. Yet here was one now, breathing fire right next to him! And two more devils by the door! Red faces and tails!

There was only one thing to do . . . empirical evidence would settle the matter: he demanded that everyone take off their shoes and show him their feet. He wanted to see their hoofs.

'Eh, maybe you'd better have a sup of this,' the devil in Kincaid's place said. He was grinning and flicking out a curved black tongue. Smoke billowed from it. Madden took the pewter flask and sipped from it, but it wasn't water, it was poison, he had drunk poison from it. He screwed the lid shut and placed it in his pocket.

'It's not right,' he said. 'Dizzy never killed anyone. You can't punish him. It was me, I did it. I killed her.'

All three devils were shaking their heads. They were laughing at him.

'What we got here? A confessor? No,' the scarred devil said. 'It was Newlands that done it. You had us going for a wee bit there, though, Mr Madden. Thought you were involved, what wae that shoe business. But when Gaskell showed us where the shoe was . . . well, let's just say he put us in the picture about why you went walkabout down there. We'll just put our hands up and say we got our man wrong.'

'But I did it, I killed her,' Madden said.

'Look, son, we know what yous lot get up to down there,' the devil went on, its face swollen, bursting. 'And if it wasn't for this other matter, we'd be doon on you like a ton of bricks. I'll not give you my opinion on what I think about your kind except to say it's a fucking crime and that if I had my own way the lot of you'd be flogged for it.' He sighed and mopped his brow, black wrinkles of soot ingrained in its creases.

The big red devil chuckled too. 'No right in the heid this wan, eh? We get a lot of folk like him down the station. Cannae resist it, so they cannae. Only this week we've had a wee wummin in confessing she done it. Reads the papers, comes in and confesses whatever she's found. Totally batty, so she is.'

'I'm telling you I did it,' Madden said. His head pounded. 'It was me! I throttled the girl and I bashed in Gaskell's head with a whisky bottle! Why don't you believe me?'

All three were shaking their heads.

'Face it,' Kincaid was saying, 'you're a hand with a surgical scalpel, Mr Madden, but you're no killer. The very idea!'

'Look, sonny boy,' the scarred devil was saying, 'the case is closed, endy story. Newlands was a big lad, he had the strength and the motivation. The fact is he's had some military training and he knows a thing or two about how to put someone out of it quickly. And that's what he done to both of them. No disrespect, but have you ever even opened a tin of mince without having to get your mammy's help?'

He could hear them all laughing, chuckling at him. And here he was about to demand to be placed under arrest for the protection of the public. The last thing he recalled before passing out was attempting to demonstrate the choke-hold on the smaller police-devil, but by then everything had gone dark.

Fourteen

Four nights before Joe Jnr set Caldwell's ablaze, it spoke to Madden again, while he waited once more for the police to come knocking. This time, the voice spoke so quietly he was hardly able to hear it. It was little more than a gurgle. He strained to catch the words the voice spoke, but they were faint, so faint it was as if he were hearing them spoken from the bottom of a well. I'm still here, he heard the voice say, I'm still here.

No, the voice said. You've not been listening. You haven't listened for quite some time. We can't stop talking now. It's all we can do. And we'll keep on talking and talking and talking and talking and talking and tal

Stop it, Madden said. Shush now. Go back to sleep.

We can't sleep. We're dead. The dead can't sleep and they can't wake. The dead can't even be. They are not. We are not. I am not. One day soon, you will not be too. Then you can say whatever you like. We'll be listening.

Madden woke, his neck stiff from the chair he was sitting in. He still had his whisky glass in his hand, but had spilled the dregs of it over his lap. He dabbed at his trousers with a tissue from his pocket and stood up, seeing the light slanting in at the edge of the curtain. Morning.

It was very early, though, that he could tell. Bright, gold-gilt clouds lay in wreaths in the sky. Madden checked his watch, then rubbed the back of his neck. Five o'clock. Seagulls were wheeling about above the tenement rooftops, screeching for the daylight. He wondered why birds always rose so early. What could they possibly have to look forward to all day? Surely even they must be bored with *flying* by now.

Seagulls. The nearest this city would get to cherubim this day, or any other. Was that the plural of *cherub*, then? What were *seraphim*? What was a *seraph*?

He went down the hall to check on Rose. She lay in exactly the same position he'd left her in the night before, the hand still unclenched, her bedside spectre having spared her for another night.

He went into the kitchen where the two pieces of burnt bread were still sitting on top of the rubbish in the bin. The life and death of a slice of bread was not something he had concerned himself with overmuch in the past. He supposed everyone was, to use a youthful expression, *toast* sooner or later. Carmen Alessandro had been for a long time, so too was Gaskell, and Dizzy Newlands had hung himself by his own necktie on his third night in a police cell. No one had cared for Madden's confession, and he did not repeat it. He had been sure, right up until the moment he'd heard the news, that Newlands would be released, and they would come for him. He had waited for it, he had believed it, and in a way he had longed for it. It didn't seem possible that he could do what he had done and still go unpunished. And so his non-life had continued. He had sleepwalked through the days, unable to feel guilt or shame or regret for his actions because, in truth, he had never felt that they had been committed by himself. They had been committed by that other Hugh Madden, the one that had learned the suffocation games from childhood.

He glanced over his shoulder at her worn face. She was definitely deteriorating. She had been dying for years. These days her life was *about* dying, it had been one long preparation for death, brought about not by the fear of death itself, but the fear of a death borne under sufferance.

Pain was more, she said, than she could bear. She had been

quite serious. If she was suffering, Madden was to help her, she said. Promise.

He had duly promised, but he wasn't at all sure that he really intended to give her the particular manner of help she desired.

'I want a *good* death, Hugh,' she said. 'One with dignity.'

Well, he'd said to her. He'd try his best. He hadn't told her that it was impossible, there was no such thing. There were no dignified exits. She had been a nurse once upon a time. Surely she knew that? It was Madden's feeling that, deep down, Rose knew it perfectly well. There were violent deaths and slow deaths and deaths that were almost peaceful (but not quite) and deaths that were very horrible, but there were no bona fide, honest-to-goodness, yes-siree-goldarn-it downright plain-and-simple down-home, old-fashioned deaths with *dignity*.

And now he was fairly certain that hers would be undignified too. Whatever manner of passing was ultimately hers. There was nothing very dignified about him suffocating her with a pillow, or giving her an overdose. It was unfair of her to ask it of him. Still, he supposed this wouldn't be suicide. Assisted death, they called it in some of the more liberal countries of the world. Murder, they called it in others. The selfishness of her request had appalled him: what did she imagine would become of him – her *husband* – for the love of Christ? Was his own life of so little consequence to her that she would have him throw it away only to speed her own demise along? What was her bloody hurry anyway? Did she not *like* him or something?

She didn't want him; he'd known that for many years. At least, not since she lost the baby. The baby that had been the reason they'd married in the first place. How laughable. The idea that they would ever have made a respectable couple! Utterly laughable. Even the way the child was conceived, on the same night he'd finished Gaskell. He'd gone to her at the infirmary, his erection painful, and she'd thrown Kathleen out. What were those blood drops on his shirt? she had asked him, but he'd pushed her on to the bed and this time he didn't need guiding in, he knew where he was going and his mind was a blank, his mind was a boil, and there he was lancing it. Of course, she had bled a little after too. That was to be expected.

But still she had stayed with him: he'd thought she liked or respected him enough not to see him in jail.

Yet it was becoming clear to him that something would have to be done. If not about her, then about Brian Spivey.

He had eaten very little the evening before and his alcohol consumption had been excessive. A woolly, doped sensation filled his head, and there were the echoes of last night's voices still ringing in it. The Spivey woman and her son, Tess Kincaid, the Loch Ardinning report, Catherine the Abscondee. And other voices.

Carmen Alessandro. Owen Gaskell. Dizzy Newlands. Kincaid. The voice of an unborn child, a child that never was, a ghost, a spectre.

It had all left him with a terrible gnawing hunger in his belly, so he forwent his usual slice of toast and filled the frying pan instead with black pudding, sausage, tomato, potato scone, mushrooms and eggs, and even heated up a small pan of beans. He ate deliberately, chewing each mouthful the recommended forty times. The pace of such a life would be too, too slow, he concluded. It was true he had never been one of life's great, well, *livers*, if such an expression did not do too much violence to the organ in question, but there were some health recommendations that ought to be banished to the monastery.

He looked at the report in the *Herald* with only vague interest: it all seemed to have so little to do with him now. Yet Brian Spivey knew of it, had somehow made the connection. Did he intend to blackmail Madden? Surely that was what this must be all about? Or had he made any such connection at all? It was conceivable he referred to some other issue entirely. Yes, much more likely. He could not know anything, it was an impossibility. The boy was simply trying for an angle, seeing how far he could push Madden. Possibly his mother was behind the whole thing, had put young Brido up to it.

He sipped his tea, the paper folded neatly in four so that he might read it comfortably while he ate. The food was not sitting well in his stomach. Yes, rather too early for breakfast. He forked a sausage – and pushed the rest of the plate aside.

There was a picture showing two or three policemen and a number of people in protective overalls lifting a stretcher into the back of an ambulance. A sheet covered it: no human shape could be seen. In black and white, the photograph could have come from any decade, or any country in the world. And the presumed body on the stretcher might have been one of anyone's victims, someone's child thrown into the loch by a desperate mother. A lost cherub. A water-baby.

Police confirm the discovery of an unidentified female body in Loch Ardinning.

He felt strangely absent. He had no idea what the thing he was reading meant. All those years, all those voices. And always other voices arriving, new voices. Every day new voices.

'Did you not go to bed last night?' a somewhat more familiar voice said, the sound of exhaustion and impatience harrowing it. Madden turned the paper over and put it photograph down on the Formica eating-surface, raising his Glasgow 800 mug to his mouth to delay the necessity of replying.

Rose moved about the kitchen on her crutches, nudging him to one side while she poured water into the kettle and set it on the boil again. Puffy with sleep, her face reminded him of an overripe peach, except that her skin was too dark. It was odd the changes produced in their respective bodies over the years. Kincaid had hardly altered, despite being dead. Yet Madden had grown *old*. Rose had grown old too. Between them, they were a veritable cornucopia of complaints, a compendium of aches and pains. Rose outdid him, obviously, since so many of her complaints could be put down to imagination, or to a disease from which she did not suffer. Still, it meant endless trips to the GP, and fortunes spent on placebo medicines that failed after a few doses, only to be dropped in favour of the next *latest*. And in the meantime, she creaked her way around the house on crutches he was convinced she had no need of, complaining of problems he had ceased to believe in, but which he was too tired to object to any longer.

'I sat up,' he said, placing his mug down, absently etching circles with its wet base on the table top.

'You look done in,' Rose said. It was a rare truth uttered in the house. Madden was shattered. He was feeling every one of his sixty-something years.

'Will Ellen not be coming back, then?' Rose said, pushing two fresh slices of bread into the toaster. Her hair hung in lustreless clumps, and she brushed it aside with one of her babylike hands, only to let it fall over her face once more.

'No,' Madden said, 'she will not. The woman is a swindler and possibly dangerous into the bargain. You'll have to keep an eye on yourself today. Just for a little while. I'll need to contact the agency, but I doubt they'll have anyone available until at least tomorrow. And I have to *work*.'

This last he said with sarcastic tone, but he knew his wife would not pick up on it. She hadn't worked in years. He half thought that this whole business was to get her out of working in the first place. It was an unfair thought, unkind too.

Rose gawped at him, wide eyed. 'No, no . . .' she said. 'I don't want anyone else. Ellen's my friend.'

'She's not your friend,' Madden said, rising and placing a comforting arm around her and drawing her to his shoulder.

'It was God's will she should go,' he added, hoping this would be enough to satisfy her. 'Ellen was like Judas Iscariot, you see . . .'

Rose pulled away from him. 'Ellen was nothing like Judas,' she said, her mouth crimped and hardened. 'Judas Iscariot betrayed our Lord Jesus Christ and as a direct result Pilate had Him nailed to the cross. Ellen nipped out for a loaf and a pint of milk. Don't patronise me, Madden, please.'

'No, you're right, dear. You're absolutely right. I shouldn't have said that. You're very sensitive about this . . . what's his name again?'

'Who?'

'You know, the beardy fellow. The Son of Kong chap. What's his name again?'

Rose sighed and put her hands over her ears. 'No, no, no,' she said. 'I can't hear you . . .'

It saddened him to goad her in this way. He didn't use to. Now some small, ugly part of him enjoyed tormenting her, poking fun at her beliefs. He hadn't minded them so much in the past. He was sure he hadn't. He had found them childish, inane even, but he hadn't concerned himself with them. He was simply unable to take them seriously. At first, anyway. When she started to hear the voices telling her she was going to die, as opposed to telling her how good her legs were, it was a bit different. Look, he had pointed out to her at the time, of course you're going to die. You're going to die, I'm going to die, everything's going to die. It's simply a fact. No use worrying about it.

She was going to die, she said, and he didn't care! O Jesus Christ, O Mary mother of God . . .

'I know you can hear me, Rose,' he said, taking the paper up again and sipping from his mug where he stood. The kettle had begun its crescendo of squealing and began to rattle on the hob. Perhaps they should get an electric one, like they had in Caldwell's. Rose took her hands away from her ears and

271

turned the gas down. Madden leaned over to her, right behind her ear.

'I heard the voice of Jesus,' Rose said.

'You've told me this before,' he said, sighing.

Rose ignored him and carried on. 'Jesus spoke to me and he said I had a good heart. He said I had a pure heart. Like his mother's, he said. D'you remember, Hugh?'

Madden nodded. 'Yes. I remember.'

'He told me that I'd have a wee baby,' she said. 'And that it'd be all ours. D'you remember, Hugh?'

He said nothing.

Rose laughed drily. 'It must have been a test, mustn't it? It must have been a test of my faith. But it was cruel, wasn't it? To test me in *that* way, I mean.'

Madden nodded slowly, averting his eyes from Rose's.

'A wee baby of my own. With you,' she added. She laughed again, humourlessly. 'Whatever you are.'

'Rose—'

She held up her hand, palm outwards, and silenced him.

'What *are* you, Madden. Tell me. What *is* it that you are?'

But he had no answer. There was nothing he could say and nothing he could do that would satisfy his wife. There never had been. He had never been able to give her what she wanted, and somehow she had accepted it. They had married in a register office, the summer he left university, the same summer after Carmen Alessandro, Gaskell and Dizzy Newlands all died. It seemed so long ago now. Kincaid and the heads of the faculty had asked him to consider leaving: if he hadn't, they would expel him for the very serious crime of plagiarism.

The fact that it was one of Newlands's – now deceased – own papers he had copied made the matter rather more serious, and, of course, distasteful. Kincaid had curled his lip in disgust, and said he couldn't fathom the damned bricks of the man. He was ashamed to admit that Madden had been one of his own, along with Gaskell, favoured students. He had believed he could have gone far in medicine. He was a natural with a scalpel. Though nothing was said openly, there had passed between them some sort of mutual agreement that Kincaid's own recreational, should we say, *proclivities* not be mentioned.

Madden felt in some way that he had made amends to Newlands at least, if not to Carmen and Gaskell. He had been indirectly responsible for the boy's death. It was good and right that he admit the charge of plagiarism and go quietly. It was better to leave than be flung out.

And so had begun the many long years at Caldwell's. He had married Rose in a civil ceremony, Rose already heavily pregnant. His father had been there, but none of Rose's own family: they were firmly against a cross-faith marriage, and were suspicious too of Madden. But the infant died, and he couldn't bring himself to repeat the awful procedure that had led to its conception. Sex with Rose would have been too unspeakable for Madden. The things he did want disgusted and appalled him even more. He had experienced *relations* only a few times in his entire life, and he had found them miserable. He felt that he had, somehow, successfully managed to suffocate any remnant sexual desires. Until recently. He had never understood it. Perhaps her illness, and her tendency towards mania, made leaving him unthinkable. He didn't know, because he had never asked.

Kincaid had stayed in the faculty, continued with his clandestine activities, and Madden worked under Joe Snr. And the years and decades had passed and now he was old and it had not been very much of a life, not much of a life at all. It had been instead a kind of stasis, a kind of rigor mortis of the soul. He had felt that Joe might make him a partner in the business, but he had died and left everything to Joe Jnr. Madden had been snubbed, but was unable to work up any resentment towards the old man. He had liked him well enough. He supposed it was natural for a father to want his son to continue in his own footsteps. But the boy was an irredeemable dolt, and had squandered the opportunity to make something really special of Caldwell's. Madden would have done that. Made it a special place. Something a bit above the average. That would have been his legacy. But the chance did not arise, and now it was too late.

He decided to walk rather than take the car, the morning being such a pleasant one and the weather still cool. Besides, it was still early, and the birds were still flying around in their ignorance. Knowledge, he supposed, was indeed the curse of humanity. As he made his way along Dumbarton Road there was only a reluctant handful of other souls on the streets besides himself. The ability to feel boredom was what did for everyone in the end. Folk took drugs out of boredom, they drank themselves stupid out of boredom, they leap out of aeroplanes out of boredom . . . they killed themselves, they killed others, they got university degrees, took up golfing or kung-fu or dressage or became masseuses, all from an inability to sit quietly in a chair. That said something about the world.

His wife became a professional invalid out of boredom, he decided. Fear of death. Fear of being childless. Fear of pain. But really it was because she had needed a *hobby*. Something to pass the time, a way to liven up the hours of the day. He didn't doubt that this Brian Spivey character had found Madden as a kind of new hobby too. An easy game to play, as far as Brido was concerned. Bully an old man into giving him money. Simple, nothing simpler. Madden chewed his fingernails as he crossed to the other side of the road. Gaskell would have been able to handle the situation better than he. Even that dashed fool Hector Fain. Even him!

'Where did you all go?' he said aloud, staring up at the gulls. 'I'm bored!'

He walked along, unconscious of the good weather, the

pleasantness of the sunlight, the silence of the waiting streets. There were thoughts in his mind about the past, thoughts about the future. There were voices speaking to him, telling him things, and this time he was lost in their cacophony; it would have taken a man with a hammer to tear him from them.

Joe Jnr took his usual amount of time to arrive at his workplace, stepping briskly in at around noon, with no explanation offered. But then why should he have to explain himself, he was the proprietor, Madden a mere lackey. Now, with Catherine gone for good, he was the only remaining one. The intention of his boss seemed to be to run the place into the ground, bury it.

It was a shame that he'd fought with the girl the last time she'd been in to work. But really, Madden's patience with her had completely run out. He supposed his response to her goading had been an overreaction, but it couldn't be helped now.

There was an air of hopelessness in Caldwell & Caldwell's these days, a kind of resignation. Yet still, Joe did not seem to care. He came and went as he had always done – except in his father's day – and carried on as if utterly unfazed by either the lack of business or the want of staff.

Madden was staring benignly at poor old Eugenio Bustamente, not fully able to concentrate. Lack of sleep or stress or both. He'd made a call to the agency as soon as it was open for business, but they'd only confirmed his suspicions. There would be no one available for Rose, not for at least a few days. He was tempted to ring Mrs Spivey up and offer her the job back, but relations between them were hardly likely to improve after what had passed between them the night before, and Rose was the paramount concern here. No, better to wait until the agency found someone else. He was apprehensive about her son too. All this made working so much more difficult: he hadn't, for some reason, been able to face Kincaid despite Joe Jnr's insistence on getting him fixed up first.

On the other hand, Mr Bustamente posed a fair old challenge. It was an unusual severance he had suffered. Vertical, instead of horizontal. Eugenio, he imagined, had been a tricky customer all his life. He had that look about him. Trust you, Eugenio, Madden mumbled aloud, isn't it just like you to go for the unorthodox cut. Reminded him of something he'd heard about the samurai using condemned prisoners to test the sharpness of their blades out on: Joe Snr must have told him, always having a thing about them. A samurai had been going to practise a horizontal cut across the hips – a very difficult cut. When he'd informed the condemned man of his intention, the prisoner had said, 'If I had known you were going to attempt that stroke, I'd have eaten stones this morning.'

As he had thought. No possibility of arterial injection being any use here: Eugenio's head was an immersion job. Two or three hours at least. The remainder of his corpse would be injected through the right carotid artery, and drained from the right jugular vein.

'What the fuck are you doing?' Joe Jnr said. Madden hadn't heard him come down. He sighed, took off his glasses and placed them into the breast pocket of his overalls.

'Listen, I was about to start on him . . .' Madden said.

'Forget about this guy!' Joe said. 'Just leave him to rot, for fuck's sake. What did I tell you yesterday? What was it that I said to you yesterday that was so important?' Joe's face was flushed and sweaty, despite the chill in the cold room. For some reason, he was wearing a mustard-coloured polo-neck. Perhaps he had forgotten how hot it had been yesterday when he'd got dressed. It was extremely unflattering, exposing as it did his flabby contours and a three-inch strip of extremely white belly.

'I know,' Madden said, thankful he had taken his spectacles

off when he saw one of Joe's hands reach around the back of his trousers. 'I'll get on it straight away.'

'We need that body on its feet as soon as,' Joe went on. 'I told you this yesterday. Weren't you listening? I've already said to his wife she can see him tomorrow.'

Joe Jnr's hand withdrew from his behind, and he casually passed the offending extremity across his nose, feigning the scratching of an itch at the end of it. There'd be no need for Madden to perform pre-embalming work on the bullet entry point after he'd shot Joe to death. It would, after all, provide a handy draining point. Then again maybe he should just shoot him through the temple. No, that'd be a shame. Swelling, and any subsequent blackening of the eyelid, would be a nuisance to relieve. And then there was his poor mother to consider. He would have to shoot her as well if he wanted to avoid her bleating over her poor butchered son.

'This guy's going to be in a closed coffin. I told you that already. You can put him through the mincer for all any cunt's going to care.'

Madden winced visibly at the word he'd used, but Joe merely frowned at him.

'Now I'm telling you,' he said, 'get this other bastard moving or we'll both be facing a law suit after his wife gets a keek. Got that?'

He wiped a palm back over his blond comb, testing to see whether it was sitting nicely.

'Right,' Madden said. 'I'll get straight on with it.'

'Man, it's going to be a late one again,' Joe said, calming down slightly. 'You be able to cope?'

'I'll have to, won't I?' Madden said.

'That's ma man. Least you won't get bored, eh?' Joe winked at him and walked over to the stairs. Madden noticed a dark patch of sweat spreading down between the shoulder blades of his mustard polo-neck, and Joe Jnr's slightly bow-legged gait. That was his daddy's walk too. Like father, like son. Strange he'd never seen the likeness until today: Joe Caldwell Snr's rickets-bent legs were his most prominently noticeable feature. Odd. Was rickets hereditary? He couldn't remember. Joe Caldwell Snr had a joke he told about his condition too – though any humour in it was gained purely from its repetition. *Here I come*, he'd say. *The Spanish Archer.*

Any addressee who hadn't heard it before would be expected to ask why he called himself the Spanish Archer. Joe, with deadpan loucheness, would point kneewards and say simply: *El Bow.* Then he would smile his slightly sad smile, the one that said, it's all right, I know what I look like to you, I know what you're thinking . . .

'I'd better get out and see about the flowers,' Joe said, as he climbed the stairs.

'I thought you saw about them yesterday?' Madden said, raising his voice slightly. Joe turned.

'Aye, well. Decided against the plastic ones, haven't I?'

'Why's that, then?'

'Plastic's good and everything, but they don't *smell* of anything. They've no *flavour.*'

A reasonable point, Madden had to concur. Flowers did smell. And perhaps they reminded the relatives of the bereaved, if only subconsciously, that what had happened to their loved one was natural. It was part of that endless cycle, and was meant to be. The sight and smell of flowers was the simplest and most obvious symbol of this process. And they were very pretty. Still, he had seen so many flowers, so many wreaths, that he couldn't help but find them ever so slightly *boring.*

'Why don't we forget about the flowers?' he said, thinking aloud. 'Why don't we offer something up to the gods instead?'

Joe looked at him. 'Are you trying to be funny?'

'No, no,' Madden said, putting his glasses back on again. 'I'm quite serious. It might provide a new avenue for the business – funerals with a twist and so forth. Cater to the diverse ethnic market out there. What do you think?'

Joe sighed and rubbed his eyes with one hand.

'Forget it,' he said. He turned and resumed climbing the stairs, leaving Madden to his white room, his delicatessen.

It was not an idea without inherent merit, he decided. They could wreathe the coffins in Inca headdresses of condor feathers, offer up coca leaves and hair and milk teeth. They could swathe them in white silk, pour goblets of beer and kill boars, arrange the pet Alsatian at the deceased's feet, loyal to the end, loyal for eternity. They could pickle it.

But no, always these flowers. When he died he wanted no flowers, no symbols. He would be dead, and that would be it. Rose could do whatever she liked with him. She could have him buried, she could have him cremated, she could have him mounted and stuffed for all he cared. He knew all this was something of an assumption. Rose would certainly be dead before him. Certainly.

And if there was an afterlife, an eternity, he wouldn't mind if he had a book with him for the duration. Endless beatification sounded so damned dull. He would likely be better off in the fiery pit: at least it wouldn't be tedious.

Kincaid was uncovered, and seemed peaceful enough. His eyes were open. He had known what he was letting himself in for. Doubtless that was why he'd had a dram to see him on his way. A wee *deoch an dorus*. Afore he ganged awa'. Quite right too, Madden decided. He reached over for his black medical bag and removed the pewter flask the good doctor had bequeathed him forty-odd years before, just before Madden had passed out in his office.

His mood improved immediately, so he downed another. It might well be an idea to be good and drunk when Brian Spivey eventually decided to put in an appearance.

He had remembered, hadn't he? the voice asked. Yes, Madden said, he'd remembered. Madden perceived it through a muted alcoholic stupor, and offered no much more to it than nods of the voice box, singular syllabic grunts.

Brian Spivey said he was on his way over to Caldwell & Caldwell's and Madden had better be alone. There were matters they had to discuss. Madden told him that Joe had gone home for the evening, that they would have the place to themselves, and hung up on Brido. He stood in the Welcome Room with a slice of Madeira cake, trying not to plan anything in advance. The whisky had helped with that, but in fact he had no plan anyway. He simply needed his senses dulled, taken down a notch or two. He sipped his coffee, and topped up the level with the whisky, setting the bottle down next to the espresso machine. The radio droned on, but the alcohol had taken the edge off Madden's nerves, and he listened to the news reports without associating them with himself. There had been nothing in the way of new developments anyway.

Nothing interesting there, then. And nothing to connect Madden to it, unless Brido had other ideas. Which, presumably, what they were about to find out.

Madden turned the radio and the lights off, and stood waiting by the window until he saw the headlights of a car draw up, stopping several metres back from the entrance to Caldwell & Caldwell's. He took another jigger of whisky and unlocked the door, then sat back down in the darkness and waited.

The big figure was outside now, and it chapped lightly on the door. Madden didn't move immediately. He felt instinctively it would be best to let the man wait for him. The figure chapped on the door again. Madden slowly rose from his chair and went to the door, opening it a fraction with the chain still up.

'That you, Mr Madden, eh?'

'It's me.'

'How's tricks? Gonnae let us in?'

'I don't know. Am I?'

'Aye, Mr Madden. Ye are.'

Madden closed the door, and let the chain off, then stepped away, into the darkness. A few seconds passed before Brian Spivey realised he was to let himself in, and when he stood inside, all Madden could see was his huge silhouette. He felt his chest tighten, the rigor returning to freeze him, and he wrung one hand in the darkness, knowing that for the moment he was invisible to Brian. It was even possible that they weren't alone, that Madden had an accomplice, perhaps several. He didn't, but Brian had no idea of that.

'C'mon now, Mr Madden, what ye playing at?' The silhouette shifted on one foot, and Madden waited. Brian was searching about for a light switch.

Madden turned on the table lamp, watching while Brian adjusted his eyesight to the unaccustomed brightness. He stood squinting, and Madden said, 'Come on through to the Welcome Room. We'll have peace in there.'

'How, ye expecting someone?' Brian said.

Madden clicked the light off again and stood. He saw visions of orange dance before him. Brian would be seeing them too. He allowed himself to take the crook of Brian's arm, guiding him through the curtains into the other room.

'I just don't want us to be disturbed when we talk business. We'll have more privacy in here. You don't mind, do you?'

Madden put the lights on, and they stood facing each other, Brian Spivey looking around at the comforting hues of the room, everything in dark stained wood, very much the same style as when Madden had first taken up his position here. There had been only minor alterations over the years, and all had blended in so well he had long since forgotten what were later additions or adjustments, and what were not. He looked up at Brian.

'So, you wanted to talk,' he said, crossing his arms.

Brian smiled, scratching his orange-stubbled head. He was

281

wearing the same bomber jacket, his face covered in minuscule red pinpricks.

'Aye. Talk, that's what I'm here for.' He winked at Madden, cocking the forefinger and thumb of his left hand at him simultaneously, like a gun.

'I have nothing to say to you,' Madden stated. 'I said everything I have to say last night.'

Brian shook his head. 'Ach, Mr Madden. You don't have to say a word. I'll talk for the pair of us. That no preferable to you?'

'That depends very much on what you've got to say.'

'Have you a drink in here at all?' Brian said. 'I could go a drink if there's one on the go. Is there?' He set himself down in Madden's armchair, the one he sometimes dozed in while listening to the radio. Madden tried to stay calm, the feeling of inflexibility spreading through him, breathing slowly and deeply through his nostrils. He retrieved the whisky bottle and a couple of coffee cups from the reception area and poured out a measure for Brian.

'Say when,' he said, then regretted it.

'When,' Brian said, snatching the bottle from him. He drained a cupful of whisky straight off and then topped it up again. Madden took measured sips from his. He didn't want to tip himself over the edge into full-blown drunkenness.

Brian settled back in his chair. He watched Madden coolly; Madden fought with himself not to return the look too forcefully. He didn't wish to provoke.

Silence settled in the room, and Brian poured himself another dram, apparently in no hurry to discuss business or anything else. After a while he leaned forwards and said simply: 'I need money.' Then he sat back again to stare at Madden.

'We all need money,' Madden said. 'It's one of the immutable facts of life.'

Brian laughed suddenly. 'Where d'ye get your patter, Mr

Madden? Amenable what? Fuck me. That's pure class that is.'
He scratched his head. 'Well, whatever, man. The thing is I
need money and you're gonnae get me it. I mean, yous have a
nice house and that. You've a nice wee earner in here, eh?
Stuffing the bodies and whatever, man, whatever the fuck it is
yese dae. There's always deid folk, in't there? Steady income
and that. Mad, man, so it is.'

Madden breathed again. 'Whatever kind of money you
need, I can't give it to you, Brido – *Brian* – I've nothing left
to give. My wife needs the help of a professional carer. That
costs money. And I have to work here for it. That takes time.
I've no more to gi—'

'Ye ever had a strangulation in here, Mr Madden?' Brian
said, sipping his whisky and staring evenly at him. 'Ever had
anyone come in that's been throttled? Have ye?'

Madden kept quiet.

Brian sipped again. 'Funny things, stranglings. I mean, you
know, right? You've seen them. Ye must have had a fair few of
the fuckers in here in your time, know what I'm saying? I
looked it up. Pure horrible, man, so it is. All that discoloration,
man. Nasty, so it is. I believe you know a bit about that.
Asphyxia, they call it. That's right, in't it?'

Madden nodded.

'You see, *I know about you*, Mr Madden. And it'd be a
shame for it to get about, wouldn't it. A shame for that wife of
yours to hear about it. Fuck that shite, eh? How'd you think
she'd feel about it? No too fucking chuffed. No too fucking
chuffed at all . . . And then there's the polis.'

Madden felt the rigor itch towards his thorax, a chill
descending. His mouth would not work properly. He feared
speaking, feared the rigor would give him away, damn him.
His face was numb. He drained his coffee cup and flexed his
left hand, the fingertips numb.

'Acht, never mind,' Brian said cheerily. 'Wan of they
immaterial facts of life, eh? There's always stuff it's best the

wife disnae know. And nae other cunt as well. Just a fact, that. Am I right? 'Course I'm fucking right.'

He raised his glass to Madden, one leg across the other, settled back in his chair, and drained it. 'So I reckon you'll be wanting to help out, eh, Mr Madden? You'll be wanting to help out any way you can.'

Madden smiled, and said, 'Since you put it like that, I don't suppose I've much choice in the matter, have I?'

'Nah, that's right. That's it, spot on. Ye any more to drink? This bottle's about done.'

Madden stood up and lifted the empty bottle from the table. 'I think there's another one downstairs, in the cold room,' he said, smoothing his overall down. 'An emergency ration, so to speak. For medicinal purposes only.'

'Medicinal purposes, eh?'

'Yes,' Madden said. 'We're not supposed to keep any spirits on the premises, but there's some down there anyway. In a bottle.'

Brian blanched, almost imperceptibly, but it was there. Just enough.

'Spirits? Down the stairs?'

'Well, where else would they be? That's the cold room. That's where I work. That's where we keep the spirits. Are you . . . *nervous*, at all?'

Brian drew himself up from his chair to his full height. He must have been six-four or -five. He towered above Madden, anyway.

'You're kidding, in't ye? Lead the way.'

Madden guided him with a hand in the crook of the elbow, as he had before.

'Not at all,' he said. 'After you. Careful of those steps. Mind your head on the way down. The stairwell was never designed with chaps of your stature in mind.' Using all the alcohol-induced strength he could muster, Madden took a step back and swung the empty bottle at the back of Brian Spivey's head. His head jolted forwards and cracked against the low ceiling; he made a grunting noise and stood swaying slightly on the top step. Madden swung again, and this time the bottle broke.

Brido turned and smiled at Madden. 'See, my ma told me about you, Mr Madden,' he said. 'She was right, wasn't she?'

Madden stood, frozen and horrified, as blood began to pour from somewhere behind Brian Spivey's right ear. He touched it with his hand and peered at it. Madden dropped the bottle and they both stood staring at the blood. There was so much of it. Brian Spivey's face turned the colour of cold ash, and if he hadn't fallen backwards down the step, Madden knew that he would have bled to death within ten minutes.

He lay at the bottom of the stairs, head twisted the wrong way round. He was still smiling. Madden stood over him, hand grasping his throat for a pulse, and it was only with the familiarity of the gesture that he knew that Brian Spivey had never known anything about the discovery of Catherine's body in Loch Ardinning. Brian – foolish, foolish man – had believed what his mother had believed: that she'd caught him in the act of attempting to throttle Rose, his own wife. Poor Brian. A mistake, a misapprehension. That was the reason he was now lying dead, but warm still, on the mortuary tiles.

He stood breathing deeply for a few minutes, unable to look at the broken thing at the bottom of the stairs, then went to the sink, ran a glass of cold water, took two sips, and vomited a bijou dollop of pungent baby food girlishly into the drain. When he had washed out his mouth he stood up and wiped condensation from the lenses of his spectacles with the cuff of his lab coat.

'Nothing to say, Doctor? Some words of wisdom, perhaps?' Madden said.

No, the voice said, so close he could feel its breath, no words of wisdom today. We have nothing to say. We're dead, remember? Ours were not good deaths. They were ugly deaths, ugly and squalid. You killed us. Remember?

Yes, Madden said. He remembered. He hadn't always remembered, but this time he did. Yes.

He unlocked the instrument cabinet, and picked out his favourite bone saw. It was one of the few remaining tools that dear old Joe Caldwell Snr had left them when he died. Most of the others had been discarded years before. They had blunted or they had broken. Not this one, though. It had a pleasantly weighty feel to it, the teeth still serviceably sharp and reliable. The man had known a thing or two about dissection-ware. More that most. Madden placed it down on the instrument table and walked over to Brian Spivey's body at the foot of the stairwell. Measuring up his twisted bulk, he sighed loudly. The time on Brido's digital watch said 12:30 a.m.

Yes. It was definitely going to be a long night.

A good hour into the procedure, Madden's face began to recognise in itself a kind of rigor, a lack of flexibility. It felt like dough, as if it could be kneaded into any practical sort of shape, pushed and pummelled into an entirely new, possibly more satisfactory one. A familiar sensation, one that normally manifested itself in his fingertips or joints. Not unpleasant. But this wasn't the time of the day to be experiencing it, not with the important job that he had to hand. Best always to keep one's pleasures for the evening, in privacy. A small libation to ease the pains and stresses of the new day.

The doctor wasn't talking this fine sunny morning, seemed in fact to have taken the huff. Madden took another gulp from his bottle and leaned over the body, a bleariness of sensation informing him that he might, now, be rather *too* drunk. Not that the doctor would have minded. Might even have approved: he'd always been so partial himself. In those days it hadn't yet been deemed so antisocial a habit unless it became a very obvious one. In the privacy of one's own home, it might even be encouraged by the old-boy network, a manly and virile practice. How often had Madden heard Kincaid slur slightly, or gesture a little too unselfconsciously? That had been his problem: a lack of discretion. But even when rumours of his most candid acts had been circulating around campus, when his habits had been more or less a matter of public record, he'd continued with such behaviour apparently unconcerned. It was known, for instance, that on more than one occasion his own department had him dressed down.

It was late in the day to be only just starting the procedure. He had been dead for many hours now. There was the beginning of a greenish discoloration on the skin of the lower abdomen. Joe Jnr was right. Madden should have got on with this hours before, on arrival of the corpse. Kincaid was *putrefying*. Madden had left him out of the storage cabinet overnight. A deliberate and calculated act of vandalism. Revenge, spite, jealousy. It was undeniable. Aye. The greenish tint was already beginning to bloom over the chest and – *damned bricks!* – upper thighs. Doubtless there was already some build-up of sulphurous intestinal gases, pregnant with liberated haemoglobin, freed finally from the walls of the abdomen. Soon, he would be ripe and rotten, a big suppurating mango of a man, ready to burst.

Caldwell's should never bother with flowers at a service: they should instead surround the corpse with piles of rotten fruit. That was the symbol that spoke. Flowers appeared *vital*, though in death. Overripe fruit appeared *rotten* as in death. The way it smelt, the way it looked, the way the dashed stuff tasted, for God's sake . . . it was just a more honest approach, and someone ought to be brave enough to force folk to recognise it. What was the point in all this stuff he was doing? Madden wondered. Comfort for the relatives? Bugger them. Kincaid wasn't going on anywhere better, wasn't living it up – ha ha – in the great beyond . . . he wasn't anywhere now.

It would be better for all those sentimental bastards out there to gaze upon the dead and see them for what they really were. Look! Here's your Lawrence, missus! Now, you may wish to remember him more fondly than like *this* . . . but isn't that the point? The fact is that no matter what we here at Caldwell's do for him, no matter how much we spruce him up for you, he's done for.

Remember him as he was when he was *alive*. This is all just a facsimile of aliveness. If I told you, missus, that even as we speak and contemplate his body, it is in fact still alive in a sense. Absolutely and completely alive! That is the true wonder of the universe, missus! Search not for gods and eternities and a spiritual realm you can never hope to grasp or understand. Such are delusions, myths, the obfuscating ink of metaphor and mirage. No, behold instead, missus, the world beneath the skin, which even now is beginning to blister and slip, like a snake shedding its own leathered raiment. In a week or two bacteria, Nature's most ubiquitous creations (and are they not wonderful in their own way too?), will gain access to every area of your late husband's body, breaking it down, returning it to the soil from whence it came . . . In time, all shall be devoured by the putrefaction process. Now, if there were a Judgement Day, is *this* how your invisible, unknowable, indifferent God intends to resurrect your Lawrence?

In truth, Mrs Kincaid, your husband's body is no mere *flower* cut down and holding its form for a brief few days. Assuredly not. It is being even now consumed by the hurried interactions of invading spores, and its own natural fauna! Is there not more to wonder at in all you can see before your very microscope than in all you imagine to be beyond death? *This* is death, and it's very much *alive*, if you choose to observe its miracle. This microscopic universe is the True Resurrection, missus.

Look on our works, ye Maisie, and decease!

288

But he was forgetting himself: it wasn't Maisie who would be coming in to see how her man was going to turn out, but his new wife Tess.

Madden unscrewed the cap of the flask, raised it to the doctor and downed another. A blurriness in his vision reminded him to take his spectacles off. Better to squint effectively than misjudge distances and objects, scalpels and haemostats through the refracted light on the lenses of his glasses and his own stupefaction. He was probably not likely to pass a breathalyser test, but as yet it was not illegal to be drunk and in charge of a corpse.

Madden sat down in a chair heavily and rubbed his eyes. Was it worth taking it a bit easier on the whisky until he'd seen Tess Kincaid? Probably not. He had decided today would be his last day at Caldwell's, whatever happened with her, or with Joe Jnr, or even with Brian Spivey, now lying in eternal repose along with Eugenio Bustamente and the good doctor. He simply didn't care any more. Not about what happened to himself, or even what happened to Rose. He was too tired.

The intercom woke him with a gentle refrain from Mozart, an allegro for clarinet, violin, viola and violoncello. It had seemed more fitting, a light and floaty piece to replace the harsh buzzer that Caldwell's had used previously. He let it ring – surely the wrong word? – for a few moments, chewing back saliva that had formed in the corner of his gummy mouth. Finally, he answered it. It was, of course, Joe Jnr. Madden could picture him closing his eyes, heard his habitual between-words sniff.

'You awake down there? What kept ye?'

'Um, working on a tricky bit.'

'Oh aye? Well, there's a visitor here for you. The cock-in-the-frock.'

Madden mumbled his jaws in a confused way.

'Who? What d'you mean?'

'You know. The drag queen. The corpse's bride.'

Did he refer to Eugenio Bustamente? Madden hadn't met any of that unfortunate's relatives as yet. Rather, he had been hoping, as he always did, to avoid such a situation.

He could hear Joe laugh at the other end of the line. A nasal static.

'Don't tell us you never knew,' he said.

Madden was mildly annoyed that he might have missed some crucial piece of information that was obvious to others. Especially Joe Jnr.

'Knew what?' he said through gritted teeth, drawing the words out of himself with barely surmountable reluctance.

'Your man on the slab,' Joe said, still laughing. 'That's the reason the old boy's daughters won't have anything to do with her. Should have clicked when I first set eyes on her. Him. It.'

'Look,' Madden said, 'I have no idea what you're talking about. To whom do you refer?'

' "*To whom do I refer?*" ' Joe Jnr echoed. 'I refer, *m'lud*, to one Tess Kincaid, wife of Lawrence Kincaid, deceased.'

'She's coming down now?' Madden said.

'*She* would have wanted to come down now. He *is* coming down now.'

Madden glanced over at Kincaid on the autopsy table.

'You're implying that . . . what are you trying to imply?'

Joe snorted derisively. 'I'm saying that the old boy's wife pishes standing up is what I'm saying. She's a fella.'

'A fella.'

'That's about the size of it. He met her on *holiday*, apparently. They were living together the last six months. They only got married a couple of weeks before he croaked. Nobody at the register office knew she was a man. Go figure, heh? All sorts of legal wrangling going on now. She claims she's a pre-op transsexual. He left her his house and a neat wee sum. Nothing for the daughters. A snub, for no seeing eye to eye with the whole thing. They claim if this new wife was a pre-op tranny, then that makes her legally a man when they got married. So the legality of it is null and void. Great stuff, heh? You couldnae make it up.'

Madden scratched his head. He felt duty bound to laugh, but couldn't. Somehow, Tess Kincaid's (or whatever her real name was) joke seemed to be on him too.

'Madden? You still there?'

He sighed and rubbed his eyes, replacing his glasses on his nose.

'I'm here,' he said. 'Send her down.'

Letting his finger off the buzzer, he reached again for the whisky bottle, but found it empty. No matter. He always kept two or three in the black medical bag, and reach in for another. He went over to Kincaid and looked him up and down, then draped the linen sheet over his face. The theatricality of the moment to come would demand some sort of unveiling to show off the work he had done on the body in its full glory. He took a gulp from his bottle, listening to the sound of Kincaid's wife's footfalls approaching down the stairs. Obviously she shared a distaste for elevators – unladylike, Madden presumed.

Joe Jnr extended a hand to guide her into the room, and she deliberately avoided meeting Madden's gaze as she swung in, the rose-tinted shades veiling her eyes as before. Now Madden saw her in a different light, tinted with whisky, a kind of baleful glow that roughened what he had previously taken for beauty, made her seem too large, ungainly even, in her taut turquoise velveteen leggings and cork-heeled shoes. Everything about her was wrong now somehow – from her too-big feet to her slight awkwardness of movement and the barely perceptible Adam's apple in her throat which gave her the look of a very large snake digesting some unfortunate mammal.

Joe Jnr looked imploringly at him, as if fearful he would say something awful, or tell an off-colour joke.

'Tess, you know Mr Madden already,' he said. 'And we'd like to apologise for the misunderstanding we had before. We can't apologise enough . . .'

Tess Kincaid raised a hand, and Joe clammed up.

'I don't know if you mean it,' she said. 'Maybe it was a mistake. Of course, you wonder why I see such a old man. Is natural, I think. All forgotten now. I just want to see my husband body one more time.'

'Of course,' Madden said, aware of Joe's look and of a slight slurriness of speech which he made no attempt to hide. 'If you'd like to come over here by the autopsy table you can see him now.'

As he led her over to the table, he was briefly aware of Joe scratching his armpit and quickly sniffing his fingers.

'I've been working on him today,' Madden said, 'and I think you'll be very pleased with the result. Some of my very best work, I think. Yes, I think so.'

Joe stepped over too, and the three of them stood before the linen-shrouded body, Madden allowing a reverential moment to pass before he coughed and said: 'Would you like to see him now, Tess?'

She pushed her sunglasses back against the bridge of her nose and took a breath.

'Yes,' she said. 'Now is a good time, no? Let me see.'

Madden took another theatrical moment, and then swept the sheet back, watching Tess Kincaid and Joe Jnr's faces for their responses.

'Jesus Christ,' Joe Jnr said very quietly. He turned around and faced the other direction, one arm drawn across his chest, and the other hand up to his mouth.

'He looks good, doesn't he, Tess?' Madden said, smiling broadly at her. She too had put a hand up to her mouth.

'Pretty as a picture, isn't he?'

Tess Kincaid let a small moan escape from her mouth, then turned and strode back towards the stairwell. By the time she reached it, she was sobbing audibly, and took the steps two at a time, the way a man would.

'You hear from lawyer about this!' she said, turning back at the stairwell. 'This time no joke!'

Madden gazed lovingly down at Kincaid's rouged face, the erratically drawn lipstick he wore, and heavily mascara'd eyelashes. Some of the make-up he had to work with was not, he had to admit, likely to be very fashionable these days, but that was not, he felt, what was required. It had taken quite some time, too, to paint his fingernails and toenails, and there'd been little he could do to disguise the discoloration spreading across upper thighs and belly. Perhaps he should have dressed him.

Joe Jnr turned to Madden. He said nothing for some time.

'Looks rather fetching, wouldn't you say?' Madden said casually, wiping a stray trail of lipstick from the good doctor's upper lip, where it had stained the edges of his moustache.

Joe shook his head. 'That's it,' he said. 'You're out of here. You're finished in Caldwell's. If you've not finished Caldwell's off first. If you've not fucking *ruined* us first.'

His grimace silently mirrored the doctor's own – Madden had stitched his mouth and lips into a parody grimace, a kind of crimped leer.

'Come on,' Madden said lightly. 'Have you never been touched by art before, Joe? This might be my masterpiece!'

'You're crazy,' Joe said, shaking his head again. 'Absolutely fucking completely crazy. Well, you can get your stuff together and get out. You hear me, Madden? I want you *out*.'

Madden shook his head, and knew that Joe Jnr would not argue with his decision. 'No,' he said. 'I'll finish here today. I've a few bits and pieces to wrap up before I go home for the night. Odds and ends. Then I'll leave.'

Joe Jnr threw up his hands. 'Fine,' he said. 'Do what you want. Just don't be here in the morning.'

'I won't,' Madden said. 'Don't worry about that. I won't.'

'Fucking lunatic,' Joe Jnr said under his breath, heading for the stairs. 'Absolute fucking madman.' When he got to the stairs he turned around and faced Madden. 'Who are you, Madden?' he said. 'Just who is it that you are?'

Then he turned and climbed the stairs, the same way Kincaid's wife had done, two at a time. Madden sighed and opened his bottle again, knowing that when he got home he still had Rose to take care of.

Acknowledgements

The title of this novel was taken from an essay of the same name in Sherwin B. Nuland's fascinating and sensitive book *How We Die*. Further ideas, images and woolly technical stuff came from *Mortuary Science*, by Frederick C. Gale. The rest is made up.